ANDALUZ BLOOD

JAMES SMITH

About the Book

Englishman, Charles Hale, is on the run from crippling debt and his own demons. He lives in a conspiratorial world in which no one is quite who they seem and from which he yearns to escape.

Inevitably, Hale's double life must be exposed, and a complex web begins to unravel when the tenacious Inspectora Jefa, Rosa María Díez, of the Policía Nacional investigates a death at a Spanish marina.

ANDALUZ BLOOD

THE ENGLISHMAN
THE AFFAIR
AND DEATH IN ANDALUCIA

'*Andaluz Blood ... stood out from the many ...*'
Curtis Brown Group, London

Copyright

Copyright © 2015 James Smith
CreateSpace Edition

ISBN-13: 978-1511774246
ISBN-10: 151177424X

All characters in this publication are fictitious and any resemblance to real persons, living or dead, is purely coincidental.

The right of James Smith to be identified as the Author of this work has been asserted by him in accordance with the Copyright, Designs and Patents Act 1988.
All rights reserved. No part of this publication may be reproduced, stored in a retrieval system, or transmitted, in any form or by any means, without the prior permission in writing of the publisher.

Cover Artwork by Sean Strong © 2015

Acknowledgements

Thank you to Sean Strong for his excellent cover design derived in one hit from my rather wordy spec; bookworm, writer, and screenwriter extraordinaire, Caroline Spence, for her manuscript proofreading and pointers regarding characters and flow; 'Joe' for his advice and insights concerning international police procedures and Special Forces operations. Last, I'd like to thank mum and dad for introducing me to Spain all those years ago, and of course, for loaning me their modest but elegant sailing yacht moored in that sleepy marina in Andalucía, and aboard which, Andaluz Blood was conceived and written.

Dedication

For Caroline

A lo hecho, pecho
(What's done is done)

.

ONE

Spain, 3:04 a.m.

The taxi flew through the night from the marina to the working town, San Isidro, a few miles inland. Charles Hale sat in the passenger seat, the dry wind buffeting his face through the open window. Too many shots of *Torres 10*, the local potent brandy, had muddled his thinking. The aroma of the desert and diesel fumes, laced with a scent of garlic, toyed with his senses. Flashes of neon, orange streetlights, and a silver moon blurred and streaked across his vision.

Hale battled to snap out of the daze.

What am I doing?

A cold shiver ran through him, a panic that alcohol no longer numbed. Leaning forward to ease the seat belt chafing his neck, a line of sweat rolled down his back. The crew at the marina, committing to a passage with criminals. A way to ease his crippling debts.

But now this. The girl in the bar. The crew might talk, but they were drunk, and would they even remember? His thoughts turned to his fiancée and the life he must return to in England.

What the hell have I got myself into this time?

He battled to concentrate over the machine-gun Andaluz dialect of the taxi driver, an older bespectacled man, happy to be busy at this hour. The football had been good that night. *El Clásico*: Real Madrid versus Barcelona. Played on every local radio and television set in the bars and restaurants, it was a tight match, tetchy as ever, the driver content with the *Barça* win.

An unsubtle tug on the steering wheel lurched the car to one side. Hale grabbed the door handle for support.

Night offered a brief respite from the all-consuming murderous heat that would make a return in a few hours. Unlike back home, here there was life at night. Vibrancy from locals who knew better than to offer themselves up in daylight hours to the choking dust and unmerciful oven of Europe's only desert.

The taxi approached the town. Figures skulked in the shadows of apartment blocks and townhouses. Local Andaluz youths, travellers, Moroccans, and flamboyantly dressed *chicas* hung around outside bars. Arguing, gesticulating, or loitering around parked mopeds. Old men sat on benches looking on, unable to sleep in the heat, kicked out by their wives to get some air. They looked as if they'd endured a lifetime of hard labour. In the fields perhaps, or manual work. Having lived through Franco's regime, civil war, poverty, and hunger, a few stoned hombres speeding around on motorbikes didn't warrant a glance.

A waft of cheap cigarette smoke met Hale's face, reminding him of the smog in the bar a few hours before, a smog lit by harsh lights over the pool table. She was there of course, and the brandies came, and so did the small talk between them. She laughed at his stilted Spanish, *Spanglish* even. He liked the conversation. Consumed by it. Hung on to every syllable, every unintelligible sentence in her thick Andaluz lilt, hardly audible over the noise of the bar and crack of the cue ball against the pack. The looks from his friends, the snide comments they were no doubt exchanging, didn't worry him. Why should he succumb to their taunts? Hale was in shape with the gym work back home, so maybe he had a chance with the girl, and they did not. They wore the look of every other middle-aged male from Northern Europe. The Spanish called them *gambas*, prawns, due to their pink bellies and faces, which they'd cooked in the midday sun. Fat tourist pigs with no etiquette. That's how the locals saw it. They were not welcome here, but tolerated for their money.

No, at the bar Hale was succumbing to it, absorbed, wanting to be immersed further by this condition, and by her.

The tyres screeched at a roundabout, snatching Hale from his thoughts. A truck shot across their path, inches from the bonnet. A cloud of diesel smoke engulfed them as the truck driver caned the engine to speed away, hooting the horn in defiance.

The taxi driver shouted, "¡Hijo de puta!" *Son of a bitch*, waving, shrugging in dismay. He looked across, smiling at Hale's anxiety and white-knuckled grip on the door handle. Hale returned an uneasy grin. This was normal. Patience was not a virtue of the Spanish motorist. You don't want to fight? Then don't go into the bullring.

"Donde?" asked the driver.

His nerves shot, Hale gathered himself. The taxi was nearing the destination, a backstreet.

"Calle Uruguay," Hale said.

The driver looked across, raised his eyebrows. "Uruguay?"

"Sí."

The driver shook his head, pursed his lips. Then made a sharp left, leaning into the turn and letting the wheel slip through his hands. He knows something of this area, thought Hale. Maybe something bad.

The streetlights were sparse now as the taxi bumped across an old car park, throwing up dust in the headlights. Back onto tarmac, they turned into a darker road surrounded by faceless apartment blocks adorned with graffiti and lit by the one remaining streetlight that wasn't smashed. Hale's heartbeat ramped up a notch. This was isolated, no place for *Inglés*.

The driver looked uneasy, parked up and tapped a button on his meter. "Por allí, Calle Uruguay," he said, gesturing to a side alley in the distance. Hale handed him a twenty and glanced to the back seat. She looked up at him, sweeping the dark hair from her face. This was dangerous, especially considering the events of the day. But his fallibility and desire, and her beauty, rendered him weak.

It was the same old Charles Hale.

Hale asked her, "Here ... this place?"

"Sí, of course," she said. "Here."

TWO

Two weeks earlier, England. A weekday in July, 7:04 a.m.

The third credit card statement of the morning's post was the worst. Hale sat in the downstairs study. His fiancée, Lucy, and his soon-to-be stepdaughter, Deborah, slept upstairs. Being careful not to awaken them, he grabbed a mug of tea from the kitchen and returned to his desk to face the statement.

The first two statements had made him wince, taking deep breaths to control a nervous panic that brought on a cold sweat. This feeling he knew from facing a board meeting, or waiting for a job interview and interrogation by some humourless stiff in the city. But the third statement had him on his feet, leaning against the desk, hyperventilating. A feeling of nausea. Drowsily, he slipped into the next room, an undersized broom cupboard posing as a bathroom. He stared at his reflection in the mirror.

Charles Hale, mid-forties, university educated, from a loving hardworking Essex family.

Is this how I end up?

He leaned forward on the sink, looked up at his drawn face and thinning hair. His sharp features, weathered by wind and a youth spent out in the elements, concealed some of the strain. The girls at work said he had something of Steve McQueen about him. Maybe they were just being kind, but at least he didn't wear the bloodshot eyes and hooded stare of the heavy drinking contingent. Men who'd started as lithe office boys, only to succumb to liquid lunches and six o' clock booze-ups.

Maybe things weren't so bad. Pull yourself together. People deal with illness, bereavement, relationship breakdowns. And debt.

Deal with it, Hale.

He rose up, straightened his back. Feeling better, he returned to the study, and the third statement. From City-Xtra Europe Bank, its position was clear: red and threatening, a final notice to pay immediately, to contact City-Xtra, otherwise legal action would be taken. They could put a charging order on the property. That was bad enough, but he glanced at the balance, giving him a taste of bile in his throat: £17,439.04. A familiar leap of his heart rate, palpitations.

Then, the interest rate for a killer blow, a kick when down at 13% APR.

"Christ, shit," he said, knowing the figure was crippling to an already dire account. He remembered some bullshit relaxation tips he'd uncovered in a men's magazine. Worth a try, anything. Deep breathing into the stomach, look outside the window, empty the mind. It had little effect. Panic returned, and tunnel vision. Reputation, legalities, professional responsibilities, relationships. Realities inextricably linked to control of his personal finances, which had run off the rails and were now careering downhill.

Calm down, Charles.

Breathe.

This was just one postal delivery. Tomorrow would bring another and the day after, another. The postman had become his enemy, the provider of two evils: bills and threats.

He heard Lucy stirring from her slumber upstairs, stuffed the statements into his briefcase, and closed the spreadsheet on his laptop. This was how his mornings began. The same routine. Only so much juggling was possible with credit cards, and the pressure was building. Using one account to pay another, taking cash advances and applying for other cards with 0% introductory deals. These were merely ways of robbing Peter to pay Paul.

It couldn't last.

The mortgage was also an issue, or was it the re-mortgage or re-re-mortgage? That hand had been dealt, but Lucy was adamant about the kitchen refit (four grand). She was developing a worrying – in Hale's eyes *unnecessary* – taste for handbags, jewellery, shoes, and 'accessories' to add to her burgeoning collection packed into a large wall cupboard upstairs. This trait no doubt born of her association with the coffee morning tribe: unbearable socialites whose appetite for trash celebrity magazines and daytime TV drivel turned Hale's stomach.

This coven of witches had acquired similarly rhyming and often abbreviated names, all ending in a high-pitched 'i'. Alli, Chrissi, Kazzi, Jenni, Traci. It grated. Hale ran into Chrissi and Kazzi when a coffee morning found its way to his home one Saturday. Chrissi looked as if her face had been painted onto a balloon and then inflated further. Such was the extent of her Botox. Kazzi sported a peroxide bob that jarred against her mahogany complexion, the work of excessive sunbed radiation.

The gaggle squawked like hyenas at a kill while Hale made his excuses to do work in the garden. Lucy fumed in the knowledge that he hated gardening and rarely indulged in the pastime. He lodged in the tiny shed out of the rain, cleaning the end of a muddy rake prong-by-prong. The better option.

He began to regret their decision to move in together two years ago. After just a year together, they had both decided they needed stability, the right thing to do. Hale never came clean about the full extent of his debts, and besides, credit was freely available. Everyone had debt, and he didn't pry into Lucy's finances, which included 'complications' with her divorce. But now the derailed train flew down the hill with unstoppable momentum.

A file on his laptop, C_Hale_finance.xls, an Excel spreadsheet, told a familiar story of personal debt running riot in the new millennium. The kind of debt that plunged the world into the abyss of recession. Sub-prime mortgage lenders, city fraudsters, loan sharks, credit card companies, and banks all had a hand in a crime that was not checked until too late. So too did ordinary people such as Charles Hale, just another guy who woke up one day to realise the game was up.

Of course, Lucy was not privy to C_Hale_finance.xls, a record that did not take into account her own stash of credit and store cards. It listed twenty of Hale's debts including loans, credit cards, the mortgage, and overdrafts. All neatly tabulated to display total debts against assets. The figures exposed, in icy clarity, Hale's predicament: deep debt and negative equity.

His twenty-eight grand annual salary as a business advisor in Fenchurch Street, plus her meagre pickings as a part-time aerobics instructor, were barely enough to cover half of their monthly outgoings. Some limited savings from Lucy's ex-husband, Ralph, made little difference. The savings comprised dwindling maintenance payments, which were now being frittered on shopping and domestic dross.

Solution: borrow more.

The pressure-cooker whistled an ominous tune, but not just from the debts. Lucy's relationship with Ralph riled Hale. They were meeting regularly for coffee, but was it *just* for coffee, or something more? Ralph hung around like a bad smell when he arrived to pick up Deborah on Sundays, putting his feet up, rifling through the newspapers.

His stomach flab spilled over his stained chinos. And what was it about middle managers with goatee beards? Hale deemed Ralph's job description dubious, a title that appeared to change monthly, including the latest version: 'marketing executive' for a software firm. Hale suspected it was a sales role of some kind, maybe flogging accounting software to mid-sized firms. Secretly, Hale dreamed of finding him sitting at the checkout counter of *PC World*.

On what was an uncomfortable weekly encounter for Hale at least, Lucy would spend a few minutes readying herself and leave the two men downstairs. Lucy thought it important that some sort of bond existed between them, and yet Hale abhorred the mere mention of the ex-husband's name, let alone engaging with him for more than a nod or a handshake.

"So, how's business, Charles?" Ralph would ask, eyeing up the women in one of Lucy's *Cosmopolitan* magazines.

"Not so bad, actually," replied Hale. "Despite the recession, we're getting more start-up enterprise enquiries than..."

"Mm, we've got a big job coming up," said Ralph, interrupting, shifting his bulk on the sofa. "Networking systems. Integrating laptops and mobile devices. Could be big money. Good thing too, since I have a new car on order," he grinned, adjusting the angle of the magazine for a better gawk.

"Yes, the mobile computing business is growing," continued Hale. "We've got..."

"And we're taking on staff," Ralph interrupted, "expanding now ... new office on the cards I think."

Ralph's habit of butting in infuriated Hale. An arrogant buffoon. Yet, despite the palpable tension between them, Hale remained civil for the sake of Lucy and Deborah.

Just ten years old, Deborah was bubbly, adorable, and shared hysterical giggles at Hale's gullible antics and penchant for old black and white movies. "Chuck's watching his Jurassic films again, mum!" she'd cry out, when Hale spread himself across the couch with tea and chocolate doughnuts on a wintry Saturday afternoon.

One of those heart-warming family moments. Deborah was active, full of energy, happy to play Frisbee in the park, or walk for miles to nearby Hadleigh Castle in the rain and mud. Lucy deemed Charles a big kid who needed to be kept busy, and Deborah made the ideal playmate.

But tensions crept in. Lucy insisted on 'private' conversations with her daughter, shutting Hale out, to his dismay. On rare occasions, he needed to instil some step-fatherly discipline on the child, and then Deborah made it clear he wasn't her *real* dad.

Kids can be cruel.

"You're up early, love," said Lucy, ambling down the stairs in a dressing gown, her blonde spiky hair ruffled in mad directions. Hale thought it better than the coiffured creation that would replace it in an hour.

"Just trying to get ahead like yesterday," he said, closing the lid of the laptop and following her into the kitchen. "Clearing some emails and stuff like that before I head in."

"Oh, okay," she said, yawning, uninterested, filling the kettle.

"You sleep okay?" asked Hale.

"Fine, until you started rustling around at five in the morning, and then came down here. Do you ever stop?"

"Not often these days."

Hale leaned against the breakfast bar watching her routine. She was attractive in her relaxed morning mode. Slim, petite, with an Essex lilt, a cheeky smile would spread across her face on the occasions Hale's dry wit struck home. But that was seldom now, and he pondered where they'd gone wrong, and how a barrier had built up between them. Maybe he should discuss the finances, Ralph, and the underlying destructive tensions. Get it out in the open.

He leaned forward, gripping a chair at the breakfast table, bracing himself.

"I've been thinking," he said, pausing while he watched her drop a teabag from a great height into the flip bin.

"Yes, love, what?" Lucy eyed him, taking a slurp, cradling the mug with both hands. Hale felt his face redden. Was this the time to broach the subject? An awkward silence, not what he wanted.

"Well, I thought ... I'd take Deborah to the cinema on Saturday afternoon. You know, something different."

Lucy looked at him, raising her eyebrows. "Oh, right," she said, rubbing her hand through her hair. "Yes, whatever. Blimey, I thought you were going to make some earth-shattering announcement, something serious. You looked like a ghost for a minute there."

Deborah announced her arrival, thumping down the stairs and into the lounge to kick off the morning cartoons on television. Another opportunity to come clean had evaporated, and Hale knew it. The strength had eluded him again for some unfathomable reason. He could face danger at sea, awkward clients at work, and years ago, tempestuous scraps on the rugby field with oafs twice his size. But in these situations, the burgeoning weight of responsibility pressed down and silenced him.

Hale hopped two steps at a time down the steep pathway, through the trees to Leigh-on-Sea station. The view out to the Thames Estuary and across to Kent, a fleeting distraction from debt hell. Container ships, tugs, and fishing boats steamed up-and-down the brown waters, most heading west to the industrial ports of Tilbury and Gravesend, while others continued, tracking the meandering river closer into the city.

Behind him at the crest of the verdant down, Marine Parade, the main road east, wound a picturesque route into Southend. Their four-bed dwelling was tucked neatly within a cluster of beech and oak on Herschell Road, which branched north off Marine Parade. Modest by the standards of surrounding properties owned by dentists, doctors, and solicitors, Lucy and Hale's house rested firmly in Middle English suburbia. With mock Tudor frontage, leafy garden in much need of attention, and Lucy's Vauxhall shopping car parked outside, it merged into a row of pleasant, unremarkable properties.

The house had become a noose around Hale's neck. The forty-minute commute on the *C2C* train line into London at least provided access to a city of wealth, a means to relieve the burden he faced. But Hale's career was foundering. As a consultant to government-subsidised *Connecting4Business* (a quango organisation with goals as woolly as its name), he was employed as an advisor for Tower

Hamlets' start-up businesses and hopeful individuals looking for a helping hand in the world of entrepreneurship. Despite noble intentions laid out in the organisation's glossy brochure, Hale knew what the clients really sought: funding.

Milking hard cash out of *Connecting4Business*, however, was about as likely as Mohammed Al Fayed receiving a Knighthood, so it was Hale's lot to palm these candidates off with presentations and 'free' courses to ease their angst. Tick accountability boxes and essentially get rid of them. Hale's boss, Martin Stack, loved to bandy around the nonsensical notion of 'mentoring' – another redundant buzzword to add to the poppycock preached in an attempt to justify the organisation's existence. Hale complied, though, and along with others born of the positive thinking era, became expert at drumming up phrases that brought knowing nods and warm feelings from management eager to report notions of 'pro-activeness' to the powers above (Government suits daft enough to plough money into the scheme). Indeed, Stack's motive should have been to promote business in the area, create new jobs, and contribute to a growing local economy, but under the surface, Hale knew he was just another box-ticker living off government handouts. Stack couldn't give rat's arse about start-ups. He was cruising along until pension pick-up day.

Hardly the entrepreneurial spirit.

Hale wondered if his own case was not too different. He'd never run a small business, so what kind of mentor was he? In fact, who in *Connecting4Business* had embarked on anything remotely risky in business at all? Employees sat comfortably on salaries and perks watching the clients pass through the system, an influx of starry-eyed dreamers and bewildered lemmings. Those clients rejected for funding (most of them, barring a privileged few whose applications met cryptic 'inclusivity' criteria) were gently notified that they were not 'investment ready'. Further 'mentoring' would be the conclusion at the end of a lengthy business analysis report (a cut-and-paste job from the archive compiled by an intern while Stack sat in his office viewing porn sites on his laptop).

For Hale, however, there was an upside to this nonsense. Unlike his previous employer, an accountancy firm, he was no longer chained to a desk piled high with company year-end accounts, tax return folders, and dubious business expense claims. He could at least ease from desk to presentation to coffee machine, and on to reception where the amiable and much harassed secretary, Pam, delivered the daily gossip with her cutting wit. In her fifties and wily as hell when it came to office politics, she would fend off Stack if Hale had escaped on a walkabout break or extended lunch. The latter would invariably be at the *Cheshire Cheese*, a discreetly hidden pub under the railway arch across from Fenchurch Street's Crosswell entrance.

At 8:05 a.m., he reached the bottom of the steps to join a gaggle of lowly commuters making their way across the road and into Leigh-on-Sea's modest station. With its view out to the nature reserve and winding creeks of the estuary, there were much worse places to begin the daily grind into the city. The temperature, too, was agreeable this month of July. Much different to winter when the breezy platform would offer itself up to a biting easterly wind, sometimes accompanied by driving rain and sleet, making commuters stamp their feet and shrink into their scarves and lapels.

Hale boarded the *C2C*'s Quiet Zone, briefcase in hand, grey suit, silk tie. He politely exchanged small talk with the regulars. Similarly attired souls whose names he should know, but never would. Anonymous faces in the relentless weekday routine.

In the carriage, he offered the first available seat to a woman, smart, forties. She acknowledged Hale's chivalry, and then continued to prod away at her Blackberry. Hale lowered himself into the seat opposite. Immediately, they were joined by two other suits eager to establish their territory for the brief journey to London.

The next station is Benfleet.

The sound of the silky-smooth automated female announcement signalled their departure. People busied themselves, engrossed in their iPhones, paperbacks, printouts from work. Newspapers were carefully, quietly folded, since rustling was frowned upon in the sanctum of the Quiet Zone.

They appeared to Hale calm and in control of their ordered lives.

But perhaps they are like me, thought Hale, as he flipped open his briefcase to peruse the morning's agenda. Surely, some have problems, personal crises.

And perhaps like me, some are in big trouble.

THREE

The next station is Laindon.

The *C2C* forged through the Essex countryside bound for Fenchurch Street in the heart of London's financial district. On board, life was civilised. Unwritten rules applied. Commuters coughed quietly, hand over mouth, conversations hushed as if in a library. Personal stereos outlawed, children frowned upon, eating scorned, sneezing winced at, and the most heinous crimes, mobile phone conversations, invited looks of derision and hatred. Hale, well attuned to this special compartment, used it as a time to take stock.

He checked the agenda for the morning, shutting his domestic worries out, occasionally looking up at the blur of fields, industrial works, and residential homes flying by. The worries would return that evening, and certainly with the next morning's post, but for a few hours he would be shielded by the bubble of the city and this therapeutic cocoon.

"So, may I ask, have you devised a business plan for your ... err, clay café, Mrs Strickland?" asked Hale, hastily referring to his notes. The morning's first client sat opposite, a dowdy woman with straw hair, which had released a sprinkling of dandruff onto the shoulders of her ruffled jacket. Early fifties, he reckoned, probably divorced and a bit spiky. Proceed with caution.

"Business plan?" she squawked.

"Yes, if you remember, I asked for an outline of your ideas. A template if you like."

"Well, it's all in my head you know."

"Yes, of course, but..."

"And my friend, Elsie, she's going to help with the kitchen."

Hale drew breath. "Okay, and have you researched the local competition? By that I mean have you considered the viability of a clay painting espresso café in the Tower Hamlets area?" Hale watched her absorb the information for an uncomfortable few seconds before her face winced into a walnut, her eyes glaring at him unblinking. She'd noticed the dry humour apparent in his comment.

"A lot of mums say this is just what they want, and their kids will keep occupied with the painting," she answered, hunching forward.

"Quite, but research is paramount if..."

"And Jill says she'll come on Tuesday," she continued. "All day if necessary. All day!"

Mrs Strickland was typical of a plethora of business 'creatives' that Hale advised. Dreamers with fickle business ideas born of impulse, but sadly doomed from the outset. Despite this, Hale tried not become a complete cynic, since there may be the germ of an idea somewhere amongst the slush pile of nutty and delusional proposals that would lead a client to a millionaire success story.

The next client before the reprieve of the coffee break did at least tweak Hale's imagination: an idea for a tapas bar. With his love of all things Spanish, a chance perhaps to brush up on the lingo.

"Buenos días señor Andrews. ¿Cómo estás?" said Hale, having prepared an appropriate greeting.

"What?" replied the client, who stood frowning.

"Oh, apologies," said Hale, "I was just saying good morning and asking how you were. Do please take a seat."

Mr Andrews, a mid-twenties illiterate with fading tattoos on his neck could have been mistaken for a football hooligan. As was the form with the more misguided clients, Mr Andrews launched immediately into a pitch, talking *at* Hale with great gusto.

"So it just came to me in the bath, like. Almost like Eureka, know what I mean?"

"Mm, yes Archimedes I believe," said Hale.

"What?"

Hale's concentration waned as he pondered how to survive the next twenty minutes.

"So anyway, I'm gonna open a tapas bar with a British twist. Great tapas at just five quid each. Then add a British menu with what people want, like cottage pie, bangers 'n mash, curry ... that sort of stuff."

"Curry, that's Indian," interrupted Hale, "and you say five pounds ... rather expensive?"

Tapas Man was not hot on comprehension, characteristic of Ralph the buffoon in that respect, noted Hale. Thankfully, however, this client was not obnoxious or bigoted, just clueless. Also on the plus side, Tapas Man was not as sensitive as Ms Clay Café, who could get ratty at the slightest cross-examination of her business proposition.

"It's gonna work," continued Tapas Man. "I can see it now and I've got the business nous and..."

"Well, that sounds fascinating," said Hale, having to barge in to break up the onslaught, "and tell me, have you been to Spain at all, perhaps to research the food angle?"

"No, but I've been to Tenerife," replied Tapas Man, with a crooked smile revealing an urgent need for dentistry.

"That *is* Spain, actually."

"And also Fuetoventorro."

"Ah, yes, Fuerteventura," said Hale.

"Nice place, great clubbing, but no one spoke English where I was, so I was a bit disappointed."

"Of course, that's the problem with foreign countries."

"Yeah, and so what I'm looking for is start-up funding to get us up and running, know what I mean?"

Hale sent Tapas Man scurrying off to draw up a business plan on something larger than the back of a postage stamp and to buy a map of Europe, and then sauntered down to reception. The ever-bubbly Pam buzzed around dealing with calls, paperwork, and sheep-like clients wandering aimlessly around the foyer.

"Ah Charles, love, so what waifs and strays did you have to contend with on this lovely day then?" she asked, in her endearing East End lilt.

"Oh, just the usual," he said, leaning lazily against the reception counter. "One damaged divorcee, bit neurotic, and a football hooligan looking to make a career change into haute cuisine."

Pam chuckled, diverted a call on the switchboard. "You're terrible, Charles. The poor souls couldn't have been *that* bad."

They continued to gossip for a few minutes about not much at all. It occurred to Hale that his humour seemed well aligned with Pam's, something he found curious, since these conversations were more relaxed than those with Lucy.

Bolstered by Pam's cheeriness, he caught the lift, walked out of the shiny foyer of the towering office block onto Crosswell, a road leading to the curiously named, Crutched Friars. He slipped into a trendy eatery with an unpronounceable name specialising in 'natural food' on the junction of the two roads. From the large glass window, he watched the comings and goings from the station and the *Cheshire Cheese*, bought a coffee, proper Italian brew. Office workers walking briskly, purposeful, many holding bundles of files, a good number of the men in pinstripe. The women, chic and slim, chose high-heels – great for poise, inadequate on the hard streets. To Hale, these were self-assured highfalutin career types. Financiers, solicitors, bankers, or criminal lawyers. No wide boys or estate agents. No badly fitting double-breasted suits or greased-back hair that would mark them as 'out of town'. People were smart in this neighbourhood, polite, well off.

Hale sipped his coffee, thought about their lives, and his. Maybe their outward appearance was a facade behind which lay customary insecurities, personal crises, and chasms of worry of the type that had beset Hale's world. Or maybe he was different. Reckless, off the rails.

Time was running out. He sensed black clouds on the horizon. Soon the storm would be upon him dark and heavy.

Hale headed back the office to do battle with his last client before giving the afternoon's presentation.

"So I want to set up a video production company with a different angle. A friendly, low cost approach to making home videos, business films, and weddings."

Video Man delivered his pitch.

Fifties, portly, beetroot complexion and intense piggy eyes, Video Man seemed to be struggling in the modest warmth of London's summer. Hale hoped he wouldn't have to administer CPR, tapped his pen vigorously on the desk to arrest his boredom. Video production ideas were flawed business models. He gave them two years before they failed, max.

"Wouldn't you say that modern technology, affordable cameras, home editing systems and so on, makes your business model a little fragile?" asked Hale.

Video Man gasped, hyperventilating. "Well that's where I've done me homework."

"Ah, good," said Hale, leaning back. At last, a client with forethought.

"Gap in the market," blurted Video Man.

"I'm sorry?"

"Gap in the market," he repeated, rustling through an unruly folder of scribbles and cuttings. "I reckon a load of people want it done proper. With titles, music, and real professional like."

"Quite."

"Like you see on telly."

"Indeed."

"And weddings ... Asian weddings are big business," he continued, beads of sweat rolling down his red cheeks. "I'm in with that crowd. I know a lot of them *people of colour* I guess you call them, what with me living in Limehouse and all."

"Yes, but I'm told that those weddings are rather long, lavish affairs," said Hale. "Wonderful events, but aren't they very hard work to cover, hard to make profitable?"

"Don't know about that guv'nor, but we could do 'em a discount if it's clocking up the hours, like. And mark my words, I'll do me research."

After lunch, Hale gathered the day's interviewees, plus a group from the business faculty at Tower Business College, in the boardroom to join him for his much-hallowed presentation: *Powering Ahead to Business Success*.

Pam hovered in the background, arranging refreshments, and much to Hale's alarm, cast him mischievous grins. This, she knew would trigger his juvenile giggling habit, which he'd try to disguise by feigning a cough or a sneeze.

After two hours of pie charts and bullet points, the room was stuffy, so Hale delivered his summing-up designed to raise the hairs on the back of the necks of 'pos-thinking' go-getters.

"And that is *Connecting4Business*, a tried and tested formula..." He deftly flipped the PowerPoint slide to a clichéd photograph of two suits shaking hands, the gleaming tower blocks of Canary Wharf in the background, "... to help *you* power ahead to business success."

A ripple of applause fluttered through the audience.

"Thank you."

Hale nodded appreciatively, smiled, genuinely happy since this finale signalled his departure to the pub. Unfortunately, Martin Stack put paid to that idea with a pile of reports, which required signing, and a menial data entry task that pushed Hale into an awkward time to negotiate the rush hour.

With the additional admin complete, and after some cursing, Hale made his customary stop at the *Cheshire Cheese* and dissolved into a throng of grey suit and tie. A more rugged crowd, predominantly traders, chatted loudly about the markets or cricket or football. Hale sat alone at a stool by the window, on the sidelines, trying to grasp a sense of their world. The crowd at *Connecting4Business* were supposedly in tune with industry and commerce, but Stack was full of bullshit, and so was the entire outfit. These pubgoers made the real money.

That's what I need to do, Hale thought. Escape the rut and generate some proper cash, nail the debts. Practise what I preach at work: take a risk.

He left the pub, walked across the cobbles to join the commuter rush back to Leigh-on-sea.

Just another day.

FOUR

Hale returned home, ran three miles along the cliff top, showered, and then hopped back down the steps to Old Leigh a few hundred yards to the east of the station.

The fishing hamlet dried out when the fierce local tide ebbed, leaving miles of mudflats and an opportunity for cockle pickers to wade out for a few hours' backbreaking work. For Hale, long summer evenings offered a chance to escape the city. This evening was typical of many. Lucy took Deborah swimming or shopping while Hale made his way to the second pub of the day, passing cockle sheds and quaint cottages along the road leading into the village. Clinker-built wooden fishing boats, all brightly coloured, slumbered at odd angles on slipways or in the mud, waiting for the incoming tide to right them.

School friend, Barrie 'Baz' Strachan, waited in *Ye Olde Smack*, their regular haunt. Here they'd chew the fat, drink beer, get away from the daily grind.

Baz was Essex-born, a chest of drawers, stocky, no neck. A heavy brow and thick head of hair, hedgehog style. Good with figures, he'd started a career as a dealer in the Square Mile, but quit to become a hod carrier. Hulking bricks around all day was, according to him, preferable to, "kissing the arse of some ponce in the smoke." During their schooldays, Hale was thankful Baz had played on his side in the rugby team. Hale had quit the game during college, but Baz played on for what he termed, "a bit of a friendly ruckus at the weekends."

Hale burst through the door of *The Smack*, late as usual. It was quiet inside. A few drinkers held pints close to their navels, other locals and tourists had opted for a view of the sultry sunset on the terrace overlooking the estuary.

These pub sessions followed a familiar pattern. Baz stood in his usual position at the bar, a permanent fixture, playing with his cell phone. A wisecrack awaited anyone familiar who approached.

"Oh look, it's the stranger," he said, as Hale entered. "Don't tell me, you had to feed your pet piranha."

Hale wiped sweat from his forehead, "Sorry Baz, in a bit of a rush."

"Leaves on the line again?" said Baz, pocketing his phone.

"Full-on day ... you wouldn't believe." Hale took a gulp from the cool pint of lager Baz had positioned for him on the bar.

"How's work?"

"It's shit. Boss needs a slap."

"Mm, I'd be happy to oblige," said Baz. "Just gimme a call."

"Will do."

"And how's the missus then?"

Baz, a fierce gossipmonger, had mentioned Hale's domestic unease on a number of occasions during the previous weeks.

"She's fine," said Hale, "but I've got hassle with work, money ... all that shit going on."

"Oh, you mean *life*?" said Baz, smiling, as was his style, more with his eyes than mouth.

"I won't bore you with the details."

"Pity. I was looking forward to some dirt about that Ralph guy or something. But, I can't see your problem, Charlie. You got a house, family life, and besides, you're going on bleedin' holiday to the Costas soon aren't cha?"

"Yes, but we won't be seeing too much of each other on that trip. I'm dropping them off with friends in Nerja. Then heading off to take the boat out sailing with the guys."

"I haven't had a proper holiday in years, so you're lucky, mate," said Baz. "Can't say much for your choice of company, though. That sailing geezer, Scottish, what's his name ... Jack?"

"Jack Weir."

"Yeah, shifty if you ask me."

"You only met him once for two minutes, but thanks for the psychoanalysis of my crewmember."

"You know me, Essex's leading conspiracy theorist."

"Accurate."

"Thanks, appreciated."

Full of worthy advice. That was Baz, the rock. A port in a storm, someone Hale could rely on. But despite his brashness, there was another dimension to Baz. Something he seemed to play down, conceal. To an inquisitive person of Hale's intelligence, it rankled.

His closest friend, the supposed down-to-earth diamond geezer, with his liking for beer and punch-ups on the rugby field, was coy about another side to his life. Any mention of Baz's weekends away, which he called the 'fishing trips', was met with a blank stare or a deft change of subject that threw Hale's line of questioning off-kilter.

Hale believed Baz could have endured city life to make a decent living, even if he hated it, especially with the escape of the Essex countryside just a forty-minute commute from the smoke. But hod carrying? Labouring was lucrative, but surely not enough to support a BMW, sizeable house, and his latest girlfriend, Georgina (a bubbly twenty-something and walking perfume factory with lavish tastes in clothes and foreign holidays). Baz's girlfriends changed with the seasons, each having unique and expensive tastes in bling and glitzy accessories, traits that seemed to amuse the jolly hod carrier.

His coyness annoyed Hale, since Baz was his closest friend and confidant harking back to the school playgrounds. Growing up, no subject – no matter how sordid or uncomfortable – had been off limits. Teachers, sport, sex, girls, or money – all open for discussion between them. But a switch had flicked after Baz quit a five-year stint in the British Army to embark on his city career. He had been purportedly ejected for an 'alcohol-related incident', after which Hale found certain subjects were not so much off limits, but rather vague and curious, and not in keeping with Baz's forthright personality.

In any 'normal' relationship, weekend fishing trips or unexplained absences would raise the suspicions of wives or long-term girlfriends, but since Baz was neither married nor *long-term* about many of the relationships with his dolly birds (his term), regular affairs seemed an unlikely explanation to Hale. For years, there was little indication of Baz's whereabouts during his fishing soirees, and never any sight of the so-called 'friends' who accompanied him.

Hale's curiosity had been heightened further by an incident, an anomaly uncovered by chance. To avoid pubs and associated beer bellies, Baz drove them both for a weekly gym workout, often stopping for petrol. After filling up and paying, Baz handed Hale the cash receipts to place in his 'filing cabinet', the glove compartment comprising a chaotic mass of crisp packets, empty drinks cartons, and random paperwork. Presumably, the petrol receipts would eventually be collated and forwarded to a beleaguered accountant to trawl through for the hod carrier's year-end accounts. On one occasion, Baz negotiated a long queue in the garage shop while Hale remained in the car, bored. This prompted him to open the glove compartment and peruse the mess. Two fuel receipts fell to the floor, the first listing a memorable date: November 5, Guy Fawkes Night, a weekend Baz said that he'd gone fishing. The receipt detailed the transaction: Saturday morning, 08:31 hrs, The Highpost Filling Station, Salisbury. The second receipt, the following day: Sunday evening 18:07 hrs, Rotherwas Service Station, Hereford. Two landlocked areas.

Odd locations, since Baz was a steadfast shore-fishing enthusiast.

Baz occasionally returned from prolonged absences with the kind of tan that lightened his stubble, drew patterns around his eye sockets. More windburn and steady exposure than radiation from a beach holiday. *Lanzarote*, his explanation. Purportedly, the Canarian island was his regular haunt for sunshine breaks with his latest girlfriend.

No fool, Hale knew that Baz had retained some army involvement, or at least maintained connections. Special Forces perhaps. But in what capacity? This question perplexed Hale. As did Baz's disinclination to divulge any information – even the most rudimentary scrap – to his closest and most loyal friend.

Baz and Hale walked their drinks outside to the terrace. Other pubgoers sat around, cradling their sundowners, taking in the view. The tide had begun to rise with its distinctive east coast scent, a cocktail of fish, seaweed, and viscous mud.

"I have money issues," said Hale, looking down at wading birds scurrying and foraging for invertebrates in the mud.

"Who hasn't Charlie?" said Baz, a grin forming across his sizeable jaw. "America's got eleven trillion dollars of debt hasn't it? Make you feel any better?"

"Maybe, but *personal* debt is different."

"What sort of figures are we talking? Maybe I can sub you some," said Baz, ripping open a packet of peanuts with his stubby fingers and tossing a handful into his mouth.

Hale remained silent while he mulled the offer. Baz was familiar with the financial plights of diamond geezers and city chancers, but the figures would make even him choke on his peanuts.

Baz raised his eyebrows, turning to Hale, "Well?"

"Thanks, I appreciate it," Hale sighed, "but this is something I need to sort out with Lucy."

Baz nodded. "Understood," he said, crunching loudly, throwing a peanut into the mud below. "And that woman's all right. Spoke to her for a few minutes with my missus in town the other day. She's a solid bird and you're not as messed in the head as you used to be with that French girl. Jesus, now that *was* a bleedin' nightmare."

FIVE

The French girl.

Hale thought about Céline the next day as he travelled on the *C2C*. The train was packed, no seats available, but standing no inconvenience since it allowed him to stretch his legs after the previous evening's run.

Baz was right. Some years before he met Lucy, Hale ran into the twenty two-year-old French 'mature' student who was spending a year in England to study at London's Royal College of Art opposite Hyde Park.

Why she was visiting *Connecting4Business*, he couldn't recall, seemed irrelevant now. Why she became interested in Charles Hale, over twenty years her senior, perplexed him, heightening his fascination and subsequent infatuation. Single at the time, Hale was plunged into a world of intoxicating obsession, a mist lifted from a dull day. The freezing London winter became a playground, something to be savoured, not squandered.

Petite, slim, with chic that French women purvey without thought, her chestnut hair curled, unruly, down to the middle of her back. Her shabby old coat hugged her figure enough to catch the glances of men passing in the street, and her oversized woolly scarf hid her sensual mouth, which blew breath into the frosty air. She wore little makeup. Her impatience and disregard for it made a mockery of women who turned their faces into oil paintings before venturing into the open. In Céline's company, Hale spotted scornful looks from women jealous of her beauty. Spite they could not hide even in public. Céline remained oblivious to this attention.

Her eyes were the darkest brown, curious, with a mischievous glint, playful, never cynical. Hale first stared into them in a faceless corridor of *Connecting4Business*.

A turning point in his life.

Their first date was for coffee at a Covent Garden café beside the Opera House. They sat outside in the cold, the table wobbled on the uneven road, splashing coffee about. The waiter fussed, cleaning up. Céline laughed at Hale's English politeness, his odd wit, as they watched shoppers, buskers, and street performers mingle in the winter air. Hale felt mildly embarrassed with the age difference, but soon wallowed in a new carefree world of infectious laughter and flirtatiousness. He caught every flick of her eyes, hung on every hastily-corrected syllable of her accented English. Her fingerless gloves grasping the cardboard coffee cup, her carelessly entangled coloured headbands, scuffed leather boots hidden to the ankle by the frayed edges of her jeans, simple gold earrings, tatty shoulder bag. These observations consumed him such that the stresses and mundane irritations of the world became the problems of others.

Moments with Céline became images stored in Hale's mind, like the folders of a digital photo album. He could replay the slideshow at will. On the train, at a presentation, or in the office, he might indulge. He'd open the relevant folder to mentally replay his obsession in exquisite detail.

Their first date. Filed for later retrieval (Folder 1, Covent Garden: The Café).

Schoolboy infatuation. Stupid, and bound to end in tears. This Hale knew, yet he willingly sank further. With Céline, the heated nature of their love spawned a taste for spontaneity and extravagance. Indulgences London was well equipped to provide for those who had cash ... or credit.

A November Saturday in late afternoon gloom, they ran through the streets, darted through traffic, hand-in-hand from café to pub, avoiding downpours and jeers from drivers of black cabs and buses. In a packed pub, they vainly tried to dry out against a radiator, drank ale, shouting to each other above noisy revellers. 1:15 p.m. was normally too early for Hale to be drinking. But time was inconsequential with the beautiful French girl squashed against him in the crowd, and no plans for later, other than to be together.

A further dash through the streets, brushing past shoppers and tramps and couples hunkering beneath umbrellas. Another drinking well offered up by the city with a pub on every corner. Afternoon melted into evening, a delirious blur that should never end.

They ducked into an unremarkable side street. Hale recognised the building opposite. Smart doorman with top hat, grand entrance, flags towering above, colour and lights blasting out of the gloom and drizzle of the wet streets.

Claridge's.

For Hale, there was only one outcome.

"Shall we?" he said, gesturing toward the entrance. He placed his hand on Céline's shoulder, guiding her up the steps and out of the rain.

The doorman smiled, exchanged some pleasantries, something about the rain.

Céline looked at Hale, puzzled as they passed into the foyer. "No, but what are we doing here?" she said.

"We can't go back to your flat tonight ... with all your student friends dossing around everywhere."

"What do you mean?" she giggled, looking around at marble floors, chandeliers, lavish furnishings. "And what is this word, *dossing*?"

Two hours later, Hale sprawled across the king-sized bed playing with the television control as Céline languished in a steaming bath, singing something in French. The bed had been turned down for the night, slippers and dressing gowns positioned. The couple could have been millionaires on a weekend having just landed in their Learjet, honeymooners, Hollywood film stars or business magnates. The staff wouldn't guess otherwise. Wouldn't guess that Céline was a penniless student, and Hale an office worker with mid-low income, rich on credit, poor on cash. No assets.

Hale donned a dressing gown, posed in the mirror. Scary sight, he thought. Then, moved into the bathroom, posed again for Céline who lifted her shapely leg through a mountain of bubbles. The bath water threatened to flood onto the floor.

"You crazy fool ... what do you look like?" she said, flicking water at him.

Hale paused, and looked blankly for a moment.

"Oh shit!" he said.

"What?"

"The rugby."

Céline rolled her eyes. Hale darted back into the bedroom, dove onto the bed and turned on the television.

Céline called after him, "You're just like those old men in Paris ... in the bars. All they can talk about is *les Bleus*."

Hale's eyes grew heavy, a daze from the afternoon's drinking and warmth of the hotel. The commentary from the match seeped into his semi-consciousness, the game played at a green and wet Twickenham twelve miles away. Céline emerged from the bathroom, naked, slipped under the heavy bedding beside him.

Later, they dressed, headed back out into the rain.

"I love the rain," she said, grabbing his arm as they bundled onto the backseat of the black cab.

"So where will it be, chief?" asked the cabbie.

"Just drive around for a bit please," said Hale.

"Ah, one of them ... just like in the movies, eh 'guv?"

"And then an Italian restaurant of your choice, West End if you know one."

"Right you are, chief."

The restaurant accepted the couple amid a throng of theatregoers and tourists. Good food, bustling atmosphere. The cash in Hale's wallet was running thin and Céline had no cash at all. Hale reached for the credit card.

The easy option.

At *Claridge's*, one night seemed too short. Rude to curtail the dream. Two nights it had to be, with breakfast of course. The best breakfast in town, not to be missed. The nervous young waiter made Céline giggle as he rattled china, spilt tea, and presented perfectly poached eggs on her plate. Hale was kinder, engaging him in small talk about the photography adorning the walls. Former guests: Monroe, Bogart, Hepburn, Hitchcock.

Céline, relaxed in the surroundings, clung to Hale's arm. Young, excited, beautiful. In the foyer on the last day, he released her arm to settle the bill at reception.

"Everything all right for you sir?" asked the receptionist. A similar accent to Céline's, Hale thought.

"Fine, thank you. A lovely hotel ... and you're French I hear?"

"Thank you, sir. I'm Italian," she smiled.

"Ah, right," said Hale, glancing across to Céline, who tutted, feigned annoyance at his doomed line.

"So, here is your bill, sir." She slid the folded invoice across the polished counter.

Hale part-opened it, focussing on the figure at the bottom, staring at the total for some considerable seconds.

£1,271.47

"And that includes our special rate this weekend, sir." Hale sensed the receptionist glancing at him, perhaps looking for a reaction. He held his breath, looked over to Céline. Now bored, she was exchanging words, flirting with the porter, a likeable Londoner in his sixties.

"Fine, thank you," said Hale, exhaling at last. "Credit card okay?"

"Of course, sir."

Claridge's. Just another folder in Hale's mental photo album. There would be other weekends, other top hotels, restaurants, clubs and bars. The extravagance built, elevating their tastes to new heights of luxury. Céline and Charles. It had a ring to it. Felt good. They gained a reputation as the city couple with cash to splash. Hotel staff, bar owners, and club managers were curious about the new 'names' in town. They were financiers perhaps, or maybe beneficiaries of a large inheritance. Pointed questions came discreetly at first, and then brashly as the alcohol flowed from wisecracking city boys, wizened women with gin breath, and drunken middle managers propping up bars after work.

The fairy tale blossomed over months. A blur of colourful characters and places, a prolonged party in the historic capital whose streets had seen wealth, poverty, disease, blitz, and destruction. A city that could turn on the lights and glamour for anyone with enough energy to burn.

And money.

The lovers' extravagance was not confined to the city. Frequent weekend dashes to the Lake District broke them out of the smoke and hubbub. As did last-minute dashes in the Friday traffic to the southwest, the Devon coast. They'd stand on a cliff holding each other in the cold, darkness and driving rain, listening to the surf crash onto the rocks before heading down into the village. A pub awaited them, typical Olde English affair. Log fire, warm ale, dogs barking at their feet. Laughter and stories from ebullient locals who gravitated to the French girl with the playful eyes.

Everybody loved Céline.

Yet, Hale refused to allow his mind veer into dangerous territory, and the possibility that their love would ever founder. Even the blandness of *Connecting4Business* could not dampen the romance. At work, Hale had a new swing in his step. Pam told him so. Said she had never seen him as buoyant, alive. At her reception desk on Monday mornings, she eagerly awaited his arrival for more news of the foreign student who had transformed his life.

But after some months had passed, Pam confided in Hale one morning. She appeared uncharacteristically sombre. Something worried her about his future.

She said she feared for him.

SIX

Then there was the sex.

Outside of Hale's credit card extravagances, Céline's student digs near Denmark Street provided an opportunity, but only when her flatmates were attending lectures and not moping around feigning illness and watching episodes of *The Wire* from a bootleg DVD box set someone had picked up from Camden Market.

The shabby third floor apartment gave them the privacy, and there was a pattern to their encounters. The door was locked, an armchair shoved against it. Wrestling like children, they bounded against each other, stumbling about in fits of laughter. They'd come to their senses, barge into Céline's room, embrace, crashing onto the single bed, which creaked under the strain, and then let out a crack as another slat broke beneath. Hysterics at the state of the trashed bed, clothes thrown off and curtains hastily yanked shut, spraying broken railing hooks across the floor. Hale hopped around the room, battling to free himself from his boxer shorts wrapped around his ankles, trying to avoid piles of magazines, unwashed cereal bowls, and CDs scattered around. Freed, he launched himself at Céline, who waited naked on the bed.

Minutes later, they lay together in silence. Just the sound of their breathing, traffic in the street, and some stoned student hollering in the corridor downstairs.

Sex injuries happened, and though accidental, added spice to the entanglements at the grubby student hovel. Few incidents required medical attention, though on one occasion Hale was pushed against the wall by a wanton Céline, only to slide down onto a rusty radiator tap. Céline dashed out through the streets of shoppers to *Superdrug* on Charing Cross Road, returning to tend a gash on Hale's hip. A case for stitches, he said. She told him not to be *such a fool* and patched it up lovingly.

Sex with Céline.

In future, Hale would recall this folder of his mental photo album with the most unease, anguish. Made him shudder.

Sex with Lucy was rare, more a Ford Escort than Céline's Ferrari. It was a different process of timing, negotiation, even diplomacy. The running and the gym work made things worse. Rather than calm him, it fuelled his interest in women and sex. The testosterone boost. Lucy was 'busy'. Busy with Deborah, didn't feel right, not the right time, out with the coven of witches, or whatever this week's or this month's reasons were.

With Céline there was no discussion, no premeditated plan or routine. Sex just happened. A lot.

Despite the action under the covers, cracks began to appear in Céline and Hale's relationship on a weekend to Paris (a trip made possible courtesy of the H-CAP Bank Gold Card with six-month 0% introductory rate and healthy £6,500 credit limit).

The first day in a cosy two-star hotel in the backstreets of the Bastille district extended the lovers' dream. Flurries of snow decorated the city's distinctive architecture, bridges, and streets. Ice crunched underfoot, the slate grey winter sky melded into evening, biting cold, encouraging tourists and locals into the warmth of the bars. Walks alongside the rivers, amongst cafés and restaurants, with piping hot vin chaud served in street markets. Frames of a romantic movie played out for real. Hale basked in Céline's company, wallowed in a heady fairy tale.

The next morning, they met with Céline's mother, Josie, a warm, outgoing woman whose striking features were identifiably reflected in her daughter. A ship in full sail, she wore flowing gowns and scarves. She greeted Hale with a hearty hug and kisses, and although spoke no English, was patient with his stuttering French, which he peppered with doses of cringe-worthy Spanglish, sending mother and daughter into fits of giggles.

He laughed with them, hands in pockets, stomping snow from his shoes, trying in vain to make snowballs from the powder to throw at Céline.

But the devil in his mind rang alarm bells.

Could this be too perfect ... too perfect to last?

In Paris, there was no outward reason For Hale to suspect trouble brewing.

Just instinct.

Meeting Céline's English father, Rex, a month later at a noisy café at Waterloo station was not such a delight. A tall man with an air of arrogance and cold eyes, Hale wondered what Josie had seen in him. They were separated, divorced, so that was no doubt the answer to his question.

"I hear you're into yachting," said Hale. An icebreaker he'd prepared by way of a tip-off from Céline.

Rex failed to meet Hale's eyes, stirred his oversized cappuccino loudly and took a slurp. Then deigned to reply, "Yes, I'm skippering forty-footers. Racing's my game." The father turned to Céline. "So how are the studies, darling?"

A snub, leaving Hale cut off. Céline seemed to feel the tension and led the conversation away from her newfound lover, Charles Hale.

Clearly, Rex did not approve of the older boyfriend. Hale was familiar with this flavour of business stiff. A middle-aged bore whose career had neither bombed nor flourished, and who'd never taken a risk in his life, opting for mediocrity. Rex enjoyed mentioning the strength of his investment portfolio, and it seemed that every other sentence he uttered contained the word 'lawyer'. Hale ached to use the term *solicitor*, a more accurate job description. A glorified admin clerk with an ego. As for the 'racing skipper' credential, Rex was in the wrong company to brag. As a boy, Hale had earned his stripes on the tricky waters of the Thames Estuary. Racing, day sailing, or just pottering on the water, he'd sailed with grizzled old sea dogs, experienced hands, and newcomers green as hell. Most skippers were likeable, coped with the highs and lows of being afloat, but there was a brand of conceited prick that tainted the mix. Rex was a shining example.

Look on the positives, thought Hale. Josie was sweet, and maybe Rex wasn't so bad. Get to know him a bit.

And yet, therein lay the problem. As Hale became closer to Céline – her family, her life, her future – the bigger the void grew between them.

A *Connecting4Business* conference in Coventry sealed their fate. A torrid four-day convention of accountancy nerds and business advisors was set to deliver a series of lectures and presentations so dull they threatened to turn sane men to drink.

"I have to go, Céline. Stack's got a bug up his arse about it and I can't miss it," said Hale, speaking on his cell phone, pacing in his office.

"But I want to *be* with you. I'll come too," she replied.

Hale considered paying for three nights at the hotel, but according to *Connecting4Business*, they would then qualify as 'a couple'. In this regard, the firm's policy on expenses was clear: couples pay. He *could* claim regardless, and kind-hearted Pam would oblige if he asked by authorising the paperwork for him. Hale, though, would not put her in that position.

The remaining option was credit.

Most of his cards were maxed-out or beyond their promotional periods. A cash withdrawal on a card would suffice, but the interest brutal. This time Hale was backed into a corner, no way out.

"It's only a week, Céline. I'll rush back on the last day to see you, I promise."

"I need you," she insisted.

Hale took a deep breath, walked to the window looking down at the office workers hurrying by.

"I'll call you from the hotel ... it's one week, that's all."

"Okay," she said, and then hung up.

"Céline?"

A week later, having cleared the remaining conference paperwork, Hale returned to the office on Monday morning. During his absence, Céline had not answered his calls. From his desk, he sent her a text:

'how r u? I haven't heard. I'm back now, can I come over later, 3pm?'

Her reply came minutes later:

'ok. cu at gareths place'

Gareth's place? A student cesspit much worse than Céline's digs, a dump Hale had visited just once. Once was enough. Incapable of working, he urged the time to pass with nothing but Céline in his head.

2:45 p.m.

Hale hurried out of the rain, entered the student accommodation block near Tottenham Court Road. Up to the fourth floor, he hopped two steps at a time, avoiding glances from students loitering in the corridors smoking joints and drinking cans of cheap lager.

Door number 406, off-white and sticky with grime. Hale knocked. No answer. Music thumped from inside. He tried the handle, eased it open. Down a musty corridor, he approached a room, the band *Snow Patrol* blasting from within. On either side of the corridor, filth, beer cans, and dirty clothing covered the floors. A fog, a pungent wall of the unwashed sat in the air. 'Cesspit' was too kind a word. He turned into the lounge, a room marginally lit from a window, dirty and stained. A battered HiFi sat on a dilapidated desk held together with gaffer tape. The sound deafening and distorted, it looked as if its last home was a charity shop and its next, the skip. Two students smoked cheap skunk, sat on the floor against a radiator, looked as if they'd be better off in rehab. Hale scanned the mess, spotted Céline seated on a mouldy sofa.

Their eyes met and he knew it was over.

She held the stub of a cigarette in one hand and her cell phone in the other. Her eyes were sunken, pupils dilated.

"Oh, you ... Charles," she said, slurring, looking as if she was having trouble focussing on him. Drunk, stoned.

"Yes," said Hale, feeling uneasy. "Said I'd stop by, remember?"

She said nothing. An awkward moment. Hale glanced around at the vagrants. A smell hit him. Urine. Hale had a nose for the stuff. Thrown about at sea in a gale, men would spray everywhere and dash back on deck, or someone would neglect to pump the toilet. The contents then splashed onto the floorboards, down into the bilges. A stench that never leaves the soul. Gareth's hellhole reeked of substance abuse and a whole load of other stuff of which Hale preferred not to know.

This sure isn't *Claridge's*, he thought.

"This is Andy." Céline flicked her eyes to a Kurt Cobain look-alike, who sat beside her, stoned and smirking. Looked to be modelling his drugged-fuelled existence on the late rock star.

"Hello Andy," said Hale, raising his voice above the music. "Look, Céline, can we go and get a coffee perhaps outside?"

Cobain sniggered. Céline looked at Hale blankly, took a drag on the butt still smoking between her dirty yellow fingers."

"Well," she said, blowing a cloud into the air. "I was..."

She was incoherent, unable to form a sentence.

Someone bumped Hale, entering the lounge. A Goth-looking student in his twenties, black jumper and too many piercings.

"Sorry dad," said Goth Boy, under his breath, and, "Who's the old geezer?" to the skunkheads on the floor. They laughed, school kid laughs, averting their gaze from Hale.

Céline was out of it, put her head back against the sofa and closed her eyes. For Hale, the coldest feeling. In one week, she'd made a dark turnaround from the bubbly French girl to this.

There was no point in hanging around. Hale turned, stormed out of the flat, down the stairs, kicking beer cans out of his way, barging past some junkies hanging around in the stairwell. Breathless, he paused to collect his thoughts at the door leading out to the rain-soaked street.

"Got any change, mate?" asked a bearded tramp sheltering at the door. Hale shook his head, in no mood for charity.

I've been a fool, thought Hale. Over the weeks, he'd detected occasional hints of cigarette smoke on Céline's clothes, sometimes a thicker, sweeter scent. Didn't think anything of it at the time. But full-on addiction? Was he so blindly in love to have missed the signs?

He fumed, hitting his fist against the wall. Idiot.

A clatter down the stairs signalled the arrival of Goth Boy, who brushed past Hale giving him a sly look. "All right mate?" he said, grinning, cocky.

"Hey son, I know you're going through your mind-expanding student shit," said Hale, "but I'm doing you a favour, okay. Clean up that repugnant cave you call your digs or the owner will evict you, no question about it."

"You reckon?"

"Yeah, I reckon, because it smells of piss and shit just like you. Oh, and I'm not your dad."

Goth Boy stood for a moment, frowned, pulled his hoodie up.

"Ciao shitweed," said Hale, left him to mull it over, headed back to the office.

SEVEN

Málaga, 2:09 p.m.

The taxi raced along Alameda Principal, a dockside dual carriageway lined with palms, leading to the Paseo Parque. A leafy frontage to the bustle of the city. They passed the Cathedral of Málaga, and soon the driver pulled up on Calle Molina Lario, a central street with the fortifications of the Alcazaba towering above a few hundred yards to the east.

"Nice area," said Hale, handing some notes to the driver and waving away the change. He swung open the passenger door.

The heat hit him, an invisible wall.

The city in August, the height of summer, thirty-five degrees and rising. On the pavement, Lucy edged into the shade holding Deborah's hand as Hale and the driver, a portly old-timer, wrestled with her huge wheelie case.

Sweat ran down Hale's face. What the hell does she pack into it? By comparison, his holdall was a quarter of the weight, *and* packed for a sailing trip.

Lucy struggled in the oven, shell-shocked, fanning herself with a magazine. The old town of Moorish architecture, street cafés, restaurants, and tapas bars bathed under intense light. But this was no time to dwell on the scenery or to be manhandling heavy bags through the streets. Hale believed he'd acclimatised on many visits over the years. Maybe he was wrong about that. His eyes burned in hairdryer wind funnelling through the narrow alleyways.

They moved off to look for accommodation. Hale had discussed it with Lucy back in England and had suggested they book on arrival, told her that in this way you could get a good deal for a night.

The first pension they happened upon questioned his theory: "Lo siento, señor, no hay habitaciones disponibles." No rooms available. The receptionist tapped on the keyboard looking for options, but the tourist season was at its height, the place packed.

Lucy sat in the foyer where it was quiet and cool, her breathing shallow and fair complexion unhealthily flushed. Deborah fared better, darting about, looking out at the characters in the street.

Students, girls with manes of jet-black hair to the base of their spines, street workers and residents pitching guttural Spanish over the traffic noise, Northern European tourists wrecked by the heat, walking like ambling sheep, the sun exposing their tortured features and pink shoulders.

The trio headed back out into the hairdryer, continued along a backstreet, Lucy not saying a word and Hale knowing the next pension would be the last chance saloon before a public strop. He imagined the scene. Old timers sitting on benches would look on at the skirmish. Another hombre with woman problems. In this country, women deemed men a necessary nuisance. Up to no good, skulking in bars, drinking shots of brandy, playing dominoes, avoiding responsibility. Hombres' number one survival rule: lie low, do not incur their wrath.

The glass doors of the second pension had hardly opened fully when Hale, desperate, enquired for an available room: "¿Tiene una habitación para tres?"

"No hay problema, señor."

Music to Hale's ears.

Minutes later, the family crammed inside a tiny lift and settled into their room on the fourth floor. Hale opened the shutters, looked over the street lined with cafés and restaurants, a pedestrianised area disobeyed by noisy mopeds speeding between shoppers and passers-by.

I must be patient with Lucy, Hale thought. Málaga in summer was an assault on the senses for anyone, and she had only been to Spain once with Ralph the buffoon. That was a holiday to Marbella, a hotel package deal rammed with Brits whose only goal was to roast in the sun around a pool. Heat up Britain and they'd stay at home. He hoped she would unwind, let Andalucían culture seep into her veins as it had done with him. But it would take time, probably longer than the two weeks available on this trip.

The first evening did not bode well for any cultural immersion. In the city of sublime tapas, Lucy and Deborah elected for burgers followed by ice cream from the many heladerías doing a roaring trade in the heat. Hale did not indulge, couldn't bring himself to. At 9:00 p.m., it was too early to dine by local standards.

They strolled along the bustling streets, back to the pension. Outside, Hale paused, mulling it over. Stepping inside would mean resigning an evening to watching television. What they did back home.

"I'm heading back into the centre for a walk, stretch the legs," he said. Lucy stood in the doorway of the pension, holding Deborah's hand, speechless for a moment.

"And I'll get something to eat as well," Hale continued. "I'm hungry at last."

"What? A walk ... to where?" said Lucy, fixing him with a glare.

"Just a tapas bar. I'll find one on this map." Hale fumbled with an undersized tourist leaflet he'd picked up at the airport. This was not going down well.

Lucy seethed, launching a tirade, "We've come all this way for a holiday and all you can do..."

Deborah tugged at her arm, "Mum."

"What? What is it?"

"Let him go," said Deborah, "It's okay. He needs some dad time."

A pause.

Lucy and Hale looked down at the big-eyed child looking up at them.

"Dad time?" said Lucy and Hale, in unison.

Then laughter. Infectious, uncontrollable giggles from the three of them. Hale staggered about holding his stomach, wiping tears from his eyes. Lucy grabbed Deborah, planted a smacking kiss on her cheek.

The innocence of childhood, the only thing that could have diffused the situation.

Hale headed out into the night.

EIGHT

Hale moved swiftly through backstreets and plazas lined with restaurants. Locals sat outside in the balmy night air. Buskers hung around tables and upturned barrels outside bodegas, chanting flamenco, beating out percussive rhythms on battered guitars. Local youths smoked dope, laughing and hollering across the streets. Impossibly old pensioners staggered on sticks through the chaos.

Hale's pace quickened, eager to retreat to a bar away from the bustle. He slipped a cell phone from his top pocket – slimmer, smaller than his main one, with a Spanish SIM card loaded for private calls. He speed-dialled the number for Jack, waited for a reply.

It came quick.

"Yes?"

"Jack, it's Charlie," said Hale. "Yep, I'm here. Free for a few hours, walking north towards that place, remember? Tapería de Cevantes." Cell phone to ear, Hale crossed a street, dodging traffic, received a yell from a youth on a moped with whom he brushed too close.

Not keen on phone calls, Jack didn't say much. Hale ended the call, "See you in ten. Bye."

Hale entered the tapería, rustic, wood framed windows on the outside. Inside, bohemian, dark, normally a quiet retreat, but tonight, rammed with students, older Spaniards, gaggles of women, theatregoers, all chatting loudly. The air was thick with smoke and wafts of heady garlic. The windows were wide open, letting the row blast out into the street, and not a word of English to be heard. Hale squashed himself into a corner, signalled the barman for two beers.

A few hours on the plane and now here, thought Hale. Hell of a long way from Leigh-on-Sea.

The beers arrived in frosted glasses. Hale took a draught and thought of the film *Ice Cold in Alex*. Knew how they felt.

"Hey Charlie, boy," said Jack, tapping him on the shoulder, grabbing one of the beers uninvited, gulping half down in one. "No smoking ban here I see," he laughed, taking a drag from a dwindling butt and shaking Hale's hand.

Jack was an imposing figure. Over six foot, bald head, stubble, prominent gut hidden under a faded grey t-shirt. With his Glaswegian accent, fair hair, and pink complexion, he stood out in the throng of black-haired Andaluces.

Hale raised his voice to be heard, "So, we need to..."

"Food first, if you please, sir," interrupted Jack, smiling, and then moving off, edging through the crowd to the bar. Preferring to let the Scot do the work, Hale watched on as Jack hunched over the bar, pointed to chalkboards on the wall listing the tapas on offer. Jack didn't speak a word of Spanish and didn't see that as a problem.

"Success?" asked Hale, after Jack had worked his way back.

"Aye, Charlie. Ordered some o' that grub. Six tapas."

"Raciónes on that board, Jack. I hope you're hungry."

"Tapas, raciónes, och, it's all the same. So, anyway, I spoke to Happy Gary and the boat's waiting. We have two crew meeting me tomorrow for the trip east. We're all happy boys and you're the skipper once again, laddie."

"I wondered," said Hale, looking up to Jack who craned down to hear over the racket, "why do they call him 'Happy'?"

"Och, I forgot to tell you, and you have no met him, eh? Well, it's 'cos he's got this weird smile on his face. Always."

"Weird how?"

"Well, it's kind of a smile, but he also has this deep tan, like them tourists who've lived out here forever. And the whitest teeth you can imagine, with one gold one. You can see his smile at night for miles. In a nightclub he looks freaky-like, under that disco lighting, but some o' those tarty women in Puerto Banús seem to love him."

"Sounds quite the cad," said Hale.

"He's a solid laddie, and he'll not shaft you, I'll tell you that."

"Reassuring."

"Aye, and he's giving us work and free rein on *Blue Too* for two weeks, man. It's very generous, so be a bit grateful will you."

Blue Too, a thirty-five foot sailing sloop, owned by Happy Gary, and moored at Puerto de Santa María, a three-hour drive east of Málaga. Solid and seaworthy, Hale had made regular sailing trips on her with Jack and a crew supplied by 'Happy' over the last three years.

The raciónes arrived. Pimientos de padrón, patatas bravas, pollo, fritas, sardinas, and ropa vieja all massed on plates and shoved on the small shelf. With bread.

"Jesus, man, they don't muck about here," said Jack, eyeing the feast.

"They don't, but you like a challenge," said Hale.

Hemmed into the corner, they remained standing while tucking in, fending off unintentional shoves of people coming and going from the bar. The atmosphere was buoyant, and building.

"The crew," said Hale, sampling a spicy potato, making him wince. "Who is it this time?"

Jack looked uneasy. "Well now, I was gonna mention that to you." He took a gulp of beer, washed down a sizeable mouthful of bread and sardines. "Remember those two, came with us a couple o' trips gone by?"

Hale eyed him, placed his beer down.

"Now come on," said Jack. "They're good boys, and they know their stuff on the water. You know that don't you, Charlie, eh?"

"Shit, you don't mean Dean, and the other one..."

"Gibby."

"Jesus, Jack, no." Hale placed his hands on his hips, looked to the ground.

"Look, Happy Gary's adamant that if you want the trip, *they go*. He's saying to me: without Dean and Gibby, there's no trip."

"Yeah, but I'm the skipper, and I don't like the smell of those comedians, especially after last time. You knew I wouldn't accept, and your Happy bloody Gary must have known it too."

Jack turned red, "Charlie, I need the money. The fishing work has dried up back home, the divorce lawyer is screwing me, my kids want money, and I owe Happy too."

"It's not just that is it, Jack?" said Hale, appetite now gone. "It's what you call *the craic* isn't it? That's what worries me. You like this macho bullshit: drinking, hell raising out here in Spain where you think you can arse around like a nutjob. But I'm the skipper. I'm the goddamn boss on board, and I say they don't go."

Jack prodded Hale in the chest with his fat forefinger, greasy with olive oil. "Then, Happy's going to screw me, and then I reckon he'll come after you. This trip's booked, money's 'bin paid, and Happy don't like losing ten quid, let alone thousands."

"You should have told me Jack," said Hale, thumping his hand on the shelf. The beers jumped, affording a glance from the barman. "You're asking me to go sailing with a criminal and a cokehead."

Jack glanced around the bar. He was looking for signs of trouble. None seen. "Look, it's gonna be fine," he said, putting his hand on Hale's shoulder. "Och, we always work through it, you and me. I didn't know you'd get a wasp up your ass about this, laddie."

Hale fumed, more with himself than with Jack. Should have checked the crew out. He said nothing.

"Charlie, you're a college boy," Jack continued, "unlike us minions down below decks, and we'll take care of you."

"Don't patronise me, Jack."

"Ha, there you go with that fancy tongue o' yours. What the 'ell is *patr-o-nise*?"

"Where are you staying tonight, Jack?"

Jack continued eating, stabbing at peppers with his fork. "Nowhere in particular. In the park. I'm not paying no hotel fee, and besides, it's eleven now and I'm waiting up a bit."

"You're staying in the park?"

"Aye, done it many a time. Know a few guys to get me a smoke, some weed, harmless stuff though."

"Great," said Hale, preparing to leave. "I'm out of here, and I'll leave you to get stoned and pissed in the middle of Málaga. You know this is my last trip don't you?"

Jack beamed, crunching peppers, "I've heard that one before, laddie. I do believe there's a little piece of the college boy who likes *the craic*, am I right? Come on admit it. *And* the money."

"When are you leaving Málaga, Jack?"

"Tomorrow. Happy's dropping Dean and Gibby off down at the park. Then we're driving east. And you?"

"Going to Nerja tomorrow, dropping the family off. I'm at the boat the following day and I expect you to be there, Jack. Sober."

"Nerja? That's a place for poofs and lightweights, isn't it? Swimming pools and lemonade," Jack smirked, wiping the sweat from his forehead. "So, you planning on doing some sunbathin' or something?"

Jack broke into a booming laugh.

Hale ignored him, made for the door. "See you at Puerto de Santa María, Jack," he said. "And remember ... I'm the skipper."

Jack clicked his heels to attention, gave a salute, grinning.

NINE

"Where the hell were you, Charles? I mean, two a.m.," whispered Lucy, leaning forward from the back seat of the taxi. They sped along the autovía rising up out of the city, heading for the Costa Tropical, a region of lush beauty. In the front passenger seat, Hale looked up at the whitewashed fincas and villas speckling the verdant rough terrain. The Sierra Nevada mountains rose above to the north. The driver tailgated a truck ahead in the outside lane, gave an impatient flash of the headlights. Hale pressed his feet into the footwell. Tense, with a mild hangover, he let out a sigh of relief as the truck relented and eased into the 'slow' lane. No quarter given to lane-hoggers on the racetrack.

"I don't know, Lucy, I..."

"You came in stinking of something. Brandy I think," she said, leaning back into her seat.

"I know, I had a few in a bar after I left Jack, that's all. Time seemed to fly. You know how it does out here." Hale cast a glance behind at Deborah. Seated beside Lucy, she occupied herself with drawings, occasionally looking out of the window at the trucks and cars labouring up the hill. He felt bad for annoying Lucy, but Deborah was excited. Her first trip to Spain, absorbing every sight and sound.

"And this guy, Jack," Lucy continued. "Charles, I don't trust him. Are you sure you want to go sailing with him ... *again*?"

"Jack's okay, don't worry about it. He lost his job fishing up there in Scotland, needs to get out to sea, and I can rely on him out there."

"Gives me the creeps, the way he looks at me."

"Knock it off, Lucy, he's..."

The driver veered violently off the motorway onto a slip road, smiled, and said, "Nerja está allí, señor."

"Sí, gracias, thank you," said Hale, grateful that the white-knuckle taxi ride was nearly over.

The villa was situated a few minutes' drive from the centre of Nerja town, a bustling coastal village mixed with attractive Spanish townhouses and purpose-built holiday apartments.

Soon, they sheltered in the cool courtyard, supping drinks from tall glasses as the heat rose into the high thirties. Bougainvillea decorated blue-white walls. Cicadas sounded loud over the fountain trickling a few yards away at the foot of the garden.

The pleasant three-bed property was loaned to Lucy and Deborah by Nerja couple, Brenda and Gerry. The plan was for Hale to head off sailing for ten days, leaving mother and daughter in what Brenda (Lucy's friend from her schooldays) made a point of repeating was 'their *other* villa'.

Hale didn't like Brenda, a snippy bitch whose looks didn't help the persona. A true lizard with an upturned loobrush hairdo, dyed jet black, hollow cheeks from a lifetime sucking cigarettes, and blue eyeliner. Not a stunner by any means, but Hale kept the peace and complimented the villa for the sake of Deborah.

Brenda's husband, Gerry, a gangly obnoxious twerp, pottered about the garden making it clear that it was no problem. By 'no problem', Hale knew he was referring to the waived rental fee the retired couple could have received from tourists staying in their *other* villa. The waiver was a relief to Hale in his financial predicament, but it rankled. If it was genuinely *no problem*, as the very affluent and vocally successful ex-banker, Gerry, stated, then why did he raise the subject every five minutes?

"It's no problem, Charles, no problem at all."

"Quite, no problem, as you keep saying," Hale repeated, under his breath.

A master of penny-pinching, Gerry had clearly retained the knack from his banking days of clawing back money, and thus, recouped one hundred and fifty euros at dinner that evening, a dinner for which Lucy insisted Charles would be 'delighted' to pay.

Another hit to Hale's one remaining credit card that was not maxed-out.

Next morning, 7:03 a.m.

Hale packed his bags in the lounge for the trip while Lucy and Deborah slept in the bedroom down the corridor. He tiptoed around the marble floor, being careful not to wake them.

He did the check, always the same routine: passport top right shirt pocket, money in wallet back right jeans pocket, UK cell phone front right jeans pocket, Spanish cell phone top left shirt pocket, one hand luggage for the bus, one sailing bag containing sailing gear, clothes, and heavy-weather sailing anorak.

An hour later, he boarded the bus bound for San Isidro.

Climbing beyond Nerja, the view opened out to the lush bay of La Herradura lined with a long white beach demarcating the village from the graduated blue of the Mediterranean. Further out, a yacht headed east, full sails in a fickle breeze. The wind strength would increase towards the turbulent area of Hale's destination, the Costa del Viento. Re-branded the *Costa de Almería* by tourism marketers, the coastline's notorious conditions had wreaked havoc for centuries, accounting for countless shipwrecks in the fierce winds and hellish seas. On land, tales handed down spoke of husbands purportedly killing their wives in rages induced by the wild winds blowing around their heads for weeks on end.

Hale knew of the dangers at sea, the elements transforming from idyllic to ferocious in minutes, and the level of respect requisite to avoid becoming another body washed up on the *Playa de los Muertos*, the Beach of Death.

At the commercial port of Motril, the bus pulled into a side street, a dusty courtyard, which turned out to be the bus station. The passengers – a mixed crowd of tourists, Spanish students, Moroccans, and Andaluces – filed out for a twenty-minute break. Hale wandered about the station, peered into the bar where the driver was enjoying a cigarette, an espresso, and a spirit of some kind. People were flagging in the heat. Now that they were further east, the atmosphere had changed. Arid, dusty. A barrage of intense heat and light.

Hale dialled Jack on his cell phone.

"Jack, it's Charles. You on your way?"

"Hey, Charlie," came a muffled reply at the other end. "I'm with Gibby, and Dean ... and Dean's got a bit of a sore head." Hale heard laughs and Jack saying something to the crew, before continuing, "Well, let's just say he met a beautiful woman of the night who turned out to be – och how do you say? – of ambiguous sexuality. But, aye skipper, sir, we're an hour away. And you?"

"Motril," said Hale. "See you later."

Hale hung up, took a swig from an ice-cold bottle of water he'd retrieved from a vending machine, wiped dirt and sweat from his forehead.

He thought about Jack and the crew: *this trip has to be the last.*

TEN

Ten miles out from San Isidro, a sea of greenhouses, known locally as *plasticos*, stretched from the foothills of the mountainous interior to the coastline. The mass-production of fruit and vegetables created great wealth in the area with the side effect of repelling the tourists, most of whom opted for less industrial landscapes. The business drew an influx of international executives and workers, the latter toiling in the heat and unsightly rubble surrounding the town.

Hale thought of what awaited at the marina. The crew would have been on board, stowed their gear and probably retreated to the bar at the end of the wharf. Hale was keen to stamp out alcoholic binges before things got out of hand. Prior to setting out, there was much work to do: preparing the yacht, running the engine, planning the passage.

On arrival at San Isidro bus station, he walked through a wind-fuelled inferno of plastic bags and dust to catch the short connection to the marina at Puerto de Santa María. Sweat poured from his face, tasted of salt and mud. He lined up to pay at the front of the bus. The diesel engine throbbed, fumes adding to the discomfort. Two wild-eyed Moroccans moved up to him, a little too close for comfort, asked if he needed a lift. One stoned, looked like trouble. Both were soon edged away by a six-foot African with impressive biceps, a big dude, someone not to be messed with. Hale nodded a 'thanks'.

On the bus, the smell of diesel, sweat, and onions threatened to make Hale giddy as workers hung to the ceiling grips. Moroccan mothers wrestled their buggies into position. Animated pensioners argued and cackled in an indecipherable stream of Andaluz-inflected Spanish. Hale found a standing position in the aisle, leaning into the turns and balancing as the driver threw the bus around. Music – Latin pop – blared out of the ceiling speakers, competing with the roar of the engine.

The bus charged through the outskirts of town, passing scrubland home to goats, rubble, and junk. Rough and dirty, the Wild West. A two-mile dual carriageway dipped and rose up to a shimmering heat haze. Beyond that, a transformation, a descent along a steep road lined with palms and tended gardens, through lavish whitewashed villas, and on to the complex of Puerto de Santa María. Low-rise hotels, terracotta roofs, restaurants, golf courses, and the marina beyond. A maelstrom of masts gathered in tidy lines along the wharfs like giant reeds rising above the cobalt water.

"Relax Charlie, boy," said Jack, standing outside *El Timón*, the bar at the end of the wharf. A lopsided sign above a battered wooden door propped open by a rock was all that signified its existence. Inside, a few hombres leaned on the bar, smoking, drinking in the darkness. Two men, twenties, unshaven, smoked and played pool. They were accompanied by women in tight jeans, laughing loudly, displaying shapely rumps as they leaned over the pool table. The clientele were happy to loiter in the dingy drinking hole out of the heat. Most gawked blankly at pop videos on a television hanging at an odd angle from the ceiling.
    "I'd rather we get onboard now and sorted the boat out," said Hale, hauling his bag over his shoulder, donning his sunglasses.
    Jack patted him of the back. "Och, not a problem, Charlie. Look, the boys are already at the supermarket getting the water and food. Let me finish here and we'll see you in ten."
    "Got it," said Hale, happy with Jack's sense of purpose.
    A hundred yards along the wharf, *Blue Too* rocked gently in the milky afternoon light, her dark blue hull contrasting with brilliant white decks.
    "It's been a while," Hale said to himself, dumping his bags, hauling the yacht in by the warp. Climbing aboard, it was clear that the crew had done little other than to open the main hatch, stow their gear, and head to the bar. Down below, the atmosphere was dim and musty. Hale opened the forward hatch, which offered little ventilation in the still air. Mould had crept into some of the bunks and the bilge needed pumping. Sweat dripped from his face onto the floorboards. He crouched, hauled himself into the navigation seat. The chart was spread out on the table, their last trip marked on it: a route to Melilla, the Spanish enclave on the north coast of Africa. Hale crossed his arms over the chart, lay his head down, and was soon asleep.
    "Hey, Charlie!" came a cry ten minutes later.

Hale went up on deck, shielding his eyes, squinting in the light reflected from the glare off the water and the white of surrounding boats and apartments. Jack stood on the wharf with Dean and Gibby, and two shopping trolleys full of provisions.

Hale jumped off to help.

"You remember the boys, Charles?" said Jack, nodding to Dean and Gibby by way of introduction.

"Sure. Hello again," said Hale, shaking Dean's sweaty hand. Dean was bare-chested, scrawny, deeply tanned, navy tattoos on both biceps. He sucked on a roll-up cigarette making his rat-face contort further. 'Substance abuser' written all over him, and a crooked smile exposing a rotting front tooth. For some reason, Jack thought his presence amusing. Hale mistrusted Dean's every move.

"All right, mate?" replied Dean in a London accent, failing to conceal a schoolboy snigger and a glance at Jack.

Jack gave Dean a frown, a light shake of the head, and then introduced the remaining crewmember, Alan 'Gibby' Gibson, a short fat man, a walking heart-attack with a pink head. Gibby stood wiping the sweat from his neck with an oily cloth, eyeing Hale wearily.

"Thanks for coming along," said Hale, grabbing his pudgy mitt. Like Dean, Gibby was good on deck and knew the sea, but equally loathed by Hale who suspected his criminal background of tax fraud and drink driving was just the tip of the iceberg.

"So, let's get the stores on board out of the sun," said Hale. "Then we'll hose her down, and get the rig sorted for tomorrow." The next line wouldn't be popular, but he delivered it anyway, "And tonight, a quiet one, boys. No booze. We're taking her out for a trial early tomorrow."

Gibby opened his mouth, but Jack curtailed the riposte. Dean sucked on the remnants of his roll-up in silence, eyebrows raised.

"Come on, lads, he's right," said Jack. "Let's do the business."

Next morning, Hale rose early as the crew slumbered in their bunks. To him, the best part of the day. He went on deck, throwing bread to the ducks, watching a red sunrise over the boatyard to the east. Today's forecast was good: a light *Poniente* wind from the west, a test for boat and crew before the passage across the Alborán Sea a few days later.

At breakfast, the wind strengthened by a few knots, signalled by rhythmic clanking of halyards against aluminium masts. At the chart table, Hale hit the speed-dial on his cell to chat to Lucy before setting out.

Deborah answered in a bubbly mood.

"Hi Chuck. Mum's in the Shower."

"Oh, okay, and how are you getting on? How's the pool?"

"Brill, and mum and Brenda went in," she began excitedly, "and then we even went to the beach, and into the town, but it was too hot and..." Running out of breath, she continued, "... and Dad's going to love it when..."

"Dad?"

Deborah paused, now awkward, "Well..."

Hale sat upright, confused, and then said, "Your dad's coming out to the villa ... to stay?"

"Chuck, mum's out of the shower now. Here she is ... I'll put her on."

Hale heard a murmur at the other end while Lucy took the cell phone.

"Hello, Charles, have you arrived?"

"Yes, I'm here, I'm fine."

"You sure? You sound weird."

"Is Ralph coming out?"

A brief silence at the other end, and then, "Only for the weekend. He's staying with Brenda and Gerry. He's golfing with Gerry. Well, you were away anyway, and..."

"I don't believe this. This was *our* holiday."

"Oh really?" she said. "Our holiday, and *you* go off sailing."

"Yes, but Ralph, your ex-husband. Are you crazy?"

Lucy's tone was firm, "I want him to see Deborah, and it was a last minute thing, decided yesterday."

"And he's staying in Brenda and Gerry's villa, not yours. Like I'm gonna believe that."

"You're paranoid, and I'm sick of it."

She hung up.

"Lucy?"

ELEVEN

"You're a sprightly one up at this unearthly hour," said Jack, heaving himself out of his bunk, his stomach a landslide of flab oozing over his boxer shorts. "Trouble with the wife?"

"Fiancée, supposedly," said Hale, pocketing his phone, organising the kettle at the tiny galley.

Jack yawned, patted Hale on the back heavily, and then said, "Och, not to worry, Charlie. Your situation will be a breeze compared to the sordid chaos of my love life. I suggest we concentrate on gettin' this tub out on the water today, and forget it all. Nice little breeze picking up."

Dean and Gibby rose thirty minutes later, slurped coffee and smoked in the cockpit while Hale and Jack struggled to attach the mainsail. Hale's cell phone buzzed.

"Jack, take the halyard for me will you," said Hale, climbing back down into the cockpit, taking the call.

A familiar, unwelcome, voice at the other end: "Charles, it's Martin Stack from the office."

"Martin, *great* to hear from you. I'm in Spain."

"Yes, I know, you lucky bugger. Look, we have a rush on. That Chinese bunch have decided to come over with their students and want the presentations on your return. Always a big money earner with them, so any chance you can slice a few days off your trip?"

Hale covered the mouthpiece, cursed. *Shit*.

"Hell, not really, Martin. A holiday is a holiday. It's booked." Hale pursed his lips, glancing at Dean leaning back, sunning his toast rack chest in the morning sun.

"Yes, and business is business, Charles," replied Stack, the irritation clear in his voice. "Can you at least do some prep out there on your laptop or something? Also, there are some typos in the training document you left behind, just minor stuff, but I can't load Pam up with more work."

"How many hours' work are we talking?"

"Um, just four I reckon. Call it half a day, something like that."

Hale sighed, looked up at the sky. Stack's half day invariably equalled one full day, minimum.

"Charles?"

"Okay, email me the details. I'll take a look if I can get online out here."

"That's the spirit, Charles, and don't get seasick out there will you."

In no mood for banter, Hale hung up.

"Let's do it," said Gibby, rising up, stretching his arms up to reveal a couple of unsightly black armpits and a pink beer gut to rival Jack's. "This bloody wind is rattling around me head, driving me crazy."

An hour later, *Blue Too* motored past the marina tower, Hale on the helm. They turned to port, heading south out to sea. White horses built on the horizon and the yacht began to pitch on the chop.

"Och, this is going to be a bitch," said Jack, stowing ropes, stumbling about in the cockpit as the boat lurched.

"Ha! I see you ain't got your sea legs yet, Jack-boy," said Dean, amidships, working the luff of the mainsail up the mast with Gibby.

"I been out in bigger seas than you've ever dreamt of," replied Jack. "So don't give me any lip, mackerel breath, otherwise I'll have you cleaning the decks later when I'm in the bar with them dusky chicas."

"I reckon it's all a lie," shouted Gibby, tugging on a line. "Maybe big bad Jack isn't the old sea dog he says he is. Reckon 'e really runs a fish 'n chip shop up there in Scotland."

"Okay, pipe down, guys," said Hale. "Gibby, you look like a damn beetroot. Put some cream on or something, will you."

"Cream?" laughed Gibby. "What is this, a boat full of bloody pansies or something?"

Jack shouted above the wind and flapping of sailcloth, "Do as he says, Gibby, otherwise you'll be out with heat stroke in this stuff. You're not off Anglesey now you know."

Gibby headed down below, shaking his head.

"While you're down there, lash down the bags and secure the bunks," said Hale.

"We got twenty-five knots already, Charlie," shouted Jack, looking at Hale, a rare serious moment. "What are we doing here, heading further out? We need a plan me thinks."

"You're right," said Hale, on tiptoes, looking ahead at the conditions, wrestling the helm. "You and Dean put a reef in and we'll push on a bit. We need to run the boat, otherwise we'll be going across in a few days' time without practice. The sails are all over the place and the helm's heavy as hell. Jesus, sort it out boys, please."

"Okay, okay, Charlie. Not so much of the stress, eh?" said Jack, clambering towards the mast.

Gibby appeared at the hatch, his face looking as if he'd smeared it with goat cheese. "Hey, skipper," he shouted, "we got a problem down here."

"What is it?" asked Hale, hauling the tiller with both hands as the boat heeled over.

"Smoke in the engine compartment, billowing. Look."

"Fire?"

"Can't see flames, skipper. Maybe she wasn't pumping water when we ran her up this morning. Looks like she overheated and burnt through a pipe."

"So, where's the smoke coming from?"

"It's steam mainly ... from the water cooling, I think. A bit of rubber smoking from the pipe maybe."

"Shit. Who was supposed to check she was pumping water?"

Gibby shot Hale a glance, "Don't you look at me, skipper, I had enough on my plate."

Hale cursed, shook his head, looked back towards the marina. The swell was now heavy and building. "Jack?"

"Checking the engine water? Well, it's your job, skipper, or mine to be fair," said Jack. "Look, calm down, boys. I say we stop squabbling like a gaggle of old hens, bring her about and head back under sail, now. What d'ya say Charlie-boy?"

"He's right, boss," shouted Dean from the foredeck, hanging on, being sprayed as the boat pitched into deep blue troughs.

"Okay, let's do it before this turns into a major balls-up," said Hale. "Gibby, call the tower. Say we've got a possible fire below and we're heading in."

"Wave!" A warning shout from Dean. Then a sickening crack as a line broke.

"Hang on," said Hale. Jack fell to the deck with a thump, held on to a handrail to avoid being swept overboard. Gibby crashed into the galley stove below. Steel pots, cups, and the kettle crashed to the floor.

The boat heeled over at forty-five degrees, frothing water just feet away from Hale's arm.

"You broached the boat, you idiot!" said Gibby, hauling himself up from the galley floor.

Hale gathered his composure, "Shut it, Gibby, we had a line go. Get your fat arse up here, now. Jack and Dean, get back here, let the mainsheet out. We'll have to gybe her around."

Jack crawled aft, out of breath, and then said, "Not a good plan, Charlie. Not in this wind."

Too late. Hale was committed. *Blue Too* lurched around. The boom swung violently across the stern, wrenching the block out of the deck with a crack.

"Jesus, Skipper," Dean said, hauling on a rope. "What the hell are you doing?"

"Calm down everyone," said Hale, leaning to steady himself. "Get control of the rig. Get the mainsheet on a winch."

The boat foundered for a minute. Then settled with the marina tower on the nose and the parched hills of the interior rising beyond. On this opposite tack, the ferocity of the wind seemed to lessen.

"You stupid bastard," said Gibby, replacing the gear in the galley.

After a few seconds of silence, Jack laughed to himself, hysterics. Then said aloud, "What a bunch of silly old sods we are. Hope no one's watching this."

Dean smiled with a cigarette lodged in his mouth, shielding it as he flicked at his lighter in the wind, and then said, "Think we're gonna need a touch more practice if we're doing a run across to Morocco, boss."

Hale ignored the comment. "Get on the radio, Gibby. Call us in," he said.

The marina staff, *marineros*, provided a tow from a motor launch, escorting *Blue Too* from the harbour entrance to her mooring.

"Two hundred euros for a tow of three hundred yards," said Jack. "Och, that's not a bit steep, no, Charlie?"

"We screwed up," said Hale, coiling some rope, "and besides, they don't run a charity here ... working outside in this wind and heat."

"Was that '*we* screwed up' I heard?" said Gibby, sucking on a can of beer.

Hale threw the rope on top of the aft hatch, and then said, "Pack it in, Gibby. We're cleaning up today, getting the boat repaired tomorrow. Then we're setting out the day after for Melillia. So, get your head in order. That's a shipping channel out there and we need to be on the ball."

"Boss's right," said Jack, tapping Gibby on the shoulder. "You boys all take yourselves a goddamn chill pill. And, tonight, we can drown our sorrows a bit, no?"

Dean gave his trademark crooked smile from the foredeck. "That we shall do. Aye, aye, sir."

TWELVE

He'd met her months before in *El Timón*, thought nothing of it, as much as men can think nothing of talking with a beautiful woman. But 'talking' stretched the notion. She spoke broken English. He, beginners' Spanish. Nevertheless, tonight, the conversation seemed easier, and the shots of rum soothed the way, helped him relax, forget the stresses of the week and the chaos on the boat earlier. Jack's gang was in good spirits, an omen for hell raising to come and some hangovers in the morning. But right now, that wasn't top of the list of Hale's concerns.

Midnight.

The crew sat around a table, drunk, jeering at what they deemed Hale's flirtations with Marta, the dark Andaluz woman who worked in the bar. She was on her way out, but made a point of rescuing Hale from the throng of Brits. To join her for a drink of what she knew was his favourite brandy, *Torres 10*. And who was he to refuse the invitation? They stood at an upturned wine barrel crowded with empty glasses. Alternately, they leaned across each other's shoulder to be heard above the din of music, mad sound effects from a pinball machine, shouts, laughter.

For Hale, everything up to that point had been a pressure cooker of stress. From stepping out of Stack's office on the Friday in London, to Lucy and Deborah's trip to Nerja, and returning *Blue Too* safely to the marina. But now Hale looked deep into the eyes of a young woman, a woman who listened without scornful replies. A woman, who shrugged at the mayhem and murky characters of *El Timón*, the maddest, baddest bar on the marina. A woman who eased his mind, as did the numbing effect of alcohol working into his bloodstream.

Marta's smile was mischievous, her skin dark, silken. Her hair long, jet-black, stretched halfway down her back. Occasionally, seemingly for little reason, she swept it across her, and then aside again. Her flimsy dress of faded red, looked cheap, but she wore it comfortably in the dry heat of the night, clinging enough to catch the eye of every man in the bar, revealing her slim figure and a hint of lace underwear beneath. Hale remained at arm's length, didn't want to look the jerk. A flash of Lucy in his mind was soon extinguished by the beauty before him. Out of the corner of his eye, the snide looks were coming from Gibby. Yet, she moved closer still, seemingly unconcerned that Hale may be just another drunk Northern European hitting on a local chica.

At first, he thought she was toying with him, but her smile and joking seemed sincere. She knew Hale as a familiar face at the marina. He'd visited *El Timón* frequently over the years, and the local Spanish seemed to know and like him. Nothing appeared unnatural or forced. No muscular boyfriend arrived with a gentle – or not-so-gentle – arm of persuasion to suggest he leave Marta alone.

"Your friends, they are funny," she said, holding the glass up to her mouth, glancing at the crew, and then smiling back at Hale.

"Funny? Well, I'm not finding them too funny today."

"No? Oh, you hombres on the boats. You always fighting, no?" she laughed, taking a sip.

"So, you've been working at the bar for some years now?"

Marta's frowned, shrugged, "Only some nights, when they need help. I want to study, not waste my life in these places."

"Good idea. And you live here, near the marina?"

A crack sounded as someone broke the pack on the pool table, startling them both. She looked around the bar, continued, "No, up in San Isidro. I go back tonight, stay with my mother at the apartment block. It's okay for now, you know..."

Marta grinned, eyeing Hale, and then glanced at his motley crew a few feet away.

"What is it? Are you laughing at me?" asked Hale, her infectious smile working on him.

"Well, it is just that my friend, Pepe, he is the tall marinero, you know the one?"

Hale shrugged.

"He said he was in the tower watching you today through the, how do you say, glasses?"

"Binoculars."

"Yes, well, he was laughing."

"*Okay*."

"He said, you English were falling around on the boat and you had not even left the shore by very much."

"Ha! You wait," said Hale. "We are highly tuned professionals and when we are practised, we will show you."

"Professionals at drinking, maybe."

"You're right," said Hale, lifting his glass, laughing, thinking he should leave the pleasant discussion as that. An innocuous, pleasant discussion, nothing more.

After a pause, and with little thought, he asked, "Would you like to go for a walk outside, get some air ... maybe on the beach or something?" He looked down at his feet, swilling the remaining millimetre of rum about in his glass.

Marta placed her glass down on the barrel, looked up to him.

"Sure, but of course."

A hundred metres from the bar, the beach stretched east, opening up to inky darkness beneath pinpricks of light from the stars. Warm wind blew sand in the air along the still-warm concrete path, which lined the beach. Hale and Marta walked along it, heading out of town. People skulked in car parks, under palms, between buildings, and in the only remaining beach bar left open, a chiringuito.

"Beautiful," said Hale, leaning against some railings, watching the moon shimmering yellow off the water.

"My home," said Marta, taking Hale's hand, leading him further along the path. "It is difficult to leave, but soon I must get away from here."

Hale felt electricity feed through him, her hand in his. It wasn't happening, couldn't be. Lost for words, he blurted out the dumbest thing that came to mind, "Do you think we should go further? Looks pretty black ahead."

"Silly. Teenagers play around on the beach all night. And you can protect, me, no?" She smiled.

Hale followed her onto the beach, near the water's edge, small waves lapping the shore. He looked inland. A black stretch of wasteland was bordered by the lights of a road and the occasional headlights of cars up on a cliff. Beyond, the hills rose, transforming into mountains. A few scattered lights low down, and then nothing but stars reaching up to the heavens.

He turned around and watched her dress fall to the sand. She removed the rest, and within seconds, gently swam out into the shimmering blackness. Hale stripped and followed, allowing the cool water to clean away the heat, dust, and sweat of the day, and with it, months of worry and fear.

He floated on his back for some seconds, locating Cassiopeia, comprehending the enormity of the universe, and his insignificant place within it.

Marta swam quietly up to him. He turned, looked into her eyes. His hand slid around her waist, and her slim figure pressed against his chest.

THIRTEEN

Hale opened the rear door for Marta. She stepped out. Seconds later, the taxi drove off, spinning dust around, tyres popping on stones. They walked into the night between apartment blocks lit with orange streetlights, the silence broken only by the sound of their footsteps on rubble and concrete, and distant dog barks.

"Do not worry, it is not such a bad place around here. This way," said Marta, leading the way, holding Hale's hand.

The warm wind had dried their clothes on the walk back to the marina. They'd sought out a taxi rank and made for San Isidro. She had said that she should go alone, people would talk, but Hale had insisted he see her to her mother's apartment. Only then would he return to marina, happy that she was safe.

Spain was safe at night. Always someone about, rarely a threatening vibe. At least that was Hale's view prior to this moment. But this was somehow different. At 3:15 a.m. in the backstreets of the working town, he felt tension in the air, sensed Marta's concern. She quickened her step, peered down darkened alleys, moved through the shadows rather than out under streetlights.

They should have stayed on the main drag, Hale thought. Kept to the areas where the bars were busy and the traffic flowed. Maybe get someone to escort them. But now they were isolated. Stupid. He urged himself to get through it. Soon they would be sipping glasses of water in her mother's apartment, whispering, laughing about their torrid dash through the rubble and rundown alleys on the outskirts of San Isidro.

But another thought, a flash of fear, shot through him like an electrical current. At the beach, in the sea. Did it really happen? It didn't happen, it couldn't. Just a brandy-induced blur.

Yes, it did happen.

Now he remembered it all. Her smooth legs had wrapped around his waist, his hands all over her breasts, down her back.

And then it was done.

Yes, it did happen.

"There, the entrance," said Marta, snapping him out of his thoughts, pointing to a door, dimly-lit through cracked glass reinforced with wire mesh. Hale didn't like the look of it. The door was positioned in a dark recess beside some underground garages.

"Not good," he said.

"It is okay, move quick." At the door, she fumbled with her keys.

Hale looked around. Something caught his eye in the shadows on the street opposite, someone watching. Blood thumped in his temples. A youth or a man, denim jacket and ponytail. "Over there. Watching us," Hale said.

Marta ignored the comment, hauled the door open. "Come, get in now."

Hale entered, she locked the door, paying no heed to the figure, urging Hale up some concrete stairs.

They entered the apartment on the third floor. Basic, clean, hard marble floors, dark wooden furniture. Their whispers echoed in the stark surroundings.

"We must not wake my mother, but you can stay until it is light maybe. You want coffee?" They crept into the kitchen. Hale pondered the options, the implications of their actions that evening.

"Not coffee, just water please. Now that you're back safely, I should go," Hale said, peering out of the kitchen window, down to a deserted car park. "That man we saw out there, you know him?"

She shrugged, "I did not look. It is best not to look."

"Just some kid, I guess," said Hale, uneasy. "Shouldn't be a problem."

"Go back to the main road, and then the bus station for taxi," said Marta, handing him a glass of water. "I write my number for you."

Hale, drank deeply, relieving his dry throat. Sobering up, he watched Marta root around in a set of draws, pulling out a writing pad and pen. Her beauty was not lost under the harsh light of the kitchen.

He thought of an option, a difficult one: don't take her number. Leave, and forget this evening.

Marta smiled and said, "You look frightened, like a mouse." She kissed him. Hale placed the glass down and let his hands glide over her shoulders, down her arms to her waist.

He took the number.

Leaving the apartment block, Hale headed across the rubble of the car park, the one he'd seen from the kitchen. Just a few blocks to the bus station. Yet he sensed eyes watching him from hidden corners of this bleak part of town. He tried not to break into a jog, but quickened his step. Sweat drenched his shirt. He sucked in the dry night air.

Two feral dogs, the kind looking for food rather than companionship, made after him. Hale hissed, shooed them away, but now they barked, echoing around the concrete jungle. He jogged, looking behind as the animals bore their teeth, snapped at his trouser legs.

"This is all I bloody need."

He crossed a street, one block from the bus station.

Hale's night was bound to get worse.

It did.

His legs flew from beneath him. Then he hit the road, hard.

The world span, ringing in his ears, a taste of blood.

Someone kicked one of the dogs and a yelp signalled its departure. Hale wheezed. A searing pain in his ribs, he spat blood and looked down to his legs. The plank of wood used to trip him clanked on the tarmac as it was thrown down by his attacker. "Let me guess," gasped Hale, looking up to the shadowy figure standing over him. "The ponytail from back there."

"¿Qué le dijiste? What you say? You Inglés, no?"

Hale was right about the haircut, but to his distress, the pockmarked man with greasy ponytail had company. Two youths, hovered in the background behind parked cars. Lookouts, thought Hale. Ready to give the signal if the Policía cruised by.

Hale put his hands on the soil ready to haul himself up.

"No, no. You stay down, my friend." Ponytail slammed his boot onto Hale's back, replaced it with the flat of his hand as he crouched down. "You lucky I speak some Engleesh, otherwise my friends over there take your money then cutting you, no?" Ponytail drew a line across his throat with his finger. With the side of his face rammed in the dirt, Hale noticed one of the youths laughing, proudly brandishing a knife, before concealing it within his jacket.

Ponytail spoke with bad breath from a mouthful of metal and black teeth, which caused Hale to gag in the dried mud.

"This is what we do, Engleesh. You see this?" Ponytail opened his jacket to reveal a handgun. A fake, Hale thought, plastic. But handguns were difficult. Sometimes the real deal resembled a toy, and besides, it was dark. He couldn't take the chance to fight or to run for it. "You stand now, quick," said Ponytail, wrenching the back of Hale's shirt.

Hale rose to his feet, groaning with the pain in his ribs. Ponytail ushered him out of the street, roughing him up, kicking, shoving his back, moving into the dark against an apartment block to join the youths. They laughed, juvenile laughs, until Ponytail slapped one of them on the neck, cursing in a stream of indecipherable Spanish.

Ponytail turned his attention back to Hale, "Look at wall!"

Hale turned, wondered if this was it. Maybe this is how it ends. Ponytail pushed Hale's face into the rough breezeblock surface of the wall, rifled through his pockets, retrieved a wallet and credit card holder.

"So, mister Charles," said Ponytail, looking at Hale's business card. "Yes, you are Engleesh. But there is problem, with the money. You only having eighty-five euros, no?"

"I can get more if..."

"Yes, more. But our fee, mister Charles, is one hundred-fifty euros."

Hale breathed heavily, gulped air. He glanced left along the alley towards a crossroads. A beaten-up van cruised by, but no way to draw attention.

"Look at wall!" Ponytail took his time to light a joint and speak to the youths. It will be risky for these people to hang around, thought Hale. Surely some curtain-twitcher would have called this in when he was prostrate on the road. But the other, less favourable, alternative occurred to him: if the gang had *influence* around here, onlookers would remain silent.

"I see you with her."

"What?" said Hale, knowing what was next.

"The girl. I know her, and you my friend, are now in the trouble. In the big trouble."

"She's a friend," said Hale. "I walked her back, that's all..."

Ponytail took a long drag, coughed, spat phlegm onto the road, and edged up to the side of Hale's head. "You speak too fast, mister. How do you Engleesh say, *no-in-ti-endo*?"

"I don't know her, I'm leaving tomorrow, and..."

"Siliencio. Look, we take your stupid eighty-five euros. We let you go, but you know that girl, she is hot, no? Nice chica ... you like?"

Hale felt a trickle of blood running down into his eye, turned to Ponytail. The youths smirked behind him.

"Sí, that is right, you look at me, man," Ponytail continued, goading. "And think hard. You come here to play on holiday with the stupid tourists, but big mistake to mess with local woman, mister Charles. Big mistake to mess with Andaluz blood."

Ponytail pocketed Hale's wallet, snapped his fingers at the youths. The three left Hale, walked off into the murk of a side alley.

FOURTEEN

At 3:43 a.m., the outskirts of town offered little reassurance that the long walk back to the marina would be a safe one. Hale's wallet and money were gone and there was no chance of a bus or taxi ride. Not that he'd risk a route leading him back to town and any further unwanted attention. He scrambled along the edge of a dual carriageway, holding his ribs, stemming the flow of blood from the cut above his eye with a section of cloth he'd ripped from his shirt. Mercifully, the injuries were light, but it would take two hours to return to the marina followed by a full day of work before they set sail for Morocco.

Through the night, lorries and scooters flew past, passengers and drivers hooting or shouting to the hapless hombre limping along the roadside. The madman, *El loco!*

Hale's mouth, sticky and dry, tasted of blood and dirt. A trough of water lay in a field of hardened mud and rocks, but he chose not to indulge since it was surrounded by a tribe of rancid-smelling goats.

His feet felt as if someone had doused them with petrol and then lit a match. Vision blurred, he made the marina in just under two hours, desperately taking water from a supply on the nearest wharf. On board, he tripped, crashing into the cockpit, cursing, scrabbling in the darkness. This arrival was loud enough to wake even Jack from his snoring on the port bunk.

"Jesus. What in God's name is going on? And where the hell you 'bin, skipper?"

"You wouldn't want to know."

Jack flicked on a small cabin light, squinted in the gloom, yawning. "Your head's bashed in, and you look like shit."

"Thanks, that's how I feel. Where's Gibby and Dean?"

"Up in the forward cabin ... I think," said Jack, dropping his head back onto the pillow. "Get some sleep, Charlie, for Pete's sake."

Hale crawled into his bunk beside the engine compartment and was soon out cold.

Morning.

Dean shouted, "Hey Charlie!"

That woke Hale. His head was lodged under the chart table in the aft berth. He looked up to see the wretched features of Dean leaning over him.

"You, wanna brew, skipper? By looks o' things, I think you need one."

"What's the time?" asked Hale, shielding his eyes from the sun streaming into the cabin.

"Eight."

"Damn."

"Yep," said Dean, placing the steel kettle too loudly on the stove, "and Jack's over at the yard getting ready to have this tub lifted out. That engine needs the piping changed. Can't do it here or we'll sink."

"Shit. Where's Gibby?"

"Dunno."

"Thought he was asleep up forward?"

"Nope."

Hale mulled the events of the previous night. Dean passed him a cup of milky coffee in an unwashed mug, chipped, and stained. Nevertheless, it tasted like heaven, and eased the headache.

"Now," said Dean taking a loud slurp. "I have just got to bloody know what happened to you. I mean, classic, and what happened to your 'ead? It looks like..."

"Leave it, Dean. We need to get Jack and Gibby together, and get the work done on this boat if we're going to have a chance of sailing tomorrow. That's what we're here for, remember?"

"And that woman you was wiv'..."

"I said drop it. And you can put that shit away ... I know you're on it." Hale nodded to a smudge of white powder on the main cabin table. "Get rid of any stuff, or you're off the crew. No question."

Dean smirked, "I'm clean, skipper, you can count on it."

Hale ignored him, climbed out into the cockpit and the blaze of the morning sun. White light flared off the water, blinding. A few hours before the full solar force was unleashed, a heady pink light enveloped the scene. Only a distant hum of motors from the boatyard and chug of fishing boats heading out of the marina broke the silence.

But this tranquillity was far from Hale's thoughts. His attention returned to the previous night's trouble. Word would get around. It always does in small towns, especially marinas.

Keep it quiet, ignore it, Hale thought. Concentrate on the job in hand, and the trip tomorrow. His fortunes must change, things would get better soon.

"Hey Charlie," shouted Jack, arriving from the yard, beaming, disturbing Hale's thoughts. "Last night, what in hell's name? We'll leave that one for you to explain in the bar later, eh?" The big man paused on the wharf, wiping sweat from his head with his baseball cap. "We're taking her over to the yard. The marineros were blabbing something I couldn't understand, but they wrote '11' in the dirt, so I'm guessing that's when they're coming over to tow us across."

"Okay, let's do it," said Hale. He called down into the cabin, "Dean, we're moving, so get the boat fixed, please, and then we're on for the trip."

"You got it, boss," came Dean's reply from below.

Jack hauled himself onboard and began adjusting the lines.

"About Gibby," Hale said, looking at Jack. "Where's he gone?"

"Beats me, Charlie. Look, forget him. He's probably in bed with that woman he latched on to. You know what Gibby's like."

"Woman?"

"Yeah, just like you, skipper. Found himself a woman in the port, headed off for a night of revelry, or shall we say, *debauchery*. This type of thing's been happening for thousands of years in ports around the world in case you hadn't noticed. We'll pick him up later, carry out a goddamn search. Now, can we please get on with the job? Those marineros don't tolerate idiots like you and me gladly."

Hale pursed his lips, took a deep breath. "I don't like the smell of it, Jack. You know what happened last time ... in Morocco."

"I know what you're getting at, Charlie, but you're a worrier aren't you? Just relax. Here they come now." Jack looked around at a dilapidated inflatable chugging towards them. A dark-skinned marinero, expressionless, cigarette hanging from his mouth sat in the stern of the small craft, waved his arms, barking instructions across the water.

"Dean, get up here," said Jack.

An hour later, *Blue Too* was lifted out by the crane, its cradle swinging, supporting the weight. The yacht hung above the dock, a temporary position while repairs were undertaken. Dean, and a wiry Spaniard with black eyes and rum breath, replaced burnt hoses and groped around in the grime and oil of the engine bay.

Hale offered to help, as did Jack, but were shooed away. Too many men in the tight confines of the boat in the thirty-seven degree oven would be a recipe for frayed tempers.

Soon, it was done. New hoses in place and hull fittings sealed.

"Good stuff. She'll be lowered back in within an hour," said Hale.

Jack shouted to Dean up on the crane, "Let's go and get Gibby. He'll be in Timón waiting for us. He'll not come down the yard 'cos you know what he's like."

"Good plan," said Dean, climbing down.

"So, you knew he was still bloody in there, eh?" said Hale, storming off to the bar ahead of Dean and Jack, who kicked up dust behind.

FIFTEEN

Gibby was immediately recognisable as Hale approached. Slumped in a chair outside *El Timón*, cigarette smoking in the ashtray, coffee in hand, and a shot of rum on the table. Gibby's way of sobering up after a big night.

"Explain," said Hale, catching his breath, craning underneath the umbrella shade. He towered over the potbellied figure squinting up at him.

"What's eating you, sweetheart?" said Gibby, slurring, knocking back the espresso, replacing the cup, and crossing his arms. "Strewth, and look at your pretty face. What may I ask did that cute piece of arse hit you with? Looks like a nice job she done on you, boy."

"You're supposed to be helping out at the yard, not getting drunk." Hale fumed, grabbed the shot of rum, emptied it into a plant pot.

Gibby rose to his feet unsteadily, eyeing Hale who stood firm.

Jack and Dean sidled up. Jack put his hand on Hale's shoulder and said, "Leave Gibby to me, Charlie. Come on, calm down, lads."

Gibby pushed the table violently, the edge hitting Hale's thighs, and then said, "You think you're mister hard nut, eh? Well let me explain a few home truths, college boy."

"Leave it Gibby," Jack said, placing his hand against Gibby's chest, separating the two.

"No, I'm not leaving it, Jack," insisted Gibby. "You see Charlie-boy here thinks he's squeaky clean, but we're all in on this trip, aren't we?"

"I'm just the skipper, Gibby. I get a fee and that's it," said Hale. "We're going sailing."

Gibby let out a laugh, looked to the heavens, squared back up to Hale. "Going sailing?" he said. "You're quite something aren't you, thinking you're just the skipper. But you see, Happy Gary don't see things that way. As far as he's concerned, we are all in the same team."

"Pack it in, Gibby, you're wasted, man," said Jack, rolling his eyes at Dean, who smiled his crooked smile, and then sucked on a can of Red Bull.

Gibby turned to Jack, seemingly gathering his thoughts, scheming. "And Jack, you've got no reason to be all high and mighty, 'ave you? Your little secret might come out *accidentally* some day if you're not careful. That trip you done with the other crew before us, remember that do you, Jack and *Charlie*?"

"What are you getting at Gibby?" asked Hale.

"Well, let's just say that Jack had his finger in the pie and skimmed a little off the top. Word got around from that crew, who as it happened, were mates of mine."

"Ignore his bullshit, Charlie, he's pissed and stoned," said Jack, looking pensive.

"And..." continued Gibby, as if on stage, "forgive me if I'm wrong, but I don't think a certain Happy Gary will be best pleased *if* he finds out."

Dean chuckled, crunched the Red Bull can in his hand and tossed it aside.

"This is why I didn't want these morons, Jack," said Hale. "It's already a screw-up and we haven't even left port."

Gibby steadied himself, sobering up in the confrontation. "Morons, eh? You see Charlie-boy, you might think you're one of them toffs or somefink, but you're one of us now. How do you say, *guilty by association?* And besides, you been slapping that hot bird of yours around or something? Looks like you came out second best."

Dean moved forward, laughing, "Well at least you got the upper hand wiv' yours last night, Gibby."

Silence.

Hale looked across at Dean, "What do you mean, *the upper hand*?"

Dean said nothing. Hale glanced at Jack, who looked down, and then at Gibby who wore a pathetic smirk.

Hale persisted, "What happened last night?"

"It was nothing, Charlie, a skirmish. Forget it, let's go now, boys," said Jack, grabbing Hale's shirtsleeve with his fist.

"And what kind of skirmish are we talking?" Hale said, pulling out of Jack's grip.

Gibby looked uncomfortable with Hale's stare boring into him, but delivered an alcohol-fuelled riposte, "That Russian girl, Alina, well she got a bit stroppy, so I gave her the slapping she deserved. Just a black eye, Charlie-boy. Sent her packing, job done."

Hale's arm swung across, delivering a haymaker to Gibby's sweaty left cheek, falling forward over the table as he did so. Gibby flew back over his chair, fifteen stones of flab landing on concrete. Glasses crashed to the floor. Jack and Dean dove in to haul Hale to his feet, pulling him away from Gibby.

A smell of diesel fumes hit Hale as he regained his composure. Gibby crawled back up to his feet, using the wall of the building to aid his ascent.

An engine throbbed loudly. A vehicle pulled up.

"Boys," said Jack, his eyes sliding sideways to indicate an arrival behind him. Hale looked into the road. A Guardia vehicle idled, stationary, windows open. Two officers sat in the front, wore dark sunglasses and looked across, the nearest with his arm dangling out of the window and a smoking cigarette between his fingers.

Hale and the crew stood in awkward silence. The officers said nothing, conferred with each other, and then looked back across to Hale and the commotion at the bar.

"No hay problema aquí," said Hale, forcing a smile. Dean helped Gibby to his feet.

The nearest officer remained expressionless. His look made his thoughts clear: *You're damn right there's not a problem*. He flicked his cigarette onto the tarmac and motioned to the driver.

The Guardia vehicle pulled off, slowly, rumbling out of sight behind the bar.

The bargirl arrived to clear the mess. Hale apologised, and then returned his attention to Gibby. "My dear friend, Gibby," he said. "We have a problem, because I know the people who work in this bar, and you come and act like the pea-brained bonehead you are. And now I have a bad reputation, *by association*, as you say. And the Guardia, who just rolled by ... if they get to hear of your assault, don't expect them to get into discussion about your human rights when they throw you into a jail full of stoned cokeheads like him."

Hale pointed to Dean, who responded with a characteristic dead look.

Hale walked briskly towards the yard, summoned Jack to follow. "Tomorrow is the last time, Jack. I'll get you across, you do whatever shit you wanna do over there. Then I'm done for good. Got it?"

"Okay, boss," said Jack, letting out a sigh, waving Dean to catch up with them. "And that thing about the last job, and the money, I can explain, you see it was..."

"Spare me the details, Jack. Don't bother."

Hale's phone rang. An unknown number. Probably Stack from the office, just what he needed.

He took the call.

"Charles speaking."

"Hello, it's me ... Marta."

SIXTEEN

"It's not good to call me here," said Hale. "I have to get the boat prepared ... and something happened to me last night." Hale looked behind at Jack following, shifted the phone to his other ear. Jack had a keen ear and must not hear this.

"What do you mean? What happened?" said Marta at the other end, her voice soft.

"I can't tell you now, but perhaps we should meet when I get back from the trip. This place is small. Too many people will ask questions."

They neared the yard where *Blue Too* rested in the lifting cradle, her sleek lines ready to leave the dust and noise ashore and re-join the tranquillity of the marina waters.

"Jack, go ahead will you, please?" said Hale. "I'll join you in a minute. Go help the marineros to get her moving."

Marta persisted, "Are you okay? You sound like you have stress."

Stress isn't the word, thought Hale. "Yeah, I'm okay, but do you remember that youth in the shadows we saw outside your apartment?"

"I did not see him. I told you not to look."

"Well, it turns out he wasn't so young, late twenties maybe, and he had company, teenagers from somewhere. They tripped me up in the street, stole my cards and money. Now I have nothing."

Hale heard Marta gasp at the other end. "We should go to the Policía," she said. "But, they will ask questions, and the jefe of the bar will get to know ... find out that we were together."

"Is that a problem? Are you seeing him?"

"No, but he thinks he owns me like he owns the bar, I..."

Hale sighed. "Great."

"In the bar, it is okay for me to talk with the customers for sure, but he should not know that you were up near my house, and..."

Hale sensed panic in Marta's voice. "Okay, don't worry, just keep it quiet," he said. "I go to sea tomorrow and when I return, I'll get some money and leave here for a while."

Hale looked over at *Blue Too*. The crane fired up, noisy, a cloud of diesel smoke surrounding it. Jack and the marineros fussed about in the heat, gesticulating. The unwieldy vehicle lurched a foot forward and the yacht swung gently in the straps.

"Marta, I have to go now." Hale took a breath, knowing the next phrase would be painful for both of them to accept. "Last night, Marta. I'm not sure we should see each other again … for a while at least. I have responsibilities back home. Do you know what I mean?"

Silence at the other end. Hale covered his ear over the noise of the crane's engine.

"Marta?"

"You have a wife, no?"

"Well, not really, but…"

"Then you must go on your trip."

"I'll call you when I return … to talk … Marta?"

The line went dead.

Hale pocketed the cell phone, ran over to the yacht now inching over the dock. Jack stood beside her on the quay, playing the lines, glanced across to Hale as he approached, "Grab the starboard line, Charlie," said the Scot. "Let's get her moving … and tell me what these marineros are saying. I have not got a clue what they're babblin' on about."

Hale took the line, not concentrating, his mind on Marta and the passage ahead. He couldn't trust Gibby and Dean, but knew that staying in Puerto de Santa María with no money and the wheels of the rumour mill now in motion, was not an option.

On the water, Jack took the helm as *Blue Too* chugged across the marina to the berth. Hale stood on the foredeck holding a bowline, looking across to the tower.

Tomorrow, he thought, we sail and I get the job done quickly. Do the crossing, get back to port, get paid, return to Lucy and Deborah. They knew nothing of his life in the marina or at sea. Best it remained that way. The thing with Marta. That would all blow over, so let it rest.

Nice and simple.

Gibby and Dean waited on the wharf as the bow edged into the mooring. Gibby grabbed the line as it was thrown, got on with the business in silence. Dean must have had a word with him, thought Hale.

"Nice one, boys," said Jack, killing the engine. "I think we're all set."

"Okay, meeting in the cockpit guys, now," said Hale, tossing a rope across the deck and making for the stern. Gibby hauled himself onto the bow, with Dean following behind still wearing his petulant grin.

"Bit of advice, Charlie," whispered Jack as Hale brushed past. "Go easy, on 'em. And if you push Gibby, well, you know what he was implying? About squealing to Happy..."

"Leave it to me, Jack."

The crew gathered in the cockpit.

Gibby broke the silence, "So, what's up, *boss*?"

"Yeah, are we grounded, skipper?" asked Dean, rolling spindly strands of tobacco into Rizla paper.

Hale drew breath, and then launched into an appeal that he knew would reveal a weakness, a chink in his armour upon which boneheads, Gibby and Dean, might thrive. "Last night I was mugged up in San Isidro," he began. "I have no money or credit cards. We should report it, but you know how long that will take and it'll jeopardise the trip."

Silence. Jack raised his eyebrows, and then looked down at his feet.

"And?" said Gibby, leaning back, folding his arms.

"Well, I need your help," said Hale.

Dean chuckled, lighting up, puffing smoke into the air, "Oh right, now you want *our* help. Peachy, boss."

Jack kicked Dean's foot, "Och, shut your nonsense for a minute, Dean."

Hale continued, "I'll need you guys to sub me some money..."

"Consider it done," interrupted Jack.

"Appreciate it, Jack. And you all need to get on my side to do the crossing. We have to operate as a team in case we meet rough weather or there's some other problem. We need to depend on each other ... and I'm in charge." Hale scanned their glum faces, looking for signs of dissent. "So, what's it going to be?" he continued. "Are we doing this, or are we going to abort following the events of last night ... and this morning at the bar?"

Dean surprised Hale, responding first, "I'm in, boss. Need the money."

Jack was next, "You know I'm in, Charlie."

All eyes went to Gibby, who exhaled, eyed Hale with contempt, and then said, "What do you think – that I've come here to sit around on the flaming beach? I'm in."

10 p.m.

Hale sat at the chart table, perusing the route across to Melilla. They'd depart in the early hours and all going to plan, be in port on the African coast in the afternoon. The boat was fuelled and prepared. Gibby and Dean had gone into town to eat, while Jack manoeuvred his bulk about the cabin, stowing clothes, organising the galley. The big man was restless. Hale's drinking ban had disrupted his routine.

Hale threw his pen onto the chart table, rubbed his eyes, sore after little sleep during the last twenty-four hours. He looked up at Jack's figure craning in the confines of the cabin, "You go, Jack. Keep an eye on the boys and make sure there's no trouble."

"You sure, boss?"

"Yep, go. I'm gonna get ten minutes' kip."

Jack needed no further persuasion, stomped out on deck, and was soon gone.

In a world of hard-drinking cohorts such as Jack and the crew, Hale knew that the effectiveness of his 'ban' was flimsy at best. It was more a signal for them to keep their noses clean and be in shape to sail the boat.

For these men, alcohol was lifeblood as vital as water.

SEVENTEEN

Hale's ten-minute nap turned into a deep enveloping sleep. He'd watched Jack through the cabin porthole, disappearing along the wharf towards the lights of the main plaza. Then, Hale's eyes grew heavy and the gentle rock of the yacht on her mooring went to work. A heavy slumber followed, which even the worst worries in the world would not disturb.

Until Dean arrived back at the boat.

"Skipper!" he shouted, uncharacteristic alarm in his voice.

Hale lurched awake violently, as if *Blue Too* had been hit by a rogue wave. He looked at his watch through blurred vision, barely knowing where he was.

1:25 a.m.

A commotion outside, created by one person. Dean banging his fist on the bow. "Skipper, Charlie! Get out here now. It's Gibby ... he's in the drink."

Hale climbed out into the cockpit, scanned the wharf for any sign of Gibby or Jack, turned his attention to Dean. "Christ, what's up, Dean? You look as white as a sheet."

"Come ashore, quick," said Dean. "Gibby's in the flaming water. He's in real trouble this time. I can't get him out."

"In the water. Where?"

Dean ran off, along the wharf without explanation. Hale pushed his feet into his sailing pumps, clambered across the deck steadying himself by grabbing shrouds and ropes, reached the bow, leapt ashore. He landed heavily, falling, cursing, rising to his feet to chase after Dean who was now moving his wiry frame into the darkness between a fifty-foot ketch and a gin palace motorboat.

"Over here, Charlie!"

"I'm here, I'm here ... what the hell?" Hale caught, his breath, surveyed the scene. "Shit."

Gibby, clearly drunk, had boarded the wrong yacht in his stupor, fallen from some height into the water, and was now holding on to the line from the motorboat's fender to prevent himself sinking further. The hull of the ketch moored to starboard was just feet away, squeezing him between the boats, threatening to trap him.

"Get a line to him, Dean," said Hale, hauling himself onto the ketch. The motorboat was unoccupied, but Hale knew the Dutch owners of the ketch and had recently seen them around town.

Please be away for a few days, not asleep below, Hale thought.

"It's not good, boss. He won't take the line, he's out of it. I'll swing down to him," Dean said, hanging like a gibbon between the boats, one foot placed precariously on a balloon-like fender, his hand reaching down with a grip on Gibby's arm.

On the ketch, Hale hung over the side, one hand on a railing, another reaching down to grab a fistful of Gibby's sodden shirt.

"How the hell did you let this happen, Dean, you idiot?"

"You know how he is, boss, he can't control his drink."

"You don't say." Hale looked around, spotted a small platform on the stern of the motorboat. "Let's drag him to the back, Dean ... pull."

"I'm not holding him, boss."

"Pull damn it."

Gibby glugged and moaned, semi-conscious, head almost under the black water. A fifteen-stone ball of pure blubber not floating well. Dean moved into a better position. Hale lodged his legs against the railings, hung down, clasped Gibby's shirt around the collar with one hand and under his armpit with the other.

"Hurry up, Dean, before I go in," Hale gasped. "I'm slipping."

Lower down, on the transom platform just two feet wide, Dean reached out, dragged Gibby across, tried to haul him up.

"Too heavy, boss, he's not coming up here."

Hale heard a voice from the wharf, Scottish. Looked across. It was Jack, who was peering into the dark, trying to fathom out what was going on. "What in Jesus name?" said Jack, crouching down, hands on knees.

Hale leapt to his feet, and shouted over to him, "It's Gibby. The drunken lunatic's in the water. Seems unconscious, maybe a blow to the head."

"Hellfire, what next?" said Jack, scratching his head. "So you got him on the stern there I see."

Hale moved aft, climbed down off the ketch, chest tight with panic. He boarded the motorboat, making for the bow. "Come on Jack, stop spectating," said Hale. "Help us. He needs hauling up."

"You'll not get a big man like that up."

"Well, we have to try damn it," said Hale, glaring at Jack, a look of disgust.

"Dean, listen up," said Jack, cupping his hands, calling to the stern. "Let Charlie hold him, he's stronger and I'll come aboard. You come ashore, Dean. Go to *Blue Too* and get the bosun's chair. We'll rig it, haul Gibby up by a winch on the ketch."

"Right you are," said Dean, breathing hard, straining to maintain a grip on Gibby while balancing on the tiny platform. Hale arrived, reached from behind, gripped Gibby under both arms and leaned back.

"Go Dean. Get the bosun's chair ... and rope."

"Christ is he breathing, boss?" asked Dean.

"Yes, yes," said Hale, feeling the full weight tugging through his arms, into his stomach muscles. "Just go, now."

Dean climbed up the motorboat's transom, rushed back along the decks towards the wharf. Jack moved past him, reached the stern, leaned over to assess the situation.

"Bloody hell, what a mess," Jack said. "I can'nae get my arse down there. Too small for me, Charlie."

"Well do something," said Hale, frantic. "Do something now!"

"I'll head over to the ketch, see if I can get a boat hook across to you until Dean gets here."

"A boat hook ... what?" Exhausted, hardly able to express exasperation, Hale said nothing, concentrated his grip on the dead weight beneath him. He sucked in the salty night air, felt helpless, watched the bulky figure of Jack climb aboard the ketch and edge along its wooden decks in the darkness. Finally, his shadowy figure appeared at the stern opposite, a long boat hook in hand.

"I can't hold him, Jack. He's going down." Hale's grip slipped. Gibby's head lurched forward. "Come on Jack, what are you doing?" Hale saw Jack come to a halt at the stern of the ketch, standing silent.

"What are we doing, Charlie?" came a reply from Jack, sombre.

Hale frowned, anger building, fuelled by adrenalin and fear.

"What in God's name are you doing? We're losing him, Jack. Get the boat hook across, something for me to hold if we go in. Now!"

"How are we playing this, son?"

"Playing this? You tell *me*, you headcase." Hale struggled to speak, tried to jam his leg against the stainless-steel fittings, which secured the platform to the transom. He looked up, incredulous, at Jack.

"If you don't get the boat hook across ... now," said Hale, pausing, sucking in air, "then later, I'm gonna stick it up your arse."

"You know what happened in Morocco, last time, Charlie. That woman. Gibby getting all violent and whatnot. Now, you turned a blind eye back then, okay, but you *know* who he is ... what he gets up to. Last night was just an example. Me and the others, we seen it many a time, laddie."

Jack propped the boat hook against a railing, reached into his pocket, drew out a cigar and lighter. Hale remained silent, looked on, saw the flash of flame and the end of the cigar redden as Jack took a drag.

"And then there's this thing with Happy," Jack continued. "Me skimming the money, says Gibby. That means we're all facing a bit of a dilemma, Charlie ... your good self included."

Hale tried to assimilate the information, comprehend the message. Jack could hold his drink, so this line of thinking was not down to intoxication. Hale looked over his shoulder, craning to see Dean. No sign. Glanced down at Gibby, a faint gurgle of water bubbled around his mouth. Still alive.

"That woman last night, the Russian girl," continued Jack. "She's in a bad way, so I'm told."

Jack took another drag, leaned on the railing, relaxed as if he was on a holiday cruise. He flicked ash into the water. "So, let me ask you again ... what are we doing here, Charlie?"

Hale blew air out of his lungs, mind racing, taking in Jack's words. He leaned back, still gripping, looked up to the inky blackness above, bemused.

"I don't know, Jack. What *are* we doing?"

EIGHTEEN

1:44 p.m.

The poorly air-conditioned room at the Policía Nacional station in San Isidro was faceless, stark white, clattering with the voices of those outside in the corridor. A mix of immigrants, pensioners, and families, all wielding forms, presenting them to unsmiling officials. They must have some gripe or issue to report, thought Hale. He sat on a hard wooden chair, staring at an off-white desk in front of him. He'd been quickly ushered past the melee, told to wait for a few minutes for the Inspector.

A clock ticked above the doorway. Hale noted that twenty minutes had elapsed. Through the frosted glass, he saw the guard move aside and the door swing open. A man walked in. Ruffled jacket, open collar, cigarette smoking from the corner of his mouth. He looked at Hale vacantly, positioned some papers on the table. Took a few paces back and leaned against the wall. A local, thought Hale, noting the jet-black hair, coarse unshaven skin. This hombre bore a distinctive look: Andalucían.

Hale broke the silence, "Inspector?"

The man shrugged his shoulders, blew smoke into the air. After some lingering seconds, he deigned to respond, "No. Soy Manolo Fernández."

Another man entered, rattling the door loudly, much to Fernández's annoyance. He was younger, of smarter appearance. White shirt and black trousers. Fernández's sidekick, assumed Hale, since he kowtowed to instructions, and appeared nervous while placing further paperwork on the desk.

Sidekick reached up, opened a small window on the left hand wall to allow a meagre amount of fresh air ventilate the room, which was now filled with smoke. It appeared to be a familiar routine.

To Hale, the scenario felt alien, bizarre. The hombres stood in silence against the wall in front of him. Fernández uninterested, as if biding his time. Sidekick pensive, playing with a biro.

Hale offered another icebreaker, this time in English: "Am I to be kept here for long? And, if so…"

"Silencio. No hablo Inglés," barked Fernández, eyeing Hale. "Cinco minutos. Cinco."

Five minutes. Hale glanced at the clock, pondered the scant information. Five minutes in this place could end up being five, ten, twelve, or any other figure, and then what? After five minutes, would the conversation begin? Perhaps he'd be escorted elsewhere. Maybe to join Jack and Dean, whom he hadn't seen since the early hours. He rubbed his eyes, breathed deeply into his stomach, not daring to let his mind drift into fraught territory: the events of last night. That pleasure, he knew would come soon.

The sound of clomping shoes along the hard floors of the corridor transformed Fernández's demeanour in an instant. He moved away from the wall, straightened his back, stamped his cigarette out on the floor.

The door flung open. A woman walked in. Sidekick bumped her unintentionally as she did so. She gave him a look: *idiot*. He closed it, silent this time, squeezing the handle down and edging it shut.

The contrast of this woman to her silent male colleagues struck Hale. Mid-to-late thirties, dark hair in a stylish bob, olive complexion, the woman was slim with a figure perfect to complement her trouser suit. She hugged a pile of brown folders to her chest with one arm, held a large leather handbag with the other. She pushed the papers on the desk aside, dumped the folders next to them. Ignoring Fernández and Sidekick, she pulled up the remaining chair, sat down, rifled around in her handbag producing an iPhone, Dictaphone, and A4 notepad.

A lawyer, thought Hale.

She looked up, paused for an instant, and then began, "I am Inspectora Jefa Rosa María Díez of the Policía Nacional. This is Inspector Fernández and his assistant, Pepe Duarte." Hale noted her English was near perfect. A slight inflection to suggest that she was not a native speaker.

She was about to begin another sentence, but hesitated. Something seemed to distract her. She looked down to her right and fixed her gaze on the floor for some moments. Fernández feigned a cough, and then moved forward, reaching down to the floor to pick up the stubbed cigarette butt. Once he had done so, María Díez's gaze shifted a few degrees to the position of the wastepaper basket beside the desk. Obedient, Fernández deposited the offending item

She continued.

"I am here to question you about the deceased, your friend," she referred to her notes, "Señor Alan Gibson."

"Yes. It was awful, and..."

"Quiet please."

Hale felt his face redden, palms grow clammy. Despite conducting countless interviews for *Connecting4Business*, being interviewed himself was unfamiliar ground. María Díez's confidence unnerved him, especially under the circumstances of the crew's detention. Her eye contact was direct, searching, uncomfortable for Hale to maintain. She dressed in plain attire, business-like, wore little makeup. Simple necklace and earrings.

Yet, despite the mental fog of stress and fear, it was apparent to Hale that in looks, María Díez was not plain at all. In fact, she was striking, and highly intelligent.

"I have come to this area from Madrid for some months on secondment. The authorities here are concerned that there has been an increase in this type of trouble. Foreign nationals, mainly from Northern Europe. Do you understand?"

"I believe so, yes."

"There are fights, alcoholism. Tourists die by falling from apartment blocks, drug money, and so on. Do you understand me, Mr Charles?" she said, leaning forward, leafing through a file.

"It's Mr Hale."

"Very well. You see, *Mr Hale*, this man, Alan Gibson, we have a file in San Isidro. My colleagues here produce this file, and I find it interesting. He seems to be the kind of Briton who likes to court trouble. And your other two friends, I have concerns there too. What are you doing with these people, Mr Hale?"

Hale clasped his hands together under the table, felt his heart pump blood into his neck, up to his temples. "I am here to sail predominantly," Hale said, "but, yes, these people drink more than me, and it can be a problem."

"Your friend is dead. That seems to me like a bit more than *a problem*, wouldn't you say?"

"Of course, but these habits – drinking – die hard sometimes."

"Why do you choose to sail with these people, Mr Hale?"

"I have done so for many years. Mostly with Jack Weir. He finds crew for me and we happened to be sailing with Alan and Dean this time. I knew they both drank heavily, especially Alan. It is a terrible shame what happened."

"And you have sailed with Mr Gibson before?"

"Once."

"And did he drink then?"

Hale paused, letting his eye contact slip away to the left to see Fernández and Sidekick seemingly hanging on his reply despite their lack of English. "Yes, he did, but we managed to keep him away from trouble."

Hale regretted his words as he said them.

"Trouble?" She raised her eyebrows. "Tell me more about this trouble you mention. And where did you sail to?"

"We were over in Morocco … but this really isn't the point. Damn it, he got drunk now and again, as many yachtsmen do. Last night, I specifically asked the crew to stay off the drink as we were sailing the next day. But of course, he didn't listen. He boarded the wrong yacht, fell in, and paid the price. That's all there is to it."

Hale looked at María Díez, and then at the others. They remained impassive.

María Díez leaned back, forming a triangle with her hands, tapping the tips of her fingers together. "So that's all there is to it, so simple. And, no doubt, how you would like this meeting to wrap up, Mr Hale."

She paused, glanced at her notes, and then back up to punish Hale with her look.

"But I've been speaking with your colleagues," she continued, "and Mr Gibson's death is not my only concern here. I would like to know more about your activities over in Morocco." She brushed her hand through her hair, picked up a pen and tapped it on the desk as if sending Morse code. "You see, your friends do not seem to be the kind to go on pleasant sailing trips, or on cultural excursions."

"I agree," said Hale, "but they like the sailing conditions in these parts, the seas … and, they like the travel, and yes, the bars too…"

"And, the women, prostitutes, the hashish. Tell me about the drugs, Mr Hale," she said, her voice now raised. Fernández and Sidekick, shuffled uncomfortably in Hale's periphery.

"You cannot accuse me of involvement in drugs. I am the skipper of the boat, we go sailing and…"

"Quiet."

She paused, scribbled notes on the pad, checked the time. "Your statement taken last night." She looked up. "Do you have anything further to add?"

Hale paused, thought about it, unsure of the best response.

"No, I think it's accurate," he said, finally. "It was dark. I sent Dean to get equipment…"

"Yes, but your friend, Jack Weir, was on hand. Explain why two men could not save him."

Hale drew breath, wondering what story Jack and Dean had given. "You have to understand that the platform at the transom of the motorboat could not support two men. Jack boarded the boat opposite to try to get a rope or boat hook across, but it was too far away, and not at a good angle. Alan was a big man. Even the marineros had difficulty hauling the body out when they arrived."

María Díez slammed her pen down. Hale jolted upright.

"There was a girl, Alina, at *El Timón* bar the night before. She left late at night and was beaten, do you know anything about that?"

Hale balked at the abrupt change of questioning, coughed, brushed his forehead with the back of his hand. "I heard that something went on, but I wasn't there."

"You know the girl?"

"I know *of* her. She hung around the bar sometimes."

"And, where were you that night, Mr Hale?"

"Well, I was at the bar, but I left early. Look. I didn't lay a hand on that girl, any girl. I was walking on the beach and I didn't return to the bar."

"You like the beach?"

"*Yes*, I like the beach."

"You must like the beach very much to have spent some hours alone on it. In the dark at night."

"Well, I…"

María Díez ignored Hale, rose, pocketed her phone. She gathered her folders and handbag to leave, and then stood eyeing Hale. "Do you have a wife, Mr Hale?"

"A fiancée."

"Then my advice is this: go to your fiancée, return to Britain, and never come back here. Be assured, this investigation is not over."

Sidekick opened the door. Hale felt a waft of warm air enter from the street.

"Goodbye, Mr Hale."

NINETEEN

"Och, she's scaring you, Charlie-boy," said Jack. "Mark my words ... and what the hell has she got on you anyway? Gibby fell in pissed, he drowned, end of story."

The taxi headed out of town, tearing past trucks billowing dust behind, mopeds ridden by mad-eyed Moroccans gripping plastic shopping bags, athletic cyclists in bright Lycra using the dual-carriageway as a sun-baked training run. Hale sat in the rear with Jack. In the front, Dean leered at women in passing cars and buses while guiding the driver by pointing.

"She's smart and she's going to dig around," said Hale. "We're getting the hell out."

Jack nudged Hale with his elbow. "That may be, but we have business to do, and when the timing's right, we make a return."

"You're deluded."

"Ha! You'll come around to my way o' thinking, Charlie. Give it a few weeks."

"No chance."

Hale opened the window, let the warm air blast his face, clear his mind. But Jack persisted, leaning over, "You see, Charlie, let's not be thinking about just us here. We have a deal with Happy Gary, and what Happy demands, Happy gets ... otherwise we'll see a darker side of the man."

"I'm shaking in my shoes."

"Don't underestimate him, Charlie."

Dean turned around, fighting the seat belt to lean closer, "He's right, skipper, a deal with Happy is a deal, whatever happened to Gibby."

"Watch the road, pea-brain," said Hale. "It's the Inspectora Jefa I'm concerned about. She'll link me to your crowd and then I'm as screwed as you."

"*Our* crowd, hey?" said Jack, scorn evident in his tone. "When in God's name are you gonna learn that you're one of us, Charlie? In fact, you always have been. And that chica's not got nothin' on us, otherwise we'd still be back there admiring her cute butt. She's full o' fancy talk and not much else. I've had harder interviews at the Job Centre back in Glasgow."

Hale's phone rang, the small one, top left pocket. The taxi drew up to the marina. "Who's paying?" asked Dean.

Jack smiled at Hale, who opened the door and moved out into the hard light of the afternoon to take the call.

"Well," Jack said, "seeing as our skipper don't have no dinero as a result of his altercation with the local muggers, and I'm a Scot, it looks like you have drawn the short straw, Deano."

Hale moved into the shade, waved the guys on to return to *Blue Too*. Baz's familiar voice was on the line.

"I checked the house, Charlie. Watered the plants, fed the cat and whatnot. You've got some post, bills mostly, flyers, that sort of thing. I won't open them unless you want me to?"

"No, don't worry Baz, I'll deal with it when I get back. I'm skipping the sailing trip, heading back to Lucy in Nerja. Look, I have to go. I'll catch up with you at *The Smack* in a few days."

"Okay, understood. We are the unpredictable jet-setter, these days, ain't we? Look, Charlie, there's one other thing before you head off…" Baz's voice sounded serious for a change. Hale sensed it.

"Yes?"

"Well, I was picking up the mail, having a nose around your fine abode, and the doorbell rang."

"So, who was it?"

"Some blokes in suits. One was a big guy, bit of a bonehead, seen him around Southend before somewhere. The other, a small stiff, funny eyes. Anyway, they asked for you and I said you were on yer' hols. I asked what they wanted, but they didn't say."

"I've no idea who…"

"Look Charlie," said Baz, interrupting, "I don't want to spoil your holiday, but I think they were debt collectors."

"Shit."

"Yeah, well, they need to write to you, Charlie. They can't just bleedin' turn up like the Kray Twins, and I had a mate once who…"

"Baz, leave it with me, okay?" Hale said abruptly.

The line was silent for a while. Then, "You okay, Charlie? You sound stressed, mate."

"Fine, Baz, fine. See you soon, bye now."

Hale pocketed the phone, headed towards the wharf.

Two hours later, the boat was secured. Hale waited in the marina office to pay the mooring fees. He'd retrieved his 'backup' credit card with one hundred and twenty euros stashed at the bottom of his crew bag. Reluctantly, he borrowed another hundred from Jack, whose response was predictable: "Now, *you* owe me, Charlie-boy."

But at least Hale was free of the crew. They departed heading west, destination Marbella, leaving Hale to deal with the admin at the marina office. God knows what plans they have before returning to Britain, thought Hale. Better I don't know.

A tall Scandinavian, bad shorts, sandals and white socks, haggled with the marina Capitán over electricity charges. Not a good idea, since the fees were hardly extortionate and the pettiness was raising the hackles of the Spaniard. The outcome for the Scandinavian would be a 'personalised' account at the marina. One in which the man's penny-pinching might yield a short-term gain, but countered later by hiked fees and much shoulder shrugging when queried.

The thrifty fashion disaster loped off. Hale took a seat, entered his card into the machine. After some seconds, the Capitán frowned at it, prodding the keys.

"Your card is not operable, señor."

Hale leaned over, stared at the display: *Authorisation failed, contact your bank.*

"It usually works fine," said Hale. "Please try again."

The Capitán sighed, pulled the card out, pushed it back in, tapped more keys. "Authorisation fail, señor," he said.

Hale stared at the Capitán for a moment, shook his head, and then said, "Okay, I have no money, no cash. I will speak to the owner and he can wire you the money or I can pay when I return. Is that okay with you?" Sweat poured down his face, voice strained. This appeal must sound desperate, thought Hale. The nerves would show. He leaned back in the chair, looked behind. A marinero strolled around with little to do in the sultry evening.

The Capitán swung on his chair. A few seconds passed, he tapped on his antiquated desktop computer, and then replied, looking above his glasses and smiling, "But of course, señor Hale. You are good customer, no? For many years we have known you here. I can simply put this on your account."

Relieved, Hale rose to go, shook the Capitán's hand. "Thank you so much, I will be back in a few weeks."

"No problema, señor."

Hale made for the door, nodding *Hola* to the bored marinero.

The Capitán called out as Hale passed through the door, "Señor Hale."

Hale turned. The Capitán smiled, waved the credit card in the air, "You forget this."

"Oh, thank you," said Hale, returning to the desk.

The Capitán held the card from him for a millisecond, smiled, and then said, "Tell me, is everything okay with you today, señor Hale?"

"Yes, of course. Fine."

Hale grabbed the card, left the office.

On the bus out of San Isidro, Hale's eyes grew heavy. Even the beauty of the golden light and setting sun ahead could not inspire him to keep them open any longer.

Yet, sleep did not come. Suspicion racked his mind. What were Jack and Dean's intentions? The Capitán. He seemed to know something. Maybe he knew about the girl, Alina, who'd been beaten. Now, everyone would learn of this news on the marina grapevine. Maybe he thought Hale responsible for the beating, or at least assumed he was a womaniser. *El Timón* indeed attracted a certain contingent, women of the night along with their cagey male admirers, but the night with Marta was different. She was not a working girl in that sense. She worked behind the bar, nothing more. Hale was sure of that.

The bus headed along the rocky coast road, the engine revving, whining through the gears. The sky was now deep red, the headlights of oncoming cars intermittently flashing white into the dark interior, lighting the faces of the only three passengers aboard: a backpacker listening to music on headphones, an old woman eating fruit, and a worker from the plasticos, asleep.

Hale instinctively looked at his wrist for the time. The watch was not there, stolen by the muggers. He pulled his phone out, illuminated the display.

9:04 p.m.

One hour to Nerja.

TWENTY

"What the devil are you doing arriving so late, Charles? My God, you've missed a *wonderful* evening."

The only thing worse than being trapped in conversation with Gerry, was being trapped in conversation with Gerry when he'd knocked back a few gin and tonics. Hale had returned to the villa in Nerja. He was greeted by Gerry, the smarmy host, while Deborah lay asleep and Lucy was out on the town with Walnut Face, Brenda. He threw his bag into the guest room, returned to the kitchen to enjoy further tales of Gerry's wonderful existence.

"The meal tonight, paella, *to die for*," said Gerry looking to the ceiling in a theatrical delivery. "Truly Spanish cuisine. Paella originated from Málaga, you know."

"Valencia."

"Mm. The girls were on *such* a high. They decided to stay in town for a few more drinks, but I sensibly came back to hold the fort as it were. Lucy's been on top form, shame you were away. Drink Charles?"

"Beer please."

Gerry handed him a lukewarm bottle from an impotent fridge. Hale gratefully received, but yearned for a frosted bottle served for a euro in any number of bars a mile from here.

"Glass?"

"No thanks."

"Good sailing?"

"Trip was abandoned, I'm afraid. Trouble with the gear. Never mind, next time."

"Too bad. I'm a landlubber through and through, as you know. All that seasickness, God, no thanks. Golf's my game."

"Quite," said Hale, taking a mouthful of a Germanic brew in line with Gerry's obdurate preference for Northern European brands.

"You know Ralph came across for a few days?"

"Yes, I heard."

"Returned the other day. Damn shame you couldn't have been around. Now, I know Ralph has a *history* with Lucy." Gerry raised his eyebrows, feigning tact. "Well anyway, I have to say he's a damn fine golfer, and his driving shot, boy, at one point he had me on the run. You should come for a game, the three of us. No really, you should."

I'd rather blow my foot off with a shotgun, thought Hale. "Yes, sounds like a plan. Must take you up on that."

A rattle at the door and a loud shriek announced the return of Lucy and Walnut Face.

They burst into the kitchen, Brenda screeching something unintelligible at Gerry. Lucy's eyes locked-on to Hale's. She looked merry, not drunk. Walnut Face, gin-pickled, definitely drunk.

"Charles," said Lucy, leaning against the doorjamb. "You look ... terrible."

"Thanks. Long trip, trouble with the boat and…"

An awkward, unexplained silence filled the room. Lucy frowned faintly, curious. She looked at her fiancée, swept the hair from her face, seemed to be gathering her thoughts. A latent switch was flicked in the moment. Something had changed between them.

Her intuition, thought Hale.

"We made some repairs to the engine," continued Hale, now tense, the three of them hanging on his every word. "Had to lift her out to the yard and it was a bit of an affair. Dirt and oil everywhere."

"I see," said Lucy. She accepted a glass of whiskey from Brenda, indifferent, her mind seemingly elsewhere. "You do look tired, and thin. You need a rest…"

"Ha!" interrupted Gerry, "I've been trying to talk this young man into taking up a real sport, on the green. Much more civilised than scrabbling around on boats. After all, he's got to keep up with old Ralph now, hasn't he?"

Walnut Face slapped Gerry on the shoulder, slurring, "*Gerrry, behhhave.*"

"Oops," said Gerry, winking at Hale, who remained silent. Didn't want to give the jerk the pleasure to know he was fuming.

"Look, Gerry," said Hale, "thanks for the beer, but I think I'd better unpack and head for the sack."

"Oh, I do believe we have a lightweight," said Gerry, tilting his elongated head back to finish his gin. Walnut Face squawked as Gerry continued, "Well, you go ahead, but you're off in just a few days, so you should catch up on the drinking stakes before you return to Blighty, where I'm sure you need to help keep the wheels of industry turning. It's all right for us creatures of leisure out here in the sun. How is business anyway?"

Gerry rattled some bottles, searching for one that was not empty, eventually selecting whiskey.

"It's okay, actually," said Hale, "always busy and we have a new training…"

"Ah, yes *training*. I remember. We used to contract chaps like you at the bank."

"Yes, we have a few clients from the financial world at Connecting."

"Connecting?"

"*Connecting4Business*, the name of the company."

Gerry sniggered, "Ah, yes, subsidy-funded sort of thing, know those types. I was almost sad to leave the bank, you know, but that was a damn good career. The payoff, God, we could have bought three of these damn villas, eh Brenda?"

It squawked again, "Four!" and then hiccupped.

"Fine, fine, bank," continued Gerry, "and in my opinion that's the path you might consider taking, Charles. If you want to get into *real* commerce."

Hale emptied the bottle of beer, placed it gently down on the kitchen surface. "Yes, fine bank indeed," he said, eyeing Gerry, preparing to escape to the sanctity of the bedroom. "But shame about that business with the board member, what was his name? Jenkins, that's it." Gerry remained mute for a change. Hale continued, "All over the papers. That thing with dirty money was bad enough, but then the extortion and sub-prime mortgages, and then … to top it all..."

Gerry slammed his glass down. "You've fudged the issue, Charles," he said. "That was *not* the case!" Gerry's nose turned red, and to Hale's delight, he wagged his finger in the air like a wizened old man. "The press got hold of that and…"

"And then there was that thing about the sex tourism," interrupted Hale. "I mean, Christ, the man bragged about his connections in The House of Lords and the next thing we know he's on trial in Bangkok having had a torrid night of debauchery with…"

"You're a damn naive fool, Charles, if you believe that ... a damn fool!"

Lucy glowered at Hale, gave a faint shake of her head.

Hale made for the bedroom.

"Goodnight everyone."

TWENTY-ONE

Hale climbed the stairs to *Connecting4Business*, greeted Pam, busy as usual, papers in hand and one ear to the phone. She gave a smile, a raise of the eyebrows, ended her call.

Before she could say anything, Hale said, "I'd better cut to the chase: How's Stack?"

"Not good," Pam replied, sighing, looking towards the glass door of Martin Stack's office. She whispered, "Just slide by and get on with something. His mood improves after about three coffees. That'll be after ten o' clock, something like that."

Hale pursued his lips, nodded, skulked past Stack's den towards his own office further down the corridor. Inside, his desk was piled with folders, in-tray crammed with letters and padded envelopes. He flicked the switch on his outmoded desktop computer. The fan whizzed, hard drive crackled as it began its intolerably slow boot-update phase. The email inbox would be worse, and include a spreadsheet from Pam with an itinerary heavily revised by Stack following the 'holiday'. Nice start, thought Hale. He grabbed a coffee from the automated machine opposite, returned to his desk, balking at the synthetic taste of the brew and mountain of work that lay ahead.

The desk phone rang, a light blinking on the unit. Pam.

He took the call.

"Hi Pam."

She whispered over the line, "Martin's on his way now."

"Okay, thanks." Hale replaced the receiver, looked blankly out of the window at the suited workers striding along Crutched Friars. Stack's feet stomped along the corridor. Hale dreaded the impending confrontation, though was consoled with one notion: a barrage of abuse from jerkoff, Stack, would be mild in comparison to Rosa María Díez's icy analysis of a few days ago.

"You're in a hell of a lot of trouble, Charles," said Stack, pushing the door open, letting it slam against the wall.

You don't say.

"You didn't even send me a goddamn email," Stack continued, slamming a folder down on Hale's desk, "and with the mess that's going on here, I'm tempted to fire you."

He looks redder in his pallid face than normal, thought Hale, put on weight.

"I booked that holiday months ago, Martin…"

"Don't go there, Charles. This is a responsible position you hold and you *have* to keep online … twenty four-seven."

"There must be a way to catch up … with the Chinese thing," said Hale. He felt his cell phone vibrate in his trouser pocket.

Stack shook his head, making his jowls wobble. "Chinese thing? Your depth of understanding is staggering. Do you realise how much money, how much is at stake here?"

"I can catch up, maybe with help from one of the interns."

"Really? So simple. We're so far behind, Charles, it's hopeless."

If you weren't surfing Internet porn for half the year, maybe we wouldn't be in this trouble.

Stack's cell phone rang, he sighed heavily, took the call. Hale reached for his, checked the text. From Lucy:

'loads more mail 4 u. also calls on answafone. can u check them, im out tonite.'

Notable that her usual 'Luce xx' was not appended to the end of her text. Hale pondered this newfound coldness. Lucy could know nothing of the events in Puerto de Santa María, the beach, Marta. Maybe it *was* intuition, or she had a hunch, but Hale searched for other reasons.

They'd visited Málaga on their return, staying in the pension for a night to break up the journey. A measure planned by Hale, and a way for him to escape a final night with Nerja bores, Walnut Face and Gerry. Especially, since Hale's revelation about Gerry's esteemed colleagues had made the ex-banker impossibly moody and petulant.

At the pension, Hale had placed both cell phones on the dresser before taking a shower. Lucy had picked up the slimline Spanish cell when a text came in, the first time she'd done so.

"Can't read it. It's in Spanish," she said, passing the cell to Hale as he emerged from the bathroom.

"Oh, okay. It'll be the marina, about the mooring fees," Hale had said, towelling his hair, studying a message from Marta. She was worried for him, wanted to meet, to talk. Tricky situation, had made Hale break out in a cold sweat.

He snapped out of his thoughts.

Stack paced up-and-down, continued to speak on the phone in loud acronyms and corporate bullshit to someone Hale assumed was higher up the *Connecting4Business* food chain. Stack finally closed the call and eyed Hale.

"Get on with it," he fumed, and then stormed out of the office.

That evening, the home was quiet while Hale perused the post. Baz was right. The debt collectors had visited, written to follow up their knock on the door. The agents had been sent by a loan company (£17,989.22 owed and five payments defaulted so far). A two-week window allowed Hale to reply, or he'd receive another visit, and any such visit with Lucy present would be uncomfortable at best.

The answerphone messages (seven of them) were equally harrowing. Lucy would have heard these, but most were automated, simply requesting a return call. Official action by these creditors could be delayed by a letter or a call. Hale drew up a priority list. At work, he would type the letters and send them off, buying himself some time, a few weeks. But in the longer run, those few weeks would not stave off the onslaught of creditors wanting blood.

Hale needed money, fast.

He retreated to the kitchen, weighing up the situation, looked through the window into the garden and the sultry English summer evening.

He grabbed his cell phone, dialled Marta. Tell her it's over, he thought. That it never really started. He had responsibilities, a relationship, and family life in England. He should say that things in Puerto de Santa María were complicated now, especially with the death of his crewmember.

After three rings, she picked up.

"Si?"

"It's me, Charles. I wanted to make sure you're okay ... to hear your voice."

"I want to see you again."

"I see." Hale paused, picturing Marta in Andalucía, a few thousand miles away. He must do the right thing. Kill this affair off immediately, so they can both move on with their lives.

"I'd like to see you, of course," he said. "But it's impossible. I have some problems."

"I know. People are talking."

"Talking? What do you mean?"

"I mean at the bar," she said, "about Alina who was beaten. About that man, your friend. The one who was killed on your boat."

"He's not my friend, just crew, and he wasn't killed on my boat. It was another boat, a motorboat."

"Maybe, but they talk about you, and some people now treat me different. Perhaps they know something ... about us."

"I might need to come out again, to finish a job on the yacht," said Hale.

"No. You must not come here."

Taken aback by her abruptness, Hale said, "But I can sort things out."

He continued, broaching territory he promised himself he would not, "And I could see you again." His other cell phone rang, accompanied by a familiar sound outside. Lucy's car pulling into the drive.

"Marta, I have to go now. We can speak again."

A pause at the other end. Hale tensed, checked the incoming call on the other cell phone.

'Jack calling'.

Keys rattled in the front door. Marta replied, "Okay, but do not come here."

Lucy entered the kitchen wearing sports gear and trainers, shopping bag in one hand. Deborah trailed behind giving Hale a wave and a big grin.

"Hi," said Hale, to Lucy. "Just got to get this call, won't be a minute."

Hale waved back to Deborah, closed the call to Marta, juggled his phones, took the call to Jack.

"Jack, what's happening?" Lucy rolled her eyes, placed something in the fridge, while Deborah bounded up the stairs.

"We got trouble, Charlie. You heard anything?"

"What are we talking about, Jack? Why haven't you kept me informed?" Hale moved into the living room, ground his teeth, urged himself to keep his composure under pressure.

"The papers in Málaga. It was all over them when we were at the airport, *El País* for Christ's sake and some other shitty tourist paper."

"*El País*. Shit, what did it say?"

"About a Brit who'd come a cropper of course."

"You get the paper?"

"No, I just saw the front page on the news stand in Departures. I didn't exactly want it as flight time reading, or even for people to see me reading it."

"Don't get paranoid," said Hale, pacing. "It's probably just a report. It'll die down in a few days, so lie low. I'll check it out on the web."

"Web? I don't do that computer crap or whatever it is, but it's not good, Charlie-boy."

"What do you mean?"

"I mean I could understand enough to know that it wasn't just a tale about a drunk Brit falling in the drink. There's to be an investigation, skipper."

"Rosa María Díez."

"Right. That bitch is on some empire-building mission if you ask me. And that's not our only problem, because guess who's blowing smoke up my ass?"

"Happy Gary."

"Yep, and he wants to know the details about how his man met his maker and how he's going to get his money."

"I told you not to get involved with those halfwits, you bloody fool."

"Pipe down, Charlie. Dean and me, we need to meet with you and sort this pile of cow dung out before Happy sends the boys around with some power tools to go to work on our limbs."

Lucy walked into the living room, tapping at her watch and mouthing, "How long you going to be?"

Hale put a finger in the air, *one minute*. Then said to Jack, "Got to go. Other problems. Call me mid-morning tomorrow." He closed the call, looked at Lucy, worry etched on his face.

"Those bills," she said, "in the post. Don't think I don't know what's up. If you need to pay them, just pay them will you? And those messages on the answerphone, what's that about?"

"Leave it with me, Lucy. I got it."

Lucy eyed him for a second. "And what was all that with Gerry and Brenda?" she said. "I was *so* embarrassed."

"He's an insufferable arse."

"They're my friends."

"Your friends or not, he's an arse."

She shook her head, seemingly lost for words, and then said, "What happened out there, Charles?"

Hale looked down at his feet, sighed, "What do you mean?"

"I mean everything was normal when you went out, but I don't like it when you go away with those people, and especially that man, Jack. And when you come back, you're always ... worried, different."

"I can't explain now, Lucy. Yes, I have bills to pay, but I'm dealing with it. I know you don't like Jack, but he gets me work out in Spain with the boat, and good money. Other types of work, not like at the office."

Lucy frowned, "I suppose you're not going to tell me about these 'other types of work', are you?"

"Let's just get through this, Lucy."

She huffed, walked off.

TWENTY-TWO

Next morning, Hale harried an intern, a polite and studious twenty-year-old, Julian, to begin compiling some inane corporate baloney within a PowerPoint presentation. This to placate Stack who prowled the offices prison warden-style.

Uncharacteristically, Jack phoned on time at ten thirty. The conversation was brief. Jack would travel down from Glasgow to London in a few days to meet Dean. They would take the short trip on to Essex to speak to Hale about 'business'. The location, Jack insisted, must be a busy pub, allowing them to remain inconspicuous in the crowd.

In the office, Hale took an hour to surf the Internet for news stories of Gibby's demise. Julian tapped away on the terminal next to him, peering over occasionally, curious.

"Research," said Hale, tapping the side of his nose.

"Got it," replied the genial assistant, who seemed to know enough about corporate politics at his tender age to mind his own business.

Hale scrolled down to a news article that made him jolt upright, splashing coffee onto a document, and giving Julian a start. He'd expected to see old news items from last week, but the Google search revealed an item from yesterday's Daily Mail:

British Tourist Drowned in Spain – Police investigation probes criminal connections.

The article quoted Rosa María Díez: "This kind of incident is of huge concern to the Spanish government…," and, "... increasing resources are being directed to the issues of drunkenness, substance abuse, and violence by foreign nationals – behaviour often linked with large mafia networks." It was María Díez's intention to investigate deaths such as Mr Gibson's in Andalucía for potential connections to mafia hits. Mr Gibson had a criminal history of tax evasion, prostitution, and drug-related offences in the UK alone. It was María Díez's belief that these people should be prevented from travelling to Spain, particularly if their offences were recent and the individuals involved had a propensity to reoffend. She was working with the British police to establish a strategy, and a treaty between the countries.

I can't go back to Spain, thought Hale. This was as bad as it could get. The news item was small, but positioned on the front page of the print version as well as on the website. In the print version, a passport-sized photo of Gibby accompanied one paragraph and referral to a full report on page four.

Not wishing to be seen on the phone, especially with Stack on the loose (it was not beyond him to monitor office calls), Hale hastily typed a text to Dean, asking him to pass the information on to Jack. Jack, the technophobe, did not entertain the idea of learning 'text shite' as he deemed it.

Hale drummed his fingers on the desk, paced about, drank more coffee, and waited for the reply from Dean. It came half an hour later:

'seen papers. jack says so wot? we meet. tell us time&place..? this friday best 4 us'

Hale replied:

'Too risky.'

Dean replied, this time immediately:

'hapy insists we do job.. we meet'

Happy Gary insists. Hale began to type another text, cursed and discarded it, slinging the phone onto the floor. No point debating the issue with an illiterate substance abuser.

A minute later, he composed himself, retrieved the phone, reattached the battery and cover, which had sprung out and crashed around the floor. Julian kept his eyes glued to the screen. Not a good time to discuss PowerPoint.

Hale typed a final text to Dean:

'Ok. 8pm, The Cocklepickers Arms, Southend-on-Sea, Essex.'

Dean's reply, again immediate:

'thx. ill wear mi best tshirt. D xx'

That evening, Hale climbed the stairs thronging with commuters towards Platform 2, Fenchurch Street station and the train home to Leigh-on-Sea. As he boarded, his phone rang. He took the call, changing carriages to avoid scorn and abuse from commuters within the Quiet Zone.

The code: 0034. Spain. Hale suppressed his feelings, but could not deny them: a call from Spain held an element of excitement. Maybe it was Marta, or a contact from the Policía Nacional and María Díez, a chance for him to explain, to relieve the tension.

"Charles Hale."

A delay, white noise on the line. Then, "You see Engleesh, I did not forget you."

Hale's mind raced to identify the voice, distant, familiar.

"You remember we meeting in the street, no?"

The mugger.

"How do you have my number? Why are you calling?"

"Your cards, amigo. Business card and number, we take them, and let me tell you…"

Hale interrupted, "The Policía know about that incident." A lie. He had not reported the incident, wary of drawing attention to his evening with Marta.

"Look Engleesh, you mention the Policía to scare me, no? But *you* should be the one to worry."

With no seats available, Hale stood near the doorway packed with standing passengers. The whistle blew. The train edged away from the platform. A passenger opposite – a suit prodding his smartphone – looked up as if sensing the tension in Hale's voice. Hale turned away, looked out at the cityscape passing by, lowered his voice, "What do you want?"

"I know about the girl."

"And?"

"She is, how do you say? *Connected.*"

"I have no idea what you're saying."

"You see, mister Hale," he said, pronouncing 'Hale' in Spanish, dropping the 'H', *Allay*. "You should not be messing with Marta, because she works for the fat man, the jefe of the bar."

Hale sighed, losing patience, "I don't know this man. What do you want, before I hang up?"

"Well, mister Allay, his name is Berto Morillo and this man is not just the jefe for bar *El Timón*."

TWENTY-THREE

"Look mister Allay, I can protect you from Berto. I know he is curious about that night and why Marta does not return until late. He considers her to be *his* woman, has people to watch over her. Understand?"

"I have no idea what you're talking about, and this conversation is over," said Hale, feeling his pulse rise, giving the suit opposite a look, perhaps unwarranted: *mind your own business.*

"No, this is *not* over," the Spaniard continued. "Listen. Berto runs many businesses and I am a good friend of his, do many jobs for him. But he does not have to know about you … and the girl."

"What kind of businesses?"

"For sure, he owns the bar and others in San Isidro. But also he works with los Rusos. Brings people into town from Africa to work the greenhouses. Also, girls ... how do you say, for the pleasure of men? He is not a man to make angry, mister Allay."

Great, a pimp and people trafficker, thought Hale.

"What do you want?"

"I can protect you."

"I don't believe you and would never trust you."

"Oh, you make me so sad when you say these things."

"I have to go, don't call me again."

Hale heard a snigger on the end of the line. Then, "You need to pay me just some small money, and then we are all good. I will call you again and we can do the money transfer. Western Union, you know them?"

"No deal."

"Berto Morillo has friends in many places across Europe. Friends who do work for him. Do you know what I am saying? Ask Marta about Berto, mister Allay."

"I have nothing to do with this girl you mention."

"Do not play games with me, Inglés. She has a sexy body, no?"

Hale cut the call.

Thirty minutes later, at Leigh-on-Sea, he walked up the path to his home. Deborah opened the door to greet him with a hug. Lucy stood in the hallway, phone in hand, "It's for you. Police," she said.

"Baz called too. Says call him back." She handed Hale the phone, walked into the kitchen, ushering Deborah away from the door.

"The police?" Hale placed his briefcase on a chair, stared at the handset, taking a moment to compose himself. "Charles Hale, how can I help?"

"Good evening, Mr Hale."

"Police?" said Hale, a hasty assumption based on Lucy's comment, wished he hadn't made it.

The reply came back with unsettling calm from an educated man. Hale guessed fifties, and without the London lilt often associated with the Met, "No. I'm Tony Hodgkinson, branch commander, International Crime Office. The ICO in London. A little like the National Crime Agency. Have you heard of us, sir?"

"Can't say I have."

"Well, there's nothing to worry about, but we'd like to ask you a few questions."

"Yes?"

"Well, we could do this over the phone, but I realise that this is your personal number and perhaps you'd like to come to our office in London."

"May I ask the nature of your enquiry?"

"As I say, nothing to worry about. We understand you were present at a recent incident involving the death of Mr Alan Gibson in Spain."

"That's correct."

"Yes, well, Mr Gibson's activities have been known to us at the ICO for some years, and this will form the basis of the questions, as well as your connection with him."

"I see."

Stack wouldn't like it, but Hale agreed to the ICO meeting the following day, 11:00 a.m., Thursday, at an office opposite St James's Park.

Life was now frantically busy. Not in the way Hale wished, but busy nonetheless, and at least it prevented him from dwelling on trouble, since there was plenty of that to dwell on.

Hale phoned Baz. Some moral support. A customary beer in *Ye Olde Smack* was arranged, and Hale descended the steps down to Old Leigh. A chance to take his mind off forthcoming meetings with two diverse and incompatible parties: the International Crime Office on Thursday morning in Westminster, and Jack and Dean on Friday night at a rock music pub.

"You look like death warmed up," came Baz's predictable jibe. He shoved a pint of *London Pride* into Hale's hand.

"Thanks, always appreciate your honesty."

"Pleasure. Good trip?"

"Nightmare."

"Debt collectors been in touch?"

"None of your business, but yes, I'm writing letters to fend them off."

"Sounds bad, mate. You should've told me, might've been able to help."

"Doubt it. It's not good, Baz."

Baz raised his eyebrows, swigged a healthy gulp of beer, placed the glass down. He nodded to the barman for another. "How *bad* are we talking?" he asked.

"Could lose the house, Lucy and Deborah. The lot."

"Flaming Nora, what happened, Charlie? After you finished with the French girl, everything was coming together wasn't it?"

Hale sighed, shook his head. Looked over at a group of men in their twenties, gawking at football on a television screen, banging fists on the buttons of a noisy fruit machine. He thought about his dilemma for a moment. They seemed so carefree. In future, would such unbearable complications afflict their lives too?

"I'll get through it, Baz. Just bad luck, I guess. You around this weekend?"

"Nope, busy."

"Fishing?"

"Yep."

9:05 a.m. the next morning.

Stack fumed, "Tell me you're joking. Humour me."

"It's an appointment with the authorities in Westminster," said Hale. "It's important, but I can't tell you the nature of the business. Sorry."

"Cripes, so now you're a secret agent. What is it, jury service, or an audition for a James Bond movie?"

"I'll be back midday."

Hale stood in front of Stack's desk, waiting for approval. Stack tapped a pen on his desk, banging the space bar on his computer with vigour.

"Get Julian working late. Get back here for noon and don't bullshit me about your delivery dates anymore."

"Thanks, Martin."

"Go."

10:28 a.m.

Hale felt nauseous at the prospect of the ICO interview as he exited Westminster Underground station on a crisp sunny morning. A full half hour before the appointment, commuters bustled past him, impatient with his ambling pace.

The ICO building, grey and forlorn, had 'Official Government Establishment' seemingly branded into the concrete. Inside, a polite receptionist took Hale's details, pointed him to a chair in the waiting area. A plain table displayed copies of *The Financial Times*, *The Economist*, and more worryingly, *Police Magazine*. A nervous-looking graduate in a badly fitting pinstripe suit sat nearby, flipping vacantly through some notes. Hale gave a polite nod, eased himself onto a chair, his cough echoing around the hard walls and floors. Sunlight streamed into the otherwise plain interior, a hint of greenery through the window over to St James's Park offering some colour.

Damn, Hale thought. Ten agonising minutes early.

Light footsteps from a corridor opposite signalled the arrival of branch commander Tony Hodgkinson, and the end of Hale's wait. Hodgkinson seemed older, slimmer than Hale had imagined. Grey-white hair, kindly face.

"Mr Hale?"

"Yes," said Hale, rising to meet him. Hodgkinson's handshake was firm, his look direct, intelligent.

"This way, please."

Hodgkinson led the way down a long empty corridor, highly polished floors, nondescript doors without numbers or signs to indicate the purpose of the rooms beyond. Hale followed. This reminded him of arriving for college interviews during his student days.

"Lovely day," said Hodgkinson. "Come far?"

"Tower Hill. Ten minute trip."

"Ah, yes, lot of building work going on around there at the moment."

"Yes, noisy."

"Mm, nuisance." Hodgkinson, turned into a corridor, knocked on a plain wooden door. He waited three seconds, opened it and peered in. "This one will do. Please..." He motioned Hale to enter.

Hale entered, mouth dry. The room was bland, and in keeping with the building, had a wartime feel about it. No windows, old radiators and furniture, cheap emulsion paint job on the walls. Made *Connecting4Business*' office decor seem like the interior of Liberace's mansion.

Hale sat opposite Hodgkinson at a Formica-covered table, Hodgkinson with a biro and small folder of notes. "This won't take, long, sir," he said. "Can I start by asking how you knew Mr Gibson?"

"He's a friend-of-a-friend, Jack Weir. Jack recommended Gibby, sorry Alan Gibson, as a crew member."

Hodgkinson made a note, and then said, "Yes, for the passage to…"

"Melilla."

"The purpose of which was...?"

"I've been sailing for years. I do it for pleasure and to earn some money as a skipper. I'm qualified for ocean crossings, and Jack likes to go sailing once or twice a year."

"The name of your vessel?"

"*Blue Too.*"

"Blue Two?" Hodgkinson made a further note.

"That's correct. With *Too* spelt T.O.O."

Hodgkinson, scribbled, corrected. "And how long have you owned the vessel?"

"Actually, I'm not the owner. I'm just the skipper, and we charter the boat. As I say, I've done this kind of work before."

"So, who *is* the owner?" asked Hodgkinson, pen hovering above the paper, peering up, brow slightly ruffled.

Hale paused, kept his reply vague, "Well, it's a friend of Jack Weir. I haven't met the man, lives over in Marbella. I believe his name is Gary. Don't know his surname."

"So, you can commandeer a vessel without having met the owner, or signed agreements, and so on?"

"Yes. For yacht deliveries or charters, one often never meets the owner. So long as the paperwork is aboard, licenses, safety papers, and so on, it's a just matter of doing the sailing."

"I see. And, do you get paid much for this type of work?"

Hale knew an establishment with the gravitas of the ICO would have no problem accessing his accounts, international or otherwise. He came clean, "I have to be honest with you, Mr Hodgkinson." Hale looked down at the table, puffing his cheeks out.

"Yes?"

"I ... I do get paid some thousands, anything up to ten thousand euros per year in Spain for these jobs. This money, I'm afraid was not declared for the last two years. You see my financial situation is not great and..."

Hodgkinson held his hand up, shaking his head, and then said, "Best not say too much more, sir. I should inform you that your financial circumstances are of no interest to us at this stage. So, let's just say you receive some thousands. Cash?"

Hale shook his head, "Bank transfer."

"Any other work ... for cash?"

Hale paused, eyed Hodgkinson, looked down, shook his head.

Hodgkinson remained silent for a second, pulled his folder across, opened it and leafed through the first few pages of the inch-thick wad. He continued, "You met my colleague from the Policía, Inspectora Rosa María..."

Hodgkinson struggled with the pronunciation. Hale assisted, "Díez. Inspectora Jefa."

"Yes, quite, and she has carried out some research on your friends. I have to say we have worked with the Inspectora Jefa for a number of years and she is very thorough." Hodgkinson continued to leaf through the documents, occasionally looking up at Hale.

"I can imagine," said Hale. "My impression too."

"Mr Gibson has some *form*. Are you aware of that?"

"I'm sorry?"

"A record of criminal activity."

"Yes, I was aware that he was involved in certain activities…"

"And you still chose to sail with him?"

"It was not my choice. Jack sourced the crew. I did mention to Jack that I was unhappy with his selection."

"Do you often associate yourself with criminals, sir?"

Hale squeezed his hands together under the table, felt nausea return to his gut. Trying to keep his voice cracking, he broached a reply, "My job is to skipper the boat, not select the crew. Admittedly, I made a mistake this time. I'll be more discerning in future. As I say, I do not own the boat, and I do not have complete control over decisions made ashore."

"Indeed. And are you aware of the type of activities in which Mr Gibson was involved?"

"He was a drinker, a womaniser."

Hodgkinson leaned back, clasping his hands together, placed them gently on the table, and then said, "Oh, I can assure you that he has been involved in a little more than womanising and alcohol. The Inspectora Jefa has uncovered some astonishing details in the short period of time since Mr Gibson's death."

"She has?"

Hodgkinson continued, seemed unimpressed by Hale's 'surprise', "He had connections with a South American drug-trafficking cartel, and was a regular participant in narcotics-related activity in and around the Cádiz area, also Morocco, and Tangier. Connected also, it is believed, with British racketeers in the Marbella area, one character in particular with a history of violence, extortion, and people trafficking."

Hale frowned, thought of Jack. It seemed that the Scot had linked him with some kind of monster.

"It's also interesting, and ironic perhaps," continued Hodgkinson, "that Mr Gibson was being pursued by other criminal groups. It appears he had a dangerous habit of double crossing his associates, and as a result, had a price on his head."

"I'm not sure where this is leading. You're not making the assertion…"

"I'm making no assertions at all. Merely collating information on this case and providing assistance to the Inspectora Jefa." Hodgkinson left an awkward silence, continued to eye Hale.

"I have nothing to do with the death of Mr Gibson," said Hale. "He was drunk. He fell from a boat, a motorboat that he wandered aboard in his stupor. Dean found him, and then alerted me."

"Ah yes, Dean. Mr Dean Oliver," said Hodgkinson, pulling an A4 sheet from his folder. "Another of your *friends*?"

"Crew member. Another referral of Jack's."

"You do seem to associate yourself with some colourful characters, sir."

Hale noted Hodgkinson's increasing cynicism, but also few direct accusations levied at Hale. It seemed more of a probing interrogation, an attempt to encourage Hale to reveal more, or implicate himself.

"I think you'll find crews, especially the older crowd of men who go to sea, have many vices," said Hale. "Drink, drugs, that kind of thing. I skipper the boat, try to stay clear of all that."

"Very well." Hodgkinson tidied his folder, looked thoughtful for a moment, and then said, "I think we're talking about a little more than the *vices* of a few old sea dogs, here, wouldn't you say?"

"I appreciate your point," said Hale, hoping the worst of the interrogation was over.

Hodgkinson stood, urging Hale to do the same. They left the room, returned to building's entrance. Hale signed out at reception.

"Thank you for your time," said Hodgkinson. "If we have any further questions, we shall be in contact."

"No problem. Can I ask, is your investigation ongoing? … Am I likely to be required again?"

"A possibility," said Hodgkinson, handing Hale a card. "Here's my number, but please be aware that this is the Inspectora Jefa's investigation and I am merely reporting to her. I think we can be certain that she will leave no stone unturned."

Hale swallowed, uncomfortable, looked at Hodgkinson, "I understand."

They shook hands. Hale departed, walking down a flight of steps leading towards the glass entrance doors.

Hodgkinson remained standing above at reception, called after him:

"Do take care now, won't you, sir."

TWENTY-FOUR

Hale disembarked at Southend Central railway station, Friday evening, 7:30 p.m. A light drizzle hung in the air, still warm from the early September day. With half an hour before the meeting, Hale dialled Marta on his cell phone. He leaned against a lamppost, peering into a wine bar opposite crowded with drinkers. Men in t-shirts, cackling women in tight dresses. Two impassive bouncers stuffed into cheap black suits manned the doors, urging sheepish youngsters to show their IDs before stepping aside to allow entry into the den of overpriced drinks and sticky carpets.

"Tell me about Berto," said Hale, when she answered.

A long pause, a pause Hale enforced until she responded. After some seconds, she did. "How do you know of him?" she asked.

"I received a call from the idiot who robbed me when I left you. You remember I mentioned the man in the dark when we were entering your apartment? I think that was him with the ponytail. He talked about this man, Berto. What a big shot he is, and then said how I'm going to be paying money to keep things quiet ... regarding *us*."

"No, no," said Marta, now sounding alarmed. "That cannot be. I am scared, we are in danger, and you more than me."

"Why?"

"Because ... because these people are known around here to get *anything* they want."

"Okay, so they're mafia. What about going to the Policía if you're concerned for your safety?"

"Not my safety, *yours*. And anyway, Berto Morillo is friendly with the mayor, and the Policía and ... the mayor was even in prison for a money scandal, but they let him out. The judge is also with Morillo, understand?" She sounded upset, hysterical. "You have no idea about what these people can do."

"So what are you going to do?" said Hale.

"I have to leave here soon, without Berto knowing, otherwise he will kill me. I mean it. I have no money. He does not allow me to work at the bar, wants me to do something else for him, carrying stuff for someone. I will not do it."

"Stuff, you mean...?"

"Yes, hashish, coke, this kind of thing."

"Okay, stay calm for a minute, let me think..." Hale walked off towards *The Cocklepickers Arms*, dark and austere-looking, out of place on the corner of a street lined with mock Tudor semi-detached houses. "I'm meeting some friends tonight," he continued. "They can maybe get you out, get some money for you."

"What about you? If you come out here, you must be careful to not be seen."

Not easy amid the prying eyes of Puerto de Santa María's gossip mill, thought Hale.

She sounded desperate, more desperate even than Hale. He sighed, looked around, crossed a road, stood at the entrance to the pub. "I might come out," he said, "but I'm not sure. People are watching me. It's risky."

"Help me. Berto watches me every day and night. I have to leave here, soon."

"Okay, I understand," said Hale. "I have to go now. I'll help you, and call you soon."

Hale closed the call, pushed through the scratched wooden door of *The Cocklepickers Arms*, entered the dim light of the ground floor bar. The room cultivated a smog transcending the smoking ban. Bodies, sweat, shouting, a thick stench of ale, cider, and noise permeated every corner of the place. Hale eased past a throng of bikers, students, stoned hippies, and 'musos' who frequented Southend's notorious music venue. Everyone seemed friendly enough, a good atmosphere. Proof that appearance can be deceptive. The wooden floorboards felt easy underfoot as he headed towards the far end of the bar. An acoustic duo banged out some 'indie' number. A song known to a group of fresh-faced students nodding their heads to the rhythm. Hale wondered if he was too old for this shit, but moved past an aging rocker proving otherwise: long grey ponytail, bald scalp, wrinkled forehead.

Warm ale in hand, Hale scanned the room for Jack and Dean, pondered the situation with Marta. He should drop it, let her deal with it. Hodgkinson and Díez would surely put tabs on him if he returned to Andalucía. But he didn't like loose ends, and his life was full of them. Methodically, if he could clear the Happy Gary issue first – and use the cash to take the edge off his personal debts – he'd be in a better position. He believed Jack when he said Happy was not to be messed with, but Berto Morillo was a greater unknown quantity. Another unwanted prospect he could do without. Best to help Marta as much as possible, silence the ponytail hombre with a payoff or something, and then get the hell out of there as quietly as possible. The only way. This time, tough discipline aboard *Blue Too* with idiots, Jack and Dean.

One more trip.

Get the job done. Get the money. Get out.

Hale felt the slap of a meaty hand on his shoulder, made him splash beer onto the floorboards.

"You surely have an eye for a cracking watering hole, laddie."

Hale turned, looked up to see Jack, his red face still sunburned, and gut contained by a flimsy black t-shirt.

"Hello, Jack. Dean here?" asked Hale.

As if prompted, Dean pushed through the melee, sporting a fresh tattoo of a cobra on his neck.

"What d'you think o' me tat?" he said, smiling with his trademark rotten tooth.

"Fetching," said Hale.

Jack rolled his eyes, "He's a bloody lunatic letting someone at his neck like that. *And* to draw blood."

Hale looked around the bar. It was getting louder. "We need to talk," he said.

"Aye we do," said Jack, cradling a glass of whiskey. "We like ya' bar, Charlie, but any room around here where we can stretch out, talk business?"

Hale nodded to a stairwell next to the Gents' toilets. Dean led the way, holding his pint of beer high in the air to avoid being barged by a throng of swaying students.

"Flamin' hell, and I thought you was a bit of a square one," said Dean, clomping up the wooden stairs, making way for a Goth-punk with jet black hair on the descent.

"I like music," said Hale.

Dean laughed, "That what you call it, eh?"

They moved towards the gig room. White noise accompanied by a low bass drone emanated like a wave from the blackness within.

"Strewth," said Jack, moving into the room, knocking back a shot. "You Southerners are into some weird shit all right."

Inside, a punk band comprising two cross-dressers and a stoned drummer played to a thrash-metal backing track. Hale moved to a shelf and some bar stools, took a seat. The sound guy, an impressive fat blob with long hair and beard, stood before a mixing desk, controlling the wall of sound with some skill. Conversation was just possible with moderate shouting.

"I know you're here to persuade me to go back out there," said Hale, eyeing Jack.

Dean smirked, gazed across at the dance floor where two punks of ambiguous sexuality danced, jumping around, barging into each other.

Jack said, "There's no persuading to be done, Charlie. Happy had an investment in that last trip ... until Gibby screwed up. Now, it wasn't your fault and all, but the way Happy sees it, he gave the boat to you and us. And Gibby ends up sent back to Marbella in a goddamn body bag."

"Gibby was on a path to self-destruction," said Hale, turning to Dean, prodding him in the chest, "and if you two go back out there like the Laurel and Hardy act again, you're going to be joining Gibby. If the Guardia don't curtail your shit, some other local individual or faction will take a dislike to your antics." Hale took a draft of beer, looked at Jack, "And then you'll find yourself dead. Dumped out in the desert, where the vultures will pick away at your eye sockets. Understand where I'm going, boys?"

Dean rolled his eyes, about to interject. Jack cut him off, "Look, we understand you're under pressure, Charlie, at home and whatnot. And, you got a beating or something up there in San Isidro ... to do with that girl…"

Hale interrupted, "Nothing to do with it, Jack."

"Well, okay, let me tell you something about Happy. He's a bloody grafter who don't care much about me, you, the Spanish, or anyone else."

"A real charmer."

"Well, he's a *family* man if you know what I mean. Has friends and family around him he can trust."

"I believe the term is mobster," said Hale.

"Whatever the term is," said Jack, becoming heated, "he won't be let down, and he *never* loses money. So, we go back out there, do the job, get the money, and Happy will be good to his word. But, turn our back on him and we're in real trouble, laddie."

"I don't see that he's lost so much money from our last trip, considering he's supposed to be some kind of big shot Marbella playboy."

Jack shook his head, "He's into big business, fingers in a lot of pies. A powerful boy in those parts doing boats – inflatable powerboats imported from Britain – and he trades cars, purebred horses, all of that kind of shite. But, you see, problem is that Gibby was one of his key boys. Had new business coming in for Happy from as far away as Colombia. You understand what I'm saying, Charlie?"

"Yeah, I do. Happy's the kind of dangerous nutcase that I could do without associating myself with, unless I want to go to jail."

Jack pursed his lips, anger ripped across his face.

Hale cut him off before the inevitable outburst, "Okay, you know I need the money. I'm prepared to skipper *Blue Too* one last time. I have other stuff to clear up out there." Hale looked across to the stage. The lead singer shouted into the microphone, removed his clothing in some kind of climax to the act.

Jack followed his gaze, frowning. "Good to hear it, boy," he said, "and tell me, why did you pick a shithole like this to meet at? We'd be proud of a dive like this in sunny Glasgow."

Hale stood up, straightening his back. "You said find a place we could have a drink … where no one would hear or recognise us."

"Aye, well, you got that one right, Charlie-boy."

They spent thirty minutes running through the plans to return to Andalucía.

Jack and Dean would drive down in a Transit van, through France and Spain to Marbella. This, purportedly to deliver a consignment of boat spares for Happy Gary. Hale would fly directly to Almería, meet them at the marina.

They clomped down the stairs to the lower bar. "So, I guess you're staying here for a bit, and then on to a guest house?" said Hale, making to leave.

"That's the one," said Dean, "and we found ourselves some women of ill repute down there near the end of that amusements strip."

"How wonderful for you."

Jack gave a haughty laugh, nudged Dean.

"Just one other thing," said Hale, eyeing Jack, unsmiling. "You remember my price for the passage?"

"Thirty grand."

"That's right. Well, tell Happy bloody Gary and his band of morons that a lot of crap is going down in my life. The trip is dangerous and I don't like working with nutters like you, or..." Hale remained looking at Jack, pointed to Dean, "...him. Therefore, the price has gone up to fifty."

Hale, turned, headed out through the door, into the dank night.

TWENTY-FIVE

Gatwick North, 4:02 a.m.

Hale drew the curtains, peered out of the window of his hotel. Drizzle streaked across the pane, blurring yellow streetlights against the black outside. The rumble of airport buses signalled the start of another of Gatwick's frenetic days.

After meeting Jack and Dean, he'd made the decision: flee to Gatwick, book a cheap hotel and early morning 'red eye' flight to Almería. Lucy was distraught, calling, texting. Cruel it may have been for Hale to leave unannounced, especially for Deborah, but he deemed this was the only way forward. And, there was another concern, a hunch. Something didn't ring true about their relationship, which was now at its lowest ebb. He'd been an idiot, run into debt, and now Marta had rekindled something missing in his life. But these personal issues were just ripples amid the turbulence.

Hale gazed below to the car park, mulling the situation, his life. Some tourists, looked American, gabbled, barking at an overworked coach driver lugging massive cases across the tarmac on their behalf. Lucy didn't do enough. Ralph the buffoon was a menace, her botoxed friends, a pain. Lucy rarely backed Hale when the chips were down. Perhaps she was unaware as to how *down* the chips actually were. He should have come clean earlier about his predicament.

Too late now.

He threw some remaining clothes into his sailing bag, made his way through the hotel, down the stairs, through reception, out into the rain. His family was an issue, one he could perhaps reconcile over time, but there was another: Martin Stack.

Another unannounced departure from *Connecting4Business*, this time for some weeks, would incur some considerable rage from the king of office stiffs. Before Hale broached that conundrum, however, a hurdle awaiting him at the terminal: Security and Passport Control. This was a routine he'd performed countless times, but now it was different. He might be on a watch list, might be apprehended. He consoled himself with a thought: neither Hodgkinson nor María Díez had refused him permission to travel, and he'd received no official instruction to that effect.

Hale crossed the road towards the terminal, the rain on his face refreshing after the air-conditioned stuffiness of the hotel. Sleepy travellers emerged from taxis and vans at the foot of the elevators. Hale moved past them, sailing bag hauled over his shoulder, laptop case in hand. The noise and bustle built. He neared the shuttle to the South Terminal. Men, women, teenagers dragged hefty wheelie cases, stumbling around in inadequate footwear. Some 'wheelies' toppled over, scraped along the concrete, causing chaos and frayed nerves at the early hour.

No queue at Check-In. Hale presented his bag and passport to the attendant, a middle-aged woman, sprightly for this hour. She tapped away at the keyboard, went through the motions. Hale thought of Jack and Dean. Rather than doing this, they'd be somewhere in France by now, sleeping in the van or a brothel on the outskirts of Paris. Both scenarios unappealing. The 'consignment', however, had piqued Hale's curiosity. Nothing was ever simple or innocent with those vagabonds, not least the supposed task of 'delivering boat spares'. An ulterior motive was likely, another deal or underworld connection made en route.

Check-In, no problem. The attendant returned Hale's boarding card and passport.

He moved on, approached Passport Control. Another unpalatable thought occurred to him: perhaps Jack and Dean took surface travel, since they knew airport security would be tighter. Hale would be detained while they made their jaunt unhindered south to the Costas. Maybe they didn't want him to skipper the boat at all, the pressure and meeting at Southend all part of some ruse to oust him. Maybe Happy Gary had ways and means to frame Hale, to tip off the UK Border Force.

Maybe.

He clutched his passport and boarding pass with clammy fingers, tried to calm his nerves, annoyed to have allowed paranoia to muddy his thoughts this early. A party of older travellers, smartly dressed on some trip to Italy, formed a queue before him. Hale fidgeted with his documents, fussed with his laptop case stuffed with cell phones, chargers, credit cards, cables, and just enough room for the laptop itself.

A couple faffed at the desk ahead of him, their passport due to expire within six months. Hale cursed to himself. An attendant waved Hale on, two desks further down. Not ideal. The male official seated at the desk, forties, stern-looking, eyed each step of Hale's nervous approach.

"Morning," said Hale.

"Everything okay, sir?"

"Fine." *Why is he asking?* "Late to bed, up early, you know how it is…"

"In this job, I certainly do, sir."

Stern-Looking swiped the passport, peered at a monitor. Hale leaned across to see, but Stern-Looking instructed him otherwise. "Looking at the camera, please, sir," he said, pointing to a camera on a post ahead. Hale eyed the lens, tried not to blink.

"Where is your hometown, please?"

"Leigh-on-Sea."

"Ah, Essex, nice place."

"It is, yes. Very nice." Hale shifted his glance from the camera to Stern-Looking, who seemed content enough, closed the passport. Hale felt blood rush to his face, anticipating the next bit. *When receiving the passport, maintain eye contact, look down, sideways? And, if maintaining eye contact, smile or impassive?*

Hale elected to lock in, met Stern-Looking's steely eyes.

"Thank you, sir. Have a good trip."

Hale moved on to the security check, relieved, but retaining some concern. Stern-Looking's gaze, a macho thing or a knowing smile? Was he aware of something that lay in store later this morning in Gatwick, or to greet him at Almería?

He queued with the rest of the sheep at security. He thought, *this sheep has GUILTY emblazoned in yellow on the back of his shirt.* He placed the laptop on the conveyor for the X-Ray, was signalled through the body scanner by a female security officer. A beep sounded. He raised his arms obediently and was frisked. Annoyed at his own fear on display, he took the walk again.

No beep.

Hale retrieved his laptop, repacked it, secured his belt, all taking seconds that seemed like minutes. He looked around and recited: don't rush, don't look nervous, you're not carrying drugs, and if they wanted to detain you, they would have done so by now.

He headed through the brash lights of Duty Free, an endless strip of clinical retail therapy for the bored or cash-rich. Then up some escalators to a café serving a meagre group of travellers seeking a caffeine fix.

With a WiFi zone on offer and strong Americano, he opened his laptop and typed an email to Stack:

Dear Martin,

By the time you read this, you'll be aware that I haven't arrived at work and you'll have left a stern message on my voicemail. You'll be aware also, that the volume of work continues to be seemingly overwhelming in my department, but that I have left some semblance of control in the capable hands of Julian, one or two other diligent interns, and of course, Pam.

Despite this, you will be correct in asserting that this does not relieve me of my responsibilities, or justify the absence of proper notice for this leave I am taking from work. I estimate the duration will be between one and two weeks, possibly more. Having read the previous sentence, you will now be in a rage and tempted to try my cell phone once again to hurl abuse and criticism at me. I respectfully advise you to pause, and read the next paragraph before doing so.

You may recall that I have backdated leave owed to me from the last two years, amounting to seventeen days. Of course, this still does not forgive the lack of notice, but do bear with me. As you know, I have visibility of the accounting software for Connecting4Business – another task you landed me with two years ago – and help Accounts to run it through HMRC for the annual returns. Not my business to pry of course, but we did have some problems balancing the figures to make the numbers go through the system. I think you'll be aware that these glitches were due to 'anomalies' on the expenses side. Your instruction to Robin in Accounts to 'fudge it through', was dutifully obeyed by him, thus, the (adjusted) figures handed on to me were processed without a hitch.

Without doubt, the nature of those claimed expenses (relating to dining, travel, hotels, 'team-bonding' weekends, and of course 'gentlemen's entertainment') would have made uncomfortable reading during last year's audit, had the receipts not enjoyed some 'creative adjustment' by your discreet and highly efficient Accounts boys – one of whom, I understand, was photographed at Spearmint Rhino in a compromising position with a partially-dressed 'professional dancer', prior to being ejected from the club for groping and lewd behaviour. The name of the Facebook page holding the photo escapes me, but with some research on Google…

Martin, I do apologise for this rather unconventional request for no-notice leave, but you do understand that life sometimes throws up complications and last-minute demands that cannot easily be resolved. Do feel free to delete this email at your discretion; I will then of course make no further mention of the matter, and will inform you as soon as possible regarding my return date.

Yours,
Charles

Hale took a sip of coffee, read the draft through once. He clicked 'send', closed the laptop, and headed for Gate 116.

TWENTY-SIX

At Almería Airport, the uniformed official seated in the Passport Control booth looked as if he had better things to do with his life. He took a cursory glance at Hale's passport, waved him through with a flick of his hand.

Hale moved across shiny linoleum floors to the luggage carousel. A few golfers outfitted in beige slacks and Fred Perrys wrestled elongated bags onto trolleys, and then sauntered out into the airy Arrivals area. For Hale, it was the same scene at the pleasant small-scale Spanish airport. Golfers and tourists met shrieking friends, and then drove off to villas and apartments. Other Brits queued at car hire booths, while Hale, backpackers, and local Spanish headed for the bus stop and a two-euro ride into the city.

Hale donned his sunglasses, took in the morning sun, the air dry and fragrant, much removed from Gatwick's industrial morning gloom. Soon, the heat would sear to intensity. Cumulonimbus towered above, shrouding the verdant upper reaches of the Alpujarras, a chance of cooler shade in the city if it clouded over.

He boarded the bus, more a coach, modern, smart. The driver listened to an animated old boy with a stick who seemed to have a free ride, gabbling, gazing through the window at the approaches to the city as he stood hanging on to a steel upright.

Outside, distinctive light, milky pink, bathed everything beneath its veil: whitewashed fincas, gravel tracks, scrubland, quaint terracotta churches, industrial buildings.

The bus entered the city, gathering a few passengers en route. On board, students prodded their smartphones. Squat women, black hair and jagged teeth, lugged plastic shopping bags. Old men waved folded newspapers, expressive, saying a thing or two aloud about the day's news.

With the central station now ten minutes away, a cacophony of noise built from a radio blaring Latin pop and passengers' conversations.

A week before, Hale vowed never to make another call to Marta. Still time to honour the notion.

He dialled her number on his cell, made the call.

"It's me. I'm in Almería," he said.

Fifteen minutes later, the city delivered something rare. Rain. Crossing the main road, Carretera de Ronda, leading away from the docks, a boom of thunder galvanised Hale to increase his pace, avoid the imminent torrent. The heavens blackened, pedestrians darted around in the charged atmosphere, brandishing umbrellas as if prepared for battle.

Yet, Hale's quickening pace was little to do with a spot of impending rain. Marta was already travelling by taxi, expensive but necessary. She was on her way to Almería and the pension Hale now sought in a shopping area of panaderías, clothes shops, and boutiques on the Avenida de la Estación.

The deluge arrived, hammered the streets. Noise enveloped the scene. Shouting, heated exchanges on car horns. Drivers strained to see the road or pedestrians making for cover through the jam. Hale moved quickly, bag slung over his shoulder. He paused occasionally under canopied shopfronts and cafés before breaking out into the monsoon for the next cover.

The Pensión Américano loomed out of the spray unadvertised, just a glass door and small blue plaque with two stars. Hale burst through into a rustic reception area of dark wood and a smell of incense. Two women, forties, smartly dressed sat chatting, looked on startled at Hale's abrupt arrival from the deluge. He closed the door, shut out the madness of the street. Inside, tranquillity, quiet. The women smiled, bustled about, happy with some new business from the lone male traveller.

In halting Spanish, he mentioned the other guest arriving soon. *Una habitación para dos*. The receptionist escorted Hale up some stairs, through a maze of darkened corridors, wooden floors clattering underfoot. The room, basic and clean, overlooked the rain-soaked street. Two beds, firm-to-hard, had seen better days, as had the battered television and tiny bathroom. The walls displayed hasty repairs covered with fading emulsion daubed onto wallpaper beneath. The kind of place Hale liked. Rustic, discreet. A repellent to the pretentious or nosey.

He lay on the bed nearest the door, his bag unpacked on the other. He stared above into the dim yellow light of the eco-bulb decorated with an ill-fitting shade. Rain hammered the window until the humidity and gloom seduced him into half-sleep.

The purpose of Marta's one-night visit to the city was for them to meet away from San Isidro's mafia and Puerto de Santa María's rumour mill. They must talk immediately, make plans for their safety.

The room phone rang, the dated ringtone jolting Hale from his daze.

Soon, Marta was at the door, dripping, beautiful with it. She stepped inside, the door locked behind her. Nothing said. Her wet dress slid down her waist to the floor. Moments later, her body splayed out on white sheets beneath him. He ran his hands over her satin skin. The rain turned to hail, beat a rhythm as the storm heightened.

An hour later.

The downpour had ceased. In silence, Marta looked through the wooden window blinds out onto the balcony. Hale tapped on his laptop trying to connect to the Internet. "Are you okay? You seem quiet," he said.

She turned, stepping back into the room. "I'm not sure of this place," she said. "Have you stayed here before?"

"No, but it's just a pension, no problem. Is it?"

"It is family business, no?" she asked.

"I suppose," said Hale, closing the laptop, packing it away. "Most of them are around here."

Marta paused, thoughtful, and then said, "Let's talk in the centre of the city, away from here."

Minutes later, they walked south along the main Avenida Federico García Lorca, a bustling boulevard of cafés, restaurants, and department stores numerous enough to appease any shopaholic. Crossing the leafy central reservation, the activity heightened to a fever pitch in La Fería de Almería, a ten-day celebration of Andalucían music and culture now under way. Marta cast a smile at young flamenco dancers, toddlers, strutting under the watchful gaze of stroppy older women, gesticulating, cajoling them into order. *Cruz Campo* beer tents shaded older revellers from the sun, the smell of garlic and tapas permeating the air. The road steamed from rain now evaporating on hot concrete.

The couple entered a tapería on a shaded corner away from the action. They sat outside. Frosted beer and olives arrived, easing the tension, since now they must talk. They were lost in the crowd, just another couple having a drink at the fería. But Marta was on edge. She donned large fashionable sunglasses, looked around frequently, glancing at passers-by, mostly men.

"You're scared," said Hale. "Are you looking out for this Morillo guy, and his friends?"

She nodded, took a drink.

"This can't go on," he continued. "This grip they have over you has to end. Explain to me who these people are ... what work you do for them."

She sighed, and then spoke softly, "My family had nothing when we came to San Isidro from Madrid, nothing, we were poor. At this time, I was young, stupid maybe. My father warned me of Berto and people like him, but this man gave me work, makes the connections with bar owners and other businesses. Shops, cafés, this kind of thing, and always I had work and money."

"And the downside?"

"He is connected with *everything* in San Isidro, good and bad. He runs his businesses strong, how do you say?" She clenched her fist.

"With an iron fist."

"Sí. No mercy."

"Mafia."

"Maybe that is a word you like, but he is connected with los Rusos, very bad people, and he gets them to do work for him. You know what I mean by *work*?"

"Coercion is the word that springs to mind." Marta shrugged as Hale continued, "I think what you're saying is that if people do not cooperate, Berto uses violence and intimidation to get things done ... and you're involved with him."

"Yes, that is what I am saying."

Hale broached a difficult subject, one he needed to confront, watched her carefully for a response, "And your relationship with Berto Morillo?"

She huffed, leaned back in her seat, "He is a pig, an animal."

"But you were together once?"

Marta looked at Hale. Even through designer shades, he could see her expression: incredulous.

"You must be crazy to think that," she said.

"But he wants *you*, doesn't he?"

"Yes, and the problem is that he never gives up. He has other women, stupid or scared, who did not fight or run away from him. I'm not ending up like them."

"Is that what you're planning to do now ... run from San Isidro?"

"I have no choice. I have no money, I cannot go to the authorities, and I cannot fight him. I must run soon. I need help and I will pay you back."

Hale leaned forward, placed his hand on hers, "Of course, I will try to help. But I have some problems as well, including this friend of Morillo's, the youth with the ponytail..."

Marta sighed, disdain on her face, "Cabrón. His name is Enzo. He is a shit and no child. He is twenty five."

"He knows who I am, and he wants money," said Hale. "Otherwise my name goes to Morillo. That is what he said to me."

Marta leaned forward on the table, held her head in her hands, "He does this kind of thing. You must run too, and now I am not so sure you should have come back here."

"I have to finish business at the marina, Marta. Then I can help you. Enzo says he will call me, so maybe I can talk to him, get him to be quiet until I figure something out."

Losing patience, she said, "You cannot talk to these people. They do things their way only."

"Okay, I know, but if I just pay to silence him, he will come back again and again. And if Morillo gets to hear about us, and then…"

Marta interrupted, sobbed, "And then you are dead."

TWENTY-SEVEN

They waited until dark and then boarded buses back to San Isidro, an hour's trip west. There would be no further discussion between them on the trip, since Hale took the 23:00, an hour after Marta had departed. They should not be seen together. Hale would return to the marina and rendezvous with Jack and Dean. There, he would discuss the passage into the Alborán Sea and put in a call to the mugger, Enzo. If Hale could silence him, temporarily at least, it would buy enough time for him to complete the sailing trip, and then help Marta flee San Isidro for good. Marta was dubious, scared, but in Hale's eyes this was a plan, and better than no plan at all.

Seated halfway down the bus, he gazed out of the window. Plastico greenhouses flew by in the blackness, partially illuminated by the glow of orange lights spaced intermittently along dark alleys – an endless maze through which workers toiled night and day. A tough life to earn a pittance, a life unknown to golfers, tourists, and other visitors passing through the richest area per capita in Spain. The vast wealth drawn from worldwide exportation of tonnes of fruit and vegetables was responsible for a commensurate level of greed and corruption within local businesses and authorities.

Hale thought about the notorious Berto Morillo. The man, the threat he posed. His wealth was no doubt partially derived from the fruit and vegetable industry, but this most likely a convenient cover for insidious sidelines and protection rackets. Narcotics would play a part. Vice creeping into the world of the rich and powerful who paraded under the guise of 'businessmen'. Morillo's connection with the Russians suggested a sinister ally. Their presence in the drug business along the coast from Marbella to Barcelona and offshore to the Balearics was well documented in the press, as was their mafia-style predilection for violence. Modern-day gangsters with intrinsic ties to the former KGB and communist party. Money was laundered from those organisations into property, taking advantage of lax Spanish regulations, inadequate or non-existent policing, or corruption within local authorities. This, thought Hale, was where Morillo was positioned. A Spaniard, a local big shot 'businessman', lured by the millionaire lifestyles and vices of the mafia: Ferraris, mansions, vodka, prostitutes, and cocaine.

With his new Russian accomplice, Morillo had raised his game and was now feared as much as the underworld factions from the Eastern Bloc.

The lights of San Isidro loomed ahead, Morillo's hometown.

Hale dialled Enzo, on his cell phone. No reply. Twenty minutes later, the Spaniard returned the compliment from the caller ID as Hale disembarked and headed for the taxi rank.

"So, mister Allay. You call me, no?"

"Enzo."

Ponytail paused at the other end. Hale kept the phone to his ear, gripped it by craning his neck to one side while carrying his bag, opening his wallet. Sweat poured down his face in the warm night. He eyed a taxi driver, an old boy with glasses who polished an immaculate white taxi with a leather.

"How you know my name?" asked Ponytail at the other end.

"People talk, maybe Morillo told me."

"Bullshit, Inglés."

Ponytail angry, the first time. Hale told him to hold the line.

The old boy grabbed Hale's bag, threw it into the boot. They took off along a dual carriageway at speed. Kids on mopeds buzzed the taxi, playing around, darting in and out of traffic.

"Continue," said Hale.

Ponytail continued, "I see him, the jefe, today, and now it is time for us to do business, otherwise my friend, you have a problem."

"I don't do business with people I haven't met, and you're the one with the problem."

"Whoa, I see mister Allay grows some balls, some cajones! Maybe we give you some more *attention* in the street like last time." Ponytail's laugh cracked into a smoker's cough, loud over Hale's earpiece. He recovered enough to say, "So, you wish to meet me again, brave man?"

"That's right, shithead. We meet to talk, and then we can make some progress."

"Okay, have it your way. You come to see me. We talk and agree. Then you pay and we are happy friends."

"No. You come to me, to the port."

"I do not come there, mister."

"The port or no deal, I don't trust any other place. I'll call you tomorrow morning."

"But, this makes a problem for…"

Hale hung up.

The taxi rumbled down the palm-lined road on approach to the marina. Lights decorated the wharfs under the summer night, thick with humidity. Further down, a few people loitered in the bars and restaurants lining the wharfs. A quiet night, not much going on.

Hale dialled Jack, who picked up after two rings, "Yes?" Noise in the background, women, music.

"I'm near the marina," said Hale. "Where are you?"

"Hey, Charlie, you're full of polite introductions as usual, laddie. I'm in a bar."

"No kidding."

"Ha. Look, we're doing some jobs for Happy in Marbella, and then we're coming across the day after next. You get *Blue Too* prepped and we're going sailing."

"Okay, and what about Dean?"

"Here with me now. Likes the dolly birds around here and says you're missing out big time."

"Breaks my heart."

"Look, Charlie," continued Jack, over the din. "I've smoothed things over with Happy about the thing with Gibby and whatnot. I think we're in the clear if we run the job and get the shit to him."

"Correction. When *you* get the shit to him, whatever shit that is. I'm just skippering the boat."

Jack's sigh was audible at the other end, "Whatever. But he's not going for fifty grand."

"Then, no deal."

"Well, you see you cannae go playing hardball with Happy like that, Charlie. He's already down on cash, and I'm saying to go back in with thirty. You know what I'm saying?"

"It's a risky trip. Fifty or no deal."

"Thirty five."

Hale paused as the taxi pulled up to the wharf. He gave a twenty to the driver, waved the change away. "Forty or no deal, Jack. Don't even bother driving your sorry arses over here. Forty."

Hale retrieved his bag, walked past *El Timón*. A whiff of cannabis, thumping music and chatter from within. He headed towards the wharf and mooring beyond, while Jack conferred with someone at the other end. Hale suspected it was Happy accompanying the Scot at the bar, or Dean on his cell relaying the deal.

"I'm giving you five seconds, Jack. What have we got?" said Hale, pausing at the bow of *Blue Too*, looking along her lines, checking her condition. In good shape despite recent strong winds, which had battered the marina. The morning would reveal a fine layer of dust on her decks. Sand carried from the Sahara across the Alborán and dumped on the Spanish coastline.

Jack came back on the line. "Deal. See you the day after tomorrow."

"ETA?"

"Midday."

Hale cut the call, longed for a frosted beer in the bar just fifty yards away. Too dangerous. He hauled his bag onboard, opened the hatches, went down below for the alternative: a bottle of warm water from the stores.

Early next morning, Hale walked to a café a half mile west, opposite a surfers' beach, the *Poniente* beach. This was a local joint. Flies, television on loud, old boys and workers drinking shots of brandy, reading the morning papers. Others ate bocadillos, drank beer, shouted to each other about football or women. Two workers Hale recognised from the marina yard sat at the bar, cross-eyed, stoned on something. The woman behind the bar, attractive, buxom, was civil but in no mood for idiots. Never was in Hale's experience. The males in the bar knew not to cross her. To do so would invite a splash of piping hot espresso in the face and a salvo of abuse only Spanish women can muster. Hale liked the place. It was private and served coffee with the consistency of engine oil, guaranteed to kill hangovers, revive the dead.

He sat at the bar, gazed at the television news. A politician being papped by a scrum of photographers over some scandal or other. Fraud or sleaze, something like that. He took a sip of engine oil, contemplated the Ponytail situation. Soon he must call to negotiate. It was madness. As with the Happy Gary situation, there seemed little choice. When you're in this deep, options dwindle.

Damage limitation formed one of those dwindling options. Come clean, ring Hodgkinson in London and reveal all? But that would involve complete transparency, the unravelling of a web, a convoluted mess that began years ago. Then, a court case, probably a sentence, and rebuilding of his life. In the beginning, it was all down to money. The involvement with Jack, the skippering, the Alborán runs, the hard cash. But now it was more complicated. He should have known that maintaining any credible distance from the devious and crooked was a flawed notion from the outset.

Hindsight's a great thing.

The driver at the bank heist remains professional, just drives, nothing more. But the clock ticks, mistakes happen, and *involvement* becomes unavoidable. Things get messy. They always do with money, especially dirty money. Similarly, Hale's notion of acting as the skipper alone had lost its way long ago.

And this was a new low point. Negotiating with Ponytail, the shithead who mugged him. Pay to leave the girl alone and back off. Once he'd done that, both Hale and Marta could flee the town. Get clear of Morillo and Happy Gary and the whole goddamn episode. Bid farewell to *Blue Too* forever, faithful servant though she was.

Nice plan, but two factors remained. First, if he meets Ponytail, where do they meet, and what boneheads might accompany him to 'influence' the negotiation? Second, what was his price? If Hale did the Alborán run, he could earn forty grand. Sterling. Happy always worked in sterling, a London thing from the boy wonder of the East End. Offer Ponytail three thousand euros to keep quiet, he'd come back with five, Hale would push him back down to four.

Hale, though, was not deluded. That would be just a temporary fix.

Powderhead that he was, Ponytail would come back angrier, come back for more cash after he'd spent his protection money on coke and weed. It would buy Hale some time, nothing more. But with that time, he could work out a strategy, help Marta, placate Happy, fend of the debts, work with Baz's contacts in the city to shift some money around with his cash and assets. There would be a way to cut the losses by selling the property in Leigh. Lucy and Deborah wouldn't like it, but that was another problem.

One problem at a time, thought Hale. He downed the last dregs and left a couple of euros on the bar.

Problem one: meet Ponytail.

TWENTY-EIGHT

10:01 a.m.

Hale walked back from the beach along the wharfs of the sun-baked marina, even with sunglasses, reflections blinding from a multitude of brilliant-white hulls and decks. He swiped his pass, entered the stainless steel security gate back onto Darsena 8 (Wharf 8) where *Blue Too* awaited. He eyed a woman hauled high up a mast, working the halyards, shouting to her husband below on the winch. Hale moved on, exchanged a nod with a German guy stretching out on deck. Knew him vaguely, a pothead rarely seen in daylight. Nice enough, but stoned mostly. The German's boat, a rusting thirty-foot sloop, needed work. The fenders, blackened with oil and dirt, hung off the side by frayed ropes in need of replacement.

Then something occurred to Hale. He stopped in his tracks, turned, cast a glance to a small doorway just to the left of *El Timón*.

The tackle shop.

Alfonso, a pensioner in his late seventies, ran the place. Short, bespectacled, always wearing a faded blue shirt, grey trousers and highly polished shoes, he was an ex-fisherman. His shop was old school, full of ramshackle bits and pieces strewn across the floor and high up on various shelves. It was chaos, in need of a woman's sense of order and common sense to sort it out. But women didn't go into Alfonso's place, only men. Fishermen looking for bait and lines, or his social group of old codgers who'd sit around on plastic chairs loudly debating football, money, politics. Their favourite subjects, in order of importance. Hale never gleaned much from their gesticulating or passionate exchanges, since they were delivered in a dialect of Spanish unintelligible to any human not born and bred within a few hundred yards of the place.

Alfonso was one of the first people to live in Puerto de Santa María when the impoverished fishing village comprised just a couple of shacks, one bar, and a mule or two hanging around. That was all before the cranes arrived to build apartments, a few hotels, and the marina development. Changed the character of the place for the worse, according to Alfonso. Another topic for the boys to sit around and rant about.

Hale had a soft spot for the shop. Reminded him of the old shacks on the East Coast of Essex, places where you'd have to climb over heaps of rope, faded lifejackets, and second-hand paraphernalia before you reached the counter to pay. And besides, Alfonso was a sweet old man. He'd root around for an hour to find some obscure bolt or fitting, and then charge Hale eighty cents, or waive the fee completely.

Hale walked back out through the security gate, approached the door with its faded sign above: *Alfonso's*. He hadn't visited for some months. The last time was to buy gas for the cooker, a couple of cleats, and a few bits of rope. Twenty euros, something like that. He didn't spend much, or on any regular basis. But in times of recession, every bit counts, especially in Spain, where the economy drew worrying parallels to that of Greece. A few years back, Hale put in a big purchase at *Alfonso's*: heaps of rope, stainless steel fittings, a few electronic gadgets, and cables. He could have gone to the other chandlery, maybe even got a better deal, but it was run by a weirdo South African guy with his stone-faced Belgian wife. Maybe they were well matched. The South African had a pockmarked face and crooked smile that seemed to match his arrogance. Their brattish child ran around the store screaming, annoying the customers. But none of this was a problem for Hale, since after the first visit, he was no longer their customer.

To Hale, *Alfonso's* was preferred, and this had been noted locally. Word got around in a small marina town, especially when you spend a few thousand euros on boat spares.

Hale pushed the door open, nodded to a kindly-faced elderly man with a stick and hearing aid who sat on a plastic chair, not doing much, and happy with that deal.

"Hola," said Hale.

"Buenos días."

Alfonso was at the counter, banging away on the till with a pointed finger, referring to a notepad in his other hand. He cursed under his breath. The damn till never worked properly. Hale weaved through some shackles and packs of yellow plastic hoses on the floor, approached the counter. Aware of a customer approaching, Alfonso glanced up above his glasses, focussing momentarily. On recognising Hale, Alfonso's face switched from mildly irritated to beaming. He tossed the notepad aside, moved around the counter as quickly as his short legs would take him, grabbed Hale's hand, shaking violently.

"Mi Amigo de *Blue Too*. Señor Allay."

Like Ponytail, Alfonso had neither the time nor inclination to grasp the pronunciation of 'H' in Hale, thus *Allay* it would remain.

It wasn't just Hale's allegiance to Alfonso's ramshackle chandlery that caused such warm and openly emotional greetings. A few years ago, *El incidente con los idiotas* (*The incident with the idiots*) raised Hale's status to legendary level, at least within the annals of Puerto de Santa María folklore.

He had returned from a boat delivery in a forty-knot *Poniente* wind. Setting out from Tarifa in the west, the forecast was good: force three westerly, calm seas. Forecasts, however, are merely approximations, estimates, and this estimate was way out. The wind whipped up to force five, and then switched to an easterly, *Levante*, force six and strengthening with seas building into choppy standing waves. Nerve-shredding seas characteristic of the Mediterranean. Now the wind was on the nose, against them. With one deckhand to help aboard the thirty eight-foot yacht, Hale's hands were full, especially with a torn mainsail and broken toilet. To address the latter dilemma, Hale employed a versatile piece of emergency equipment. The bucket. Both Hale and the deckhand made use of it to deal with copious volumes of urine, vomit, and faeces.

After a two-day battering, heeled at forty-five degrees, Puerto de Santa María's white tower loomed into view amidst a haze of dust from the land and sea spray from rollers crashing against the breakwater. Hale's mood was edgy, ragged. Once the yacht was secured on Darsena 8 with the aid of two gesticulating marineros, he grabbed a sail bag containing the shredded mainsail and leapt ashore. He stormed down the wharf in no good mood, wind still buffeting around his head. Salt encrusted across his face, the heat of the day built, niggled at him.

He was heading for the sail repairer a few hundred yards away. Once he'd dumped the sails, he could catch a shower. Then make for the bar and an ice-cold *Estrella* served in a frosted glass. What you do this sailing shit for. That was the plan. But plans don't always work out, and this one changed when Hale glanced into *Alfonso's* as he rushed by.

He stopped dead in his tracks, did a double take. Two men, both shirtless, sunburned with tattoos were crowding Alfonso, getting in his face. One of the thugs, a fat slob with jeans partially exposing his arse crack, prodded the sweet old man in the chest. Alfonso was clearly distressed. The other, a pallid skinhead with a nose ring, laughed, threw packets of screws and fishing products around the room, and at Alfonso. A real jerkoff.

The aged shopkeeper was disadvantaged by the modest frontage to his shop. Just a single door signified its existence. The upper section of the door was glass, so at least Hale was able to peer in when passing. Other passers-by were oblivious to the commotion inside.

Hale recognised the thugs. Peabrains who hung around an Irish bar getting drunk, looking bad, giving Britain and Ireland a bad name. He felt his heart pump and fury build.

The red mist came down.

Hale stormed through the door. The fat guy turned, met Hale's stare, dumbstruck. Alfonso frowned, adjusted his glasses, squinted. The other dimwit stood motionless, gawping, still clasping packets of plastic fittings in both hands ready to hurl.

Hale moved towards Fat Guy, grabbed the nearest thing to hand, a fender, gleaming white. No conventional weapon, he held it by the rope at the top end. A metal bar, a club, an oar would have made a more standard implement, but Hale, not ordinarily predisposed to violence, was not thinking in terms of ideal weaponry.

Twisting the rope around his fist, he swung it full force in a wide arc at Fat Guy who squealed loudly like a pig as the fender slapped against the red skin of his chest. Fat Guy made for the door, bolting away from Alfonso. Hale swung again, catching the freckled cooked meat that comprised his upper back. The ball of blubber smashed into a rack of pennants and steel fittings, fell to the floor with Alfonso's products crashing around him. In Hale's periphery, the accomplice made a move, also bolting for the door. Hale put his foot out. Dimwit tripped, flew forward, crashing into his friend. They both rolled around on the floor, a lovers' clinch. Except this was no gay couple. Gay guys were not this dumb, and certainly not this ugly. His rage unquelled, Hale reigned down a further series of blows, the fender making its target on Fat Guy and Dimwit, both of whom scrambled across the floor, and then struggled to their feet. Dimwit wailed, tried to remove fishing hooks stuck in his arm. Fat Guy made the door, fell out into the road, pulling his jeans up to hide his ugly backside. Dimwit soon followed, blood streaming down his arm.

Following *El incidente con los idiotas*, Hale gained local notoriety, though he sometimes wondered about the nature of the reputation he'd acquired. The Englishman who beat the shit out of a couple of thugs with a boat fender? Regardless, it seemed to elevate Hale's status, such that old men in town raised their walking sticks in greeting, came up to him in cafés specifically to shake his hand, or to exchange small talk about the fishing forecast.

Life went on as normal for Alfonso, and apart from some reorganisation required following the fracas, the chandlery was undamaged. Alfonso, however, seemed indebted to Hale, frequently asked him to visit, have coffee, chat with his friends.

Hale, however, was embarrassed by the incident. Out of character, played it down, wouldn't happen again. It certainly never occurred to him to ask a favour of Alfonso in return.

Until now.

Hale looked around the chandlery, awkward, not knowing how to broach the subject. Alfonso looked up over his glasses, seemed curious. They spoke in Spanish, Alfonso reverting to an odd clipped version so that Hale could follow.

"My friend, mister Allay, I have not seen you for so long. You must come in sit down, with José, have coffee."

"That's kind," said Hale. "You are always so kind."

Alfonso grinned, apparently amused at Hale's English reserve. Politely, he moved the situation on as if to make Hale more at ease, "So, what can I do to help you today, my friend? I can get you a deal on some lines, some steel … you tell me what you want, no? Alfonso helps mister Allay, always."

"Well, it's a difficult problem I have," said Hale, looking down at his feet, and then casting a glance towards the door.

Alfonso paused, shouted something abruptly to José. The old man obediently rose, staggered to the door with his stick, took a seat positioned outside.

Alfonso frowned, hung on Hale's reply.

"You see," continued Hale, "I need to find a place where I can meet with someone."

"Ah, a woman?" Alfonso grinned.

"No, a man. Someone I do not trust."

Alfonso's grin evaporated. "I see."

"I am alone here as you know, and when I meet this man, there may be a problem."

Alfonso murmured something, scratched his head.

Hale continued, "I need to talk business with this man, but if he does not like what I offer…"

"Then he will become angry," said Alfonso, completing the sentence.

"Yes, I think that is possible."

The door rattled open, the bell rang. A youth wearing shorts and flip-flops entered the shop. Alfonso tutted, shooed the kid off to look at the gear in the back, to not interrupt. The youth skulked off, happy to peruse fishing rods and reels.

"And this man," said Alfonso, "he will have friends, no?"

"Yes, that is possible."

"And what kind of place you want to meet?"

"Somewhere quiet, but not too quiet. A bar, a gas station or something, so I can be safe with some people around."

Alfonso's eyes flicked from side-to-side as he mulled the request. "I think I understand this," he said. "And what time?"

"Tomorrow afternoon, 2 p.m.," said Hale. "I'll call him today, tell him where to meet."

Alfonso paused, smiled, looked up to Hale, "Esto no es problema, mister Allay. I know a very good place for you to do this business."

"You do?"

Alfonso scribbled a note on a piece of paper, handed it to Hale: *Bar de Pedro, 2 p.m. mañana.*

TWENTY-NINE

The next day, 13:45 p.m.

The box shape loomed in the distance, a remote place inside the harbour wall, just as Alfonso had described. Hale walked the long dirt road, which ran along the length of the wall. A few blue-and-white fishing vessels and a rusting dredger, ugly and imposing, were moored on the dockside. Dust blew up in his face, getting on the inside of his sunglasses. Choking heat formed a thick haze that hugged the earth ahead. The place was deserted apart from a few terns diving into the water and a tall African with a straw hat tending some nets on a fishing boat.

Hale had made the call when he'd left *Alfonso's*. Ponytail had said he didn't know *Bar de Pedro*, said it was rumoured to be a shithole. Hale said he didn't know it either, but assured him that it was private and quiet, a place where they could talk business.

There must be a way to strike a deal, silence Ponytail, but Hale knew he was dealing with a proper slime. The Spaniard would duck and dive and bullshit and raise the price. Whatever price Hale suggested. A low-life like this would most likely bring company, added problems. People like Ponytail didn't operate alone, always someone else on hand to do the dirty work.

On approach, there appeared to be another issue. The bar Alfonso described, 'this place looking like a box', didn't seem to be a bar, more a shipping container, or at least two welded together. One half yellow, rusted, paint peeling off. The other, dull red with skilfully airbrushed graffiti. On the marina side, two square holes a few feet wide just above shoulder height had been carved out of the container with a grinder. The windows. Buckled, rusted holes of shoddy workmanship. Hale moved closer, rose up on tiptoes, peered inside through one of them. Darkness, virtually black, but some movement within. Hale walked around to the rear, stumbling over rocks, broken bottles and driftwood, moving between a snug two-metre gap separating the ugly box structure from the harbour wall.

At the other end, he spotted a steel door, something he'd missed on his approach. 'Door' stretched the meaning of the word, more a sheet of buckled metal hung by a few makeshift hinges. An offcut piece of wood the size of a shoe was bolted to one side. The door handle. The container real estate was raised on blocks. A wooden box, the type used to pack oranges, provided a step up to the door. Above that, a sign sprayed with white aerosol: *Bar de Pedro*.

Hale stood for a moment, mulled the situation, flies buzzing around his face. Still time to back out. It didn't feel right. Isolated. Maybe Alfonso didn't get the gist of what he was saying, and what the hell kind of place was this anyway?

He stepped up, swung the door open. The inadequately-engineered hinges shrieked, announcing his arrival. Hale stepped in, rubbed his eyes, waiting for them to adjust to the murk. Two white shafts of light streamed across the room from the irregular shapes of the 'window' holes. Against the harbour side, the bar was formed by a buckled sheet of metal propped up by wooden crates. A few stools were lined along it. Hale walked across the chipboard floor, pulled up a stool, sat down.

Flamenco singing wailed on a crackling radio. The type Hale preferred, not koshered for tourists. A smell of acetate permeating the air. At the far end, a woman, thirties, black curly hair, painted her nails. She half-nodded at Hale: *Just a minute*. Hale nodded back, looked behind. A man, sixties, mahogany skin, sat at a table cradling a brandy glass half full, looked drunk.

Hale gazed through the buckled window ahead, squinting to the outside. The bridge of a dredger dominated the scene, rust stains streaking downwards from the doors and fittings upon white marine paint. No one appeared to be aboard. Abandoned, thought Hale, until he caught sight of a worker on deck, hauling a line from the ship's crane.

The barwoman approached, attractive, but hard in the face. Gave him a dead look.

"Si?"

"Una cerveza."

She walked off, Hale eyed her curvaceous figure for a second, being sure to divert his eyes before she turned back. She flicked the cap off a bottle of *Mahou*, placed it in front of him.

"Gracias."

Anchovies and olives followed on a small plate. Hale had no appetite, but took a lengthy swig from the bottle while running through the options.

13:55 p.m.

The options didn't look good, and this plan, doomed. Flee now while the going was good. Pay the woman for the beer, get out of the only exit while he had a chance. Run down the other side of the harbour wall, missing Ponytail if he was making his way along the road.

Too late.

The roar of a vehicle sounded outside, a truck or 4x4 with a clanking diesel engine. Whatever it was skidded to a halt and the first door opened, and then slammed shut. Ponytail, alone? The question was answered when the second door opened, slammed.

Maybe this wasn't such a great idea, thought Hale. Alfonso had led him somewhere isolated, a remote death trap. What was the old man thinking?

The beer did little to quench his thirst. Hale's mouth was dry, hands clammy. This was definitely a shit plan. Alfonso had not understood, and now Hale was vulnerable, some distance from help, and only the barwoman and a drunk for company.

The door swung open, a blast of warm air. Dust billowed, now dancing within a third shaft of white light.

Two men stood in the doorway, silhouetted like the alien scene from *Close Encounters*. Ponytail strolled over, cigarette hanging from his mouth, almost comically. Clint Eastwood, but much shorter. He sat down on the stool opposite Hale, the stream of light hitting his face from the window hole. Daylight didn't do him justice, thought Hale. Looked uglier now than at the mugging.

In terms of dubious associates, Ponytail had pushed the boat out his time. Subtlety not being his strong point, he'd invited a gigantic meathead along to the occasion. Looked Russian, thought Hale, as he glanced up to the formidable sight. A goon from the Eastern Bloc, sweaty bald head and hooped earring wobbling about from his pudgy lug. Give him an eye patch, he'd make a pirate. A faded vest, belly hanging over his belt, and chain around his neck complemented an unwashed *Shrek* image.

The barwoman came over. Another dead look, deader when she saw the new arrivals.

Ponytail grunted something at her, returned his gaze to Hale. Shrek stood beside Hale, trying, and succeeding, to intimidate. The meathead reached over, grabbed some anchovies and stuffed them into his mouth, the tails of the fish slithering between his dewy lips. Then he wiped his oil-soaked hand on Hale's back. A real charmer.

They sat in silence for a moment, knowing the woman must return before business would commence. She did, planted a glass cup with something hot inside. Looked like something you'd pour out of an aging truck's radiator.

"This is my friend," said Ponytail, flicking his eyes to Shrek.

"Delighted."

Ponytail didn't catch the dryness of Hale's reply, sipped the radiator oil, gurned at the taste, and then said, "You have an offer, no?"

"I'm going on a trip," said Hale, taking a slug of beer, trying to keep his hand from shaking. His elbow brushed Shrek's gut to his right. "When I return," continued Hale, "you get one payment, you then leave the girl and me alone. End of deal, no complications."

Ponytail rasped a cough, stubbed his cigarette out in the coffee cup. "Mister Allay, you are funny." He looked up at Shrek, exchanged a smile.

"Am I?" said Hale.

"Yes, you come to this shit bar that I not know. You talk like this to me and my friend. But look, you are in Andalucía, no?" He prodded Hale's chest, hard. Shrek leaned in, his garlic breath mixing with the tang of cheap cigarette smoke. "Listen to the radio, look at the women," continued Ponytail, "feel the heat of the sun. This is not your home. No Londres, no Mancheeester. You alone here."

Ponytail leaned back, smirked. In character, Shrek belched.

"Are we doing business here," said Hale, "or did you come to talk about the weather?"

"You crazy man, loco," said Ponytail, shaking his head slowly. "Come here to make the deal, but now make the fun. My friend can cut your throat in this bar and no one know."

Shrek reached into his pocket, pulled a blade, slid it back down out of sight. Hale felt his stomach turn, looked around at the girl. She avoided his glance, looked ahead, vacant. Ponytail reached over, grabbed Hale's face, squeezing the cheeks by thumb and forefinger, wrenching his head back. "No, no, mister Allay, you look at *me*." Ponytail raised his fingers to his eyes, the whites tinged with yellow. "This *my* country, *my* town. I make the deal. Berto knows nothing, but I must tell him about you if the price is not good, because me and my friend here we have to eat." Ponytail pushed Hale's face away. "So, now we talk money. How much?"

"Three thousand euros," said Hale, working the feeling back into his jaw. "I'm going on a trip, so I'll get it for you in five days. Then we're finished."

Ponytail looked down, clasped his hands, sniggering. "No, no, no."

"Three thousand, that's my best offer."

Ponytail nodded to Shrek. The meathead grabbed Hale by the collar, hauled him across the room, slammed him up against the metal wall. Hale felt blood in his mouth, winded. Shrek held him up high, off his feet, and then released. Hale fell to the floor prone, gasping. He wretched, was hauled to his feet again, his vision blurred. Shrek pulled him back to the seat before Ponytail who chewed on a toothpick.

The drunk across the bar looked up. Shrek shouted something at him in bad Spanish. The drunk looked back down at his drink. Hale cramped over on the stool looking at the floor, taking gasps of the thick stale air. Needed a solution.

Shrek stood over him. Grab the knife from his pocket, thought Hale. Too risky, and maybe I'm dead anyway.

"We continue business?" said Ponytail.

Hale sighed, rose gradually. He reasoned: I'm not dead yet, so they want my money, or they would have killed me by now.

A noise from the other end of the room. Hale looked around, glimpsed a crack of light shining through the wall at end of the bar. In a split second, movement out of a side door, a door Hale hadn't previously noticed. A man, a Spaniard, small, squat, ushered the woman out, took her place, and then stood motionless behind the bar, paying no attention to the commotion at Hale's end.

Ponytail slapped the side of Hale's neck, "Hey, Inglés. Look at me."

This is how it works, thought Hale. Man-to-man, behind closed doors. No one messes with Morillo's business. Not even in *Pedro's*. Ponytail calls the shots and Hale must comply.

Hale straightened his back, composed himself. "Okay, so what is *your* price?"

"Ten thousand," said Ponytail, flicking the toothpick at Hale.

"I don't have that kind of money, no way can I…"

"You asked my price, you have it."

Hale shook his head. Shrek tapped his trouser pocket, the one with the knife.

"Four thousand," said Hale. I can get the money for you in a few days."

Ponytail hissed, looked down at the floor, as if wondering what punishment to dish out next.

Hale sensed movement in the periphery to his left. A clang outside. The door on the bridge of the dredger had swung open. Dark figures were climbing out into the sunlight. Hale maintained his gaze on Ponytail who looked up and said, "This trip, mister Allay. Where you go?"

"Out into the Alborán, near Melilla."

Ponytail raised his eyebrows, smiled at Shrek, who shrugged, grunted.

Ponytail said, "So, you sail on boat, no? You go alone?"

"I have friends, crew."

"Okay, mister Allay, you will go to Melilla to get money. I am interested in this business."

Hale took a split second glance through the window. Then feigned a look to the opposite side of the bar to cover it. The figures, were walking down the deck, onto a gangplank to shore. Four of them. Some in overalls, one in a white t-shirt.

"Someone owes me money over there," said Hale. "I just need to collect it."

"Lies," said Ponytail. He flicked his eyes to Shrek, who planted a close range punch, an uppercut, into Hale's ribcage.

Hale huddled over, held his side, pain working through his torso, and then gasped, "The truth … four thousand."

A screech announced the bar door opening, white light streamed in again. Hale, glanced up, remaining on the stool, hunched in pain.

Three men walked in. The first, a giant in a white t-shirt filthy with oil. The man rubbed his eyes, adjusting to the gloom, scanning the situation. The other two, blue faded overalls, ripped and grimy, pushed in. They eyed Ponytail, who sprang to his feet, and then froze.

These were rough men. Oil ingrained skin, thick set, black hair shorn up the back. Hale had seen men like these in nearby mountain villages. The kind of men who moved barrels around on their shoulders all day, hauled ropes, and worked heavy machinery. Men who, besides cheap pornographic magazines, hadn't seen women in weeks, probably months, and whose faces had become black and maddened by the sun. These men came down from the hills to work on the dredger. To Hale, they looked mean and pissed off.

The big man in the white t-shirt sucked on a spliff the size of a celery stick, had an irritated expression, as if Shrek had slept with his wife. Shrek shifted uneasy, side-to-side, weighing up the threat, looked at Ponytail for a command. But Ponytail remained frozen, jaw gaping.

The big man looked across at the barman. The barman nodded in the direction of Shrek, and then looked away.

A third overall appeared at the entrance to the door. The first two overalls took positions at the bar: one beside Hale, the other beside Ponytail, pushing past him heavily. They ordered beers, but Shrek wouldn't be staying for the party.

The big guy in the white t-shirt moved up, stubbed the spliff out on the meathead's forehead. Then spun him around, bent down and yanked his leg into the air. Shrek's sweaty face nudged Hale's thigh as it fell to the deck. The big guy hauled Shrek across the floor like a golf trolley. Shrek dug his fingernails into the chipboard to no avail. The big man pulled him through the door, Shrek's flabby head slapping the wooden orange box as they dragged him out into the light. The third overall made a grab for Shrek as the door slammed shut, returning the bar to gloom.

Hale looked up at ponytail, who sank back down to the stool. "So, my offer was four thousand," said Hale. "This is a good offer, don't you agree?"

"Morillo will hear of this," said Ponytail.

The overall seated nearby turned, lit a pungent spliff, blew smoke into Ponytail's ear.

"No deal," said Hale. "Four thousand, and Morillo hears nothing about me, or the girl. Nothing."

A splash sounded through the window as if someone had thrown a bag of cement into the harbour.

"Where are they taking him?" asked Ponytail.

"At a guess, swimming," said Hale. "Nice day for it."

Ponytail pursed his lips, and then said, "You think you smart, mister Allay, but you do not know how it works."

Hale glanced outside. A line was being lowered from the crane of the dredger.

"I *do* know how it works, Enzo," said Hale, prodding him in the chest. "You take the deal, I get the money for you, and in two weeks this is over. I am gone, and so is Marta."

Ponytail looked down, mulling the situation. Hale took another look outside. A diesel engine thumped, a generator from the dredger. Shrek swung by a line from one leg. They'd hauled him up by the crane, arms flailing, shouting. The big man operated the cab, the third overall manned a hose from the deck, dousing Shrek with blasts of water.

"Okay, have it your way. Four thousand," said Ponytail. "You get money to me in five days, or Berto will know about this and the girl."

Hale ordered two more drinks for the overalls, left a twenty on the bar, walked out.

The wind was now fierce, blasting dust into his face. He stretched his back, the pain now easing. No broken ribs. He clambered up to a rocky path running beside the harbour wall, and started the mile-long walk winding back to the marina.

A Guardia jeep cruised by, approached the dredger. Hale ignored it, walked on.

THIRTY

Next morning, all was set for the passage. Hale had called Marta, told her things had been taken care of. He'd pay Ponytail off and they'd flee this place together when he returned. Jack and Dean had arrived on time, and relatively sober. *Blue Too* was gleaming, fuelled, sails prepared and tied off. A swift return trip across the Alborán would see Happy Gary's job done, money exchanged, and Ponytail's deadline met.

These ideas seemed rational, but one element wasn't ideal. The weather.

A thirty-knot *Poniente* turned the marina into a shrieking cacophony of swaying masts and rattling halyards. Waves crashed against the breakwater, hurling spray into the marina area. The marineros cruised up and down the wharfs, cocooned in their vans, smoking, gazing at the moorings, on the lookout for frayed warps and yachts edging too close to the concrete. The mood of the town changed. People hunkered in cafés, shops, or apartments, away from the chaos as restaurateurs battled with flying chairs and ripped canopies.

"It's blowing a goddamn hooley," said Jack, holding a rail to prevent himself toppling into a bunk. "The forecast was crap."

"Nothing we can do about it," said Dean. "Just chill out."

"We cannae chill out you idiot. Happy is taking no excuses this time."

Hale remained silent as they sat it out. Even in the mooring, the boat lurched about violently. To set out would be madness.

"What's the plan, Charlie?" said Jack.

"We sit tight for another day," said Hale, looking at a weather website on his laptop. "This is how it is in the summer sometimes. This shit comes out of nowhere."

"Yeah, but it can blow like this for days, weeks even. You know that, laddie."

Hale shook his head, knowing Jack was right, "It's clear we're not going today, so let's regroup tomorrow morning. Then I make the decision. And no drinking, please ... you need to be ready."

Dean let out a groan, "I'm gonna die of boredom."

"We *will* die if we go out in those seas," said Hale. "If you doubt me, take a walk around to the harbour wall by the dredger. Do yourself some good, get some exercise."

Jack shook his head, cursed, and then slumped down into his bunk.

At night, the storm built. By 3:00 a.m., Hale and Jack went out on deck into the gale, which blew under intense moonlight. *Blue Too* snatched at the warps, leapt around, heeling onto the vessel to starboard. The marineros passed by, spotted the problem, bathed the scene in the headlights of their van. They helped set another line to shore, bringing her stern across to port and away from danger.

"We're not going tomorrow," shouted Jack over the screaming wind, holding his balance by leaning inboard against the mast. "Not in this blow."

"Let's get below, look at the forecast tomorrow," said Hale, waving the marineros off, thanking them with a thumbs up. Down below, Hale noticed that Dean looked green. Seasick in port. Not ideal.

By 6:00 a.m., the storm had abated. Completely. Absolute calm in a millpond. Hale rose at seven, threw bread to the ducks that bobbed about on the water, now glassy, golden-red in the morning light.

The calm brought with it another problem: no wind by which to sail. Hale couldn't believe the run of bad luck, though characteristic of a region notorious for driving people over the edge with its climatic oddities. The conditions would make the passage uncomfortable. They'd have to motor in a big swell without the benefit of some wind in the sails to stabilise the yacht. Could be risky, especially at the other end where the swell at the entrance to Melilla could get big. That was if they had to make for Melilla in an emergency.

Melilla was the cover story.

By eight, Jack had risen from his slumber and was out on deck. The wind had now risen steadily to twelve knots. Hale felt his spirits lifting, the run of bad luck perhaps over. Perfect sailing weather.

Half an hour later, they motored past the marina tower, *el torre*, and hoisted the sails in the rolling swell. They turned to port, heading south. *Blue Too* pitched heavily. Jack took the helm, Dean forward on deck, and Hale down below at the chart table.

No going back, thought Hale. Time to get this done. In a year's time, Jack and Dean and this boat would be relegated to the memory bank, a series of risky adventures and turbulent times never to be repeated.

The passage to Melilla was a convenient ruse. Many vessels made the trip due south to fill up with cheaper diesel, do the tourist thing, or add another passage to the log. Box tickers looking to impress gin-soaked buddies at the yacht clubs back home. But Hale and the crew wouldn't be going to the Spanish exclave. They'd make approximately two thirds of the way across the Alborán to rendezvous with Happy's RIBS – rigid inflatables – heading out from Melilla and stashed with 'the cargo' as Hale preferred to call it. Whatever was in the sacks hauled aboard *Blue Too* was Jack's business. Hale was the driver at the bank heist, didn't need to know – or want to know – the details.

But in his heart, Hale knew the consequences, the implications, and what was likely to comprise Happy's precious cargo. Hashish and cocaine. He'd become used to the skippering money over the years. Dependent on ten or twenty grand coming in now and then. Used it to beat his debts down when they rose uncomfortably high. But now the debts were at an exorbitant level, and he could only hope to stall the spiral with the money from Jacks's trips.

Shifting cash back to the UK – being investigated for money laundering – was another issue. The bigger the debts back home, the more Hale needed to transfer by some means to address them. Packing cash into luggage, shifting money between bank accounts, or getting other people to carry it, all held risks that would eventually catch up with him.

For Hale, this trip marked a watershed. His last chance to get out, end his double life.

"It's building again," said Hale, standing on deck, looking west through binoculars at white horses gathering on the horizon.

"Don't tell me," said Jack, hauling on the tiller. "What's our position?"

"Not even halfway."

"Forecast?"

"Strong to gale from the west."

"Christ, rough stuff again. They didn't forecast it this morning did they?"

"Nope."

Dean popped his head out of the hatchway, battled to ignite a roll-up with his oversized paraffin lighter, and then said, "I say we break out the rum, drown our sorrows. Prepare us for a rough ride. If it's coming, it's coming."

Hale ignored the banter. It *was* coming, and it *was* serious. Making any kind of rendezvous with the RIBS would be tricky enough, but in rough conditions under cover of darkness, virtually impossible.

These are the stakes, thought Hale. To play the game, you have to run the gauntlet. A perilous game played out in rough seas, in the dark, avoiding the law. Like days of old. "You're just another bloody smuggler," he said to himself. He sighed, shouted to the others, "Guys, reef the main, please, and change the jib. I'm on the helm, we're pressing on."

Blue Too heeled over hard as she pounded through steep chop. Jack and Dean sat on the windward rail, cold and silent as the sun set over their shoulders, spray hurling against their backs, sent in sheets from the pitching bow.

Darkness fell. Jack got on the radio to deliver coded calls. Hale knew nothing of the details, other than they were instructions to Happy Gary's crew setting off from the African coast.

Jack yelled up to Hale from the chart table, one hand on the radio handset, "What's the ETA, Charlie? We gonna make it in these bloody seas?"

Hale looked at his watch: 10:50 p.m. "Looks like midnight," he said. "I think it's moderating a touch. Ask them what's happening at their end. We'll press on."

Rain fell, unusual in these parts, increasing Hale's unease. A squall in the Solent, or The English Channel, you may be able to predict an outcome, hazard a guess. But out here in the Alborán it followed neither the sayings of old sea dogs, nor predictions of modern gadgetry.

Jack emerged from the dim cabin lights, hauled himself into the cockpit donning a heavy weather jacket. "Looks like we got a bit of everything on this trip, Charlie," he said. "Rain out here? Never thought I'd see it."

Hale steadied himself in a gust, working the tiller, "I don't know what it's going to do. What did they say … about the sea state their end?"

"Couldn't understand 'em much. Moroccans I think, one Portuguese, but they've got the stuff aboard two RIBS and they're out there somewhere."

"RIBS? I'm hoping they're big, Jack."

"Knowing Happy, they'll be the biggest … he's into all that marine engineering business, and Happy don't do things by halves."

Hale noted a change, a slight lull. The dark skies upwind to the west, darker, angry. "Wind's shifting, Jack. What have we got here?"

Dean rushed back from the foredeck, "Oh shit, man!" he shouted. "It's a flaming squall."

"Clip on now," said Hale.

Jack and Dean rummaged in a locker for their harnesses. Too late. The squall hit, a frenzy of hammering rain, wind buffeting, driving the sea into angry spume. Hale lodged his feet against the cockpit seat opposite, now virtually standing, as the boat broached, heeled at an impossible angle. Sheets of rain hammered down, the wind shrieked, tore at the sails and rigging. Jack clung to a handrail, shouting something unintelligible in the chaos. Dean wrapped an arm around a winch, grabbed a metal stanchion, his legs dangling in the sea.

"We got too much sail up!" shouted Hale. Spray smacked his face, silenced him as he took a choking mouthful of brine. A crack of thunder. The rain turned to hail, hammered the decks, frozen pellets collecting around their feet. The sea formed a white torrent around them, blasted by sheets of ice, the chop blown flat by the ferocity of the squall.

"Shit, shit!" shouted Dean, losing control, panicking.

Jack reached out, grabbed his arm, tried to shake sense into him, "Shut it, will you. Stop your howling you damn fairy."

Blue Too sprang upright in a violent wind shear. The three men fell to the cockpit floor, scrabbled, slipped on the ice.

The melee ceased in an instant.

"Jesus Christ," said Hale.

Silence.

The wind abated. Then vanished. The sails flapped limp without a breath of wind, and *Blue Too* wallowed on a large swell.

Jack heaved himself up, and then said, "In all my days, I've nae seen the likes of this nonsense."

"Let's get the engine fired up," said Hale. "Leave the sails for the moment."

Dean stood motionless, stunned.

Two minutes later, they were under way, motor-sailing in a three-knot breeze, the three of them silent, ready for another assault should the weather turn once more.

11:45 p.m.

Lights on the horizon appeared intermittently. These were not flashing lights from any shore. Huge swells hid the RIBS momentarily in the troughs, and then lifted them skyward, their lights visible at the peaks.

"Sketchy, Jack," said Hale, watching the vessels' approach through the darkness. The clouds had cleared swiftly, and now there was at least good visibility under moonlight. "The problem is that we're not going to be able to tie up alongside."

"We'll have to, Charlie. To get the gear aboard," shouted Jack, making his way amidships, preparing lines. "The sacks are big and we have to manhandle them aboard. They cannot be thrown. That'd be impossible, you understand."

"Jesus, this is going to be hell," said Hale, reaching down to a lever beside his knee, throttling back the engine.

The RIBS approached line astern, a single nav light shining above each on a steel post, their crews huddled in black heavy weather coats. *Blue Too* pitched, sails thumping as they filled with each descent into a trough.

"Steady, Charlie, steady!" shouted Jack. "Dean, get forward, grab a line from 'em."

The dark-skinned crews from the RIBS peered about, fear in their eyes born of hours in the perilous seas. But now, more danger.

The first RIB slammed into *Blue Too*'s side, and then squeezed against her. Dean hurled a line across.

Hale looked down at the RIB crew and their terrified faces looking up to him. An instant later, he looked up at them as *Blue Too* dipped into a trough.

"Hold her in, Dean, for a moment will you," said Jack leaning out to grab a brown sack bound with gaffer tape from the RIB crew. The RIB slammed in again, trapping Jack and the sack between the vessels.

Dean shouted, "Port, Charlie!"

Hale swung the tiller around, creating a gap of a few feet. Jack hauled himself up with a moan, but the sack was gone.

"Jesus Christ, man," said Jack. The RIB came in again before Jack had composed himself. The Moroccan crew hastily launched another sack towards *Blue Too*. Dean lunged for it, but it too sank to the depths with a splash.

"They're too goddamn heavy," said Dean, running back to the cockpit. "And we can't see a damn thing."

Hale steadied the yacht, put some distance between the first RIB that now wallowed abeam. "Put the mast lights on, flood the decks," said Hale.

"No," Jack said, "we're already letting the bloody world know we're here, with those nav lights on the RIBs. Dean, get back here," he ordered, "another one's coming across."

Dean returned to Jack, clambered on all fours, holding his balance in the pitching swell.

The RIB approached again, but then, disaster.

THIRTY-ONE

On the starboard deck, Dean lay on his stomach, reached for the sack held out by the RIB crew. Jack held a stay with one hand, made a grab with the other.

But Hale saw a problem beyond. The second RIB had come too close, descended into a swell and was now surfing uncontrollably close to the first, rising up towards it.

Hale shouted, "Look out, hold on!" He rammed the tiller over to the right, shifting *Blue Too* clear of the inevitable. The second RIB continued to rise, and then rose under the first, catching it at the bow. Cavitating props screamed, a smell of diesel fumes. The first RIB capsized, hurling the crew overboard into black water.

Jack stared at Hale, stunned, terror.

The second RIB crew motored around, looking for the three swimmers, hauled one up. Hale caught sight of the other two on a peak of a breaking swell, white water gathering around them as it broke. He gunned the engine, made for them. The second RIB fell out of sight into a trough.

Hale barked commands at his shell-shocked crew: "Jack, Dean, get the lifebelt, get a line ready. Point to them, keep their position." Dean obeyed, stretched his arm out, pointing to the swimmers, one of whom was distressed, flailing arms, panicking. Neither wore life jackets.

Hale's mouth was dry with stress, tasted of salt and diesel. He glanced at Jack, who was sluggish, pondering. "What in hell's name are you doing, Jack? For chrissakes move your arse. The line."

Jack stared at Hale, hanging on to a shroud. "It's not happening, Charlie," he said.

Hale cursed, "The bloody line!"

Jack remained motionless, and then said, "We have to get out of here, Charlie. This isn't happening and we're going to get caught up in this screw-up."

"We're helping the swimmers," said Hale, battling to steady himself as the yacht lurched. He craned his neck to follow Dean's line of sight to the swimmers.

"We've been out here too long, Charlie. We have to run, or we'll be in jail, simple as that."

Hale shook his head, looked to starboard. The second RIB had recovered. Dean was up on the foredeck pointing, waving, guiding them to the black objects bobbing on the mountainous swells."

Hale looked at Jack, a look of fury. "You selfish shit."

The second RIB reached the swimmers. Hale throttled back, watched them being hauled up, requiring two men for each swimmer. *Blue Too* wallowed for a moment. Then Hale made the decision: "Dean get back here now, Jack too. We're aborting. Hang on, I'm going about."

Jack clambered back into the cockpit. Dean cursed as *Blue Too* swung around one hundred and eighty degrees. Jack and Hale ducked under the boom as it swung above their heads. Hale gunned the engine, this time with the yacht heading north, back towards the Spanish mainland.

Minutes later, they sat in silence, riding the swell as rain returned, washing down the decks in floods back to the cockpit. Hale looked behind, shivered as water ran down his back. The RIB was heading south, fading into the night.

"A massive balls-up," said Dean, over the clank of the engine, trying to break the mood. "So, now what?"

"We're screwed, that's what," said Hale.

Three hours on, rain continued to lash down. A dark outline of the Sierra Nevadas lurked on the horizon, a faint glow beneath from the lights of the coastline. Around the yacht, darkness, broken only by the occasional splash of white water from a breaking swell. *Blue Too* half motor-sailed, half surfed the swell north, with Hale vigilant at the helm. Dean kept lookout while Jack monitored the radio for coded news of the RIBs.

No news.

Hale looked around, sensed something. A presence. Dean too, remained quiet, experienced enough to know when something was amiss. More gut instinct than superstition.

The wind eased further. *Blue Too* was now under motor, the sails flapping lazily.

Hale called down to Jack, "Anything?"

"Nope, nothing. Just static, and no one out there. No one stupid enough to be out here tonight, apart from us, boys."

"Okay, pack it in, just leave it on monitor," said Hale. "Come up and be on lookout with us."

Jack killed the cabin light, eased his bulk up on deck. In the blackness, the water bore streaks of phosphorescence, the stars emerged above as the clouds flew east. Beautiful, thought Hale. If only, I could appreciate it.

Jack said, "You gone quiet on me, boys. What's up?"

Dean shook his head.

"Don't know," said Hale. "Keep your eyes peeled. Hear that?"

Jack paused, turned his head, listening, "Nope, not over this engine. You hear something Dean?"

Dean looked at Hale, "Low hum?"

"Yep," said Hale. "It's gone now."

"What do you say we kill the engine for a minute, skipper?" said Dean.

Hale thought about it, reached behind him to the control panel, turned the key. The engine clanked, stopped. A two-second beep sounded from the controls, and then silence, apart from the sound of the wash as *Blue Too* wallowed on the swell.

The three stood still, looked about, occasionally casting an inquisitive glance at each other. Hale heard it again. The low hum, now a thunderous drone. He looked northwest. Just to the left of the mast, he saw its approach. A towering shape, heading straight towards them.

"Shit, Jack, eleven o' clock," said Hale.

Jack swung around leaned out, peered into the gloom. "Jesus. Headin' straight for us, Charlie. What the hell is it, lifeboat, coastguard?"

Hale shook his head, turned the ignition. The diesel engine wined through a few turns, and then bit and fired up. "It's got no nav lights, Jack. What does that mean?"

Dean stared at Hale, as if he knew the answer. Hale gunned the engine again, bearing away on a heading north to Puerto de Santa María. Jack made his way up to the foredeck for a better angle, hung on the stays to prevent himself being thrown overboard as *Blue Too* pitched.

The vessel was almost on them.

"Goddamn!" shouted Jack, turning, heading back along the deck. A swathe of blinding light illuminated him from the vessel ahead, his bulky frame silhouetted as he fell back into the cockpit. "Bloody Guardia," he said, breathing heavily. "That stealth thing from Almería."

Hale squinted, covered his eyes, barely able to steer the yacht. Something boomed through the vessel's loudspeakers, Spanish. Its engines roared. Jet thrusters, not conventional propulsion. *Blue Too* was headed off in an instant. Hale slammed the engine into neutral, looked up at the Guardia vessel now illuminating *Blue Too* from three angles with powerful beams forging through the dank air. On board, uniformed crew moved up and down the decks. On the bridge, Hale made out the Capitán speaking into a microphone.

The loudspeaker boomed out again, this time in English.

"Vessel ahead. Identify yourself, channel seventeen."

"Jack, take the helm," said Hale. He went below, grabbed the radio handset, spinning the channel selector to seventeen.

"This is yacht *Blue Too*, over."

White noise. Hale clenched his fist, cursed to himself, waited for the response. He peered out of the window from the navigation table. The Guardia vessel was manoeuvring around, checking them over. The deep thunder of the vessel's engines resonated through Hale's ribcage, diesel fumes hung in the cabin, forming a heady, nauseous stench.

The radio crackled. Then a command issued: "Your destination and crew, over."

"Puerto de Santa María. Three on board," said Hale.

"Nacionalidad, over."

"British. We were heading..."

The Guardia interrupted: "Standby."

Jack shouted from his position at the helm, "What's up, Charlie? Tell 'em, we got caught by the squall, had to turn around."

"Leave it to me," Hale said, waiting for the Guardia's response.

Dean lost his nerve, leaned down into the cabin, "This is shit, skipper. Tell 'em we're in trouble, need assistance or something. They won't buy any cock and bull story, not this lot."

"Dean, take the sails down," said Hale, "they're flapping like a bitch. Do something."

Dean moved to the foredeck.

The radio fired into life: "Yacht *Blue Too*. You follow us. We escort you to Puerto de Santa María for checking. Understand? Over."

"Understood," said Hale.

"You take sail down, use motor. Understood? Over."

"Understood."

Hale threw the handset down, went up on deck. Dean had already dropped the jib.

"Follow them, Jack," said Hale. "They're taking us back."

Jack edged the throttle forward, cursing, "Shit, bollocks ... I knew it."

Hale stood at the mast, helping Dean haul the mainsail down, more to keep his mind active than anything else. Better than standing at the helm, agonising on what the next few hours would bring. Always best to work.

The thundering bulk of the Guardia vessel rumbled ahead, control tower swaying, surrounding *Blue Too* in whitewash from its jets.

The lights of Puerto de Santa María loomed beyond.

THIRTY-TWO

4:07 a.m.

The Guardia vessel – a stealth machine bristling with technology, deployed to track modern-day pirates, immigrants, and drug smugglers – moved into position at the marina tower. Spray and smoke swirled about the decks under the brilliance of its lights, the twin jet turbines churning up the water, turning it to foam. The boat edged into position against Puerto de Santa María's quay.

Behind, *Blue Too* rocked gently. Hale idled the engine, waiting for instruction. It soon came as the radio burst into life over the deck speaker: "*Blue Too*, moor at the tower. *Blue Too*, moor at the tower."

Jack acknowledged on the radio handset. Hale brought her about in the damp, the rain having now turned to drizzle. He moved her in closer to the quay, opposite the lights of the marina office, the office that never slept.

Over the years, Hale had often been out on deck at night, unable to sleep on board. Looking west, there was always someone operating the marina tower night and day. Marineros – smoking, bored, looking to pass the hours – hung around waiting for a call. Holidays, fiestas, or normal working days, it made no difference. Vessels were always at sea or visiting the port for some reason.

Dean threw a line from the bow to the marinero ashore while Hale mulled the inevitable question from the authorities:

What was your business at sea tonight, Mr Hale?

On approach, he'd spotted two figures standing to the right hand side of the marina office entrance, waiting, huddled out of the drizzle. One, a woman, smart, dark hair, clutched a folder to her chest. She stood upright, confident. The other, a man, ruffled suit, looked Almerían. The end of his cigarette glowed orange as he sucked on it intermittently. Hale knew these people. Inspectora Jefa Rosa María Díez and Manolo Fernández. The welcoming committee.

Blue Too was tied up, Dean and Jack led away to a 4x4 Guardia vehicle. María Díez directed an armed, uniformed official, in full gear and heavy boots, towards Hale. He held Hale by the elbow, escorted him away to a room in the tower, an admin office filled with uninteresting paraphernalia: printer, ancient personal computer with bulbous screen, and filing cabinets crammed with fading folders and ring binders. Could be a mouldy solicitor's office back in Britain, thought Hale. This one, however, had marble floors, and terribly outdated advertisements of Spain dotted about the walls – fading mementos of the tourism boom years.

Hale was left in the office for some minutes until the official returned, gave Hale a hard look.

"Café?"

"Como?" said Hale, not expecting pleasantries.

"Café?"

"Sí, con leche."

The official walked off, returned a minute later with steaming black liquid in a plastic cup. He handed it to Hale, and then slammed the door as he left, locking it.

Forty minutes later, Hale was about to put his head down on a desk, get some rest, but the official returned, rattling the key to unlock the door. This time he had company. María Díez stood at the door for a moment eyeing Hale, folder still clutched to her chest.

"Shall we?" she said, motioning Hale to the office across the hall.

Hale walked across to the main office. In the daytime, addled marina staff sat in this room around a long desk, typing at computers while clients – gin palace owners and yachties – vainly haggled prices for marina berths. But Hale wasn't here to negotiate mooring fees. Unfortunate, since that would have been easier.

María Díez took her position at a desk, an antiquated computer to her left. Hale sat pensively in the visitor's chair opposite, felt a chill despite wearing the foul weather jacket. Fernández loitered in the doorway. María Díez shooed him away with a flick of her wrist, upon which he loped off to join the Guardia men who could be seen through the window chatting outside.

"Mr Hale, we meet again," she said, clasping her hands on the desk. "How nice. Now, can you tell me … What was your business tonight on the boat?"

Hale shifted nervously in his seat, looked down at his hands, and then said, "Well, it's all rather a long story, really."

"Is it? Well, you have heard about summary, no? So how about you try to make it short and then we can progress."

"Yes, of course. Well, we planned to head across to Melilla this year, the boys and I, and…"

"Purpose?"

"Sorry?"

"Purpose of the trip." She tapped her pen on the desk, an unsettling habit that made Hale uneasy.

"Leisure," said Hale. "We often sail together in these waters and…"

María Díez sighed, leaned back, looked at the ceiling. Hale continued for a few seconds, muttering to a halt, since she was clearly not listening.

"Your friends," she began again. "Mr Weir and Mr Oliver. They do not look to me like tourists, holidaymaking. They do not look like such people, would you say?"

"Perhaps not, but…"

"And wouldn't you say this is a strange way to enjoy your sailing, to go out in storms, at night? I assume you know about weather, have experience?"

Hale glanced through the window, caught a shrug of a Guardia official who had joined the group outside. A shrug directed at Fernández. Hale looked back at María Díez, who demanded his attention with two clicks of her fingers in front of his face.

"You must realise we have some serious issues with your behaviour, Mr Hale," she continued. "You return here to this town, to this marina. When we spoke last, I specifically said that it would be unwise for you to do so. And now you leave me no option but to expedite my investigation. We are searching your boat now, questioning your friends, Weir and Oliver, and we do not believe their stories. Stories that do not align with yours, sir." She slammed her fist on the table, the sound echoed through the room, catching the attention of a marinero, who peered in frowning.

"*And*, Mr Hale, there are traces of cocaine on your vessel."

Dean's coke-snorting habit. Taking lines on the chart table when Hale wasn't around, something the Guardia's dog would have sensed in seconds. Hale cursed Dean under his breath, shuddered at the thought of the ongoing investigation. He remained silent for a moment, weighing up the situation. The vagueness of the Inspectora Jefa's approach had not been lost on him. And, the official's shrug to

Fernández outside. Fernández had responded by shaking his head, blowing smoke into the air as if disappointed. Perhaps they'd searched the boat, found nothing.

Despite the chaotic events at sea, and the technological wizardry at the Guardia's disposal, perhaps María Díez had little evidence that they were rendezvousing with Happy's RIB crews. In fact, *Blue Too* was clean. That was a certainty, since most of the contraband was now on the seabed. Jack and Dean were seasoned criminals, too wily to divulge anything other than the kind of drivel alcoholics and powderheads rattle off their tongues in bars. Even to Hale, a seemingly simple conversation to ascertain facts from the Weir and Oliver comedy act invariably led to claptrap wavering from one subject to another.

Hale sensed frustration in María Díez. Her standpoint perhaps weak. What *did* she have on him? Too weary and punch drunk to debate, Hale said nothing, and felt bad for doing so. Holding his cards close to his chest, evasive, protecting his interests. The traits in others Hale despised. Games played by bullshitters in the city. But he was in a corner. Not much better than Jack and Dean, he was a criminal. He thought about it: if there was any excuse or factor that set him apart from them, it was that his dream was of a new life away from this skulduggery. He wanted out. But for now, he needed to buy time.

"If you don't mind, Inspectora," said Hale, "my yacht needs to be returned to its mooring and prepared, and my crew are tired from what turned out to be a dangerous trip."

María Díez glared at him.

Hale continued, "So, if you don't mind … if your business here is complete."

She looked down, scribbled notes on a pad. Then said, "Inspectora Jefa."

"I'm sorry?" said Hale.

María Díez looked up. "I am the Inspectora *Jefa*. My colleague, Manolo Fernández, is the Inspector."

"Of course," said Hale. "I do apologise."

"I would like you to remember our names and our titles, Mr Hale," she said, continuing to scribble, "because we will be contacting you when we have progressed this investigation.

Extended to include the events of tonight. Do you have anything more you wish to say to me?"

Hale shook his head, remained silent, looked down. He jolted upright as María Díez slammed her pen down, leaned on her elbows forming a pyramid with her hands.

She glowered at Hale unblinking.

Uncomfortable, Hale zipped his jacket, shifted in his seat, feeling her eyes burning into him. He met her stare again, "Is that all ... shall I?"

María Díez flicked her eyes to the door and back.

Hale took this as a dismissal, rose from his seat, and walked out.

Two minutes later, Fernández joined María Díez at the doorway outside, looking on as the Guardia group split up, heading to 4x4s or the stealth vessel. Hale approached Jack and Dean who huddled beside *Blue Too*, smoking.

"Same thing as before," said Dean, smirking. "Bitch knows nothing, has nothing on us."

"If you believe that, you're even dumber than I originally thought," said Hale, turning to Jack. "What did they ask *you*?"

Jack flicked his cigarette stub into the water. "Och, not so much, Charlie. Destination, purpose of trip, that kind of shite." He looked at Dean with a glint in his eyes, and then smiled at Hale, "To be honest, skipper, Dean and me had the impression that they were more interested in you. I mean, we're in the clear, laddie, or so it seems. Question seems to be: what have *you* been up to?"

Hale fumed. Dean broke into a husky laugh, holding his stomach with hysterics.

"Fine," said Hale, throwing a rope against Dean's chest. "Take this, and let's get her back."

They boarded *Blue Too*, and minutes later, eased away from the quay. Hale swung her around to port, heading for Darsena 8. He cast a glance astern, alerted by the throaty roar of the Guardia vessel firing up. Further right, María Díez and Fernández stood talking, looking out towards *Blue Too*.

THIRTY-THREE

After a few hours' sleep, Hale called a meeting in the beach café, 8:00 a.m. Get Dean away from his spliffs, and Jack away from *Blue Too* where he'd otherwise fiddle with ropes and gadgets, being evasive rather than sticking to the point of the conversation.

At the far end of the bar, the usual scene: a few grizzled workers ate bocadillos, drank beer from bottles, gawked at the news on a television high up. Hale took a stool at the bar, ordered three cortados. Dean and Hale sat down, reluctant, uncomfortable in the surroundings.

"What's this, a gay surf bar?" said Jack, gazing up at a yellow surfboard strapped to the ceiling.

Hale nodded to the workers, "Do those guys look gay or into surfing? Why don't you go ask them?"

Jack ignored the comment, knocked back the cortado in one hit. "That was fun last night, eh, boys," he said. "So, what's the plan now?"

Dean appeared more sombre than usual, remained silent, looking around as if someone might be watching.

"The plan now," said Hale, "is that there is no plan. We're finished. You guys go back to Marbella and explain to Happy Gary that things didn't work out and we had to abort. That's life." Hale shrugged. "Things don't always go to plan, he should know that. He still has *Blue Too* in fine shape. I'm out of here in a few hours."

Jack sighed, looked at Dean, who said nothing. Jack said, "We're splitting, skipper, sailing west."

"West?" said Hale.

"Happy's not gonna go for our story, or *your* story. We're taking *Blue Too* to Ceuta."

Ceuta, the Spanish exclave on the north African coast, three hundred kilometres west on the Strait of Gibraltar. Hale mulled the idea of running from Happy, someone whose reputation alone suggested that running was a brave choice, or stupid.

"What's in Ceuta for you?" Hale asked.

"We're picking up another skipper, Charlie, on account of your good self not being up for more trips and our fine company. Och, he's a good man from my neck of the woods. Knows the route well."

"The route?"

Jack glanced at Dean, who shrugged. Jack continued, "We don't have to tell you, but what the hell ... you're gone later and our business is done, so keep your mouth shut if you will. We're heading to the Moroccan coast, across to the Canaries. Then west from Tenerife."

"Caribbean?" asked Hale.

"Panama, and then South America."

"On business?"

"You could say that," said Jack, delivering a smile that vanished on seeing Hale shaking his head.

Hale looked at Dean, "When are you guys going to quit this life?"

Jack changed the subject, tapping Hale on the bicep, "Never you mind us, laddie. Look after yourself, and speaking of which, had you noticed we got company up at *Blue Too* early this morning?"

Hale frowned, "Company?"

"Aye, some lad hanging around the wharf. Thinks he's being all undercover and whatnot. Playing with some ropes and on his phone all the time. Looks dead outta place to me."

"What does he look like?"

"Black hair, white skin, bit of flab. Stocky. Might fancy himself as a tough boy."

"Can't say I've seen him. Spanish, you'd say?"

Jack shook his head, "Nope. From east of Europe maybe, like them nutters we see in the bar now and then. Mad bunch drunk on vodka. Not much between the ears."

Rich coming from you, thought Hale. "What makes you think he's interested in us?" he said.

Jack shrugged, "Instinct."

"And the Guardia in their jeep," said Dean rising to his feet.

"Yeah, I saw them," said Hale. "But we often see them around, so no big deal is it?"

The three said nothing. Hale threw some coins on the bar, thanked the barman.

Jack broke the silence, "The heat's on us, Charlie. We're splitting late afternoon. You?"

Hale, paused, thinking about his present status. No money. No transport. Enzo's crowd pursuing him. Happy Gary oblivious to their latest failure, but not for long. Under observation by María Díez. Marta in danger.

There was little deliberation required: get some money and run.

"I'm out of here midday," said Hale.

Hale lodged himself in the forward cabin, throwing clothes into his sailing bag. Checked his passport, placed the laptop in the bag. Jack's footsteps thundered through the glass fibre deck above him, voice booming out to Dean who prepared lines in the cockpit. Never seen them so focussed, thought Hale. Amazing how fear galvanises people.

But Hale needed them off the boat for a while. There was only so much packing and document checking he could feign, and there would be only one chance to flee. He clambered out into the cockpit, up towards Jack on the foredeck.

"He around?" said Hale.

Jack shifted his eyes left, and then back, said nothing. Hale nodded, climbed over the stainless steel pulpit at the bow, leapt onto shore. On the wharf, Hale moved clear of *Blue Too*. Then glanced over to an area to the right of *El Timón*, the area Jack had indicated. The Eastern Bloc guy loitered, too obvious. He ambled in front of a boat adjusting some fenders, as if it were his own. But Hale knew the real owner, a Frenchman he hadn't seen for months.

Hale pulled his cell from his trouser pocket, dialled Marta.

Three rings and she answered, fear in her voice, "You should not call. There is more danger, something has happened and they watch me most times now."

"I know," said Hale. "You need to leave right now."

"But how?"

"Is there a way you can get to the bus station unseen?"

"Maybe. I do not know."

"Do it. Board the bus heading for Málaga, but get off before, at Torrox."

Silence at the other end. Hale sensed Marta weighing up the danger.

"Torrox?" she said.

"I have a friend there who can help us, someone I can trust with my life. You have a pen? I'll give you his number."

"What about you?"

"I'll travel later this evening, meet you there. I need to get some money, sort some things out here."

"I'll wait for you," she said.

"No. We cannot be seen together, not here." Hale scanned around, sweat poured down his back, the stress making his mouth dry and sticky. In his periphery, Hale felt Eastern Blochead glance across.

Jack was right, the pressure was on.

"You need to go. Now," snapped Hale.

"Okay, okay. Your friend, his number."

Hale recited the number, closed the call, and then called an old friend from university, Rupert Lloyd-Evans. Not much was said, no time. Hale apologised, said he'd explain when he made it to Torrox. One more call to make, this time to the ponytailed mugger, Enzo.

Phone in hand about to dial, he looked up at Jack on the bow, his huge frame lugging sail bags around the deck. The days of *Blue Too* were over. Later, the boat and this crew would be gone, perhaps signifying the end of a dark chapter in Hale's life. He needed to disassociate himself from these rogues before he could reform, move his life forward. But first, he must delay Enzo and Berto Morillo. Make time to run, to plan, and for Marta to get clear of San Isidro.

He listed Enzo's number on his phone, hit dial.

THIRTY-FOUR

Hale moved slowly towards the group of buildings surrounding *El Timón*, listened to the dial tone, and then instinctively glanced to his right. In the distance, Eastern Blochead was rustling in his trouser pocket, drew out a phone, Hale heard it ringing. Coincidence?

A voice answered on Hale's phone.

"Si?"

"Is that Enzo? It's me, Hale."

"You want Enzo?"

Hale heard Eastern Blochead from across the way, an echo. This was him on the line, no doubt about it. Hale turned away, moved out of sight, beside *Alfonso's* tackle shop.

"Yes, I want Enzo," said Hale. "This is his number?"

A pause, "You Allay?"

"Sí."

"Enzo muerto. Dead." Hale heard Eastern Blochead cough and spit at the other end, and then continue, "We have your number, English. We know your boat, so now you work for us or you end up like Enzo. You need money, yes? We know about Marta and I tell you, boss very unhappy. You crazy for messing with girl. You understand this, English?"

Hale hid behind a tall plastic garbage bin, peered along the quay to Eastern Blochead positioned on the quayside, still loitering at the bow of the Frenchman's yacht.

Blochead continued, goading, "You still there funny man? You come to San Isidro and we give you work or we come get you. We hear you do work on this boat. We need boat like this for business."

"Not my boat," said Hale.

"Well okay, but what you say about working for us, English? My boss reasonable sometimes, but, other times…"

Hale cut the call, watched Blochead curse, pocket his phone.

He needed to get back on board, retrieve his gear without being seen, but Blochead eyed *Blue Too* like a bored security guard on duty. Berto Morillo must have stationed the goon, perhaps to track Hale's movements before abducting him somewhere more discreet. There may be more goons around.

Hale peered around. Not many people about. A family strolling along the wharf with a pram and a dog. A fisherman washing a bucket, throwing it into the water, pulling it back up with a rope. He looked back to Blochead who'd rolled a cigarette, poked it in his mouth unlit. Now he was walking over to the café opposite the French yacht, looking for a light from the waiter.

Hale moved, eyes fixed on Blochead, tripped over his own feet entering the Wharf. *Blue Too* was thirty yards away, and Hale out in the open. Blochead leaned over as the waiter presented the lighter. Hale moved faster, sprinting now. At *Blue Too*'s bow, he hauled himself up, falling onto the foredeck. Looked up. Blochead was turning around. The forward hatch was open. In one movement, Hale eased himself down, fell heavily on the floorboards below.

"Jesus Christ," said Jack from the main cabin. "What's got into you?"

Hale gathered himself, regained his breathing. "Need to get moving, Jack … bus time's earlier than I thought." Jack shrugged, gave him a look. Dean peered into the forward cabin, smirking at the sweat-soaked skipper. "Problem, Dean?" said Hale. Dean walked off. Hale shoved his gear bag aft through the bathroom area, into the main cabin.

Jack sat at the chart table, tapping buttons on the radio set. "So, Charlie," he said, continuing to select channels. "I guess all good things must come to an end, and lovers must part."

Hale straightened his back, adjusted his sunglasses, which had been thrown off and bent during his descent into the forward cabin. "Yes, so sad," he said. "Breaks my heart to be leaving you boys like this."

Jack turned, gave him a hard stare, offered his massive hand. Hale shook it, trying to read Jack's thoughts.

"We've had some adventures," said Jack, with a grin, "and at least we'll come out the other side with some tales to tell the grandchildren, wouldn't you say?"

"Let's hope so, Jack. Let's hope so." Hale, turned to Dean who was stretched out on his bunk, smoking. "So long Dean."

Dean raised hand in farewell, said nothing.

Hale hauled his bag out into the cockpit, fearful of what lay ahead. A daunting prospect. How to get past Blockhead again, get out of Puerto de Santa María, help Marta, avoid Morillo, get out of Spain.

He donned his sunglasses, peered through the rigging of several yachts to Blochead beyond. The goon was still speaking with the waiter, looking about occasionally, clearly bored with the task Morillo had assigned.

Hale clutched his bag, swiftly moved along the deck, grabbing the stays for support. Blochead was heading back. Hale froze, crouched down. Blochead returned to the bow of the French yacht, throwing seeds or something into the water. He looked across to *Blue Too*. Hale remained still, hoped his image would be lost through the forest of rigging and masts.

A few metres ahead on the wharf, Hale spotted two marineros doing their rounds on an electric golf buggy, checking lines, passing the time. Hale knew the older one, a friendly, gregarious Spaniard with a chocolate tan, spoke no English, not even 'hello'.

Blochead turned, ambled along the quay in the other direction. Hale seized the opportunity, jumped off the bow and mingled with the marineros on the far side of their buggy. They idled the buggy at Hale's walking pace, exchanged some pleasantries with him, moaning about taxes, wages, or something. Hale couldn't fathom out the flood of unpunctuated Spanish, but smiled and laughed nonetheless. Blochead was alerted to the banter, looked on, returned his gaze to *Blue Too*, and then turned away again.

Outside the steel wharf gate, the marineros sped off jauntily. Hale darted into *Alfonso's*.

"Hola, buenos días," Hale said, throwing his bag to the floor, interrupting a debate. Alfonso and the old boys were seated in a semicircle on their plastic chairs. There was a second's awkwardness, before Alfonso rose to his feet, walked across to Hale, while the cacophony continued.

"Ah, mi amigo, señor Allay, so good to see you, and you have been sailing, no?"

Hale asked him to slow his delivery to follow the accent even thicker than the marineros', asked if he could wait for a few minutes to 'sort out some business'.

Alfonso raised his eyebrows, curious, and then smiled. "But of course, you can stay here as a friend of mine. Until we close, if you see fit. I make coffee, and then you join us, no?"

"Thank you, but no. Really, I'll just look at these ropes here," said Hale, kicking his bag to the side of the door.

"No hay problema, my friend. You stay here, and ..." the old man, looked around, mischievous, continued, "... you find the service at *Pedro's* to your satisfaction?"

"Ah, yes," said Hale. "Nice place, and the staff ... so friendly. Thank you for the recommendation, señor."

Alfonso patted Hale on the shoulder, returned to the debate.

Hale peered through the glass section on the door, which was plastered haphazardly with fading stickers and advertisements. A final visit to *Blue Too* was required. Hale's only chance for money lay aboard. Despite their foibles, Jack and Dean were creatures of habit, a routine that had perhaps kept them clear of prison cells for a remarkable stretch. They were unaware that Hale knew of the money aboard, money allocated to pay the RIB crew for delivery of the contraband. A year ago, Hale had caught Jack rustling around one day, and later found a screw to the aft compartment laying on the floorboards. When Jack was ashore, Hale had removed the remaining screws, eased away the panel behind the engine, and looked around in the grime. Beneath the cockpit floor, Jack's fresh handprint was smeared along the side of the plastic fuel tank. Hauling himself further in, Hale had found a bundle of cash strapped behind the tank, sealed in foil and bound with gaffer tape.

Prior to a trip, Jack or Dean would access the 'bank' when Hale was absent ashore. In this way, only Happy Gary's crew were aware of the funds, regardless of any skipper they'd need to hire.

The thought of boarding once more placed butterflies in Hale's stomach. To run the gauntlet, avoiding Jack and Dean, would have been madness had it not have been for the duo's predictable nature. Now that Hale was gone, it wouldn't be long before the two figures loped across to the bar. That would just leave Blochead to contend with.

Ten minutes passed. Hale's view of *Blue Too* was clear, although Blochead loitered beyond the field of view. Occasionally, Dean wandered on deck, hands in pockets, before returning below.

No sign of Jack.

Eighteen minutes, no sign.

Hale peered around. The debate behind was in full swing, and only one visitor had rattled the door open, soon leaving with some small item of fishing gear.

For now, Hale was unseen, safe.

THIRTY-FIVE

Twenty-three minutes elapsed, and true to form, Jack and Dean emerged. Dean swaggered along the wharf, mock-punching Jack in the arm, both heading towards *El Timón*. They'd be watching Blochead, thought Hale, but not worrying him. Without knowledge or comprehension of Berto Morillo, his influence in the area and connections to the Russian mob, they'd consider the visitor as a bit of amusement. Sport.

Hale watched them move out of view behind a concrete wall leading to the bar. They'd be inside for an hour, minimum. Hale grabbed his bag, nodded to Alfonso, and then edged the door open. His foot was on the step when Blochead appeared beside the concrete wall, just yards away. Hale froze, still holding the door, moved his foot back inside. Blochead looked into the bar, seemed in two minds. Then turned to watch *Blue Too*. Hale remained still, the door half open. If he let it close, it would rattle and the bell would sound. Alfonso would soon come to question him, wondering why he'd frozen in the doorway. Two seconds seemed like a minute. Hale's eyes locked on to Blochead.

Then Blochead moved. Swiftly, he marched, almost ran, towards *Blue Too*. Pausing at the bow, looking either side. He then leaned out and banged his fist on the glass fibre hull. Blochead would have seen Jack and Dean leave the yacht, but he was clearly tasked to watch Hale.

Hale eased the door shut gently, looked behind. Alfonso eyed him, gave a smile as if aware of Hale's predicament, but made nothing of it. He looked away, continued the debate.

Hale continued to observe through the window. Blochead ran back along the wharf, his chest heaving, gait ungainly, and then into the bar and out of sight.

Now or never. Hale opened the door, stepped out into the sun, and ran back towards the wharf gate.

Don't look back to the bar, keep going, walk naturally.

He imagined the three of them in the dinge of *El Timón*. Jack and Dean would be seated near the pool table, hunched over scotches, rolling cigarettes. Blochead might take a stool at the bar, order a coffee, try hard to go unnoticed. Dean would smirk over at him, the game would begin.

Let them play their game.

Hale, neared the bow of *Blue Too*, tucked his bag out of view behind a plastic electricity box on the wharf, climbed up onto the bow. He made his way aft, keeping low, affording one glimpse at *El Timón*. All quiet within the black entrance, music blaring out.

In the cockpit, Jack, lax as usual, had left the main hatch open. Hale took a breath, eased himself down into the familiar smell of diesel and bilge water. He crawled into the aft berth, behind the navigation table, saw the panel secured with the four screws. Heaving himself back out, flies buzzed in his face and sweat dripped onto the floorboards. He cursed, grabbed some kitchen towels from the galley, wiped his head and kneeled down to clear the floor. Stuffing a batch of towels into his back pocket, Hale removed the tool bag from a locker beneath the chart table. Rooted around, pulled out a medium-sized screwdriver.

I've already been here too long, he thought. The urge to go back on deck, look across to check the bar was overwhelming, but he moved back into the aft berth, this time crawling to the end. His heartbeat ramped up. His shirt now wet, his hand slipped on the handle of the screwdriver as he worked each screw out. One out. Two out. The head of the third was gnarled, difficult to grip. He applied hard pressure, and then it moved. Three out.

A heavy thump at the bow.

Hale held his breath, stalled unscrewing the fourth. Shit. Jack, he thought. Back to get some change, his cigarettes, his lighter? Hale remained still, heart pounding in his chest. Jack's temper would erupt if he confronted Hale on board, especially when realising his intent to steal the money. And, especially when Jack had been drinking. There would be violence.

Another thump on the bow. This wasn't Jack or Dean. They would have boarded by now. Hale's mind raced for an answer, until it came with a woman's voice:

"Tortas!"

Hale exhaled, wiped sweat from his face. *Tortas*. Cakes. The Spanish cake woman doing her rounds. Once a week, she worked the darsenas, tray in hand, offering cakes for sale to the crews.

The cry came once more, "Tortas!"

Hale took a breath, shouted his reply, hoping it would be heard from his concealed position, "No, gracias!"

Silence. He waited, breathed again when he heard the "Tortas!" cry further down the wharf. He worked the remaining screw, which came out in seconds. The panel fell against him and he peered into the murk, dull light filtering through the semi-translucent hull.

Placing the panel aside, he moved into the compartment. The stench and heat were thick, made him nauseous. He eased his hand behind the rear of the fuel tank, felt the package, the size of two margarine tubs, soft to touch and smoothed with tape. He gripped the far side and tugged. It wouldn't budge. He worked the tape on the nearside, peeling up a strip, and then edging his fingers under the main bulk. Tearing up, it peeled away, the strips of gaffer tape ripping at the hairs on his arm.

Hale hung on to the package, pulled himself out of the confined space, scraping his arms on glass fibre and wood. In seconds, the panel was back in position. One screw in, top left. Two, bottom right. No third screw. Hale cursed. Looked about. Two screws were missing, gone completely. He peered down, saw them wedged deep between the bunk upholstery and the wooden framing. No room for his fingers to retrieve them, no time to get some long-nosed pliers or a magnet. No time.

Spent mentally and physically, Hale moved back out into the cabin, felt the veins pumping in his forehead. He replaced the screwdriver and toolbox, lifted his shirt, securing the package to his waist on one side with the remaining gaffer tape, thick, sticky, and more than adequate to grip his skin.

On deck, he moved more quickly than he should, leapt off the bow, grabbed the bag, and donned his sunglasses. The doorway to *El Timón* was blocked by an hombre holding a pool cue, speaking into his cell phone. A few other Spanish locals approached the bar, brushed past the pool player, moving out of the sun into the melee within, momentarily blocking the door. Hale used the block, moved past the bar, out of the wharf, and towards the town.

The next problem: transport.

In the marina toilets, Hale ripped the money out of the packages. Fifty euro notes in two packs, roughly two hundred and fifty within each. Twenty-five grand. Paying for car hire would not be a problem.

Hale knew a guy called 'Dutch' from a car rental outfit, a guy who would remain tight-lipped if challenged by an outsider or the Guardia. Problem was, Dutch liked to sit around socialising, talking with Hale, or rather talking *at* Hale. And time was something Hale could not afford, since Jack and Dean may wish to dip into the 'bank' at any moment, should their taste for more booze, coke, or prostitutes beckon. Blochead might also get twitchy when he realised Hale was gone. Worse, Jack and Dean might try to work with Blochead to find Hale in the hope of money or future 'business'. Bad move, thought Hale. They'd end up like Enzo.

Hale walked up to the car rental shop in an area surrounded by upper-crust restaurants overlooking gleaming gin palaces moored at the quay. The shop was one of those multi-function places you find in marinas, in this case operating as a launderette, car hire facility, and retailer of electronic paraphernalia.

If he could withstand the ear-bashing, Dutch would always get Hale a good deal. The man from Holland appeared to have no Christian name, surname, or salutation. *Dutch* appeared as his signature on all documentation, a man with a shady background. Scrawny with pink skin and an odd stare, Dutch was a likable substance abuser, a kind of wheeler-dealer common to the area. Leaving the 'shit home' and the 'shit wife' and the 'shit weather' back in Holland, Dutch enjoyed what he deemed greater leeway afforded by the Spanish authorities by which to practise his illicit business ventures. A deluded notion, since he frequently enjoyed prolonged attention by the Policía who cruised past his shop on a regular basis.

Outside the shop, Hale glanced around. Seemed quiet. No one paying him any undue attention. He pushed the door open. An assault of detergent and bleach stung his nostrils. Dutch was seated behind his desk, looking blankly at a washing machine whirring around. He turned slowly, became animated on recognising Hale.

"Charlie, my friend," he said, stubbing a cigarette out on top of a Coke tin. He leapt from his desk like a coiled spring, moved across to hug Hale.

"How's it going, Dutch," said Hale. "You look good." Dutch looked bad, much worse than Hale remembered. Hair greasy, eyes red, like he'd been snorting some bad stuff.

"Thank you, Charlie, I am good. Come, sit down." Dutch dragged a chair, screeching across the lino floor.

Hale took the lead, "Dutch, I have a rush on. Really, I do. I need a car now, and I have to go. Now."

Dutch raised his eyebrows, delivered his special grin. Hale realised his own approach, his psychology, was not great. Should have reversed it with Dutch, since he was the kind of guy who tired quickly with people who hung around, deemed them freeloaders. Conversely, he was intrigued by evasive, impatient people. People going somewhere, in a rush, in trouble. People like Hale. Dutch was an opportunist, and essentially bored, needed things to break the tedium before his next fix.

"Charlie, you seem stressed, man. Look, I was like you last year, until I got on to that new stuff. You know what I'm talking about? You wan' me get you some skunk?"

"I don't smoke, remember, Dutch?"

"Yeah, of course, but there's always time to get into some chill-out gear. You know, for busy men like you and me … businessmen."

Hale shuffled his feet, looked out the window. No one about. "Yes, I understand, Dutch, that's cool. But, as I say, I'm in rather a rush, and that car. It needs to be a small car, just for a few days."

"Ah, yes, of course. I do you nice price. Nice price for Charlie." Dutch returned to his desk, opened a drawer crammed with papers and receipts, pulled out a price list. "You going far then, Charlie?"

Hale sensed the prying nature of the question. "Just up the coast, west."

Dutch nodded, donned some bent spectacles, drew his finger down the list. "Okay, Charlie," he said. "Look, seventy euros normally, but for you, nice price, fifty five for two days."

"Perfect."

"And some stuff?"

"Sorry?"

"You nervous, man. More than I seen you before, you need to relax."

"I'm okay, Dutch, relaxed."

"I can get you some coke, man." Dutch looked up, removed his specs to reveal a couple of mad-eyes, barely aligned. "Nice price."

"No really, I'm fine for that stuff, really. But thank you."

"Okay, man," said Dutch, rattling some car keys, scribbling on a form. "But the shit I get is hot. And you can be new customer for Dutch, with hot stuff for cool price…"

Dutch is on a ramble, thought Hale. A ramble that could go on for thirty minutes, minimum. Needed to be out of there in five.

"And the car, Passat, very economical. But I let these dumb surfers have one a month ago, and guess what Charlie, guess what?"

"What Dutch?"

"They put their shit boards on the roof, five boards okay. And they turn the roof into … how do you say ... cave?" Dutch cupped his hand, moving it back and forth in an arc.

"Concave, concave," said Hale, impatient, twitchy. Dutch had the keys ready, the form placed on the desk, ready. Hale leaned over, ripped it away from Dutch, spun it around, signed it, and threw two fifties on the desk.

Dutch's eyes widened at the sight of fresh notes. "Ah, but we need the change, I will have to…"

"Keep it," interrupted Hale, grabbing the keys, and snapped, "Where's the car, Dutch? Now. The car?"

"Jesus, chill out, man. It's parked over by the Pizza restaurant, dude. Look for the white car."

"Thanks." Hale hauled his bag over the shoulder, walked out, leaving the door to slam in the breeze.

Dutch called after him through an opened window, "The car door is shit, man. Banged up by that German bitch from the video shop. Just use passenger door, okay?"

Hale held up his hand up, headed for the pizza restaurant.

THIRTY-SIX

Dutch was right. The car was banged up. So much that Hale had to climb in through the passenger door, over the gearshift, and edge out the same way at the gas station. But at least now he was on the winding coast road, clear of the marina town and heading west towards Torrox. He sent a text to Marta, juggling the phone in his hand while the Passat climbed, tucked in behind a cement truck labouring up a hill. A tense few minutes waiting for Marta's reply. It came with a beep on his phone as the road levelled out and he downshifted to overtake. On a precarious bend, he couldn't resist it, picked up the cell up from the passenger seat, peered at the message:

'on autobus. circa Almuñécar. no folowed. but i am scared.'

Hale glanced in the rear-view mirror, thought about her text. *i am scared*. Knew how she felt. Every car, every motorbike rider, every innocuous look across from a motorist fed his paranoia. The arid moonscape of Almería now miles behind, a golden swathe of evening light bathed increasingly verdant terrain lush with orange trees, palms, and groves rising up to the Sierra Nevada. Hale motored through the coastal towns of Calahonda, Salobreña, and on to Almuñécar. Opened the window to allow air to blast in, air scented with mimosa, garlic, and diesel. In the streets, Spaniards, old women in black fanned their cracked faces, men in grey shirts clutched walking sticks, began to emerge from the heat of the day. Dazed by the heavy air, locals sat on doorsteps, congregated in clearings, around bars. Others languished outside restaurants staring blankly at the traffic. Teenagers buzzed around on mopeds, gangly shirtless boys hunched over the handlebars, girlfriends clutching on behind. Grizzled men, unshaven, sat in bars watching football, drank flutes of beer, distracted only to eye women in the street or signal the barman.

Hale thought about the locals, their life. Thought about his own.

With Marta, it could have been different. In another time, things might have worked out for the better. Funny how situations, people, events are not always well aligned to deliver the outcome we wish. The Chaos theory at work, something like that. In Hale's life, things began predictably, normal, and then became convoluted, chaotic.

He could have met Marta at the bar, yes, but under different circumstances. He would be in the town to sail or go to the beach, nothing more. Could have been single, or perhaps younger, like the kids on the mopeds, or older, like the content old men on the street. At a different time, maybe family life with Lucy and Deborah would have worked and they'd immerse into Spanish life, integrate. A simple existence in a finca with a few goats and a cat or two, unremarkable, less stress and more contentment.

In another life, Hale could be like the locals back there in the towns. Sitting around, not doing much, sipping a beer, and he would be amongst them, holding hands with Marta. Making plans to go travelling, build a house, buy a boat, or settle in some little-known town up in the mountains.

But that was not this life. Inadvertently, this life had become complex, and now dangerous.

The evening was turning to night.

The sun, a burgeoning orange ball, sank down upon Málaga and Cádiz beyond, blasting Andalucía with sultry colour and light. The road climbed up to La Herradura, and then back inland a few hundred yards, and on to the quaint village of Maro, a modest yet prominent pueblo on the cliffs. Torrox was not far now, through some tunnels, twenty minutes maximum.

The traffic built. Beyond Nerja, Hale descended back down to the coast road, which filed along ordinary streets lined with bars, hotels, and apartment blocks. He tried to find the route, slowing to catch the names of roads, veering off at the last moment. Mopeds buzzed him like flies, youths hanging off precariously, waving, shouting, venting frustration at his wayward driving. He failed to remember the turnoff, a road leading north into the hills and to the home of dear friend, Rupert Lloyd-Evans. A lover of practical jokes, Rupert had clearly sensed that Hale was not the greatest navigator on roads (belying his abilities at sea), and thus, conveniently neglected to provide detailed directions to the concealed road heading inland. Thus, Hale cursed, pounded up and down Torrox Costa's main drag for a quarter of an hour. He'd retaliate later with extensive use of 'Rups', an abysmal abbreviation the ex-Professor of Economics hated.

With a taxi driver inches from his rear bumper, Hale happened upon the turning, Calle Rosal, a tiny street nestled between a fruit stall and a bar. He swung the car into the road.

This route did not accommodate conventional vehicles well. Potholes and crumbling concrete thrashed Dutch's suspension, and within ten yards, turned to hardened mud and pitch black as the track threaded into the hills.

"Shit. Christ."

Hale cursed continually as the Passat caught the edges of ditches or pitched onto rocks or fallen fence posts.

"You Bloody joker, Rups. Shit."

Higher up, the track led to a tarmac road, precarious in the night with sudden bends. Pitch black other than the distant twinkling lights of pueblos nestled in the hills and the orange glow of Torrox Costa receding in the rear-view mirror. Hale vaguely remembered the route into the mountains, wondered if Marta had made it. Should have called in earlier, but now may be a good time with another fifteen minutes' drive remaining. Check she arrived safely, confirm the route. He pulled over to the side, skidding to a halt on the broken asphalt, reached for his cell on the passenger seat. No signal. Peered through window into the blackness, down to the cluster of lights on the coast, and then up to the inky heavens sprayed with swathes of blinking stars. He crawled over the gearshift, out of the passenger door, surveying the scene in an enveloping silence broken only by his own breathing and the white noise of cicadas. Not long now. Talk to Rups, have a drink, see Marta, take stock.

Some headlights lower down caught Hale's attention. On the route he'd just taken. A car moving swiftly, taking the bends well, gear shifting and engine working with purpose. Just another car, thought Hale. But tired and hungry, rational thought eluded him. Something didn't add up. Who would be taking this route at such a pace, and to where? Only Rups' villa was up here plus a couple of farmers, and then the road meandered beyond towards Cómpeta. And there were better routes, so who would bother with this one? Morillo, or Happy Gary's boneheads on his trail? The cell phone. Maybe they could track it.

The car, now a few bends below, built momentum, roaring into the night. Hale launched himself back into the car, over the passenger seat, killed the headlights on the dashboard, and then fired the engine. Into first gear, the wheels spun on the broken asphalt, and then bit on tarmac, lurching the Passat forward into pitch black, the tail snaking wildly behind. Hale stooped forward over the dash, straining to see the road ahead. Sweat and dust ran into his eyes. He pursed his lips, hand hovering over the right stalk, the headlights' switch. If Morillo's gang caught him, he was dead, but he'd die in a ravine if he couldn't see.

He hit the headlights.

Rocks and scrub ahead, he veered away, smashed into a fence, jolting the car, slamming his head against the windscreen. The wheel whipped his hands away, lashing his finger, spraying blood across the windscreen. The engine revved, screamed out of control. Somehow, the car snaked back to the middle of the road. Now the rear-view mirror was brilliant white, flashing. They were all over him. So bright, he could hardly make out any form, any shape of vehicle or humans. His neck strained. Too much time fixed on the mirror. Looked ahead, trouble again as the car edged off the road, slamming into rubble, hardened mud, throwing dust up around him. Now the Passat was side-on, spinning in the road, slow motion. Hale looked across, the pursuers passed as he spun. Figures discernible in a split second. Two men in front amidst the dust and light, horn blowing, engine revving, screaming above the wail of screeching rubber on tarmac. Hale spun the wheel to no effect, the Passat whipped around another one-eighty degrees. He kept his foot to the floor remaining momentarily in a cloud of choking smoke, burning rubber. The pursuers had stopped in the road ahead, the tires of the Passat bit again, accelerating it at crazy speed. Hale shot past them again, stealing another glance, inhaling dust and smoke into the dryness of his choking lungs. Four men. Two in front, two in the rear, looked Spanish.

A hit squad. Morillo.

Hale swung around another bend. Shouted, "No!" Pulled the vehicle away from a sheer drop. The road was now winding, tight, becoming more precarious as they gained height. "You go off there, you're dead, fool, dead." Blood smeared across the steering wheel, slippery at first, and then sticky against the plastic grip. Morillos's gang were all over his bumper, veering, revving, sounding the horn.

The Passat's straining engine blasted their car with an eerie smokescreen illuminated by their full beam.

"Come on, how far? Give me the turning."

The track to Rupert's finca led off from this road, but how far and on which side, Hale could not recollect. On his last visit, Rups drove, and Hale was drunk on rum.

The split second lack of attention gifted his pursuers. Morillo's gang were now alongside. Hale swung the wheel, veering across, blocking them. A screech, they hit the brakes. A glimpse in the mirror and they were ten yards behind, and then more. Hale wheeled around another bend, leaning into the turn, losing the tail again. He threw the wheel to counter the oversteer, the wheels bit, saving him from a two hundred foot drop into blackness and certain death.

Morillo's car was on him again, now aggressive, pitching to overtake. Previously, their horn was intermittent, now it blasted continuously. Hale blocked them again, they span out. One-eighty degrees. Saw them in the rear-view. Their car was side-on in the road, stationery, smoke settling around.

Hale, smiled, let out a small cheer, looked ahead.

The slip road to Rupert's emerged to the left. He recognised it immediately, now he remembered. Marked by an abandoned fruit stall on the apex, the mud track led steeply down for a hundred yards, a track comprising rocks and potholes, accessible only by a 4x4. No time to back out. He pulled off left, headed towards the crest and entry to the track. Headlights emerged from the bend behind, shafts of light searching through the dust. Hale gritted his teeth, bracing for the impending bone-jarring impact of rock on metal when the Passat grounded.

A split second thought changed everything.

A surge of electricity ran through his head, an adrenaline-fuelled reasoning tore at his mind as the vehicle shot towards the apex. To go down the track would lead Morillo to Rupert. Worse, to go down the track would lead Morillo to Marta.

Hale wrenched the wheel right. The car heaved on the suspension. A tire blew as he struck a rock the size of a football. The engine screamed out of control, Hale was whipped away from the wheel, slammed back in his seat. Smoke, dust, a glimpse of the fruit stall ahead. Hale picked out the individual planking, the nails, the faded 'Fruta' markings in a slow motion nightmare.

And then the impact.

A flash and muffled shot released the airbag, slamming into Hale's face. He slumped forward, a rag doll out cold for seconds, and then came around, looked across to his right, neck stiff and aching. Morillo's car skidded to a halt, throwing stones against the metal of Dutch's trashed Passat.

His pursuers' car remained there. Still. Engine ticking over, dust settling around.

THIRTY-SEVEN

Drowsy, Hale unclipped his seat belt, lifted his gaze to the driver in the car. Out of focus. He'd have to clamber out of the passenger door to escape. If it opened. He'd then have to sprint ahead into the blackness, out of sight, if his legs were uninjured. Difficult to tell, he was numb, dazed. Morillo would hunt him down, four against one.

A shriek of laughter and a thump against the driver's door snapped him out of oblivion. He looked down. A bottle of beer glugged out into the dirt, he smelled the alcohol, looked up.

This was not Morillo. A youngster, barely twenty, waved from the driver's seat. Maddened eyes, stoned, jet-black hair, dark skin. In the rear, another youth hung out, shouting obscenities, a girl behind him screeching something, waving her fist. Then revving, violent revving that made their car rock with the torque of the engine. These were kids, petrolheads out in the hills for mischief.

The driver released the clutch, the car swung around, and he held it in the dirt, spraying the Passat and Hale with grit and stones, smashing into his face. He ducked down, across to the passenger side, closed his eyes until the noise of the engine and laughter faded into a distant roar as his pursuers climbed the roads into the night.

Hale remained motionless for another minute. Stupid, he thought. How could he be so stupid? He'd seen four men, Morillo's men in that car. But that was paranoia, fatigue. He'd imagined it. There was a girl in the back. Stupid.

A stench of fuel galvanised him to move. He pushed the sagging remnants of the airbags aside, crawled out, and rose to his feet. The noise of cicadas and stillness of the night returned. He opened the boot, grabbed his bag, unzipped it and pulled out the first piece of material to hand: a white sock. He wrapped it around his finger, now caked in blood and dirt. He abandoned the wreck, descended down the track, stumbling over boulders and rocks towards Rupert's finca.

Hale's eyes adjusted. He could make out the track, but not much else. To the left, a dirt ridge rose up to dense foliage. To the right, a gully filled with olive trees. Ahead, black nothingness. A dog barked, deep and throaty, echoing in the night, the sound building with Hale's approach. He spotted the tail end of a 4x4 in a driveway, and Rupert's finca amid the shrubs and trees beyond. The dog barked louder, sounding from the rear of the property, resonating. A light flicked on. Hale walked down the darkened path, knocked on the door with his fist.

Bolts clunked for an instant, and then the door swung open with a creak. Rupert stood with a pipe hanging from the corner of his mouth, a large brass lighter in one hand. Sixties, his thinning grey hair, neatly trimmed beard, half-moon spectacles, and studious air were at odds with his brash Hawaiian shirt, chinos, and sandals. Short and portly, his eyes were sharp, inquisitive, but kindly.

"Charles, at last. Come in, come in." Not one to fuss with handshakes or hugs, Rupert ushered Hale into the hallway and wandered ahead into the lounge, fussing, and snatching at the lighter to ignite the tobacco leaves sticking out of the pipe. "Dog was driving me bonkers, knew you were coming," he said. "Damn heat, God this place is not for the faint-hearted." A few yards in, Rupert turned to look at Hale, eyed him over his spectacles. "Crikey, man. Which bramble bush have you been dragged through? You look like you been keel-hauled and thrown to the lions."

"Thanks, Rups."

"Don't mention it," Rupert said, returning his attention to his pipe.

Marta emerged from a bedroom, stood looking tired, eyes drawn. She wore a black dress. Almost too much for Hale as he took in her beauty. Her hand rose to cover her mouth, conceal her shock. "Charles, what happened to you? Your hand, your face."

Hale dropped his bag to the floor, felt emotion well up. A tear rolled down his cheek. Marta moved close, threw her arms around his chest.

Rupert, honourable enough not to goad, broke the tension, grabbed Hale's bag. "Look, you youngsters go and sort yourselves out," he said. "I'll throw this bag in the room and leave you to it for a couple of hours. Help yourself to the house."

"Thanks, Rups," said Hale, embarrassed, trying not to blub in the presence of an old friend.

"Think nothing of it," Rupert called, from the bedroom. "I'm going to dine with Humphrey. Then, Charlie, we'll have a chat later."

Hale clung to Marta, one arm around her waist, his other hand swiftly wiping the tear with the heel of his hand before Rupert noticed. He tried not to croak, tried to disguise his emotional state, "Ah, Humphrey, and how is the old man?"

Rupert re-emerged from the bedroom, wheezing, pipe waggling from the corner of his mouth, "Oh, he's fine, temperamental old sod that he is. Took him to the vet and he wouldn't take his damn medicine, same old stuff."

"Bit like you then."

"Probably. So, anyway, let's have that chat later, Charles, because I have the notion that you and your delightful friend here will need to scarper tomorrow morning, rather sharpish."

"I see."

"Nothing to do with me, you understand. Nice to have company of course." Rupert gave Hale a look above his spectacles, a look reserved for rare moments of seriousness. "It's just that various things seem to have *transpired* since your hasty S.O.S. call."

"I understand. Thanks, Rups."

"Don't mention it." Rupert walked off, down some steps into a sunken living room overlooking a concrete porch and garden beyond. He called out again, "And there's some Betadine in the bathroom, wash that wound for cripes sake. Loads of food in the kitchen, get stuck in." His voice faded as he disappeared outside.

Marta washed the wound and dressed it. A deep gash on the side of the middle finger, a case for sutures, but no time for that. Hale showered, holding his hand out of the water, dressed into fresh clothes and joined Marta in the kitchen. Nice kitchen. Rupert seemed to have it all worked out. A finca, beautifully rustic Andalucían style, stone floors, and Moorish furniture. Set in the hills, cool, and above all, private. Having lived in Spain for over a decade, Rups seemed to occupy himself by writing and painting, and kept the company of various obscure friends, some local Spanish, a few Brits, none of them known to Hale. Plus of course, Humphrey, the pampered old black Labrador. No wife or kids, the unfortunate conclusion of turbulent relationships gone by. A touchy subject that Rups rarely broached.

Marta and Hale stood either side of the breakfast bar, saying little, knowing that this was not the time for deep discussions, questions about the near future, about Morillo and the dangers. Too tired, too late. Nevertheless, Marta quietly mentioned one thing. "There was a problem," she said, handing Hale a plate stacked with tortilla, peppers, bread, and Russian salad. He contemplated the feast for a moment, savoured it, drinking deep from a glass of ice water.

"A problem?"

"At the bus station. Your friend, Rupert, he pick me up, but we were followed."

Hale returned the glass to the table, frowned, "Do you know by who?"

She shook her head.

"They followed you in a car?"

She nodded.

"But you lost them?"

She nodded again. Hale preferred not to pry further, though he sensed there was more to the story, and to the reason why Rups suggested they 'scarper' tomorrow.

"Rupert will tell you about it," she said, sweeping her hair across her shoulder. "I am tired, must go to bed now. You should talk to your friend, he will explain. He is kind man. I thank him that he help me."

Hale nodded, held her hand until she moved away, extending her arm until gently releasing her grip.

Midnight.

Hale and Rupert sat on the porch, both cradling shots of rum, *Ron Arehucas*. Rupert puffed his pipe. Humprey slumped on the floor beside them, occasionally twitching in his sleep or snapping awake in response to the barks of distant wild dogs from the surrounding hills.

"You haven't quit the smoking I see then, Rups," said Hale, leaning back in the chair, letting the rum work into his bloodstream, relaxed for the first time since leaving Puerto de Santa María.

"Keeps the mozzies away, old boy. A pipe and the rum are my vices I'm afraid." Rupert shifted in his seat, tapped his pipe on the armchair, something on his mind. "Charles, I know from your call and hasty explanations that you're in a barrel load of the old merde at present. So, I won't pry, nothing worse, but it seems your dusky maiden had some friends in pursuit."

"So I'm told."

"Mm, I picked her up from the bus depot. Striking girl, spotted her straight away. Those legs…"

"Behave."

"Sorry. Bad form, won't happen again. Anyway," Rupert looked sheepish, smiled at Hale, continued, "I happened to spot a couple of chaps seated in a white Audi. Powerful car, actually. Wouldn't have noticed anywhere else, but I know that depot like the back of my hand. Drop the gardeners off there all the time."

"Get a look at them?"

"Mm, yes. Not Spanish. European maybe."

"Russian, Eastern Bloc?"

"Possibly. Anyway, we set off in the 4x4 and they were certainly tailing us. Quite professional, knew what they were about. As I say, wouldn't have noticed normally, but when they were still hanging off us out of town, I smelt a rat." Rupert paused, swilled rum about in his glass, clinking the diminishing ice within.

"So what happened?" said Hale, frowning. Rups the great storyteller, loved suspense.

"Well obviously I couldn't lead them back here on the usual road, so took them the scenic route."

"The one I came up," said Hale. "Calle Rosal?"

"Yes, that's the one."

"And?"

"Took them on a flying lesson."

Hale closed his eyes, looked to the ceiling, "Shit. The bend of death?"

"That's it, *Horquilla de la muerte*. They didn't see it coming. You see, Charles, they became aggressive, climbing all over my bloody bumper. Your lady was agitated, bad show all round, so I floored it going down into the bend, and then pulled across to the wrong side of the road. Then off they went. Ears are still ringing from the girl's scream in my ear, but job done."

"Christ, Rups." Hale knocked back the dregs of rum in his glass, looked across to Rupert, who appeared unruffled. "Straight down the ravine?"

"Yep, three hundred feet. They're a gonna. Saw it in the mirror."

"Anyone around … anyone see it?"

Rupert scoffed, leaned forward, stroking Humphrey's glistening coat, "God, no. Not a soul around. The land below is owned by Alberto, a farmer with one eye and he's hard of hearing. Doubt he'd see or hear much, and besides, he's seen a few flyers in his time on that bend. Practically a spectator sport for him."

"So, what happens now?"

"Oh, dear boy, please relax. The usual. Alberto phones it in, Policía drop by. They sit around in the shade drinking coffee and that one-euro wine they sell around here. They'll bitch about the mayor, football team and so on. Then call in the investigators. Eventually, a truck rumbles up the road to haul it out of the bloody ditch. But, of course, depends who's around and what's on. You know how laid-back they are around here. Probably make a news item on the telly, day after tomorrow I'd say."

Hale breathed deeply, let out a sigh, "*Okay*, right."

"Look Charlie," said Rupert, shifting his position to speak directly at Hale. "So, you've got the bloody Stasi or Christ knows who after you, and there's other nonsense going on that I can't fathom, so what do you say we top up the glasses and get to the bottom of this caper you're involved with? Quite frankly, I like all this stuff. Gets boring all the way up here for Humphrey and me."

"You're bonkers."

Rupert smiled, "Well I'm a writer these days, need some inspiration." He grabbed the glasses, retired to the drinks cabinet situated conveniently close behind. "So," he continued, rooting through the bottles. "You knock on my door looking like you've been in a punch-up on the Lions' tour of South Africa. How the hell did you get here?"

"Car hire from the marina. I trashed it after some bloody joy riders decided to play stock cars with me. A write off, unfortunately."

"Joy riders and not your pursuers?"

"Nope, just kids racing around. Definitely Spanish."

Rupert laughed, "Well, doesn't surprise me. Your driving was never up to much."

"Thanks."

"Pleasure," said Rupert, returning to his chair, shoving a drink into Hale's hand. "And where might this wreckage be now?"

"End of your road, if *road* is what you call it. Near the fruit stall. Correction, now part of the fruit stall."

Rupert frowned, "Hell, really?" He grabbed his cell phone, tapped away at it, and then peered over his spectacles to the bottom of the garden. "Better get the gardeners to sort it out, don't want to cause a stir and all that."

Twenty yards away at the foot of the garden, a ringtone sounded and a light illuminated a window of a flat-roofed white building. Rupert gabbled Spanish into the cell. Seconds later, two men emerged from the building, walking in the darkness along a path boarded by thick shrubs and hibiscus. One of the figures waved. Then both loped on towards the garage.

Hale waited until they were out of sight, and then said, "What do you do here, Rups?"

Rupert placed the cell on the nearby coffee table. "Thought we were talking about you," he said. "Much more interesting."

"The night is young."

"Indeed it is," said Rupert, bashing the side of his pipe against the chair, letting tobacco fall onto the stone. "Well, writing the damn book of course, painting."

"Yes, caught a glimpse in your room, nice work."

"Watercolours, bitch to master."

The 4x4's engine sounded from the front of the finca. A slip of tires on gravel, and then it took off.

"So, you left the college, what, a decade ago?" continued Hale. "That was a few years after I finished the course. Then you came out here after that thing…"

"Mm, nasty business," said Rupert. "Of course, you were just another student in my class back then. You didn't know the gossip and so on."

"No, they had it in for you … about that girl?"

"Well, admittedly, she was one of my pupils, twenty four year-old stunner. But it wasn't really the professional conduct thing they had a problem with, Charles. It was those turgid old fools in the college. Jealousy, you see." He lit his pipe, puffing away until an orange glow lit the tobacco. A glimmer of bitterness in his eyes.

"That's life I guess," said Hale. "So, they ditched you, and then you picked up the redundancy and some inheritance, and escaped out here for a new life in Andalucía."

"Partly true. It wasn't strictly *redundancy*. They paid me off, Charles, to avoid a court case and publicity. Frankly, redundancy would have paid better, but it wasn't just that. You remember that Hollingsworth chap? Dipped his finger into the candy jar a bit too often. He knew I knew about the artistic side of his bookkeeping."

"Well, you were the Professor of Economics for chrissakes. On the board of directors, *and* with access to the college books I assume."

"Quite correct. Not his finest hour. He should have guessed I'd rumble him, but I kept a lid on it. Ashamedly, I used our little secret later to keep him off my back. That was until they uncovered what they deemed to be *the scandal*. Silly old goats."

Hale was shot, his eyes heavy, but enjoying the measured drift into numbness. Rupert, wily and coy, rarely opened up, but here was a chance Hale would not squander. "So, the money got you this place, but I see it's expanded over the years, Rups. Fancy jeeps, land, staff. Where'd the rest come from?"

"Oh, you know, I dabble. Fingers in a few pies out here. Also, do a bit of writing related to the college, economics. A bit like your course, dull as hell. Speaking of which, you still with that shower at Tower Hill?"

Hale sensed Rupert's deft change of direction. "Sure am."

"What's that chap's name?"

"Martin Stack."

"That's him. Total clod. Tried to work with us at the college, but for no money, usual story."

"I had to wrap his knuckles a bit recently. Enjoyed it," said Hale.

"Good man, that's the spirit."

Hale brought Rupert back on track, "And those gardeners, Rups. Not much land here."

"Oh, hell, Charles, I help them out with a bit of business here and there. They look after the place when I'm back in Britain, that sort of stuff. I mean Humphrey gets on with them, don't you Humphs." Rupert nudged the dog with his foot. Humphrey exuded a grunt, uninterested.

Hale rose, still holding his drink, paced about the porch, looked out to the distant glow of light rising up from the coastline ten miles away.

"I'm in trouble, Rups."

Rupert scoffed, "Ah, Charles Hale, always was the master of understatement."

"I'm serious."

"And I don't need to be a psychologist to ascertain that you, sire, are in the centre of a busload of cow dung."

"I've got into some bad stuff over the years, Rups. Bad people."

"Excellent, now we're getting down to it. How bad?"

"Let's just say I got involved in the *transportation* business. At sea."

Rupert sucked on his pipe, looked skyward, thinking. "Ah, and let me hazard a guess as to what one might be transporting in these parts?"

"Please do."

"Charles, I'm a polite old fellow as you know, so shall we just call this said cargo 'stuff'?"

"Fine by me," said Hale, emptying his glass, taking a refill from the bottle on the table.

"Motive?" said Rupert.

"Debt."

"Ballpark?"

Hale paused, figures running through his mind. "Getting on for a couple of hundred thousand. Loans, credits cards, other stuff," he said. "Give or take twenty K."

"Cripes."

Hale leaned against a wooden post, his back to Rupert, wiped sweat from his forehead. The heat of the land still engulfed the finca, the night rich with the scent of jasmine.

Rupert rustled about for a moment, staggered to his feet, and then joined Hale at the lookout. Humphrey stirred, rose, plodded out into the garden, yawning, sniffing plants. "Look Charles," said Rupert. "Everyone's into some sort of thing, especially out here. Job to meet someone who isn't corrupt, stoned, drunk, or all three. Look at the governments around the world, the bent politicians, billionaire ponzi fraudsters, drug barons, sex tourists, and gangsters. Who really *is* straight, Charles? The problem with you, son, is that you're deluded enough to think you're straight as a die. The sooner you realise you're no Little Red Riding Hood, the sooner you can deal with your dilemma, face up."

Hale sighed, shrugged, "You're right, Rups ... I guess."

Rupert smiled, patted him on the shoulder. "Good man. Now, you mentioned something about that incident ... on the boat, what do you call her?"

"*Blue Too*."

"That's the one, odd name. Now, you say this chap fell into the briny and he was part of your *stuff* transportation business. That right?"

"Yep, one of the crew. Dead."

"Yes, saw a clip on the news. Fascinating, made a good story." Rupert grabbed Hale's glass. "Come on, old fellow, let's top these up, and then you can let me know the details. We'll get to the bottom of this, so do take a seat."

Hale paused, felt better. Needed a release, to open the floodgates of pent-up worry and stress.

Rupert filled the glasses.

Hale took a seat.

THIRTY-EIGHT

"It got ugly, Rups," said Hale, slurring.

"These things invariably do, especially where stuff is involved," replied Rupert, throwing peanuts at Humphrey who snapped at them with his jaw, catching them mid-flight.

Hale continued, "I was hanging around on the boat, not doing much, and then Dean called me over to the scene in a panic."

"Dean?"

"Crew. Scrawny runtish guy, never liked him."

"Mm, know the type. Go on."

Hale took another slug, continued, "Well, Gibby was in the water when I turned up. Hell of a state, pissed, puking, drowning, not good."

"Common story. Brit gets drunk, falls in the drink, dies."

"Indeed. Then I start flapping around like an old woman at a tea party. Pulling at him, calling out, that sort of thing. Trouble is, he was a dead weight, and I was wedged on a tiny platform on the stern of this gin palace stinkboat."

"Where was runtface during these heroics?"

"He was hanging between the motorboat and the ketch, couldn't get into position, too high up. Then Jack turned up on the wharf."

"*Ah*, the not-so-mysterious Scot, Jack. Met him once, didn't I?"

"Yep, that's him, Jack Weir. Anyway, he climbed aboard the ketch, grabbed a boathook, and sent Dean to get help."

"Strong boathook was it?"

"*Exactly* my thought at the time. He had no angle, and what the hell would he do with a boathook anyway, other than to drag a dead body alongside? Then – you won't believe this – Jack casually lights up and starts lecturing me."

"I believe it. Go on."

Hale shook his head, remembering the moments as if they occurred an hour ago. "To cut a long story short, Rups, he implied that I should let him go."

"Cripes. Doesn't surprise me though. And did you?"

Hale eyed Rupert, and then lowered his gaze to the floor, pondering an answer. The learned professor would sense anything other than the truth. "Let's just say I didn't push him down, and ..."

Rupert raised his eyebrows, "And?"

"Well, I didn't exactly help him up either."

Rupert sighed, leaned back in his chair, and then said, "Well that'll go down well with the judge, Charles. *I didn't push him under, Your Honour, honest.*"

"Be serious for a moment, Rups. Gibby was a problem, real trouble. He was aware that Jack and Dean had been skimming cash from their boss, a guy from Marbella called Happy Gary. Know of him?"

"Oh *him*, of course," said Rupert. "Crooked wideboy, total airhead, but dangerous as hell. Seems to elude the authorities, God only knows how, as he's as visible as a bloody fireworks display."

"My impression too, though I haven't had the pleasure of making his acquaintance. Well anyway, Gibby was going to let the cat out of the bag, but for me, that wasn't the main issue. On the ketch, Jack was goading, reminding me of Gibby's trait: heavy handedness with women. Just a few days before, he'd been beating up on some girl from the bar."

Rupert shook his head. "Big problem out here with the domestic violence and all that, but foreigners getting stuck in as well ... that's not clever."

"Precisely. I saw red, especially when Jack revealed a few truths about other trips to Melilla. Apparently, it went on over there when this shithead was unleashed on the local girls, the ages of whom, I shudder to think."

"Bad business, Charles. Money and stuff transportation is one thing, but that behaviour ..."

"Yep, so there was Jack smoking, relaxing on the ketch as if he was in his local boozer, and encouraging me to let Gibby go."

"So you let him go. Good riddance and all that?"

"As I say, Rups, I didn't exactly help him up, and by the time Dean returned, he was a gonna."

Rupert slapped his thigh, making Humphrey twitch, and then said theatrically, "Your Honour, I have some unsubstantiated notion that this rogue, with whom I was engaged in the stuff transportation business, beat up on women and girls and was going to grass to our bent boss, therein informing him that my equally roguish associates – namely, runtface and Mr Weir – had skimmed money from him, money that was dirty in the first place. Thus, I felt it appropriate, Your Honour, not to push this scoundrel down into the murk, but not exactly help him up either."

"Give me a break, Rups."

"Just, weighing it up, Charles. Don't think it would wash, do you?"

"That's not quite the end of it."

"Really? Marvellous. What d'ya say we have one for the road and you finish your tale in style?"

"Go on then," said Hale, handing him the glass.

Rupert walked off, swaying somewhat. Hale managed a smile at the English eccentric.

"It does seem to me, old boy," called Rupert, "that you are in a bit of a quagmire, but let me and old Humphs put our minds around it for you."

Rupert returned with another two glasses clinking with ice as Hale continued, "So, we got hauled in by the Guardia of course, and next day interrogated by the Inspectora Jefa."

"Name?"

"María Díez."

Rupert shook his head, frowned. "Strange, never heard of her," he said. "Should have. Know the other inspectors in the region."

"She's down from Madrid apparently, working on this kind of business."

"The business of stuff transportation?"

"Yes. Seems to hold weight, tough cookie, that's my impression," said Hale.

"Attractive?"

"Very."

"Yikes, almost tempting to get arrested."

"I wouldn't if I were you," said Hale. "She'll fry your balls."

Rupert feigned a shiver. "Perish the thought ... and so *after* the interview?"

"Not much, really. Appears they had nothing on us, let us go the next day. But that's not really the issue. What I was getting around to is that Jack and I were being watched."

"During Mr Gibby's demise?"

Hale nodded.

"Egads, that's tricky. And whom might our voyeur be?"

Hale stretched his arms behind his head, closed his eyes for a moment, and then slumped back down, "Some little Belgium shit aboard the ketch Jack was standing on."

"Gosh. Know the man?"

"Mm, seen him about the marina, nasty little short thing with greasy hair, fifties. Has some stupid made-up name: Zac or Zick or something."

"Shall we call him Zit?"

"Perfect. Anyway, it seems that Zit chartered the yacht from a Dutch couple who supposedly developed some daft cabin fever thing. A phobia I guess. They'd rented an apartment to get onto dry land, and unbeknown to me, left this seedy character skulking around on the ketch. I'd known of him when he was on another yacht – now sold – with his wife. I say *wife*, but it was a grubby situation. He'd effectively bought her over the Internet. *Mail order brides* I think they call them. She was Taiwanese, something like that. Anyway, she always looked unhappy, hanging around his boat, cleaning the decks, polishing the steel, getting the shopping and whatnot."

"Effectively his slave," said Rupert.

"Seems that way. And the real blow is that, like Gibby, I reckon he could be heavy handed."

"Evidence?"

"Swollen black eye one day."

"So, Zit's a real shitbrain too."

"Yep, and with that in mind, I wasn't in best mood to be lenient with this brand of smalldick. So, can you now comprehend why I didn't exactly help Gibby up?"

"Absolutely," said Rupert, nodding. "So, was the 'wife' on board the ketch when you were teaching Mr Gibby to scuba dive?"

"Probably, but it seems that Zit was peering through a porthole lower down by the waterline. So he would have seen everything, maybe heard too. Thin glass fibre hulls these days."

"How would you know?"

"Next day, after we'd returned from the Guardia interviews in San Isidro, Zit was hanging around on the wharf. Every time I passed by, he'd come up and taunt me with some stupid comment, giving me knowing winks, nods, that sort of thing. I thought I'd let it go, but then he amped it up by saying he'd keep his mouth shut about *the accident* if I did some work for him."

"What kind of work?"

"Didn't say, but the slime was into all sorts of rackets. A cokehead too. You can just imagine."

"Not the ideal employer."

"Quite. Makes Happy Gary seem like Peter Pan."

"You try to negotiate with this cretin?"

"Well," said Hale, shifting awkwardly in his seat, "*negotiate* is perhaps too sophisticated a term for my actions, but hell, I was tired."

Rupert did his old trick: raised his eyebrows, waited silently for a reply, swilling his rum around in bottom of the glass. "Well?" he said, finally.

Hale sighed, "Christ, I explained to Dean that we had a bit of a problem with Zit. Told him to pay him off with something, anything, to keep the little creep's mouth shut. Dean, being a coke-snorting pothead himself, suggested he gift some of his stash to Zit for the purpose. I never wanted any of that crap on the boat anyway."

"My God, Charles Hale, the master tactician at work," said Rupert, and then theatrically, "Your Honour, I thought it prudent to pay one crackhead off with another, thus silencing the wife beater who witnessed the semi-enforced drowning of my colleague, the drunken stuff smuggler."

"Oh Rups, do back off. As I say, I was tired, not thinking straight."

"I'll say," Rupert laughed. "So, how were Dean's negotiating skills?"

"Not refined."

"How did I guess?"

"Bit of a screw up," said Hale, "and yet strangely gratifying."

"Really?" said Rupert, beaming. "Do go on, we're loving this, Humphs, aren't we?"

"Well, Dean hated Zit even more than me. Seemed to relish the opportunity to pay him a visit when I was away in the shower block. Needless to say, he didn't take an ounce of stuff along for the negotiation, and subtly not being his strongpoint, went on board the ketch, grabbed a pair of mulgrips, and proceeded to remodel Zit's nose with them."

"Impressed. Using his initiative."

"Yes, well I can't stand the sight of Dean as I've mentioned, but I had to take my hat off to him on this one. Never heard a peep out of Zit after that."

"And the wife, or shall I say, *slave?*" said Rupert.

"Still with him I think, but last I saw of them was in the supermarket near the main road out of town. He had some extensive bandaging around his head and a plastic tube thing sticking out of his nose."

"Dean did the business then."

"Yes. And the best thing was that Zit pushed the trolley around, while his wife was zipping around looking quite chipper. Maybe Dean threatened Zit with a follow up nose job, I didn't like to ask."

Rupert's chest heaved trying to contain his laughter, seemed then to change the subject to avoid breaking into hysterics. "So, this young lady, Marta," he said, playing with his pipe once more, loading it with tobacco. "What's the story there, and who the hell were these goons crawling all over my arse this morning?"

Hale paused, mulled the sequence of events, and then said, "We had a thing back at the marina ... the trip before this one."

"Mm, I see. And Lucy?"

"Been a bit rocky between us for some time."

"Yes, sensed that. Nice enough when I met her that time, seemed distracted though. Spain not her thing."

"No, she hangs around with a couple of dullards from Nerja. Also, her ex-husband, Ralph, pitched up recently believe it or not ... on the pretence of coming out to play golf. They congregate with other Brits, mostly drinkers, go to English bars, that sort of thing."

"Sounds inspiring."

"Yes, awkward as hell for me. Worse thing is, Deborah ... she's a nice kid, we get on."

Rupert lit his pipe puffed it thoughtfully, "Kids, always the most tricky in these situations, Charles. That's not going to get easier, you know that don't you?"

"I do. And I'm concerned that this whole thing may get back to Lucy and Deborah somehow."

Rupert nodded gravely, said nothing.

Hale turned to him, serious now, "Those people in the car following you, I believe they're connected to a big shot from San Isidro called Berto Morillo."

"Know of him," said Rupert, "but you continue."

"Long story," said Hale. "Basically, he employed Marta, but the way he works is through protection rackets, intimidation, that sort of thing. She hates him, terrified, but he *wants* her. Deluded enough to think she'll be his wife probably. I didn't know of the guy until I escorted her back to her place in San Isidro. Creepy area of town, I got mugged on the way back by three nutters. Some lowlife called Enzo was the ringleader. He hung around Marta's apartment, made the connection with me when I was seen around there. Later, this got back to Morillo."

"So, this Enzo is now tracking you down, keeping an eye on the girl, and you?" asked Rupert.

"Was. Now he's dead, and seems to have been replaced by some character of equal intelligence, Eastern European."

Rupert nodded. "Adds up," he said. "Those two tailing me would have been from Morillo's lot. You see, Morillo isn't the big shot you think he is, Charles. I've read about him over the years in the papers, but learned more on the grapevine to be honest. He calls himself a businessman, but in fact, his property development outfit is just a cover. He operates a system over Almería way – coerces local businesses, backhands authority figures, the mayor, the Guardia, that kind of sinister stuff, mafia-style. But he's really just a poodle to the Russian mob. Nasty bunch led by a short-arsed bully called Sergei Karzhov, a relic of the KGB. I'd say he's responsible for sending the goons in the car. Morillo is weak, just a pawn whom Karzhov uses to mediate, work his way into the system out here. Morillo's deluded enough to believe he has some long-lived position or status through these endeavours. He's always having his photograph taken with damn government figures, celebs and footballers. Makes me puke, but Karzhov looks at the bigger picture. He has an international network spanning France, Italy, Britain, out to the Caribbean, South America. Almería is just playtime for him at the moment. From there, he's expanding east and he'll know people around here already. Drug runners in Marbella, pimps, organised crime. He kills anyone deemed to be out of line, or surplus to requirement. My guess is Morillo will be on his list before long."

"Not good for Marta and me," said Hale. "To add to my woes, the mugger, Enzo, stole my wallet with business cards, addresses, and numbers in it. If they do some digging around, these could potentially connect them to Lucy and Deborah."

Rupert shook his head. "Not good, son."

"And this guy ... Happy Gary. Jack and Dean were talking him up, maybe to intimidate me," said Hale.

"Different creature," said Rupert. "He's just a money man, small fry compared to Karzhov, more on Morillo's level. Thinks he can make some sort of bizarre mark in the world, and if that mark is tainted by corruption or jail time, it doesn't seem to bother him. Potentially, it sounds like you could run from Mr Happy, go back to Britain. He'll have little influence there, forget the whole thing if you lie low."

"Could do the same with Karzhov. Maybe change my name, hide out?"

"Possibly, but something doesn't add up." Rupert looked up thoughtfully for a moment, and then said, "You must have ruffled his feathers somehow, can't just be the girl, the jealousy thing. Seems like they hold you in some kind of respect, standing. Maybe they deem you as some sort of hotshot on the loose. Perhaps you now have a reputation as someone slippery, a useful criminal ... *if* they can control you."

"I'm not sure that's their view."

"You'd be surprised. You seem to be leaving a string of incidents – and now bodies – in your wake."

"Great."

"And this Díez woman appears to be throwing the kitchen sink at you. Maybe she thinks you're a Brit version of Karzhov, something like that."

"You're scaring me, Rups."

"Just trying to get into people's heads, Charles. Everybody seems to want a piece of the action when you turn up. Strangely, all seems to have kicked off after this ding-dong with Marta. On the beach you say?"

"I'll spare you the details, Rups, if you don't mind," said Hale. "Though I know you'd love to hear them."

"Mm, shame."

Rupert heaved himself out of his seat, wandered over to the edge of the porch, looked at his watch. "Well, that was a damn good natter, Charles. Very enlightening, bit worrying to be honest. But I think Humphs and I are going to turn in and mull it over."

"You're right, Rups," said Hale. "I'm beat."

Hale rose, motioned to leave.

"Before you go," said Rupert, still looking out to the blackness, "let me give you a helping hand."

"Yes?"

"Tomorrow morning, early, take the jeep, not the 4x4, the other thing. Head somewhere away from here and lie low as we discussed. I have your Spanish cell number, and I'll give you a ring pronto if I come up with anything. Tricky, I have to say. Tricky, son."

"I know, Rups, it's a mess. Thanks for the jeep. You don't need it?"

"It's just the gardeners'. Bit of a wreck, watch it on the bends."

"I will. Appreciate it."

"Don't mention it. I won't bother to see you out and all that, just get up with the birds and be gone."

"Okay," said Hale, turning to leave. He paused for a moment. The two old friends said nothing in the silence, until Hale broke it, "I'm scared, Rups."

"I know, son. Life sometimes leads us down these sorry roads. You could return home, come clean, but it will get murky. You're implicated in some business that could see you inside for years. Some kid lawyer for the prosecution, looking to impress. Could wrap you up with Mr Happy's circus, blame you for Gibson's drunken scuba diving adventure, and link you with a string of stuff transportation escapades you weren't even aware of."

"I'll run with Marta."

"Best way," said Rupert, turning, eyeing Hale. "Let it all blow over for a while, return to Britain, and see how it pans out. Got anyone you can depend on over there?"

"Baz."

"You're still in touch, excellent. Good chap, Baz. Knew his father, military man."

"Yep. Baz knows something's up. The debts and all that, but of course I don't let on too much. He normally reverts to rugger tales anyway, gets bored easily."

Rupert laughed, scratched his beard.

"His father," Hale said. "What regiment?"

"Paras, then Special Forces I believe. Always on aircraft shooting around the world. If only they had air miles back then. He used to regale eye-watering tales when I knew him, quite the storyteller. Problem was, he was cunning, even when blind drunk … you never knew whether the stories of his daring raids were factual or a load of bloody hokum. Probably the latter, swine that he was."

"Yep, and Baz seems to take after him somewhat," said Hale.

"Oh, undoubtedly, I would imagine."

"Tell me, Rups, you know anything about Baz? His dad say anything about his work?"

"You mean army stuff?"

"Mm."

"Well, as far as I'm aware, Daddy owns a big outfit running private security services, international consultancy that sort of thing. Private Military Companies they call them … PMCs."

"Mercenaries."

"He'd probably slap you if you said that to his face, but yes. They dress it up with corporate baloney to provide training courses in hostile regions, but essentially, they are guns for hire."

"Baz doesn't broach the subject, doesn't go near it … even with me. You reckon he's involved?" said Hale.

"I would guess so. And it doesn't surprise me that he's tight-lipped. It's a funny business, lucrative too. They have offices in London, Hereford, around the world. They say it's all legit, but I'm convinced some things are swept under the carpet … too uncomfortable to divulge politically." Rupert knocked back the last few millimetres remaining in his glass. "Christ, I'm sounding like a bloody conspiracy theorist."

They strolled back into the house.

Rupert placed his hand on Hale's shoulder, and then said, "You know, Charles, I've been coming out here long enough to know that the likes of Karzhov and Mr Happy come and go. If it's not one mobster, it's another. Stay around long enough and they eat themselves. Get greedy, someone sees them off, or they end up in the clink. In the long run, it's not tourists of their creed that worry me so much. There will be a way for you to hide from them, pay someone off, or simply wait long enough until they disappear down the cesspit of their own creation. But it's María Díez, and this local thing that worries me."

Hale frowned, "Not sure I'm following you, Rups."

"Unless you've forgotten, you're in Andalucía, Charles. Stigma doesn't die in these parts. My concern is that if you raise your profile inadvertently – say to the lofty levels of Mr Happy – you're labelled for good. The people around here will never forget. You'll find that even if you run to some remote goddamn sun-ravaged town in the middle of the desert – somewhere you happened upon that no one knows – the women, the kids, the Guardia, even the old timers playing dominos, will give you a certain look. A look that says word had spread and that you, Charles Hale, are now a threat, disrespectful to the very fabric of their local life, their culture. And that's the bit that worries me. You'll never be able to come back here. Should you dare, someday there'll be a body found in the hills, and not much else said about it other than a small news item in the bottom of a local rag. And that'll be the end of Charles Hale."

Hale looked down at his feet, absorbing the graveness of Rupert's words.

"I understand, Rups. I'll sort this out."

"I know you will, son," said Rupert, grabbing Hale's hand, shaking it vigorously, looking into his eyes. "Go tomorrow. Go early, and run."

THIRTY-NINE

8:23 a.m.

Marta drove the open-top jeep. Hale nursed a hangover in the passenger seat wearing mandatory sunglasses. They twisted down the mountain roads, around rubble-strewn arid hills interspersed with shrubbery, farmland, and olive groves tended by old men in straw hats prodding goats with crooked sticks. Hale didn't say much, admired the scenery. How a sunny morning in Andalucía can make everything seem okay.

But not for long.

The first problem was Rupert's jeep. Bright yellow, albeit battered and rusty, it was in line with his taste in Hawaiian shirts: loud. The open design of the vehicle was not the height of discretion, and neither was the beautiful woman in the driver's seat with flowing black hair, and long bronzed legs exposed by the breeze hiking the dress up to her thighs. This broadcast their presence, made Hale feel uneasy.

They had money for a hire car, but this would require time, answers to questions, forms, passports. Marta shrugged off the notion, keen to push on and run as Rupert had suggested. Maybe she was right. Just another couple in a jeep on their way to the beach or to hang out in the shops and cafés.

Heading west, Hale insisted on a stop at Vélez-Málaga, a small market city, traditional and bustling. Scope for them to meld into the crowd unnoticed. Hale had kept his eye on the rear-view mirror. They were not followed. In Vélez-Málaga, they would stop to talk in a café, plan a route, drink coffee. For Hale, coffee was now imperative.

Marta parked the jeep down an alleyway, a dead end with a few half-built apartments, rocks and rubble strewn about. They walked into a café on a sloping road filled with shoppers, workers drilling holes, and surrounded by rustic whitewashed buildings leading up to a church. They sat at the bar. Hale ordered a cortado for Marta, a café solo for him, asked for strong. Strong is what he got, made him wince.

"We'll go west beyond Marbella," said Hale. "These people, they'll expect us to hang around Málaga or go inland, but I doubt they'll expect us to head towards Cádiz. Let's head that way."

Marta shrugged, and then turned as the door clattered open. Two Guardia officers walked in. Hale gazed at her, questioning, alarmed. She gave a faint shake of the head, drank her coffee, and then said softly, "It is nothing, relax. They come in these places like everyone else."

Hale wasn't so sure, scanned about the room. An old man at the bar, kid at the fruit machine, two women at a table eating tostadas. Nothing out of the ordinary. The officers sat down at the end of the bar, ordered something from the girl working behind it. Coffee and spirits of some kind. One lit a cigarette, the other read a paper. Marta was right, nothing unusual.

Hale kept his voice low, began to feel more comfortable as customers crowded around the bar and sat down at tables, the noise building. "I'm feeling better now," he said. "More relaxed."

"I have nothing, no place to stay and nowhere to go," said Marta.

"I have money," said Hale. "I'll help you until we get this sorted out, but we need to hide for a while before we travel further." Hale glanced around. One Guardia officer caught his eye for a second, looked away, uninterested.

Marta nudged his arm, told him to be calm.

"Tarifa," Hale said.

"I know of the town, but I cannot remember it. I go there when I was small," she said.

"We can get there easily. No one goes there other than local people and surfers."

"And then what?"

"Where is your family, Marta?"

"My father and brother in Madrid," she said. "Some friends in Almería, of course."

"You should go to Madrid," said Hale, "maybe in a week. I'll pay for you, but you need to be careful how you contact your father and brother. They should know that you are in trouble, but that they can only see you and contact you in certain ways. I'll tell you what you have to do ... to prevent Morillo from finding you."

She nodded. "And you?"

"I have to go to back to Britain, but I'll wait before I do. Morillo and this man from Marbella, they might stake out the airport."

"Stake out?"

"Wait for me there."

"Berto will never give up," she said. "You know that?"

"Rupert knows of this man, Morillo" said Hale. "He's not the main problem. It's the Russian people as well. They're a big deal, dangerous mafia. If I can get back to Britain, I may need to take action to hide."

Marta's eyes narrowed, "Action?"

"Change my name, my identity. You should do the same. Go to Madrid by train, and don't use any cards or your phone. Everything has to change."

A tear formed in Marta's eye, ran down her cheek. She wiped it away. Hale held her hand, looked around, nervous.

"My life is over," she said.

"It's not over," said Hale. "It's just different now. And what life did you have working for Morillo anyway?"

She nodded, wiped her eyes discreetly.

Her distress riled him. He cursed Morillo, Enzo, Happy Gary, the whole goddamn mess. Most of all, he cursed himself.

"There's a way out of this, Marta," he said. "I'm going to find it."

Hale left five euros on the bar. They moved out into the sun and heat, passed the Guardia vehicle parked outside, headed back towards the jeep. Hale's cell rang. They moved under the shade of a shop canopy to take the call. A voice, unfamiliar, at the other end, a London accent:

"We're looking for Jack and Dean, and we have the impression you know where they are."

"Who is this?" asked Hale, looking at Marta. She frowned, questioning him with her eyes. Hale shook his head.

"I'm with Happy," the voice continued. "And you're in trouble, sunshine, unless we know where the boys are and where the boat is. We understand each other?"

Hale saw no reason to withhold the truth. "I think they've left the marina, Puerto de Santa María," he said. "Heading west, and that's all I know."

A moment's silence at the other end. Then, "We're going to go looking for them, and then we're coming for you. We'd like to ask you some questions as part of a friendly little chat."

"I have nothing to say to you."

"Really? Well, Happy might like to make your acquaintance, mate, especially if we can't find our crew."

"I can't help you."

"Is that a fact? Well, hear this. Happy's getting a bit narked because it seems like some geezer going by the name of Charlie Hale is losing him crew members ... and more to the point, money."

Hale remained silent, waited.

Then finally at the other end, "We'll be in touch."

The line went dead.

"So?" said Marta.

Hale looked at his phone, pocketed it, thoughtful. "It was Jack and Dean's people," he said. "Don't worry, it's okay ... let's go." Marta seemed unconvinced that things were anywhere near okay. She stood for a moment. Hale grabbed her hand, urging her to walk back towards the jeep.

Hale drove this time, out of Vélez-Málaga, along barren country roads, and then out onto the faster autopistas. He floored the wrecked jeep, gunning the engine as the warm breeze whipped around their faces. They shouted to speak over the blast of the air and din of the engine.

"Too fast," Marta said.

"It's okay," said Hale. "We have to push on. I'm within the limit ... it just *seems* fast in this thing."

A loud blast as a taxi flew by. Marta waved him off with a finger. Hale had lingered a split second too long in the middle lane, soon darted back to the inside.

They drove on for another hour, heading west, steady speed.

"We need the coast road," said Hale, working the gears.

They climbed, and then descended to a treacherous stretch beyond Málaga.

"You need the other road, *a la derecha*, to the right," she said.

Confused, Hale craned his neck to read the blue and white road signs flying past above the autopista. "But it must be left," he said. "The coast it to the south, so surely we need the left autopista?"

The motorway dipped sharply, widening into four lanes, and then splitting into two of each: left and right. An iron apex separating the two would greet ditherers with spectacular results.

"No. Right!" she shouted, pointing.

Hale moved over to the right, but then panicked, swung wildly back and took the left. Marta shrieked, held the roll-bar above as the jeep shot past the apex throwing up dust, a metre to spare. Now on the left carriageway, a truck veered to avoid them, the driver delivering a continuous blast on the horn. Another car shot across them in anger, a few metres separating the vehicles. Hale braked to avoid the car. The passengers waved fists madly at him. He glanced at Marta, who shook her head, fumed.

The coast was on the left, to the south, thought Hale. Therefore, the coast road must be the left road.

A hundred yards further on, Hale was proven wrong as a sign loomed and the road veered right. This route was not for the coast road, but for Algeciras, the inland route. This choice had a further problem, something Hale had wished to avoid: it was interspersed by toll stations.

They may have escaped any notice from the Guardia in Vélez-Málaga, but if Karzhov had the power and influence Rupert had implied, the Russian would almost certainly pay off gas station attendants, officials, or even the Guardia at key points for information leading to the whereabouts of *Morillo's woman*. Including the toll attendants. The first was two miles ahead, no exit road, and no choice but to continue.

The twenty five thousand euros stuffed into the sailing bag made Hale uneasy. Should have left it with Rups or hidden it. But he had no plans to return to Rups' finca any time soon. If they were searched by any officials, questions would be asked. And then there was the question of authenticity. Happy's money was bound to be dirty, perhaps counterfeit.

They approached the tolls, the road opening up into a vast concrete expanse. Most booths were free. One attendant waved them over, looked angered when Hale chose to ignore him, joining a small queue to mingle with other cars.

All looked normal. The attendant ahead, bored, took money from the first car, waved it on. Then the next. Hale edged forward, handed him the note, engaged first gear. The attendant fiddled with the change, looking at the till. Then glanced down and left to something else. Hale tapped his fingers on the wheel. This was slower than the first car to have passed through, certainly slower than the second. The attendant looked across to Marta, and then to Hale who smiled nervously. Ahead, Guardia officers were parked in a lay-by under bright sunshine to the left. Three of them hung around their vehicles, smoking. One was older, attentive. He stood watching the tolls, arms folded, legs astride.

The attendant handed the change across. The barrier rose and Hale eased the clutch, moved off. Hale recited to himself: *Don't stall, look ahead, relax*. Marta remained silent, didn't seem phased.

The Guardia officer watched them as they passed. Looking cool, thought Hale. They always did. Armed, hi-vis jackets, smart green uniforms, boots, and most importantly, expensive shades. Would make a movie extra no problem. An air of intimidation. In Britain, you could taunt or throw stones at the Police, and then maybe you would be arrested. In an interview, they'd consider inviting you to discuss the reason behind your actions. But here, it seemed simpler: you might be shot.

They drove on, normal speed. Hale checked the rear-view. The officer was still watching. Nothing unusual with that. He was probably looking at Marta, those legs.

The officer turned away at last. Dangerously glued to the rear-view, Hale snatched glances to the road ahead. He noticed one of the other two gaze across at the jeep, distracted from his conversation. Something had alerted him. Now the guard moved, animated, towards the door of their 4x4, still staring at Rup's jeep. The other two seemed uncertain, but turned to look and then also moved with urgency.

Hale cursed, picked up speed. "We need to get off the autopista," he said.

"Why? They were okay back there, no?"

"They know something," said Hale, glancing in the rear-view. The officer was now on a handset, while the other two were boarding their 4x4.

Edging around a long bend with the tolls now out of sight, Hale floored it, straining the engine. He looked ahead for an exit. In the distance, a sign emerged: Fuengirola. They climbed up a hill. The jeep slowed, labouring. Hale watched the rear-view. No sign of the Guardia as the exit approached. One hundred yards. Fifty. Marta gripped the seat beside him. Hale felt the tension between them. They said nothing.

Another glimpse in the rear-view. A truck and other vehicles were emerging in the distant heat haze, unclear if the Guardia 4x4 was amongst them. Hale took the exit, moved across in front of a slow-moving lorry. Two hundred yards on, he took another road off to the left, which soon turned into a dirt track with little indication of its destination. Other tracks intersected. Hale took them at random, used the position of the sun and glimpses of the ocean to gradually head south.

An hour later, no Guardia, and the industrial sprawl of Algeciras loomed.

Next stop: Tarifa.

FORTY

Griffon vultures circled above as the jeep descended from the hills into Tarifa, Spain's southernmost town, a sandblasted outpost with a history of Roman and Moorish conflicts over the centuries. Wind battered the jeep, causing Hale to yank the steering wheel erratically to compensate. The Guzmán el Bueno castle rose from the centre of the walled old town, a traditional area of cobbled streets, whitewashed apartments, rustic shops and restaurants leading up to the port and ferry terminal to Tangier. Colourful fishing boats and yachts sheltered in the small marina. Vessels of the brave or foolhardy in these seas, or those running for shelter, retreating from the hellish wind and chop offshore.

The road behind was clear. Marta was more relaxed now, but Hale was shredded, eyes straining in the heat and dust blasting around. They entered the old town, drove around in circles a few times, before finding the familiar blue two-star sign of a pension. Hale drove past. Then pulled up in a side alley some streets away. The town was quiet, just a few locals shifting around in the shade. Siesta time. Within the walled town, there was relief from the wind in some places. But here, people were on guard, edgy. Around any corner, a fiery gust could beat a man down, slam grit into his face, have him running for shade and cover.

Hale pulled their bags from the jeep, scanned the street. Nothing suspicious, no cars rumbling by with curious passengers, no Guardia 4x4s, no Eastern Bloc characters skulking around in the backstreets. They walked back around the corner to the pension.

"It should be okay at this place," said Marta.

Hale was confused by the comment, "What do you mean?"

"The pension is okay."

"Why would it not be okay?"

She paused at the steps, looked about, and then said, "Morillo is connected with everything, everyone. Even some hotels, bars, places like that in Andalucía. Family businesses especially."

Hale shook his head, too tired to reason. "You sure? Otherwise, we can go somewhere else, a bloody campsite or something."

"No, it is okay in these small places, but all I say is that we should be careful."

They booked a twin room, one night. Hale paid cash to an old woman, kindly, partially-sighted. She wore an apron and brandished a stick with which she occasionally prodded a noisy rat-sized dog. The room cost fifty-five euros, but Hale gave her two fifties, said to keep the change, though he wasn't sure if she could understand or see the notes anyway. Marta clarified for him. The old woman smiled, and escorted them to an undersized room. It was basic, dark, with hard mattresses and a tiny balcony overlooking a scruffy back yard leading to an alleyway. Facing south to Tarifa's port, the Rif Mountains and Africa rose up blue and distant beyond.

Hale hit the bed face down, and without another word, fell asleep.

Gut feeling, the noise of the wind on the shutters maybe, but something woke Hale from delirium. Marta was standing by the window. She turned and they locked eyes. Without words, a connected intuition that something was wrong.

He looked at his watch.

8:13 p.m.

"What's up?" Hale said.

Marta eased the shutter away from the window, letting a pale shard of light strike the off-blue of the wall. She peered down into the alleyway. "I don't know," she said, concern on her face. "Someone down there. When I woke up, I went down into the main street to buy water. Someone was there too."

"Who?" asked Hale, rubbing his eyes.

"A man, hanging around. Not Andaluz, not from here."

"So a surfer, some kind of guy from out of town. Big deal." Hale moved up to the window beside her. "Let me look."

"He is gone now," she said.

Hale sighed, "One man or two? Did the one in the street look different from the guy down here?" He scanned the alleyway, empty, wind whipping up dust. Golden light shone from the terracotta roofs of surrounding buildings, shuttered and quiet.

She shrugged. "Two, I think."

This is paranoia, thought Hale. Mental fatigue, stress fuelling deep suspicion.

"We're okay," he said, rubbing her shoulders. "We're going out now, into the town, just normal. We go out to have a drink, tapas. We come back here, just like normal tourists. Tomorrow, we have coffee. Then we head west to Cádiz. Simple, nothing unusual. After a while, I go back to England and you travel to Madrid. Who comes to Tarifa? No one comes to Tarifa, other than travellers and surfers, okay?"

Marta nodded, "Sorry, I worry too much." She went into the bathroom, started the shower running. Hale looked back out of the window for reassurance.

They could not have been followed, not here.

No one comes to Tarifa.

Darkness fell with a massive red glow to the west. In town, they found a small taberna packed with locals crammed in, some speaking animatedly around them, others gawking up at a television screen. Flamenco dancing, a talent show. The wine was cheap and people friendly. Made the couple from out of town feel good, free from their woes. The tapas came, as did more wine, and conversation from townspeople who appreciated these outsiders. The striking Andaluz woman, and the man with foreign looks. A nice man with poor Spanish, but not accented like the tourists.

The flamenco on the television intensified and chanting heightened within the confines of the small taberna. Like the crowd, Hale found himself drawn in, mesmerised by the screen. Colour, rhythmic passion, and percussive beat of the *guitarrista*. He glanced across to Marta who'd been caught in conversation by a one-toothed man who beat his chest with his hand, venting his love for the art, the heartbeat and blood of Andalucía. She returned a glance to Hale, smiled, sipped her wine. If Hale had not known love before, he did now. Not just for this woman, but for Andalucía too. Rupert had implied that his actions might prevent him from ever returning to Spain.

An intolerable thought.

Hours later, they stepped out into the street. The night was building. People thronging in alleyways, white taxis cruising for business, mopeds buzzing, and surfers hanging around in sandals, their sun-bleached hair stark against mahogany flesh.

Hale and Marta moved through the streets, close, intimate. Laughing, dodging blasts of wind and sand forming eddies in the street, while Marta held her flimsy dress down against her thighs. They found a late-night bar, stood amid a crowd of surfers, a bunch getting high on weed – watching extreme sports videos on the televisions above the bar, and talking about whatever shit they talked about.

Hale thought about what would happen later. In the early hours, they would return to the pension and their tiny room. Hale would sit on the end of the bed, look on in silence for a moment, doing nothing. She'd move close, her navel inches from his face. Then, he'd watch her dress drop slowly as she stood before him. She'd remove the rest – what little there was – and that too would join the dress on the floor.

These moments were how it was supposed to happen.

Just like the first night on the beach in Puerto de Santa María, just like with Céline, just like in his fantasies.

But that's not what happened.

At the surf bar, Hale's head was fuzzy after the taberna, but cleared fractionally with a sip of cold beer. Marta said something, something innocuous, but it was lost on him when he clocked a man entering the bar. This man took one glance, as if he'd made some sort of mistake, and then exited. Nothing wrong with that, thought Hale, trying to rationalise. But two things. Firstly, he walked out immediately he saw Hale. Secondly, he looked like Eastern Blochead. A different man, but the same breed, heavy brow, same dull lifeless look in his eyes. Same menace.

Hale rose, held his hand up to Marta, who looked confused. He moved to the window, looked through its iron bars out into the street, being careful not to be seen. Diagonally opposite, the man was speaking to Eastern Blochead on a corner. They looked so alike, they could be brothers. Hale leaned back against the wall, out of sight, as Blochead and Heavy Brow took a glance across to the bar. Blochead looked annoyed, as if he was shouting at his friend. Then they both moved into a side street and out of sight.

Hale returned to Marta, flung a ten euro note on the bar. "We need to go," he said.

Marta rose to her feet, "Why? Who was…?"

"Now."

Hale's tone, grave and tight-lipped, indicated that trouble had caught up with them. He took Marta's hand, moved towards the doorway, looked outside. A black shirt at the corner. Then, Blochead eased his distinctive thick face into view for an instant. This was no hunch. They were watching the bar, waiting for the couple to emerge.

"Who?" said Marta, holding her position behind Hale, keeping out of view.

"Karzhov's people," Hale said. "The Russian partner of Berto Morillo."

Marta swept her hair back, clenched a fist of it behind her neck. More terror than fear on her face. She peered behind into the darkness of the bar. "Back there," she said, pointing to a throng of twenty-year-olds, speaking loudly amongst themselves, cradling bottles of beer and waving cigarettes about.

Hale looked through and beyond the crowd. A small door onto the street, hardly noticeable, strings of beads hanging down through which people occasionally crept in and out of the place.

They moved swiftly without a word, brushing past the group, one of whom apologised as he inadvertently barged Marta. Hale drew the beads apart, peered out into the alley. Too many people about to make any clear assessment: a few taxis parked up on the opposite site of the street, the drivers leaning against them talking, two old women with sticks moving slow arm-in-arm, some surfers and tourists moving about in the thick heat of the night. If Blochead had planted another lookout at this exit, there was no way to know.

Hale grabbed Marta's hand, moved out into the street.

The pension was a few hundred yards away. Straight on a hundred, take a left and a hundred more would see them to the rear of the place. They shuffled along the street, slowly. Fast would look obvious, draw attention. But Marta drew looks from men anyway, always did. Hale chose to ignore any attention, to keep moving.

He considered the options. The jeep was too conspicuous and could be on the radar of Karzhov's mob, maybe Happy's too. They needed their bags from the pension, no doubt about it. Money, passports, everything. There was a back entrance to the pension down an alley, dark and discreet, the only option as the goons could be staking out the front. Then they'd need to flee, move on foot somewhere out of sight, regroup overnight, and somehow throw these people off their trail.

"We'll get the money, enter through the back way," said Hale. "Then get a taxi, and leave the jeep here."

"No taxi," she said. "Too dangerous."

"Dangerous?"

"Morillo knows the firms, owns some of them. He uses them for moving people around, getting information. He is everywhere."

"He can't own them all, we'll risk it."

"No taxi."

Hale felt his mouth dry, pulse ramp up, and not through the pace of their walk. He cast a glance behind. Nothing yet, but how long would Blochead stake out the bar? He looked across to Marta, worry etched on her face. They'd escaped the bar, but they could sustain the walk no longer, too slow and nerve-racking. She moved first, running ahead. Hale followed, grabbing a final look behind. Movement in the distance, youths perhaps, difficult to tell with sweat pouring into his eyes. He broke into a run.

They took the left, Marta still ahead. Her heels were low, but she struggled on the cobbles. The alleyway leading up to the rear of the pension loomed, half-lit by an orange streetlight across the road. No one around, and no one following. A dog ran across the road, a few mopeds buzzed by, nothing unusual. A blast of wind whipped dust into their eyes as they settled back into a walk and moved into the alley, beyond some bins, through a wooden door and into a yard big enough only to house a few chairs and a barrel. A dog barked a few houses away, wind rattled the fence and howled above the rooftops, whistling, groaning.

Marta rapped lightly on the door. No response. She tried louder. The old woman's rat-dog burst into life, a light came on. The door opened and the woman spoke through a two-inch gap held by the chain. Marta gabbled quick-fire Spanish, urgent, breathless, and soon the door opened.

Marta continued to speak to the old woman under the harsh glare of a light bulb hanging from the ceiling. They spoke about mafia, bad men. Hale could barely understand the woman's strange dialect, picking up only an occasional word.

Fuelled by fear, Hale's impatience grew. After a minute, he said, "I'll get the bags, and then we should go soon."

Marta nodded as Hale burst up the stairs and rattled the key in the door. Moving into the room, his hand reached for the switch, but he pulled it away at the last moment.

Think Hale. Don't show your position.

In the dark, he threw clothes into his sail bag, felt around towards the bottom for the pack of money. Still there. He gathered Marta's scant possessions from the dresser and bathroom, shoved them into the bags, and then hauled them onto the bed. Then moved to the window, easing the curtain an inch away from the wall to see the back gate and street below. A shadow moved, passing the alley, which led to the street. Could be anyone, a dog walker, a kid on a bike. Impossible to tell in this light and with no angle.

He grabbed the bags, moved out of the room. Marta was waiting at the foot of the stairs, pensive.

"We can't go out the front," said Hale. "We'll go back the way we came, the alley."

"I know," she said, taking her bag. "And then where?"

A good question. A question Hale hadn't thought through. "We need to go on foot, fast ... somewhere we can lose them. Here in the town they might have people positioned, waiting for us."

She nodded, "I understand." Hale noticed determination behind her eyes, but also a hint of resignation. As if going into battle against the odds. You might win if you're lucky, but losing could mean paying the ultimate price. He sensed the fear in her. A fear born of years under the rule of Morillo's heavy hand, aided now by the sinister force of Sergei Karzhov.

Marta held the old woman as she would her own mother, kissed her on either cheek, and then directed her to the living room, consoling, assuring her that things were okay for them.

If only they were, thought Hale.

They killed the light and Hale set his watch for five minutes. Don't be rash, think it through. If Blochead knew of the pension and of the exit to the alleyway, they were doomed anyway. But if they were followed to the street, might as well give them time to look around and move on. Hale was sure that he and Marta were not seen moving into the alley.

He couldn't help but to ask himself a question, hated himself for doing so: What if the old woman was with Morillo? Hale whispered, posed it to Marta.

She shook her head rolled her eyes.

They stood in silence by the back door, looked at each other. Racing clouds cleared intermittently, allowing monochrome moonlight to splash across their faces. Sand blew beneath the door as the gale intensified, shrieking through the telephone lines outside.

A magnet seemed to hold the hands of Hale's watch back, but four minutes came and went, and then five.

Only fools venture out on nights like this, thought Hale.

He opened the door, held it hard to prevent it slamming. They moved out into the alley.

FORTY-ONE

They ran west towards the edge of town, staying in the shadows, stumbling through the rubble of half-built apartments and rough ground of hardened dirt, littered with broken bottles. A football ground, just an illuminated dust bowl, blocked the way to blackness and possible safety of the beach beyond, *Playa de los Lances*. Hale turned briefly, saw the figures, knew immediately who they were. Two hundred yards away. One stocky, struggling behind a marginally fitter form, both leaning into the wind, shielding their eyes from clouds of swirling dust and litter.

Not good, thought Hale. His efforts to avoid attention had been in vain, and for Blochead and his accomplice, there could be no mistake: a woman and a man, both lugging bags over their shoulders, running out of town at 2:10 a.m.

Hale knew Marta had seen them too, but she said nothing. No decision and no words required. They must simply run. A gulley, shallow and dry, two metres deep, thwart the beach before them and led out to sea. They scrambled down it. Marta's wholly inadequate footwear made her trip and fall. Hale pulled her to her feet and they splashed through a few inches of water, climbed the other side up to the loose sand of the beach.

Wind and sand slammed into them as they emerged at the brow. Marta screamed, Hale tried to reply, but stinging particles smacked his face, drowned any sound he made. Blochead and the ape with the heavy brow were approaching the gully, waving angrily. Blochead seemed to be clutching his waistline. Maybe holding a gun beneath, thought Hale.

Marta removed her shoes and ran, dragging her bag behind with one hand. Hale moved after her, the sand now impeding his progress, every step sapping the equivalent energy of five on hard ground. Ahead, Marta was oddly silhouetted against a sea of white sand whipped up by a fifty-knot gale. Hale's mind was shot, waves crashed to his left. The shorebreak provided a guide, since looking ahead into the blast was impossible.

"Come ... come!" shouted Marta, moving faster. She was fit, nimble, but Hale was weighed down, not only by the bag, but also the alcohol in his blood and too many weeks away from the gym. Paying the price. He fell, clawed at the sand, desperate. On all fours, he gathered himself, breathed deeply, glanced over his shoulder. Behind, the pursuers were equally shredded in the blitz, Blochead walking, staggering into the wind, Heavy Brow moving faster, but pummelled by the onslaught.

Marta shouted again, "Come now! They are slowing." She grabbed Hale's shirt, tugging at him, raising him to his feet. He hung on to her, leaning forward, pumping his legs into the deep sand. They moved faster, gaining momentum. The sand firmed slightly underfoot. Blochead was down, and both were falling back. Two hundred yards and increasing.

Marta moved ahead again, urging Hale on. She made twenty yards on him, but then stopped, looked lost, crouched down to shield herself from the sandblasting. Hale caught up, dumped his bag down, and then saw the problem. A lagoon blocking their path. He waved his hand, motioned to move inland, to go around it. They set out, but a scramble of just thirty yards revealed that it was more river than lagoon. It stretched far into the gloom of waste ground, and then on to flow under the main route into Tarifa from the west, a road illuminated by yellow lights half a mile away.

Marta moved to Hale, spoke close up to his ear to be heard, "Can we go through, swim?"

Hale shook his head. "Too deep ... and look at the current. And what about our money, passports?" There was no option. Blochead was moving again. "We go inland," he said. "Your shoes ... put them on." At least it was darker inland, away from the sand, and perhaps easier to evade the goons in scrubland. Then head to the road, maybe hitch a lift.

Marta slipped her shoes on and moved into the dark, Hale followed behind.

Branches, thorns of bushes, bent and disfigured by the wind, scratched their skin. Rocks threatened to break their ankles as they sprinted through the bush, hunching low to avoid their forms being seen against the road lights and those of fincas dotted in the distant hills. They were making ground. Hale felt better, keeping pace with Marta who threaded through the maze of broken fences, scrub, and wrecked fishing boats. The river narrowed, and a rotting wooden bridge five metres wide took them across.

The road loomed. Hale saw occasional trucks, taxis speeding along it. With luck, they could flag someone down quickly, or if not, head further into the hills beyond and hide out. But first, there was some distance to cover, and a building, rough and dilapidated surrounded by barbed wire to confront. And another problem.

Dogs.

Marta stopped in her tracks. Hale caught up, gasping, dry air filling his lungs. He heard the problem. "Shit ... dogs."

"Which way?" she said, looking over Hale's shoulder. Her expression prompted Hale also to glance back. Two figures moved towards them in the dark, surrounded by scrub and dancing eddies of sand. Three hundred yards and gaining.

"We'll go left, around the fence," said Hale, trying to conceal his fear. The dogs were not of the rat-variety. Going by their barks alone, these were big dogs. Hopefully contained within the fencing, hopefully not wild or stray.

They moved left. Nothing was seen in the direction of the barking, though it sounded as if the dogs were moving closer. Hale wondered whether they should double back, sprint. Which was the better option: being mauled by Rottweilers or shot by Blochead?

Marta grabbed Hale's arm, clearly fearful that the dogs would attack. The noise, close now, just metres away. Hale pulled at Marta. They were the hunted. He kept moving across the scrub and rough ground, head down, looking for a branch, a piece of driftwood, anything to fend off the inevitable attack from rabid jaws.

They neared a clearing. A small light shone on a post to the right. Seemed to signify an entrance. Vehicles were parked beyond. The dogs were not gaining, not any closer, perhaps chained or fenced in. Hale was confused, but kept running towards the light. Like Hale, Marta's fear had turned to terror. They both ran, shouting, gasping above the incessant noise of wind and barking dogs.

They hit hard ground at the clearing. Dirt in the form of a car park as they passed the light. Camper vans lined the edge, two either side. Three were white and shiny and new, the other one old and battered. Hale ran into the centre of the clearing, gripped Marta's hand, pulled her into a dark area under cover of a van to the left. He paused, looked back, catching his breath, clocked a figure running through the wasteland, further east than the route they had taken. But now the figure seemed to be changing direction, coming their way.

Hale's shoulder was red raw from hauling the bag. He threw it across his other shoulder, urged Marta to move on. She wrapped the handle of her bag around her other wrist, and then turned to move. As she did, the door of the battered camper swung open, missing her by inches. A grizzled-looking man, hunched, thin, wearing shorts and sandals waved his hand at them. "Come," he said, appearing to urge them into his van.

Hale was taken aback, but made a snap decision. "Let's get in," he said to Marta.

She didn't hesitate.

Soon, the metal door was slammed shut and they stood inside the van motionless. The man held his finger to his mouth ... *silence*. Outside, running footsteps were just audible above the gale. The van rocked as the storm made good work of its high sides. Hale could hear the thud of his own heart, the blood pumping around the arteries in his neck and temples. His eyes adjusted to the darkness, but there was little to see. A few shapes, presumably a bed of sorts, a surfboard lashed up high, and junk scattered about. A smog of stale sweat and smoke hung in the air. This was no palace, but better than being outside.

The man broke the silence, smiling in the darkness, "So, welcome. My name is Hans. Español, Italiano?"

"Yo soy Marta, Español," said Marta.

"Inglés, Charles," said Hale.

Hans leaned to his right and slowly reached over to flick a switch. A dim table lamp – the type you find in second-hand shops, yellowed and grimy – illuminated their faces.

"So, my friends, we speak English, no?" said Hans.

Hale guessed Hans was in his fifties and likened the man to the table lamp: grimy. He wore a faded *Neil Pryde* t-shirt, leather sandals that had seen some miles, and a bandana to hold back wild hair. His eyes were intense. Fuelled by some strong stuff, thought Hale. Some shit other than the gel he was rolling into a joint. Hans gave a friendly, mischievous smile as he sat down on a grubby sofa, leaning back nonchalantly.

"Please," he said, motioning with his hand that they sit. Marta dropped her bag, sat on a cheap plastic chair, her chest still heaving, her dress torn and wet with sweat. Hale opted for a wooden box.

"Let's be calm for a minute shall we?" said Hans, licking the *Rizla* paper and sealing it. "When we are sure that your friends outside are not coming back, I will see to your troubles." He pointed to Marta's legs, which were covered with deep scratches, blood trickling down to her feet.

"Thank you," said Hale. "I can explain, we were..."

"Look, relax," interrupted Hans. "I like visitors, and you do not have to explain much to me." He laughed to himself quietly, and then continued, "But I have to say, I am curious about you English and Spanish locos running around in that shit out there."

Hans lit the spliff, blew a cloud into the air.

Hale looked around the junk shop that comprised Hans' mode of transport. This looked like something more permanent than just a vehicle.

"You hang around Tarifa a lot?" asked Hale.

"Look. I travel, but I come here always."

German, thought Hale. Often prefix their replies with 'look'. "And you live in this van?"

"But of course, I am a lucky man."

I've met luckier men, thought Hale.

"I also have good friends around here," said Hans. "But look, enough about me. Those people that follow you, they are not coming back and I will get you some beer." He rummaged around in a dwarf-sized fridge.

Marta cast Hale a worried glance. Hale shook his head, held her hand for a moment, reassuring. Hans cracked open the lids, tossed the opener into a sink piled with plates, and passed the bottles to them. Hale sucked half out of his immediately.

"So, look," said Hans, pulling a small cardboard box out from behind the driver's seat, "here I have some stuff for your legs and we talk." He sat cross-legged on the floor at Marta's legs, hunched over, pouring some liquid onto a cotton wool ball. Hale sensed that Marta was distressed by the pursuit, but not so by their strange new companion. "Look, this will hurt, no?" Hans said, dabbing the first scratch. Marta winced, squeezed Hale's hand.

"What if they come back?" said Hale.

Hans shrugged, took a slug of beer, and then continued the first aid. "He would have come back, man. He thinks you are over the road, in the hills by now, or whatever."

"You say *he*. What about the other one?"

"Yes, I saw him too. But maybe the dogs got him or something like that."

"Really?"

"Well maybe he got – how do you say? – bitted by the dog and ran off."

"Jesus."

"For sure, the guy who owns the dogs calls himself a farmer," said Hans, looking up to Hale, rolling his eyes. "But he is just a junkie I think. Look, when he hears some noise from the dogs, he gets crazy and sometimes opens the gate. And the dogs are crazy, more crazy than him. You are lucky. You got away maybe before he opened the gate."

"Thank you for letting us in here," said Hale, finishing the beer. Strong stuff that made his head spin.

Hans' spliff wobbled about in his mouth as he spoke, "No problem, man." He finished the first aid, and then stood up, stretching his back.

"You saw us running in the dark?" asked Hale.

Hans reached across to the driver's seat, pulled out some binoculars. "Most nights I watch with these," he said. "You see, sometimes people come out of the town and get me some stuff, you know what I mean?" Hale didn't know, but nodded anyway. Hans continued, "So I watch *a lot*, man." He laughed, choking on his cigarette. Then eyed Marta and Hale in turn. "Well, anyway, tonight I see a woman go into the *Poniente* wind on the beach as if she enjoys pain or something, and then a man follows. *Locos*, crazy people, so Hans continues to watching the action. And then I see you fall, have hard time, and some other dudes come out to join the fun, chasing you."

"We need to get away from those people," said Hale, interrupting. "They're dangerous, they will kill me, and maybe you too if we're found."

Hans stiffened for a moment, nodded at their bags, and then asked, "You have some shit in there that they want, no?"

"No, it's not like that. They want Marta. They want money from me probably, I don't know."

Hans shook his head, and then said, "I saw his face through the windscreen when we were standing quiet. He is not Spanish, and I know some people like this have been hanging around the town today."

"We think they're Russian," said Hale. "Can you help us? We need to rest, eat. Tonight, maybe tomorrow too, and then get out of Tarifa. I have money."

Hans puffed his cheeks out, looked at Hale, "For sure, I can help you to get away. But Tarifa is cool, man. And like I say, I have friends who help me here. Back in Germany I worked in the factories, not good for my lungs you know, but here I come and everybody nice, everybody cool. Now I do business for some people. People I can trust."

"I don't understand."

Hans shrugged. "Man, all I am saying is that Tarifa is cool for business, and I can help to maybe do a deal with these people. Maybe the dog got one," he laughed, "so only one now to deal with. And then, if you have money, we do some business, longer term. Know what I am talking about?"

Marta sighed, shook her head.

"Thank you for the offer," said Hale, "but it's not that simple. I said these people are dangerous and I mean it. They're connected."

"Connected?"

"Mafia."

Hans shrugged, "Okay, so give me a name, man."

"Morillo."

Hans coughed, stubbed out his joint into a coffee cup. Then nodded, looked at Hale, "Shit, man, you must go. I have a friend who can help."

FORTY-TWO

Hale peered out of the window of an apartment a mile west of Hans' mobile home, watched the morning sun rise over the hills, sipped water from a plastic bottle. Marta slept on a bed made from a strip of foam in a small room down a hallway. The aging surfer had called one of his 'crew' to drive them to this place, small and unfurnished, two rooms, clean and tidy, lodged on the side of the road. Hans rented it out to tourists. By 'tourists', Hans meant surfers of the holidaying variety, flying in from their conventional lives in Germany or Britain. A different breed to the hardcore surfers and accompanying potheads and groupies who lived around the beach.

Hans' bravado and nonchalance had been lost on mention of Morillo's name, and now he wanted rid of the hapless couple. Hale, though, was grateful for the shelter and few hours' rest before they fled Tarifa.

The plan was simple and, Hale thought, relatively safe. The crew would pick them up at the apartment in a Combi, a surf wagon loaded with boards and suntanned guys. A common sight in these parts. Hale and Marta would hide under the stack of gear and they'd cruise out of town. Taxis and buses were too risky, as was the jeep. In fact, the jeep had drawn interest from Hans. The type of vehicle every surfer coveted, it was part of the deal. Hans' reward was the keys to the jeep, and whether it was being watched by Morillo's crew or not, time was on the surfers' side. In the early hours of some night, the crew would turn up and drive it off. A few days later, with different plates, resprayed and covered in stickers, Rupert's possession would have a new life. A dog would sit in the passenger seat barking at the shore-break, waiting for its master to come back from the surf. Just another stolen vehicle ending up on some wind-hammered beach.

10:06 a.m.

Sun blasted through the apartment. Hale and Marta sat against the wall on the floor, speaking in hushed tones. Even these whispers echoed through the vacant building. The unmistakable rattle of a flat-four VW engine signalled the crew's arrival. Hale tensed, looked at Marta as footsteps sounded on the gravel outside. Time to go.

A fist thundered on the woodwork and Hale swung the door open. A muscular cover model for *Surf Magazine* stood before him. Shirtless, board shorts, sandals, shades, tanned biceps riddled with veins, and a goatee beard.

"Morning, I'm Charles," said Hale.

Biceps ignored him, looked over his shoulder. "The girl?" he said.

Marta appeared. Biceps nodded, flicked his head towards the Combi. "This is what you do," he said. His English was clipped, German or Belgian. "The door slides open, you crawl under with the girl, you stay quiet, we drive, we go out of town, maybe to Algeciras, you get out, we leave you. Understand?"

"Seems clear to me," said Hale.

"If we are stopped you stay quiet, we deal with it, understand?"

Hale nodded, but curiosity overcame him, "Deal with it how?"

Biceps looked at Hale beneath reflective shades, mouth a straight line, impassive. Hale saw nothing but his own reflection looking back.

"I *said* we deal with it."

Biceps nodded to the driver. The engine fired up and the Combi inched a few feet forward, opposite Hale and Marta who stood just inside the apartment door. The door of the Combi slid back with a metallic clunk against the stops. Biceps looked around, and then motioned Hale and Marta in.

Hale noticed other surfers in the van. One sat towards the rear, long black hair. Another in the front passenger seat, smoking, tattoos on his neck, wore beads in his hair. Marta climbed in under the boards and Hale followed, laying on his side on the buckled metal floor. Biceps tossed their bags in, shoving them against the far side under some surfboards. Sail bags and wetsuits followed, rammed against Hale and Marta, covering them and releasing a stench of neoprene, salt, and sweat. Biceps climbed onto the remaining back seat and slammed the door.

"Hit it," he said, slapping the back of the driver's seat.

Hale felt the Combi reversing out onto the main road, a deafening noise from the engine rattling behind. This was not discreet, and the crew didn't bother to hide their faces. Maybe a routine of theirs in and around Tarifa: escorting holidaying surfers to and from their accommodation, bus stations, and airports.

Marta shifted awkwardly. They both moved into the fetal position to make room. The Combi's suspension was beaten, the shock jarring their bones when they hit rubble and potholes.

Further on, Hale checked his watch. Ten minutes had elapsed. They'd be on the edge of Tarifa, heading east and nearing the climb into the hills. The Combi pulled up somewhere, engine idling. Maybe some lights. Hale looked through a crack of light between wetsuits and bags. The driver was lighting up, relaxed, and then released the clutch violently. They rattled along for another minute, and then stopped again. This time, an air of tension.

Biceps gave a command to the driver: "¡Vamos! Look ahead, fool."

The Combi lurched forward, and then swung hard. Marta hung on to Hale as they slid some inches across the floor, hard up against the door, trapping Biceps' feet. Biceps nudged Hale roughly with his foot to get back. The couple did so, edging back to the other side.

Hale sensed the road smooth out, the speed increase. They were on some sort of autopista or dual carriageway. But soon, discomfort overwhelmed them as the vibration worked into their blood. Hale's arm was numb, irritated from leaning his weight on it. Marta groaned, trying to settle into any position tolerable for more than a minute.

After an hour, Biceps spoke, raising his voice above the noise of the engine and air rushing through the open windows.

"You and the girl, listen. We leave you soon up here just off the road, okay? Do not come back, because Tarifa is crawling with those people. For me, I do not like the smell of those ugly mothers. You understand?"

Hale said nothing.

Biceps continued, "They hang around bars and bus stations asking questions about the English guy, no? And that means *you*, amigo. I think they want your woman too, and if they get her, I believe they will do bad stuff to her, and then kill her, yes? Personally, I do not know what shit you are in and I do not care, but maybe if you want to live, you go far away. For sure, these people are pissed about something and I think they look for blood. Understand?"

Hale said nothing.

"Good."

The side of a road, ten kilometres to the east of Algeciras on the outskirts of San Roque. That's where Biceps had stopped the Combi, slid open the door, and dumped them. Not much around, an urban sprawl and no shade out in the open. Flies buzzed around Marta's legs. The wounds needed tending. Hale felt bad. She needed clothes, a shower, food, but they must keep moving.

They walked on fifteen minutes to the middle of nothing, continued through more residential roads, until breaking out of bland nothingness beside the Autovía del Mediterráneo to the south. Traffic sped in both directions, blurred in the heat haze.

The sun dogged Hale, beat him down as he tried to work a rational solution. This was not good. The Englishman and the Spanish girl out in the open, worst case scenario. He cursed the surfers, and then himself. Marta remained silent as if she knew he was tormenting himself. He opened his mouth to speak. Then, a car, an old Mercedes, pulled alongside, the sound of the engine cutting him out. Hale gripped Marta's arm, ready to run, but Marta pulled free as the window wound down. An old man, kindly face, big square glasses peered out.

A minute later, Marta was in the front, Hale in the back. They were heading east on the Autovía. The old man looked down at Marta's legs, tutted, chatted continuously. Marta seemed happy to be moving, out of the sun, and for some minutes at least, away from the eyes of anyone apart from the old man and a few motorists flying past.

After five minutes, the driver was prompting for a destination. *Este*, east, was Marta's original instruction, but now he was curious, wanting to know where the foreigner and the girl with the scratched legs wanted to go. Hale heard *farmacia*, from the old man, a stop to get medication, dressings. Marta turned to Hale, looking for an answer.

He had thought about it. They should not go, under any circumstances, to one place.

Puerto Banús.

And certainly not the main strip by the marina, Muelle de Rivera, or the seedy Calle del Infierno behind. At night, an area of drunkenness and crime. A tourist glitz-hole, haunt of pimps, wannabes, and high-class hookers. Here, English bars entertained wide boys and dolly birds getting ruined on gin and British beer. A place where city slickers flew out for the weekend to snort coke, race around in Ferraris, and burn money on priceless tat. A place where people who hadn't quite made it, headed to posture as if they had. A place where crass vulgarity ruled and Spanish culture was banished to the outskirts and pueblos inland. A place where Hale would never normally go unless someone paid him or put a gun to his head.

There was another reason why they should not go to Puerto Banús. It was overrun, not only by the cream of the British criminal underworld, but also by the Russian mafia.

Hale leaned forward, said to Marta, "Puerto Banús."

FORTY-THREE

The Mercedes pulled up to the Pyr Hotel in Puerto Banús. "You're very kind, *eres muy amable*," said Hale, presenting a twenty euro note. The old man waved it away, laughed to himself.

Hale grabbed the bags and they walked into the reception as the car pulled away. The hotel, leafy and cool, just a few hundred metres from Puerto Banús marina and the main strip, was discreet enough, but Marta seemed worried.

"Why here?" she asked, moving quickly inside the doors, looking around, nervous.

Hale scanned the foyer area. A few tourists waited at reception. A cleaner in smart blue uniform with white apron wandered by. All normal. "They could not have followed us here, unless they're psychic," said Hale. "You should stay one night here, and then go tomorrow, early. We have to split. We cannot be seen together. I'll give you plenty of money so that you can buy clothes this evening. You have to go tomorrow morning on the bus to Málaga, and then the train to Madrid. Buy different clothes than you would wear normally, wear sunglasses, and no one will know who you are. Just another woman travelling. But with me, you're noticed. Do you understand?"

Marta nodded. "And you?" she said. "This place, Puerto Banús, is full of people we run from. Morillo's people, you know that."

"Yes, I know. But this thing has to end. I have an idea ... to strike a deal."

Tears formed in Marta's eyes, "A deal?" She shook her head, incredulous. "A deal with these people is death ... it will be nothing other."

Hale nodded, "I know you think that, but we can't run forever." He glanced across to the reception desk. The tourists had moved on. The receptionist, a man in his fifties, looked over, smiling, urging them to the desk. "This madness has to stop," continued Hale, "and I need to speak with the people I was working for."

"The people of the boat?"

"Yes, and then Morillo. If he wants *me*, fine, but he must know that you are gone and nothing can be done about that. You must go to Madrid and hide out for as long as possible. Throw your phone away. Buy another one and text me in one month, not before. Hide near your family, but use a different name. Tell your family of the danger."

Hale unzipped his bag, drew out a small wallet and handed it to her. "This is for the hotel, your clothes, and the trip to Madrid. In your bag, I placed another package. It has a lot of money in it. Take it with you, and try to forget everything when you are in Madrid for a month. Spend some money on yourself, find a place to rent, maybe look for a job."

Marta wiped tears from her eyes, nodded and straightened her dress. Despite the dirt on her face, scratches on her skin and rips in her clothes, her allure was untainted. Anguish tore at Hale, but reality demanded that they separate. Hale didn't say it, but this was likely to be goodbye. Forever.

Hale looked to the receptionist, words hardly needed. *Look after her.*

The receptionist nodded lightly.

Hale kissed Marta's forehead, picked up his bag, moved out through the hotel doors without looking back.

The taxi east to Marbella took fifteen minutes. Hale had made his decision: he would no longer hide from this burden, the criminal factions on his tail. He'd retained three thousand euros from the stash he'd stolen from *Blue Too*. Marta would find three hundred in her wallet and a further eighteen thousand in her holdall. It was of no use to Hale, since boarding an aircraft with this sum of hot cash would be foolhardy.

He booked in to Marbella's *Hostel Pepe*, a whitewashed building on a quiet side street, Calle Bermeja, away from the city's central bustle and traffic. The modest family business was denoted only by a doorway surrounded by flowers, but which opened up into cooling courtyards, walls of Moorish tiles, tiny fountains, and dark marble-floored corridors. The type of place any traveller or backpacker would choose, a retreat for those tired and weary from the heat and monotony of travel. The receptionist, a woman in her forties, did not linger on the discrepancy: Hale's disinclination to produce a passport. She smiled, accepted his name as 'Smith' when the one hundred euro note was slid across the counter.

Hale guzzled a cold bottle of water provided by the room's mini fridge, gazed out at the golden light now settling upon rooftops and whitewashed architecture. He rummaged through his bag, pulled out a phone charger, plugged the adapter into the wall. A good signal. Flicking through the menu, he located the 'received call' from Happy's bonehead a few days ago. Without hesitation, he hit 'call'.

The dial tone rang for five seconds, ten. Hale looked out into the inviting street, thought about beer, about food. Thought about cutting the call. Then it was answered. The same voice as before: "Yes, who is this?"

"We spoke before," said Hale. "Skipper of *Blue Too*. I'd like to speak to Happy Gary."

There was a pause, a muffled sound, the mouthpiece being covered at the other end, and then, "Happy doesn't like phones."

"I need to speak to him, about money ... and the boat."

"Where are you?"

"I cannot say."

"You're dead."

Hale felt his stomach turn. Then composed himself and said, "Mr Happy might have an issue with the boat."

Another pause, a shuffling sound, and then, "What d'ya mean *issue?*"

"As I say, if Happy has the ability to speak, I'd be glad to…"

"No phones."

"Then we'll meet."

"Where?"

"A place of your choice. Morning, somewhere public, no tricks."

"Alone?"

"Alone."

"Stay on the line."

Hale released his grip on the phone, realised he'd pressed it into the side of his head with stress, causing sweat to run down his cheek. After a minute, Bonehead came back, "Happy will meet."

"Delighted."

"No pigs, no stunts, and then you won't suffer."

"How kind. And no games your end, please," said Hale. "Where and when?"

"Sammy's, Puerto Banús. Know it?"

"Know it. Time?"

"Ten, and..."

Hale cut the call.

FORTY-FOUR

Maybe I was wrong about this place, thought Hale. He walked west along Calle Ribera on Puerto Banús's opulent quayside. At 9:41 a.m., a few people, Spanish locals and Brits, strolled around, gazing at the blinding white yachts, mostly motorboats tied up to the marina wharfs. Sunglasses mandatory. The atmosphere was pleasant, easy-going, made Hale feel better. Like those early summer mornings in Britain down at Leigh-on-Sea. Sunshine, the smell of salt in the air, the sound of crews readying boats for a day on the water.

Maybe Puerto Banús wasn't so bad. Maybe night-time was the problem, when the boozers, chancers, the addicts and the posers hit the strip and the underworld of the backstreets.

These were musings, distractions Hale toyed with to keep calm. To keep from thinking of what lay ahead in fifteen minutes. The meeting with Happy Gary. Leaving Marta to run alone to Madrid tortured his mind. He ran through their final minutes together, the trip in the car, her face as he walked away.

Tough it out, Hale. You want her, miss her, but at least she'll be safe.

Calle Ribera split and doglegged. Hale took the route south beside the quay. To his left, shining gin palaces outnumbering smaller sailing yachts. To his right, the road lined with Mercedes, BMWs, and other expensive rides parked before a strip of bars and designer clothes shops. He kept a steady pace, looked into the distance. He spotted *Sammy's*, the last café to the right on the corner of a busy intersection. Hale had frequented the place one night years before, having just delivered a yacht for a rich trader. He'd left the boat in the marina and headed off to grab a drink with the crewmember who insisted on *Sammy's*. Hale had downed one overpriced beer, and then left for Almería. Not his kind of place.

One hundred yards out, Hale clocked a goon on the quay at eleven o' clock. An unmistakable bonehead, he leaned against a black BMW parked diagonally opposite Sammy's and beneath some attractive pseudo-Spanish apartments. Suit, shades, hanging around like a bouncer outside an Essex wine bar. Happy Gary was not a bright spark if he was looking to be discreet.

Seventy-five yards out, another goon to Hale's right, peering into a shop window, feigning interest in women's clothes. A real dumbnut.

Hale took a breath, swallowed, trying to moisten his mouth, which was dry with nerves. Thirty yards, and the first clear glimpse of *Sammy's*. Looked pleasant in the sun. A few chairs and sofas positioned under a cover. One client, seated, a woman. A waiter roamed around. No sign of anyone who may be Happy Gary. Hale glanced at his watch. 9:48 a.m. Cursed. Too early. He stopped, leaned against a lamppost, looking out to the marina tower. An inflatable with outboard motor buzzed around in the water, breaking the peace. The goon by the BMW shifted in Hale's periphery, seemed to notice his approach. Happy had flouted Hale's stipulation of 'no tricks' and to arrive alone. No surprise there.

Hale remained still, feeling nausea build up in his stomach. His mind drifted, thought about Marta, and where she would be now. In a pension, or already on the train to Madrid. What clothes she had bought, where she had eaten.

His reverie was broken by the blast of a turbocharger behind, a low yellow sports car being put through its paces on a twenty-yard strip. Hale looked at his watch.

9:54 a.m.

He walked over to *Sammy's*, looked ahead only. The goons moved in his periphery again, but maintained their distance. Hale moved into the terrace area, took a seat, a soft chair near the road. A polished coffee table was laid out before him, a leather sofa opposite. The barman, tall, grey, clearly British, nodded at Hale with a faint smile.

Two minutes passed. Hale practised his breathing, tried not to rub his hands, play with his shades or fidget. The barman stayed clear, must have been told to do so. The only client, the woman at the table, fifties, maybe Russian or Polish. She flicked through a paper, seemingly bored.

Hale eyed a figure dead ahead across the street, a stocky man dressed in black. He approached with a waddle, almost a limp, head tilted slightly to one side. His build was low, stocky, common to many older Spanish men. But there was something different about him. Hale expected him to veer off, head left or right, but he kept coming. Hale noticed the goon to the left across the road stiffen, and then move away from his position against the car.

The man in black threaded his way through some chairs, turned to acknowledge the barman, sat on the sofa opposite Hale.

This man was ugly. Hale felt a strange tinge of disappointment. Jack and Dean had portrayed Happy as flamboyant, yet here was a man of diminutive stature, a wideboy cliché stuck in the sixties. His face was bloated and complimented with a blotchy orange complexion jarring against a mop of pitch-black hair positioned on top of his head. A wig, thought Hale. A type of hairpiece preferred by Argentinean gentlemen of advanced years. His shoulders were narrow, supporting a weak freckled chest on display by way of an open-collared shirt. This man had no neck, as if the head had been removed, and then glued back onto the shoulders with *SuperGlu*, the join concealed by a gaudy thick gold chain. He sat looking dead ahead, hands in his lap. Hale enjoyed a distinct height advantage from his armchair.

The standoff continued for ten seconds, neither person saying a word. Hale removed his shades.

The man sighed. "I'm Happy," he said, finally.

Hale responded immediately, "Well, you don't look it to me."

Happy tilted his head, and delivered what Hale assumed was his trademark smile: a permanent smirk on the left side of his face, a scowl of derision. Occasionally, it transformed into a wider grimace such that Happy's gold back teeth would glint.

Hale offered his hand, "Apologies. I'm guessing you've heard that pun before … Charles Hale."

Happy remained impassive, hands on lap.

"You bought your monkeys," continued Hale, pulling his hand back and flicking his eyes to the goon by the car. "On the phone I said no tricks."

Happy ignored Hale, looked to his left as the barman approached, placing a mug of tea on the table, the kind you'd be served at the British seaside. It looked like Happy's special mug sporting the St George's Cross.

"You want one?" said Happy.

"I don't drink milkshakes," said Hale.

An awkward silence. The barman looked at Hale, frowned.

After a beat, Hale said, "Café solo."

The barman walked off, Happy watched him go, waiting for privacy, looking around. Cagey. "Look sunshine," he said. "Happy doesn't have time – like some people might 'ave – to make clever conversation and sit around like a couple of ponces. You wanted to meet, so here I am and you can start explaining right now…"

"I was the skipper of the boat," said Hale, "you know that much. We had trouble with the passages across, you know that too. It was not my intention for things to go wrong. Can we at least agree on that much?"

The barman returned, placed the coffee down. Hale picked it up, being careful to steady one hand with the other, not to show the tremble.

Happy waited for the barman to be out of earshot, and then replied, leaning forward with his smirk, "You know who I am, okay. So, you know what shit you are in, sonny, don't cha?"

"I think we should move things forward positively."

"What happened to Gibby?"

"Same old story."

"What?"

"Men who go to sea often return to port, get drunk, fall in, sometimes drown. Gibby got drunk, fell in, drowned."

"Not what I 'eard."

"What did you hear?"

"I heard that you are some kind of bleedin' cad who thinks he can pull a fast one over his mates, *and* over Happy."

"I can assure you…"

"So, how about you tell me now where Jack and Dean are." Happy leaned forward, glared at Hale with black eyes. Hale noticed his habit of staring intently while speaking, and then shifting his eyes sideways when listening, as if not offering the courtesy of eye contact when the other party spoke. "And before you give me an answer, 'fink carefully, 'cos someone owes me money *and* a boat. And somehow, every bleedin' bit of hassle I've had over the last weeks points to you. Me and Gibby go back a long way, and we 'ad plans."

"I'm sorry for the loss of your colleague, but neither his death, nor the disappearance of the crew, is my fault."

"Who you working for?"

"No one. I skipper boats, deliver them, do trips."

Happy sniggered, "What do you take me for?"

"Look," said Hale, also leaning forward, getting into Happy's unsightly face. "I'm not into trafficking, money laundering, prostitution, cock-fighting or whatever other crap you're into, but there are other forces at work along this coast as I'm sure you're aware. Your threats are quite frankly tiresome and the only way forward is discussion."

"What do you mean other forces? This is Happy's patch."

"No it's not," said Hale. "You're not *that* dumb are you?"

"Watch it shitface."

Hale noticed the goon to his right enter *Sammy's*, take a position at the bar.

"Jack and Dean have taken the boat," continued Hale. "Moved it somewhere west, maybe further out this way. Who knows, if you look out to sea, you may spot them passing by now. To be honest, I think they received a better offer."

Hale leaned back. Happy frowned, staring at him.

"Go on," said Happy.

"Some outfit from Puerto de Santa María, where the boat was moored."

"Brits?"

Hale knocked back the coffee in one, replaced the cup, shook his head, "No, Eastern European as far as I can make out, Russian maybe. Small-time operators, a few youngsters, thugs. I see them on the beaches sometimes. Gym monkeys doing a bit of low-level dealing, running boats across the Alborán."

"So, Dean and Jack are working with this outfit?"

"Can't be sure, but let's just say they were hanging around with them a fair amount, especially when I was trying to sort out this thing with Gibby and when we were around for the second boat run."

"Who's the leader … of this mob?"

Hale shook his head, "I don't know for sure, but there is a rumour that he's Spanish. Goes by the name of Maradona."

"Like the footballer?"

"You're very perceptive."

"Never heard of a dealer going by that name, and he's not on my patch anyhow."

Hale sensed increasing tension in Happy. Despite his diminutive stature, this was a dangerous man with blood on his hands. Hale tried to keep that fact in his mind. "I think we should move the conversation to resolve our differences."

"How?" said Happy.

"A deal."

"Happy doesn't do deals."

"Call it an agreement."

"Go on."

"You seem to have power, influence. You're looking to find the whereabouts of *Blue Too* and get your money…"

"Get to the bleedin' point."

"Okay. I think these people will be intimidated by you."

"What does that mean?"

"*Afraid* of you."

"Go on."

"Well, they may meet and come to a settlement figure."

"So, you're in touch with them?"

"No, but they call me occasionally. Hassle me. They do this every few days, will probably do so today or tomorrow. It follows a pattern."

"How much money does this outfit turn over?"

"Difficult to say, but enough to pay for *Blue Too* and…" Hale stopped himself mid-sentence before making the blunder of mentioning the hidden cash, "...the inconvenience."

Happy's orange tan reddened, his snarl creeping up the side of his face. He thumped his fist on the table, giving the woman nearby a start. "Look here. No one mucks Happy about. This is not just about the money."

"Really? I'm told you're an astute businessman in these parts, *business* being the priority."

"Shut the crap up, you toffee-nosed ponce. This is what you're gonna do. You're gonna arrange a meeting with this Maradona geezer, so I can pull his head off and shove it up his arse. And then I'll send his mates back to the Iron Curtain or whatever shithole they come from."

Hale puffed his cheeks out, shrugged, "Okay, leave it to me. You could strike a deal, maybe work with them, get *Blue Too* back. As I say, they're not big players."

"You really don't get it do you?"

"Get what?"

A white Bentley pulled up in the middle of the road to Hale's left, the driver waiting, engine idling, holding up traffic. Hale nodded to it, "What's this?"

"My ride," said Happy.

"I didn't know you did weddings," said Hale.

"Oh, so you're the funny guy ain't cha? Well, you haven't seen the news then?" said Happy, straightening his collar, clicking a finger at the goon, making to leave.

"I haven't?" said Hale.

Happy rose to his feet, an act that did little to increase his overall height. "Well then, you wouldn't have seen that my boat, *Blue Too*, was attacked by some pricks in a RIB. Sprayed it with a bleedin' machine gun that tore through the hull killing Jack and Dean. Then, they set fire to it and scarpered. So, the way I look at it, mister ponce, is that these Russian shitheads are going to pay and you're coming to work for Happy."

Hale's mind raced to assimilate the course of events. While Marta and Hale were on the run from a faction of Karzhov and Morillo's mob, another was hunting down *Blue Too* and its temerarious crew.

"I wasn't aware … how?"

"So you're gonna let me know when I can have a little chat with these amateurs," said Happy, "and then, as I said, you're coming to work for me."

"I am?"

"That's right. Just so happens I'm in need of a skipper, since everyone else seems to be dying on me. So you's going to be manning one of my RIBS on some little jaunts I 'ave planned."

Happy limped out into the street. "Call us," he said. "I'll leave you with the bill for my tea and that shit you drink."

The goon out on the street gave the irate driver of the car behind a stern look: *don't try it*. Then opened the back door of the Bentley. Happy stepped in.

The Bentley crept off, taking a right at the corner towards the centre of town.

FORTY-FIVE

Back at *Hostel Pepe*, Hale lay on the bed in the cool and dark, staring at the ceiling and listening to the cry of parakeets from a palm across the road. He couldn't think about much other than Jack and Dean. Both dead. He held little remorse for Dean, though for Jack there was at least some latent bond, the companionship of men who work together at sea regardless of background or differences.

One thing was clear: Karzhov was, as Marta had alluded, powerful and ruthless. And Morillo's extended network within Spain, born of his eagerness to comply with and impress the Russian, was an extra asset to an already revered mafia ring. Hale worried about his own tactic to play down Morillo's influence and lead Happy Gary to him, or at least to a man going by Hale's hastily-contrived pseudonym, *Maradona*.

He went to the window, looked down into the street, pondering the whereabouts of Marta, Morillo, and Karzhov. This plan could backfire, he thought. Neither party will hesitate to kill me, should this fabrication be uncovered.

In the street, a slim woman dressed in red overalls and a Hi-Vis jacket, attractive, forties, pushed a trolley, cleared litter from the pavement. Bin workers looking like fashion models, thought Hale. Only in Spain, or maybe Italy too. A couple walked along the street, their child swung from their hands, laughing. Hale missed Deborah. He could be taking her to the park or driving her to the pictures. He thought about the treadmill back home. The *C2C*, heading back to Leigh, looking forward to the rugby on the television or a pint in the pub.

That world has gone now, Charles.

Now you're alone. Marta has gone, as have Lucy and Deborah. You're alone in a hostel in southern Spain, calculating, theorising about how you may set one faction of ruthless criminals against another.

Nice one, Charles.

But what of the alternative? To run forever, to always be looking in the rear-view mirror, over his shoulder? Happy Gary had plans for Hale: to run the boats, the RIBS. Hale knew this would immerse him fully into criminality and drug running across the Strait. Happy would no doubt place Hale on the riskier missions that cropped up, leaving his more trusted companions to run easier routes or coordinate the retrieval of hashish burlaps from the beaches. The tale would be a simple one, hardly making the headlines of some English rag hitting the fish and chip shops in Torremolinos:

British boat handler arrested for drug smuggling – Spanish court appearance set.

Hale spent the afternoon not doing much, in deep thought. Not about the danger, his predicament, but about his position in the world. The future. This moment, these weeks, would come and go like clouds sweeping across the sky. But what of the future for Charles Hale? *If* he survived?

He walked to a supermarket two blocks away, bought some fruit, olives and bread, returned to Calle Bermeja and the hostel. All quiet, no Blochead on the corner, no shady people hanging around, just the kindly receptionist shuffling papers and a cleaner mopping the already-pristine marble. Hale spent the evening in a bar across the road packed with local men who played dominoes. As evening turned to night, the beer fuzzed his mind and the scene transformed to a younger, louder crowd watching football. The next morning, much the same. Sitting in a café next door to the bar. Three coffees, tostadas. Hanging out, living a Spanish life.

These hours he knew he must enjoy. The calm. His life may take a turn for better or worse, probably the latter, though he shuddered at the thought. His liberties snatched from him, shot or thrown in prison, his life ended or damaged irreparably.

In the meeting with Happy, Hale was right about one thing: Morillo's goons would call. While paying for the coffees, his phone rang. He handed ten euros to the girl at the bar, shielded his ear from the noise, took the call.

"Charles Hale."

"Mister Hallay, we speak before, remember?"

"I do remember." Hale recognised the voice of Blochead.

"We have problem and, like I say before, you come work with us. You see, you cause big trouble with boss. Boss gives shit, so I come to you for help."

"How sad for you," said Hale, crossing the road, stepping into the hostel, "and what problem might you have?"

"When I say *problem*, mister, I mean both. *We* have problem. Especially you. You see, your friends they were..."

"I know what happened to them," Hale whispered as he entered the silence of the hostel, nodded to the receptionist, and climbed the stairs.

"Good, now you know what happen to people who screw with Morillo."

"And Sergei."

"Yes, and Sergei too, clever man. Berto is our friend. You should understand this, because Sergei is not so nice a man." Hale rattled the key in the door, moved into the room, pacing as Blochead continued, "You know in Tarifa, you lucky we not get you and girl, because out there, no one around ... we make fire and barbeque, and girl watches us feed you to dogs and vultures, yes?"

"Sounds pleasant, however, I don't have time to discuss your cooking ideas. I'd like to meet with Morillo ... to talk business."

The line went quiet, just static. "Hello?"

"Yes, hello mister," said Blochead. "Berto will meet. Where are you?"

"Nerja."

"Why do I not believe you, mister? Anyhow, Berto will not go to this place."

"I want somewhere out in the open, a public place," said Hale. "I can go to Málaga."

A pause, more static. Hale picked up voices, the tail end of an animated discussion, and then, "Berto will meet you in Málaga. You know Teatro Cervantes?"

"I know it."

"Nine tonight, you stand in open square in front of theatre. There is your public place mister English."

The line went dead.

FORTY-SIX

Hale chose not to hide in the shadows, the recesses, or to stake out the place beforehand. Rather, he stood dead centre in the Plaza de Jerónimo Cuervo, looking ahead towards the Teatro Cevantes, modest and elegant, a classical building dominant amongst surrounding cafés and restaurants. The night, hot and balmy, a few lovers and families strolled around, busy, but no tourists. Theatregoers mingled in the brightly-lit reception area beyond glass entrance doors. Tonight's performance, of strangely Anglo origins: *Enrique VIII*, Henry VIII.

8:56 p.m.

A few minutes to go. Hale scanned around, felt exposed. But what harm could come to him out in the open like this? Beads of sweat rolled down his back to the base of his spine. Normally he'd wear shorts and a t-shirt in this weather, but a shirt and jeans were more apt for these surroundings. His heart rate was up. Same old Charles Hale, stressed up with the latest situation, the latest crisis. Just like the meeting with Happy, waiting, trying not to think the worst.

No one conspicuous around, no one looking like Happy's goons, or Blochead. This place was as relaxed as any place he'd been. He could be out in the hills in some pueblo, the residents of whom herded goats, tended their homes, drank wine, and didn't think about much else. That's how relaxed this was. Not the atmosphere in which he'd expected to meet the infamous Morillo.

Hale's phone vibrated and rang, giving him a start. He grabbed it from his trouser pocket, calming himself before answering.

"Hale."

"Buenas noches. I see you have come to meet, so look to your right."

The man spoke with good English, accented. Hale looked to his right. A few passers-by strolled before a rustic restaurant and bar situated off to the left on a corner.

"Morillo?" said Hale.

"What do you see?"

"Restaurant, a bar on the left."

"That's correct. Go to the bar."

"You alone?"

"Go to the bar." The man hung up.

Hale pocketed the phone, moved off as instructed, looked around as he did so. No goons, no Blochead. Ahead, the bar was quiet, bright inside. He could see through the wooden framed windows. A group of people stood in a group, theatregoers, drinking, having tapas. The main doors were open, a waiter standing on the step, rising onto his tiptoes, passing the time, greeting customers. Beyond the waiter, a figure leaned at the bar. Fat. Moderate height, black hair, fifties, white shirt and trousers, smart. He stood alone accompanying two glasses of red wine on the bar.

Hale acknowledged the waiter, stepped inside. The man at the bar was eyeing him all the way, tracking him. His skin was dark, naturally so, with a thick mop of hair neatly combed. His eyes were hard, but not without intelligence, curiosity.

"Berto?"

Unlike Happy Gary, the man offered his hand with a hearty smile revealing expensively-capped teeth. And unlike Happy, unyielding eye contact. Hale accepted a strong handshake. Firm, dry, not that of a pen-pusher.

"Please," said Morillo, motioning to the glass of wine. Hale was taken aback by the man's politeness, took a sip from the large glass graced with a splash of red ink at the base. This was good wine, this was a fine bar, and this was a man of education, culture. Hale forced himself to switch his thoughts to Marta, her fear, the power Morillo imposed upon her, the brutality she'd described.

"So, we finally meet Charles Hale," said Morillo, pronouncing his name as if double-barrelled and with a slur, *Sharles-Ale*, an inflection of which Hale was not opposed.

"I think it was inevitable that we'd meet," said Hale.

Morillo ignored the comment, took a sip of wine, slowly lowering the glass towards the polished dark wood of the bar. "You know I am glad you chose the beautiful city of Málaga for our meeting. This wine they serve here, *Pinot Noir*, is one of my favourites. It comes from a producer near Cádiz. Natural, you know. The farms grow almonds, vegetables, and even pigs run around in the dirt, unlike purpose-farmed places."

Hale said nothing.

"You know I went to London one time," Morillo continued, "and had wine in some place – at least they called it wine – tasted like *Red Bull*. Shit, not to my liking."

The first sign of Morillo's less polite side.

"Am I here to learn about the history of Spanish wine, or is there another reason?" said Hale.

The barman placed the tapa in front of them. Morillo frowned at Hale, popped an olive into his mouth, and then smiled, "So, Sharles-Ale, I see you are a man who likes to get down to business. Very well."

"Before we do," said Hale, looking around. "Are we alone here?"

Morillo laughed, "Alone? You think I bring protection, no?"

"I know who you are."

"Well, it depends what you mean by *alone*."

"I find the meaning of the word quite simple."

"Indeed. But I must inform you, that although I have no bodyguards with me, that we are in Andalucía, señor." Morillo's eyes were dark, narrowing as he spoke. "And here, in my home, I am never really alone. These people in the bars, in the road out here, they all know me. Even the people who pick up the rubbish know me."

"How wonderful, so you're famous. Or shall I say, infamous?"

"Ha. My colleague said you like to joke," said Morillo, emptying his glass. His faced hardened, a look Hale had expected sooner. "All I am saying, Inglés, is that out here in my country, wherever I go, I am never really alone. But you, well…"

Hale interrupted, switched the subject, looking to establish a position, any position, "You should leave Marta alone, forget her."

Morillo stared at Hale, the mafioso's eyes steely, and early glimpses of his candour now gone. "Where is Marta?" he said.

"Travelling. She'll be in another country by now," Hale said. "I don't know where. We agreed to separate for her safety and I won't see her again."

"You lie."

"She's gone. Accept it."

Morillo laughed to himself, a conceited gesture. It riled Hale.

"Marta is not a problem for me, Sharles-Ale. I will see to her."

"See to her?"

"We need to talk about *you* Inglés," Morillo said, tapping Hale on the bicep, grinning. Hale felt uneasy with this new direction.

"Me?"

"But, of course. You are of great interest to me and my friend."

"Sergei Karzhov?"

"So you know we are friends, very good. I know Sergei like a brother and we have an understanding. But unfortunately, you seem to have created much interest from Sergei by leaving a trail of dead bodies and men with injuries behind you. And, we all need to keep Sergei in good spirits, otherwise he starts making plans for people. Do you know what I am saying?"

"What do you mean by dead bodies?"

Morillo caught the eye of the barman, issued an order: "Dos mas vinos."

The barman immediately refilled the glasses with a bottle reserved for Morillo.

"There is the case of an incident in a bar in Puerto de Santa María," continued Morillo.

"*Pedro's.*"

"Yes. And this, I understand, was a meeting for friends … to negotiate."

"Enzo used force, intimidation."

Morillo ignored the comment. "Sergei and me, we heard about this man, Sharles, who runs the boats. Then I hear about him with Marta, and then I hear about Enzo." Morillo clenched his fist, his anger now clear. "Then I hear about two more dead in the hills, and then I hear about another in Tarifa…"

"Tarifa?"

"Yes, *perros*, by dogs. Then I hear that this man Sharles-Ale has, how do you say? Escaped me."

"Evaded."

"Yes, *evaded* me again." Morillo calmed himself, returned his gaze to the wine glass, urging Hale to indulge. "So you can see, it is a pleasure for me to make the acquaintance of the crazy Inglés. The crazy Inglés who Sergei wants dead."

Hale said nothing, took a sip, leaving Morillo to play the next card.

"Who do you work for señor Ale?"

"I don't work for anyone."

Morillo shook his head, tutted, continued, "I find this difficult to believe. Many people are now talking about you, this man who drives the boats, who goes with Andaluz women, who plays games with me."

"These rumours are unfounded."

"Look. I have respect for men who are ambitious and I happen to have a need for someone who can run boats. You can make your life easy, Inglés, and you can have any car you want, any woman, a place to live in safety."

"I'm not looking to do your kind of work."

Morillo sighed, delivered a condescending smirk. This man knew how to belittle, make his opponent feel an inch high. "Look at you Sharles-Ale," he continued, "what are you doing with your life? You taking these risks, you running, always scared. You can change this, no?"

Hale inched away from the bar, pushed the wine glass aside. "The yacht," he said. "Why did you kill those people offshore near here?"

Morillo shrugged, shook his head, said nothing.

Hale continued, "You thought *I* was aboard didn't you?"

"Things happen out on the sea every day," said Morillo. "Stupid people try to steal other people's stuff, the guns come out. La Guardia sometimes get involved, sometimes not. You read the news, no? You say Sergei sent his people, but who is to say what those people on the boat were doing. You think they were nice people, you're sorry for them?"

"What I feel is not the issue. I was working for someone, and now this person has no crew and no boat. I can tell you this: he is not pleased."

Morillo's eyebrows raised on hearing this new information, "So you *are* working with someone?"

"I was. He wants me to work with him again, but he doesn't like complications."

"Complications?"

"You and your idiots following me. You killing the boat crew, destroying the boat. If this continues, I cannot work with them again."

"These people are responsible for the two people dead in the car crash, and the man who met his fate with the dogs?" asked Morillo.

Hale shrugged, "Maybe."

"Who is this man, your jefe?"

"Goes by the name of Happy Gary."

"I've heard of him, another Inglés."

"Yes, a businessman with many interests."

"They are all the same, this type of people. Fools who come and go, usually killed by their own kind. You should come work with me, forget this hombre."

"I don't work with people I don't know."

"Then you will die Sharles-Ale, and that is not my problem." Morillo signalled the barman for the bill, "La cuenta." Hale balked at his abruptness.

"This man, Happy Gary," said Hale. "He wants to talk, make a deal."

"A deal?" Morillo laughed. "What kind of deal?"

"He has work coming up, big jobs. Boat runs across to Tangier, and he needs boat handlers. I'm the best, so he wants me. But he needs you off my back. He'll pay for you to stay away from me."

"How much?"

"Half a million."

Morillo nodded. Proper money. His face now serious, he said, "Half a million euros for Berto to do nothing, it sounds impossible."

"Pounds, sterling."

Morillo frowned, "This man only works in English money?"

"Yes."

"So, if we agree to this English money from your friend, how do we get it?"

I arrange the meeting, no tricks, somewhere open, public.

"Maybe I can talk to this Happy man, because I see there is a way we can work together."

Hale shrugged, "Whatever. But that's not my business. You can talk, but I just drive boats."

Morillo huffed, "You know, they say the English are crazy, and I have to say this is funny. But I like that you are professional, and that you also take risks. You are a risk-taker, my friend. I was like this when I was very young, but not at your age. My worry for you is that these risks are too high and too plentiful. Soon, like a cat, you run out of lives. Like those greedy pigs in Las Vegas and Monaco in the casinos, they put too many chips on one last bet, and then they go down."

"Very eloquent," said Hale, "but do we have a deal?"

Morillo paid the barman, handed over a fifty, more gift than tip. The barman was effuse with thanks, Morillo waved him off.

"A deal, no," said Morillo. "That is up to your friend, the Happy man. I will, however, meet with him to talk about his plans. You call me to arrange." Morillo made to leave, offered his hand. Hale shook it, squeezed, held on.

"One other thing," said Hale.

"Sí?"

"There will never be any agreement, no money, no nothing, unless you leave the girl alone."

FORTY-SEVEN

Hale pondered the rationale behind his audacious plan, a strategy *evolved* rather than calculated. Maybe suicidal. Yes, these were drug barons and crooks, but also killers. Was it fanciful to believe that both sides would attend the so-called 'meeting' that Hale had arranged?

Both parties insisted on open, public areas. When Hale phoned Happy Gary's bonehead, there was little discussion. A beach location just east of Marbella, in broad daylight at noon suited Happy. Similarly, Morillo had no problem. Hale was surprised at the ease at which the arrangement was made. Both views seemed clear: we're a powerful outfit, and besides, what could go wrong on a tourist beach in broad daylight? A few guys would meet, strut around in Armani getting sand in their two hundred euro shoes, and discuss money. Discuss Hale's employment as the boat runner, and from Morillo's perspective, agree on a collaboration with Happy's operation, or a buyout.

But Hale knew more than either party. He lay on the bed at *Hostel Pepe* mulling the intricacies of this engagement. Happy Gary believed he was meeting small time drug dealers headed by the little-known *Maradona*. His intent boarded on revenge for loss of personnel and cash, whereas the more powerful and connected Morillo was perhaps less perturbed by the loss of a few of his foot soldiers flying off a mountainside in a car. Morillo was intrigued, desired control over Hale, extending it to make a move on Happy's operation, and moreover, to keep tabs on Marta. Hale was in no doubt that torture would be on the cards for him. Hale would break, reveal that Marta had travelled to Madrid, and then Morillo's network would come into play. They would track her down. But no matter how perverse and deluded the mobsters' motives, there was another.

Greed.

Morillo might get out of bed to negotiate, make a deal, for any figure amounting to six figures or beyond. Similarly, Happy saw in Hale the potential for numerous boat runs and deliveries in the dead of night. Runs that would yield countless burlaps of hashish and coke. 'Stuff' for distribution to the clubs and bars across the English-dominated stretch between Gibraltar and Málaga. This contraband to be handled by gangsters and pushers, most of whom were high on the shit themselves, all being sure to return Happy's beloved sterling currency. And no one crossed Happy. That was the rule, the word on the street. At least it was before Hale's arrival on the scene, a man who'd set a precedent that Happy would be eager to quash.

In Hale's mind, this *Meeting of the Mafiosos* was a diversionary tactic while he and Marta fled Andalucía. Confusion would reign. A conflict between the factions might buy time for the couple, and an alternative to submitting to either side. In Madrid, Marta could at least be with someone, her family, explain the situation, hide in the metropolis. In Britain, Hale would disappear, change his name, and let time take its course. Wales or Scotland came to mind, remote. Morillo's reach would not extend to Britain. Sergei Karzhov was another matter, the lesser-known quantity, but not one that Hale could contemplate now.

He rose from the bed. He'd become fond of the hostel and the cool tranquillity, the anonymity. No one asked questions. The bars and cafés accepted him, and were mostly indifferent to the Englishman's presence. But that was beginning to change. The questions from waiters and old men were coming, friendly, but inquisitive too. Occasional looks and smiles he'd earned from a girl who worked in a leafy café both warmed his heart, but also chilled him. Time to move on.

This is how it would be now in Spain, and Britain too.

10:00 a.m.

Two hours before Happy Gary and Berto Morillo would meet. Two days ago, the meeting date was set for noon on the beach in front of a tennis and golf resort. Hale tried to imagine the sequence. Holidaymakers would cook themselves on sun loungers, a few boats and swimmers messing around as they do on countless beaches along Spain's coastlines. Happy and Morillo would come together on the patch ten metres in front of a chiringuito called *Sally's*, a Brit place selling cool drinks, sandals, inflatable toys and other junk. The meeting would be convivial for two to three minutes, but then it would break down. Confusion. The goons on both sides would become aggressive, shit would happen, and the Guardia would arrive promptly. The Guardia would arrive promptly because they don't like shit going down in broad daylight in tourist resorts. They don't like shit going down because the resultant bad press turns tourists away, and along with it, millions of euros. Those numbers go upstairs to the local authorities, and then to the government who kick the Guardia's butt. The Guardia doesn't get its butt kicked needlessly, if at all. The Guardia would arrive promptly for that reason, and for another. A tip-off. A tip-off from some crackhead who lived on a steel boat in Puerto de Santa María. Some crackhead who had long owed Hale a favour and whose brother worked for the Guardia in Málaga. Hale had taken the crackhead up on that favour.

That was the rough sequence of events as Hale predicted. Following this, the mob convention would be hauled into some offices and cells for prolonged questioning, forms and paperwork shoved before them, all taking considerable time and deliberation. Time Hale would use to get out of town.

Tomorrow, he would take the 5:50 a.m. flight from Málaga to Gatwick, the earliest day he could book. In Britain, he'd recover for a day, retrieve some possessions, take care of business.

And then vanish.

FORTY-EIGHT

12 noon.

Seated on the pavement under some palms, Hale ordered a second coffee. The café overlooked a line of parked scooters. Across the way, the cleaner tended to flower pots decorating the entrance to *Hostel Pepe*.

Hale smiled to the waitress. She returned the compliment, spoke no English, not a word. A good chance for Hale to practise a few words of Spanish. They spoke about Marbella, something about it being busier and the weather very hot, *muy caliente*. Hale knew this was the last time they would speak. He'd leave early tomorrow and must then stay clear of Spain, maybe forever. But it was good to talk. She was young, pretty, bright eyes not tempered or strained with worry or responsibility.

It made life seem normal, as if everything was fine under the sun and amidst the bustle of an ordinary day. In the street, cars and trucks bolted up and down, somehow having no impact on the ambience of the café. As with many Spanish cafés and restaurants, this one nonchalantly teetered on the edge of traffic mayhem. A light breeze ruffled the palms above and the parakeets swooped from building to palm and back for no apparent reason other than to fly free. A few students chatted on the next table, prodding iPhones, drinking glasses of milky coffee, one with a bottle of beer.

Normal life at five minutes past noon. No one looked at Hale, asked any questions, suspected anything. Just another guy in a café.

His mind rode the caffeine buzz, heart rate down, thinking good thoughts. There was no turning back, since the point of no return had elapsed. An hour ago, he could have made some calls, pulled the plug, but not now. There was no point in contemplating events on the beach, no point in doing anything other than ticking the minutes and hours away until the taxi to the airport the following morning.

An hour later, he ordered some food, *Ensalada Rusa*, and a beer. Doodled on a pad, made some notes. He thought of Lucy and Deborah, their whereabouts. Then of Pam and Stack and Baz and how he'd enjoy a pint of warm ale in the *Cheshire Cheese* when autumn turned to winter. The cosy nights, cobbled streets of London, a world of which he was fond, far from the gregarious people, heat, and colour of this place.

Hale peered up at the television in the bar. No news flashes, no people crowded around watching an event happening live. No 'incident' or disturbance on a nearby beach. No break in the music on the radio, no heated discussions amongst the clientele.

That evening, much the same. No news, no calls from Happy's bonehead, none from Morillo or anyone else. Hale packed his rucksack, connected up to the hostel's WiFi, checked the weather on his laptop: a misty late September in London. Unremarkable conditions, no delays predicted. Tonight, he'd drink water, eat fruit and bread, read.

8:16 p.m.

Hale's cell rang. Caller ID unknown. He took the call.

"Hello old boy, me here."

Rupert's voice, immediately recognisable. This was unusual. Baz phoned once every two weeks, once a month sometimes, but Rupert, once every five years, sometimes less frequently. Rups was more of a face-to-face person, or email from a Hotmail account, an account that seemed to change frequently such that Hale had to call to reconfirm it when his messages bounced.

"Rups. Gosh, this is a surprise, how are things?"

"Marvellous."

"Humphs okay?"

"Fine. Out in the garden chasing bumblebees today. Never seen him so lively. Must be the biscuits I'm feeding him."

"So what's up?"

"Where are you? Got a minute for a chat?"

"I'm still in the country, west of you," said Hale, sitting up, placing his book on the dresser.

"Good, good. Need to show caution on this line, understood? Walls have ears and all that."

"Of course," said Hale. Despite the usual banter, he sensed a tinge of concern in Rupert's voice.

"Seen the news?"

"Nope. Do I need to?" said Hale.

"Are you in Spain for long?" asked Rupert.

"No, leaving tomorrow."

"Good. Do that."

Hale craned his neck, held the phone to his ear. Then switched on the battered portable television, plugged in the aerial to get a signal, and flicked through the channels. "My TV's on now, Rups, what am I looking for?"

"It's not showing now, but caught a glimpse of something ten minutes ago."

"Something?"

"Mm. Seems there was a beach party recently."

"*Okay…*"

"Yes, how can I describe it? A soiree with some undesirables. Wouldn't be anything to do with you would it?"

"Can you elaborate?"

"Well, let's just say I had my suspicions about what you said when we met. One of the partygoers seems to be a Brit. The other faction, indeterminate bunch, maybe Eastern European. Reports are sketchy at the moment. I reckon the authorities are drip-feeding it to the press, lessening the impact."

Hale felt a familiar dryness in his mouth return, clenched his fist, a mild grind of his teeth.

"And what happened, Rups? Any details?"

"Seems a bit of a shindig went on, old boy."

"Bodies?"

"Bloodbath."

"Shit."

"Quite," said Rupert. "Thought I'd give you the heads-up."

"Thanks, Rups. You okay? Anything on the flying lesson?"

"God no. Usual stuff, made a column in a Spanish daily, and that's it."

"Good."

"Look, son, you keep your head down now, won't you?"

"I will, of course," said Hale.

"Be safe and let's meet up in the smoke for a pint of *Bombardier* sometime."

"Say hi to Humphs."

"Will do, ciao now."

"Ciao."

Hale closed the call, searched the television channels. He caught the tail end of the report, a shot of journalists and cameramen held back by Guardia officers, 4x4s and ambulances attending a chaotical beach scene. Something about *tres muertos*, three dead. Hale fumed when it switched to a report of a Papal visit, and then to football.

He had a choice: sit up all night, scanning the channels for news, or let it go and shut it out of his mind. In some ways, any knowledge of the events might be a good thing, helping to form a strategy. In another way, perhaps bad, increasing his anxiety when he needed to be calm at airport Passport Control and through security. Tomorrow, the news would break all over the television, radio, and newspapers. An incident of this magnitude on a tourist beach, involving big players in the criminal underworld would make headlines, create a stir internationally. That would all come in the morning, but he needed to remain focussed on the goal: get out of Spain.

Hale switched the television off, placed the remote on the windowsill, far enough away so that he wouldn't be tempted to grab it from the bed. With his bags packed, he positioned them in the wardrobe. Then headed out into the night to a store, returning with a few bottles of beer. Brands strong enough to fuzz the worry, whilst leaving a clear enough head when the alarm on his cell sounded at 4:00 a.m.

FORTY-NINE

1:13 a.m.

Hale awoke.

Without a thought, he rose, grabbed the remote from the windowsill and switched the television on. The glare of the display hurt his eyes. He trawled the channels: a music video with Enrique Iglesias, *Discovery Wildlife*, *Canal 24*, the news.

The 'beach party', as Rupert has described it, was all over the channel. Recorded footage of bodies being loaded into ambulances, or bloodstained, laying on the beach. Three dead, a shootout. The newsreader interviewed a local authority figure, a woman from the government. They were trying to determine whom the factions were, what happened. One tourist was injured, shot in the leg. The bar owner, a Brit from the chiringuito was interviewed, her English dubbed over in Spanish. She described the chaos, people running, terrified. Something about others joining the firefight, and then fleeing to the car park and speeding off when the Guardia and Policía arrived.

Happy Gary's picture appeared, followed by Morillo's. Archived press photographs. Happy looked younger, more thuggish. It appeared Happy was injured, shot in the hand, a common and instinctive reaction to block shots fired. Morillo was arrested. Footage from a television camera operator showed him being roughly manhandled into a police van, his suit ruffled. The lens received the heavy hand of a Guardia official pushing the media away. Further handheld cell phone footage showed the scuffle on the beach. Not much to see other than a few dark shapes on the sand, bodies down, and suits fleeing the beach.

There was talk of an investigation, the impact on tourism in the area, emergency meetings about thuggery and violence on the 'Costas'. Among the officials, Hale recognised one figure. The old jacket, the stoop, a mildly gaunt look born of overwork, cigarettes, and coffee: Manolo Fernández, the Inspector and assistant to María Díez.

Hale switched the TV off.

It was now two and a half hours before the alarm would sound. He cursed, knew he shouldn't have watched the news.

4:06 a.m.

Hale placed the key on the reception desk. Someone moved in the back room, the night attendant stirring from slumber. He eased the front door shut and headed along Calle Bermeja, the early hours dry and still, a contrast to its frenzied daytime buzz. A few cars and motorbikes broke the silence accompanied by a slow-moving garbage truck and a few gabbling workers surrounding it.

He'd lightened his bag, which would now qualify as hand luggage. Having checked in for the flight online, a simple passport check would see him through security. Something Hale had done countless times before. No problem. No cause to worry.

At the end of Calle Bermeja, he looked across the main street to a rank of three taxis, crossed the street, headed towards the front. Three drivers chatted in a huddle, looking down at a newspaper held open by one of them. Sensing Hale's approach, the driver holding the newspaper flung it through the window of the taxi and opened the passenger door. Two minutes later they were on the dual carriageway to Málaga, Hale in the passenger seat, window wide open, radio loud, speed excessive. On hearing Hale's Spanish, the driver somehow deemed him fluent, thus hammered out a stream of unfathomable Castilian. The driver's speed put Hale's already-frayed nerves on edge, as did the snippets he was able to glean from the driver's barrage: *football is not like it used to be, they get paid stupid money, that thing on the beach is outrageous, the town is ruled by mafiosos, the Guardia should do more, they are paid too much to cruise around in fancy trucks like they do.*

Signs for the airport shot overhead, bright white and blue illuminated by streaming headlights in the darkness. The taxi shot ahead of a truck, swerved off a tight bend and onto a slip road to the airport. They climbed up to the new Departures area. Recently refurbished, a huge glass structure with coaches and taxis unloading hordes of passengers.

Hale paid the driver, left a tip, walked quickly beyond the throngs of luggage and confusion. He slowed, paused as he took the escalators to the first floor. No need to rush, look normal. Just another flight.

The Departures area was busy. People hustling through a queue at the security scanners, their voices echoing through the vast soulless atrium. Good, get lost in the crowd. He threw his bag on the floor, placed some liquids in a plastic bag, checked passport and boarding pass. The remaining euros, around a thousand, were tucked in his laptop case and in the bag and wallet. No big amount, no big deal.

All set.

A snaking line of passengers queued towards two security checkpoints, each with body and hand luggage scanners. Hale took the right, guided by an assistant checking boarding passes and handing out plastic bags for liquids. It was going well, moving swiftly. People seemed relaxed and the officers on the far side of the scanners were smiling, in a good mood. Beyond them, armed officers, Guardia, two women and one man, looked on, also relaxed, chatting.

Hale removed his cell phones, watch and laptop, placed them in a plastic box, slid them onto the conveyor. He moved behind a middle-aged couple, both in matching golf shorts and polo shirts, fussing with oversized hand luggage. Too slow. People streamed by in the other queue. Self-conscious, Hale felt his face redden. Tried to remain calm, looked around, and then down to his feet.

The couple ahead still fussed, argued. Hale tried to slip past them, but was directed back by the assistant. Flustered, he cursed quietly. Then did what he vowed he would not: locked eyes with the officer beyond the scanners. The eyes reveal much, and in Hale's case, they said one thing: I'm jumpy.

The polo shirts went through, the man holding his shorts up to his bulbous belly to prevent them falling to the ground. Hale felt sweat on his brow, heart pumping. His plastic tray and bag were in the scanner. He stood before it, waiting for the attendants to wave him through. The woman did so, the same woman who had locked eyes with him.

He walked through. The scanner beeped. Hale looked down, brushed his pockets, checked for his watch. They were all in the tray.

The woman blurted something in Spanish, pointed to his waist. The belt. He removed it, went back. She waved him through again.

No beep.

Hale recovered his tray and calmly redressed.

He was through.

A wave of relief eased through his mind and body. He strolled dreamily through the Duty Free area looking at products he had no intention to buy: perfumes, bottles of liquor. Into the lounge, he checked out bookshops and retailers selling newspapers, tourist souvenirs, shiny electronics goods, designer sports gear. But his mind was elsewhere. He was through security, practically back in Britain. And in Britain he could work things out, be clear of the relentless pursuit by mobsters and the authorities.

A plastic-looking café sold bland coffee and pastries wrapped in cellophane. Hale gladly paid the extortionate price, sat on a hard chair bolted to a table, savouring every sip, every bite of the stale-sweet offering. A television aired the news on a screen in the bar next door. A group of three men with pints of *Guinness* gawked at it. Hale changed seats so as not to see the screen. No point in worrying further.

An hour later, the gate appeared on the Departures board. A gaggle of holidaymakers headed for Passport Control, and beyond, on to Gate 102. Hale moved past most of them and queued, once again behind the polo shirts. It seemed they were destined to be in his way.

Hale stopped at the red mark. The polos went through, Hale followed, stepped forward to the booth, calm.

"Hola, buenos días."

"Hola."

The guard, thirties, impassive, swiped the passport, waved him through.

No problem.

Hale felt a mild high, euphoria. He climbed the shiny linoleum slope towards Gate 102. In Britain, he really could sort this shit out. The runs with *Blue Too* were always numbered. He had always aimed to quit, and this trip was part of that objective. With Marta, he could perhaps re-establish contact when it was safe. And hard though it was, things with Lucy and Deborah would be different now. They would split, but he could maybe see them from time-to-time under different circumstances.

The debts were more problematic, but he'd need to take the fall. Both he and Lucy would have to receive advice from lawyers and solicitors. The house would have to go, something that Lucy would find more difficult than Hale. Damage limitation. Cutting losses was the only way forward.

Perhaps he could pick up the pieces at *Connecting4Business*, get some cash coming in. Pam and the team below Stack made it bearable. The daily grind, his old life in London giving him a thread to cling to until he hauled himself clear of insolvency.

He found a seat overlooking the runway. The Gatwick flight was being prepared in the darkness. Vehicles sped about the concrete, headlights streaming. Workers loped around, not in any particular rush, same scene for them: packing British tourists with a handful of Spanish nationals into a flying sardine can. Hale chuckled at the notion. In under three hours, that sardine can would somehow be on the concrete in misty old London.

Maybe Marta could come to London. She'd like that, so different. The notion filled him with a buzz. He scribbled notes on a pad, the priorities. Hide out for some weeks, head north, hold the situation at work, ring them and control Stack. See a solicitor about the house and finances. Contact Lucy when the time was right. See Baz discreetly, and after a few days, check the news and the status of Morillo and Happy Gary. Rups would help with that. Then, with time, ease back into society.

Fanciful thoughts perhaps, but there was hope.

His eyes were sore. Thirty minutes to boarding remained. He put his head back, pulled Marta into his thoughts, and drifted into blissful unconsciousness.

FIFTY

Marta and Hale sat around a table in a café in Covent Garden, just off the cobbled street, the morning bright and frosty. She smiled, flicked her eyes, indicating something, someone to the left. They both laughed at a busker waving to her, trying to catch the pretty Spaniard's eye. So different with Marta in winter clothes. She felt the cold, but loved the eccentricities of London's people.

Hale's delirium was shattered by a sharp feeling on his right wrist. Cold metal. He snapped awake, squinting under the pale yellow light of Gate 102. Two figures stood before him, gradually came into focus.

He began breathing hard, looking around, trying to assess the situation. Reality, dream, or nightmare?

Like a winded blow to the stomach, it struck home: this *was* reality.

A call came over the tannoy: the flight to Gatwick was delayed by thirty minutes. Passengers were to clear the Gate area while an 'incident' was dealt with.

An incident.

Hale sat up, composed himself.

Ahead, Rosa María Díez stood, smart black trouser suit, clipboard in hand, glaring. Stern. To her left, Manolo Fernández, the Inspector, with his hands in pockets and wearing a look of satisfaction.

Hale looked down to his right. Handcuffs attached his wrist to that of the person seated next to him. He looked up to the face. Pepe Duarte, Fernández's sidekick, expressionless, looking ahead.

"How does it feel?" said María Díez.

"I'm sorry?" said Hale, grabbing a look over his right shoulder. Passengers for the flight were crammed against a yellow tape demarcating the Gate area. They appeared disgruntled, gossiping amongst themselves, pointing in Hale's direction, tutting.

"They are not happy, Mr Hale, since you have delayed them."

"I have?"

"You have. And how does it feel?"

"I don't follow you."

"To have the handcuffs."

Hale said nothing. María Díez continued, "You see, this is a feeling you must get used to. To be arrested, to be incarcerated, to be held or imprisoned by the authorities. This is what it feels like to be a criminal, Mr Hale."

Hale noticed her eyes, deep black, were beautiful, direct, but never shifted. Many people's eyes scan, shifting from one eye to the other of the opposing person's. María Díez's did not, such was her control, her focus. Her aura unnerved him, as it had done each time they had met.

"I'm going back to London," said Hale. A vacuous statement issued to play for time.

"Really? I do not think so," said María Díez, taking a step closer, so that Hale was required to look up at an angle. Hale noticed she lowered her voice as she continued, conscious perhaps of the nearby passengers, "I have some questions."

Hale said nothing.

"You seem to be gathering a reputation."

"I do?"

Beside her, Fernández sighed, shook his head. María Díez looked left two degrees, shifted her eyes, a silent riposte to the Inspector. "Can you explain, Mr Hale," she continued, "anything about the death in San Isidro, of a young man, Spanish? A man by the name of Enzo Martínez?"

Hale pursed his lips, said nothing.

"No. I thought that would be the answer," she said. "And I suppose you have no knowledge of the deaths of two people – foreign people – in the hills just east of here? An *accident*, so we are told by the newspapers."

Hale shook his head, shrugged.

She went on, "And it seems interesting that my people discovered a vehicle, burnt-out and abandoned in a ravine not far from this area. The vehicle seems to have been registered to you, Mr Hale, from a rental company in Puerto de Santa María. Can you explain this for me?"

"I…"

María Díez moved the clipboard from her chest, drew a pen. "I am waiting."

"It was stolen from me," said Hale. "I was merely travelling to Málaga, when…"

"Interesting route," she said.

"Sorry?"

"Strange route to take." She turned to Fernández, switched to Spanish, annunciating such that Hale could follow, "Wouldn't you say, Inspector ... if you were travelling from Puerto de Santa María to Málaga, would you take this route into the hills?"

Fernández shook his head.

"And," continued María Díez, back to Hale in English, "it is interesting that in this particular area, on these roads into the hills, there are very few people to speak of."

"I don't understand," said Hale, working the handcuff, which was now digging into his wrist.

"Well, let me explain." She placed the pen in her top pocket. "The good Inspector and I have done some research and all we find are goat farmers and a mechanic who lives in that area. But we know of one other man, a Mr Richard Evans. Do you know of this person?"

Rups has changed his name again, thought Hale. 'Rupert Lloyd-Evans' was clearly too distinctive for his liking.

"I'm not sure I do," said Hale.

"Really? Strange, since it seems you have some things in common."

"We do?"

"Yes. Like you, he is English, evasive, and we have been watching him for some years. His activities are suspicious and a mystery to us at the moment. But I am very good at solving mysteries, Mr Hale, and I actually enjoy them."

"It's nice to have a rewarding job." Hale regretted the quip as he said it. María Díez's face hardened, she moved across to his left, placed her clipboard down, and lowered herself on the seat next to him. A light waft of shampoo, conditioner. Hale took an instinctive split-second look towards her legs as she crossed them. She seemed to notice. She leaned towards him slightly, one arm leaning against the back of the chair.

"Everything is catching up with you isn't it?" she said, tapping her forefinger lightly on his shoulder, goading. Glancing sideways,

Hale looked down at it as she did so. Nicely manicured, no varnish. "And the pressure must be bad," she went on, "with what happened in the news, the beach incident. The people involved are dangerous, and although these criminals, these thugs, are detained or being treated for their injuries, their networks are still in operation. You know what I mean, Mr Hale?"

Hale said nothing, looked down to his lap.

"This case fascinates me," she said, pulling her clipboard across, leafing through the papers, tapping the top of the board with the nail of her finger.

"And I suppose you are to tell me that this woman, Lucy Stanford, is your fiancée."

Hale looked up, taken aback by the mention of Lucy, and failing to see the relevance. A faint smile now apparent in María Díez's gaze.

"She is," Hale said.

"*Of course* she is. But isn't it interesting how you never seem to be involved with anyone with any plain motive, a plain motive such as getting married or being with someone you love, just because you love them?"

Hale shook his head, now lost, "I'm sorry, but I really have no idea what on earth you're saying, and furthermore, these people behind me are waiting and…"

"How touching that you are concerned for them. But I suppose you have no idea that Ms Stanford was detained for eighteen months for money laundering operations..." She flicked through the notes, "... let me see, *that* was three years ago. Community service as well, so my London colleague tells me, and I suppose…"

Hale shook his head, looked blankly to the floor, tracing when he'd met Lucy, her jobs, trying to think. But María Díez wouldn't let him. She continued, "You have no idea, I suppose, that she is linked with another man by the name of Ralph Pilkington, previously imprisoned for this work of receiving cash from Germany, Switzerland, and then routing it through Spain to Britain. And you, *of course*, have no idea that they were linked to other English people in Nerja town, who were involved in fraudulent banking practices, laundering, embezzlement, which caused them also to pay fines and serve sentences."

Ralph the Buffoon, a crook. Brenda and Gerry, *The Perfect Couple*. Both crooks.

A vague smile crept across Hale's face.

María Díez seemed to notice Hale's reaction, seemed to pique her curiosity rather than throw her off guard. "Something funny, Mr Hale?"

"No … it's just that, despite what you think. I was not aware…"

María Díez rose, indicated something to Fernández with a nod, and then walked off. Hale prepared himself for humiliation. Prepared to be cuffed on both hands, led past sniggering hordes of tourists wearing bad football shirts and pastel-coloured frocks, out into Departures where disparaging glances would be cast, until finally taken to a stark room blasted by fluorescent strip lights for his interrogation. This would mark the early stages of a long trawl through the Spanish justice system.

FIFTY-ONE

Fernández blurted an order to Duarte. The cuff was released and they both walked off to follow María Díez, leaving Hale looking on over his shoulder. He rubbed his wrist, racking his mind to reconcile the impromptu interview of the last thirty minutes. They'd left him to board the flight, and face the scorn of three hundred passengers.

The crowd did not waste any time.

A sweaty plump oaf wearing a West Ham football shirt ambled up, leaned over the back of the chair. I know what's coming from him, thought Hale.

"You wasted me time you stupid shite," said the oaf.

Next, a woman with an orange lizard face, decorated with red lipstick and eyeliner, walked over especially to deliver a similarly-inspired line. "You make me sick, your bloody type," she huffed, stomping off whilst receiving nods of approval from other lemmings in the queue, those less committed to losing their place.

Gradually, they lost interest, filed through, and boarded. Hale joined at the back. A kindly man, seventies, patted Hale on the shoulder as he passed, a welcome gesture of civility.

On board, the budget flight was packed. Hale took his position towards the rear entrance, crammed against the window next to a brash portly couple who spoke loudly to friends across the aisle about their Spanish villa and new car.

None of this mattered to Hale. He watched through the window as the aircraft rotated, took to the air and circled around Málaga before heading north to Britain. Below, the lights of the vast sprawl petered out as they stretched up to the Sierra Nevada. Hard to believe that down there, within the centre of the fibrous network of streetlights, was the small bar beside the Teatro Cervantes, the venue of Hale's meeting with Morillo just days ago.

Much had happened since that meeting.

His mind switched to the overriding question: why had María Díez not hauled him in for further questioning? The series of incidents leading up to the confrontation on the beach alone were surely enough to warrant his detention for days, weeks even, while they investigated. Perhaps Spain did not want the burden, and a welcoming committee would greet him at Gatwick.

A further question regarded Lucy.

Hale paid three euros for a coffee from the trolley. The couple next to him seemed to have bored their friends and now targeted Hale, speaking to the side of his head about their grandchildren. Hale, polite, but clearly uninterested, watched the dawn rise and retraced his life with Lucy. She seemed to have cash in the early days. Cash that a temporary secretary and aerobics instructor would find difficult to attain. Ralph's maintenance payments ceased when Hale arrived on the scene, further reducing any possible income. The pressure Hale was under over years was now placed in a different context. He'd used any means to arrest the debt, pay for the upkeep of the home and their lifestyle, and some of these means were dubious in nature, criminal acts that he now regretted. But now it seemed that Lucy was not the innocent he had been led to believe. Like Hale, she too harboured demons, secrets that she could not or would not reveal to her partner. Hitherto, and unbeknown to Hale, she had a criminal record, had been sentenced. Hale shook his head at the notion, sipped his coffee, staring at cotton wool clouds as the aircraft climbed.

And the thought that she was somehow embroiled with Ralph, Brenda, and Gerry in money laundering was astonishing, difficult to comprehend. But he replayed the story in his mind. The trips to Spain, and Lucy's insistence on meeting these people, now made sense. She had no interest in Spain, never did. These trips were made to bring cash back to Britain, packed into her oversized luggage. Hale had always loathed Brenda and Gerry, but now he knew the truth: they were corrupt, common criminals.

Ralph, however, was the bonus prize, the icing on the cake. Whatever the future now held for Hale, he silently thanked María Díez for this enlightenment. Despite his posturing, Ralph, the arrogant buffoon, was a fraud and an ex-convict.

He returned his thoughts to the plan. To disappear, go off the radar. María Díez did not seem the kind to let criminals walk free, nor hand glory to the British authorities, especially when crimes had been committed on Spanish soil. She, after all, had done the groundwork in this investigation. If she had uncovered Hale's work, plus that of Morillo and Karzhov, this would be a win for Inspectora Jefa Rosa María Díez of the Policía Nacional, and for Spain. Something to celebrate, to release to the news-hungry press.

Something was amiss, and a thought depressed Hale: at Gatwick, he'd be led away from Passport Control by security officers, passing the line of holidaymakers looking on, smirking, as they had done in Málaga. It was time to face the music. Hale's last few hours of freedom were likely to be spent on this very aircraft.

Gatwick.

The airport was busy, so busy that they were instructed to walk down the steps and crowd into two buses. A tedious inconvenience, but there was no waiting committee for Hale on the tarmac. He assumed they'd be waiting at Passport Control.

He assumed wrong. No one at Passport Control other than throngs of passengers shuffling about. Hale chose the *ePassport* gate, since it was manned by just one woman whose time was spent coaxing passengers through the digital passport scanners, most of whom placed it the wrong way up or on the wrong page. Hale placed his passport on the scanner, looked up at the security camera as ordered by the display. He was resigned to the inevitable: a beep would sound, the barrier ahead would remain closed, the woman would come across telling him to step aside. Meanwhile, a queue of flustered passengers would build. Passengers who were placing their goddamn passports upside down without the woman's help. Finally, two officers would arrive to lead Hale away.

But again, Hale had assumed wrong.

The barrier ahead opened.

Minutes later, he entered the Customs declaration area. Took the green *Nothing To Declare* route. He thought about the money in his bag. The quantity was insignificant, but could pose a problem with a diligent Customs officer if the quality of Happy Gary's counterfeit product was poor.

No Customs officer apprehended Hale.

He kept moving through the Duty Free area, eyes forward, relaxed, as if he was becoming accustomed to controlling his outward appearance and behaviour. A seasoned criminal.

The double doors opened automatically ahead. He stepped out into the Arrivals hall, loud and brash. People stood around waiting. Families, grandparents, taxi drivers holding up boards, groups of teenagers, all watching the double doors eagerly, waiting to meet passengers. Hale moved on. No one greeted him. No lover with a warm embrace, no elderly mother smiling and concerned, no Deborah running up with a laugh and holding a cuddly toy, no one. And most notably, no Border Force officers or police.

Confused, and surprised though he was, Hale was free to travel.

He took the inter-terminal shuttle to the North Terminal, crammed in with travellers from across the globe, many hulking massive cases too heavy for their inadequate frames. On arrival, Hale threw his bag on the floor near the overland train terminal, rummaged through it to retrieve a jacket, find credit cards. Travellers bumped him as they moved by, rushing for their trains. Hale, unprepared for the prospect of freedom, made a hasty decision: return briefly to Leigh-on-Sea, visit the house, retrieve warmer clothes, maybe see Baz, and then go.

He slid his debit card into a nearby cash machine, hit the button requesting a balance.

£177.41

Enough to travel home and to eat, but he'd need more. Nine hundred euros in cash remained. He exchanged it at the Bureaux de Change, where no questions were asked about the currency, potentially counterfeit. He had cash for a week, maybe more.

Things were coming together.

He queued for ten minutes, bought a ticket straight through to Leigh-on-Sea from a smiling Jamaican woman at a booth. Headed down the escalators, past a group of Japanese students to Platform 2 bound for London Victoria.

The Gatwick Express train waited, with five minutes before departure. Hale took a carriage towards the rear, empty apart from one woman struggling with a bag while speaking on her phone. He helped her with the bag, heaved it into the overhead, shuffled down to the rear of the carriage.

Three minutes to go.

A few people arrived, took their seats. A worker, big man in boots, hardwearing clothes. A woman with a child, Spanish. Hale caught her accent, maybe Canarian. Another, an office worker, a man with cropped hair and badly fitting suit, the only other passenger in the carriage. The whistle blew and the train moved off. With less than forty minutes to Victoria, and the Circle Line Underground to Tower Hill, the journey would be straightforward. Hale eased back in his chair, relaxed.

The trolley service rattled up. He ordered sandwiches, biscuits, and water from a Romanian attendant who exchanged some friendly small talk in broken English. Hale looked out of the window at the scene racing by. A contrast to the arid landscape of southern Spain. A crisp late September morning, the green Sussex countryside soon transformed into the industrial outskirts of London, traditional Victorian factories and mills. Then, Battersea Power Station and on to the conglomeration of pristine glass tower blocks striking out against the historic monuments and landmarks of the city.

At Victoria, he disembarked, anonymous in the crowd, looking around, reflecting as he walked towards the barrier. He tried to remember his previous trip at this point. Back then, he would have either headed straight to the office (and to the delights of Stack's empire) or back to Tower Hill, where he would travel on to Lucy in Essex. Couldn't recall.

He swiped his ticket through the barrier, avoiding tourists jammed in an aisle to his left, walked out into the vast open complex of London Victoria rail station. People on business, tourists, shoppers, and rail staff crisscrossed in ordered chaos, most purposeful, others confused, lost, asking directions or gawking at train times on overhead boards.

A presence behind. Hale noticed it ten metres beyond the ticket barrier, ignored it, moved diagonally across the white floor in the direction of the Underground entrance, and the Circle Line.

Halfway across the open expanse, he sensed it again, glanced to his right. In his periphery, two men. Another ten yards, and they were closer now, each to his flank either side.

Ahead, an outside area led down a flight of steps. If he continued, he could be caught out in the open, led away outside. Hale responded to this thought, changed direction, moving to his left, testing them. He remained inside the public station complex, keeping with the crowd, headed for a café ten yards ahead. They followed, and now it was unmistakable. They were on him, no doubt this time. Hale cursed under his breath, joined a small queue of people at the counter of the café, a chain serving numerous types of coffee. The same shit marketed under different options. The staff addled him with choices.

"Just a damn white with no sugar," Hale snapped, "to take out." The barista hustled off banging the machine loudly.

Hale glanced around. The two men queued one customer behind, fierce in the eyes, a dead look that chilled Hale to the core. He cursed himself for being lax. He recognised the first character, the businessman on the train. Cropped hair, badly fitting suit. While chatting to the Romanian trolley girl, drinking water, daydreaming, Hale had noticed tattoos on his one hand and concealed behind the collar of his white shirt. Thought nothing of it at the time. He should have thought something of it. The second, the worker, big, muscular. Not typically someone you'd see on the Gatwick Express. Possibly a rail worker en route, but they'd not often be amongst the passengers. He *should* have noticed and it *should* have registered.

Hale dialled Baz, cursed under his breath as it rang, "Come on, Baz. Jesus, come on."

Hale took the coffee, ignored the men, moved to a stand-up table near the entrance. Struggling with the phone to his ear, he placed his bag down, looked across faintly. The men had left the queue without buying anything.

They were heading directly over to Hale.

Baz answered, "Mate, how's the wandering gigolo? I'm gonna…"

Hale interrupted, "Baz, I'm in trouble…"

"Haha! Aren't we all…"

"No, look, Baz, no time to explain."

Silence from Baz.

The goons arrived. Time up.

"Baz, serious trouble. Help. Mayday. This is…"

FIFTY-TWO

Both men moved up to Hale, in his face, too close for comfort. The short guy snatched Hale's phone from his ear. "I redirect call for you," he said, and then dropped it into the coffee carton, replaced the lid and tossed it into a bin beside the table. The short guy looked fit and nimble, wore an open collar revealing more of his neck tattoos. His winced face bore cynical green eyes. The other man watched on, a meathead with coarse black hair, big boned, supporting the type of muscle that bulges through thick clothing.

Hale sized them up, and guessed that, unlike Happy and Morillo, these men would not be negotiators, disliked chitchat. Both of Eastern Bloc origin, no doubt about that in Hale's mind.

"If you are from Sergei Karzhov, I can explain and we need to talk," said Hale, making the first move, trying to control the pitch of his wavering voice.

The Small Guy replied, "You see my friend's knife here." He nodded down as the big guy revealed a weapon in his hand, a nasty type, more a knuckleduster with a ragged blade. "Well," continued the Small Guy, "you come with us now, otherwise he gut you like a fish in this shit café, and before Police over there come," he jerked his thumb over his shoulder at two unarmed security guards mingling in the hall, "you bleed to death on floor."

"I said I can explain … about the incident in Marbella."

"Some advice, mister. You quiet up your mouth, because you not in Spain now. Sergei is in London and he don't play games like those monkeys in Spain, you shitbrain, understand?"

The big guy grabbed Hale's arm high up near the armpit. The Small Guy looked around, as if checking for trouble, led the way out of the café with Hale's bag over his shoulder. Hale thought about shouting, making a scene in public, but then thought about the knife. Chances are they wanted him dead, and the big guy might not be bluffing about the fish-gutting idea. He said nothing.

Play for time, Hale, think.

They moved fast across the station, almost lifting Hale off his feet. They were jumpy, scanning the place. They'd be seen on CCTV, seemed to be aware of that fact, raced at crazy speed, stumbling down steps, barging people, swearing at them as they went.

Hale felt sick. Knew he was as good as dead. These people were focussed, not playing around. Best scenario: he'd be beaten, knifed, and thrown into the Thames. News would get back to Spain and Morillo would give a wry smile over a glass of *Pinot Noir*. Hale's deeds avenged by way of a favour from his dear friend, Sergei Karzhov.

Seconds later, they were out on the street, down an alley, a grim faceless place and home to wheelie bins overflowing with black bin-bags butted up against the unsightly backyards of kebab shops, launderettes, and grubby newsagents. A transit van drew up, white and battered, like any other beaten-up piece of shit driven by downtrodden plumbers or deliveryman. Hale was bundled into the back, his bag hurled in. They both followed, chopping Hale's legs away with a kick and holding him face down on the floor.

"Shut up, stay down," said the big man. First time he'd spoken.

A bang on the side of the van by the Small Guy's fist signalled the driver to pull off. He did so with a mild screech. The engine was thrashed as it climbed the gears, jolting Hale, smashing his face against the rusty metal floor. He felt a boot resting on the back of his neck, holding him down.

Hale battled to calm himself, think logically. This didn't look like the beginning of a business proposition. This was no job interview to hire him as a boat skipper, as Blochead had originally implied back in Puerto de Santa María. About as far away as you could get from one. To escape death, Hale needed a break, contact with the outside world to cry for help.

He shuddered at the prospects, or lack of them. His one chance may have evaded him back at Victoria Station. Idiot. Should have splashed coffee in the meathead's face and run like hell. Should have caused a scene, should have done something, anything.

Too late now.

Hale estimated fifteen, maybe twenty minutes had elapsed since they'd sped away from Victoria. Impossible to ascertain the direction. The noise on the floor was deafening, but the going smoothed at one point for some minutes, a dual carriageway perhaps.

Then back into side streets, some with speed bumps making Hale head-butt metal as the wheel axle vaulted over them.

Meathead and the Small Guy yelled at each other over the din, sometimes laughing, sometimes exchanging unintelligible banter in some guttural slur not fit for sane humans.

We're still in London, thought Hale.

The van stopped, started, staying within the confines of tight roads and heavy traffic. Maybe south London or the East. Either way, not out in the countryside or isolated, not yet. That was a scenario Hale dreaded. At least in the city, eyes were everywhere, so were CCTV cameras, so was security. The closer to the centre, the more chance there was of causing some noise, giving a sign to passers-by, or even the police. But further out, towards the outskirts or beyond, no hope. They could carry out their grim work somewhere remote, maybe an abandoned farm. He'd be found months later by a walker and his dog. Or never.

The Small Guy shushed Meathead. They seemed to be approaching something. The van slowed. The Small Guy said something, moved around within the dull interior, kicking Hale's legs aside as he moved to the rear. Hale turned his head, peered up to Meathead, who looked ahead over the driver's shoulder.

The van pulled up to a curb somewhere, idled for a moment, and then stopped. The driver said something quietly in the unspeakable drawl. Five seconds later, blurted louder, more punctuated.

The rear doors were flung open. Meathead leapt into the road, dragged Hale out by his feet. The Small Guy assisted him. Standing up, Hale looked about, his vision blurred from the dark and vibrations during the hell ride. A London street, definitely. Georgian houses, something like a strip club or restaurant ahead. Black windows, a white and gold sign, the wording of which he could not decipher. Looked closed for business, in dire need of refurbishment. They pushed him to the right side of the place, through a gate and down some steps, a fire exit. The Small Guy pushed past, tripped, cursed, grabbed the front of Hale's jacket in his fist, hauling him down the steep metal steps with Meathead steadying the whole show from behind.

Hale, desperate, looked above at blue-grey sky, a wall to one side, but no windows. He shouted in vain, "HEY!" provoking a predictable response: a fist in the stomach from the Small Guy. Hale gasped, taking the shock of pain. A black metal door was opened at the foot of the fire escape, and Hale thrown into a narrow corridor, musty and dark. It led to a room in the distance with stainless steel shining from within, a kitchen. He stumbled to the floor. Meathead delivered a blow to his thigh.

"Up, up!" shouted the Small Guy, his face contorted, more fierce than before, and seemingly happier. Dangerous in his own domain.

Hale rose, held his hands up, "Okay, okay." Then saw the Small Guy's fist rise up. A split-second blackout signalled it landing on the side of Hale's face. It stung, as bad as any haymaker he'd received on the rugby field. And that was from the Small Guy.

Meathead barged into Hale, urging him ahead, around a corner. Dingy stairs covered with gaudy red carpet loomed ahead. Meathead grabbed Hale's collar, hauling him back before he reached them. Other goons arrived at the foot of the stairs, two or three of them, seriously ugly just like the two manhandling Hale, brothers maybe, or inbreds. They exchanged words with Meathead, and then filed past, laughing.

Behind, the Small Guy fumbled with some keys in the lock of a plain white door to the left, slid a bolt across. Hale was pushed in, kicked to the floor. He surveyed his surrounding in an instant. Not much to survey. Small, square room, concrete floor, one desk and a bare bulb hanging from a ceiling. Maybe an old storeroom. Notably, dark stains adorned the floor in one corner.

Hale rose to his feet, looked at Small Guy who stood before him, more pockmarked under the stark light than he'd remembered from the café. Silence for five seconds, just hard stares.

Then it began.

Meathead shut the door, and then another blow arrived from the Small Guy. Landed on the same place. This time, a small 'crack' sounded, maybe a broken cheekbone. Hale grabbed the slime's throat with one hand and squeezed. The Small Guy pulled clear, laughing. This prompted Meathead to shoulder-barge Hale against the wall behind, winding him, causing him to bend over. He gasped for air, looked left to see a boot coming at him, and then lights out again for a split second. He felt his head clatter, rebound off the wall.

Warm liquid run down his cheek. The sight in Hale's one eye had gone, the other blurred. He made out the Small Guy heading for him again. Hale reached up, grabbed a handful of crutch, squeezed. A yell, and a laugh, this time from Meathead, who shoved the Small Guy aside.

Meathead towered above, a fuzzy silhouetted image. The giant bent over Hale, frisked his pockets, removing his wallet. Then his Spanish mobile from Hale's top pocket, his last hope of contact with anyone outside this hellhole. With a smirk, Meathead rose up, dropped the phone from his considerable height, and then serviced it with his hobnailed boot, leaving splintered plastic and crushed circuitry littering the concrete.

The goons left, the door slammed. The bolt rattled across, and then a clink of keys as the latch of a mortice lock made good Hale's incarceration.

Hale was finished, lay on the floor in the fetal position, grabbed his stomach. The floor felt good, warm, his head numb.

You asked for it, Charles, didn't you? You thought your calculated stunt with Morillo and Karzhov – the beach party – was a clever ruse. But now look at you, Charlie. This is it.

Silence.

Hale remained on the floor, dabbed his head with one hand, trying to assess the injuries. His head felt like a beach ball. Blood was oozing, but not gushing above his temple. It might congeal before he bled to death. He thought of his cheekbone, moved his hand towards it, but then pulled it away. He'd rather not know. His breathing was steady despite the kicking, though his stomach was cramping, pulsating with pain.

He lay there for thirty minutes, maybe an hour. Difficult to estimate. Heard muffled voices from upstairs in the restaurant or lap dancing club or whatever den of iniquity this place purported to be. This was a private club, some kind of base or cover for their nefarious operations. In the kitchen, he heard pans crashing, men shouting in Russian, and some swearing in English.

More hours passed. He hadn't moved, still on his side in the fetal position. Must be dark outside. He'd regained vision in both eyes, though his right was blurred and now swelling, caked with blood.

He thought again about options. The voice in his head, the one that sounded like Rups, was all he had now.

You're always banging on about 'options', Charlie. So go on then, what options are we going to run through now, old boy?

Above, in the corner of the ceiling, a small unit was visible. A surveillance camera.

Well done, Charlie. Well spotted ... they're watching you too. So, even if you did come up with some bloody master plan, they'll be down here like a shot to work on that other cheekbone.

What were they waiting for?

Hale suspected that Karzhov was likely to put in an appearance to make an example to the dumb schmucks under his command. He'd pop by to deliver a few choice words, and then give a knowing nod to Meathead, who'd return a grim smile. The rest would be incidental thuggery of which Karzhov need not be privy.

Yes, that is the 'option,' old boy. Singular not plural.

He thought of Marta, the night on the beach, her smile, her smooth skin. The cramped bar in Tarifa, watching flamenco on television. How people loved her, how *he* loved her. So far from here, this dire place. He banished the thoughts from his mind. Too painful. Concentrated on quelling the physical pain.

This is how it ends, he thought. And this is how it ends for countless victims who dare to cross mafiosos.

Only one tenuous hope remained.

The call to Baz at Victoria.

He'd not conveyed much in the panic, and Baz, the practical joker, had most likely deemed Hale's bizarre call nothing more than a revengeful joke. In return perhaps for the multitude of past stunts that Baz had pulled over the gullible college boy.

That's the problem with serial pranksters: how do you get through to them when things *do* get serious?

Hale recalled his last words to Baz on the phone:

No time to explain.

Serious trouble.

Shit, help.

It wouldn't wash with Baz. No way. Those words would not resonate, would not impart the graveness of his predicament.

Game over.

But there was another word in his panic and fear at Victoria that he had managed to blurt out in desperation. A word different, unique from the rest.

A word that gentlemen who played the game for ruffians understood all too well. A word no man used in vain, and every player from ale-drinking boozer to public schoolboy, respected and honoured. A word that might save a man at the base of a pileup or scrum from injury, or worse, lifelong paralysis.

This word, Baz would understand.

Mayday.

FIFTY-THREE

Hale was jolted from unconsciousness by a noise, a muffled thump vibrating the floor. The dead of night, hours since Meathead's boot last slammed into his face. His eyes barely focussed on the naked bulb above.

Then the light was extinguished, sending the room into pitch black. Not a glimmer of light seeped through the doorframe from lights in the corridor.

Inky nothingness.

A power cut.

Another thump, louder this time. Voices in Russian, men moving, shouting above. Hale leaned up on his elbow, looked around. But whether his eyelids were opened or closed, made no difference. An eerie tomb.

More footsteps above, moving fast. Meathead and the others trying to get the power sorted, thought Hale. Now screams. Panic. Noises, drumming, like an anchor being hauled up on a chain. Hale smelled something in the air, smoke, metallic, sulphur. He rose to his knees. Still no light, a faint flash, and then blackness again.

The room shuddered.

A flash.

Brilliant white surrounded the doorframe reaching out in straight lines, lighting the entire room. Hale was blind, nauseous, mouth dry with fear. Then another flash, numbing whiteness, and then smoke, thick and acrid. Ringing in his ears, a high-pitched tone, dominated his head. Still blind, he fell backwards, knocked his head against the wall. He regained his breathing, sucked in a breath of hot soot. Then, shouting, muffled, as if someone was wearing a gag. He rose up, his sight was returning, blurred. Ahead, a figure filled the doorway, and then entered, bulky, silhouetted against dim yellow light in the hallway. A beam forged a shaft of light from the figure's weapon as it swept the room. Another from a figure behind. The weapon swung back, pointed at Hale's torso.

Death had arrived.

Hale rose to his knees again as if praying. The weapon light flashed in his eyes, and then back down to his chest. Another shape, a man, moved behind Hale, grabbed his wrists, bound them. Cable ties.

The figure ahead shouted from behind a gas mask, big black eyes like those of a monster bug. A deep, gruff voice enhanced through electronics of some kind on the mask, "Hale. Charles Hale?"

Hale nodded.

The other figure moved back to the doorway, moved his gaze from Hale to the corridor and back again. Keeping watch, making calls, presumably to others in the building. *"Power. Hale located. How long?"* he said.

The light came on. Smoke hung in the room.

The man ahead was dressed in black. Weapon at the ready, the Heckler Koch drove a white beam through the smoke to Hale's sternum.

Stunned, Hale's vision was blurred. He struggled to hear over deafening cracks and thuds from out in the corridor and upstairs.

"Get up, get up!"

Hale rose to his feet, unsteady, instinctively put his hands in the air.

"Put 'em down. Down!"

Hale, dropped his arms.

"Two lower clear. Three lower clear."

Figures moved across the doorway behind, shadows. The door itself had been blown off, some remnants hung from the hinges. Hale's thoughts were muddled. Who were they? Karzhov's crew? But he was hearing stabs of English, not Russian.

"Lower four. Hale located. Move."

"Are you okay? Can you walk?" said the figure.

Hale nodded, and then said, "Who are you? I'm..."

The figure cut him off, "Hold steady. Wait."

Hale swayed, disorientated, ears ringing.

"Twenty seconds. Move."

The figure from the door re-entered, fast, took a position behind Hale, grabbed him under the armpit. The man ahead exited the room, dragging Hale by his waist belt.

"Who are you? Where?" said Hale.

"Move. Go! Go!"

A shove in the back.

Out in the corridor, debris, smoke and a dim orange light. Hale tripped, was hauled his feet. Then pushed manhandled over broken doors, chunks of smashed masonry.

He gagged on the smoke.

"Ten seconds."

They came to the foot of the stairs. Hale's legs were weak, jelly. He stumbled again, fell onto sticky red gloop running down the thickly carpeted steps.

A heady smell, coppery.

Hauled to his feet again, he limped on one leg, pumped the other to stay upright. Glanced down. To his left, a torso, shoulder and arm missing.

At the top of the stairs, a large expansive room. The club, brash and ugly. Now even uglier with debris, blood, and body parts adorning the floor. Other figures brandished weapons, headed for the double doors ahead, which opened out onto the main road lit with yellow-orange streetlights.

"Clear building. Go."

Hale was shoved out into the night. A van ahead, a Transit, idled on the curb. The rear doors swung open.

Sirens sounded from a few blocks away. Multiple police units. Response vehicles.

Manhandled towards the back of the van, Hale fell onto one knee. Three men hauled him up, launched him into the back of the van.

"Get in for chrissakes. Now!"

Cold metal again on his face.

Time for another tour of London.

Bang. Bang. The two doors slammed behind, the van accelerated, the tyres biting, releasing, fighting to grip.

A flash of white light and then orange illuminated the back. Then a deep thud.

"Jesus," someone said.

Men were crowded inside. One barked instructions. *"Right. CCTV. Left. Then one hundred, exit."*

Heavy wafts of sweat and diesel.

"Sit up," came a voice. Then arms behind helping, heaving Hale into a seating position.

A figure, still masked, hung onto some metal framework to steady himself and Hale as the van sped, lurching, braking hard. Racing. "You okay? Can you speak?" said the figure.

Hale nodded.

"You're bleeding, mate. From the head. We'll sort you out. Hang tough, okay?"

Another figure emerged, struggling to balance in a kneeling position, held a dressing to Hale's head.

The van took a violent turn, throwing the medic aside, and Hale back to the floor.

The van slowed. The front wheels rose up onto a bump, and then back down. The rears wheels did the same.

The van stopped. A clang, doors closing. A garage.

The driver killed the engine.

FIFTY-FOUR

The garage was sizeable, gloomy. Hale stood at the rear of the transit, leaning back against the doors to prevent himself from collapsing. He could make out engine spares, bits of old motorbikes strewn across the floor and upon workbenches. In the bay to his right, a vehicle, an ageing Cortina or Granada, a relic from the seventies. Movement in the back. The men stashing equipment into bags, busy but not frantic. Ordered instructions came from one of them. No panic, suggesting that this was a routine, trained and familiar.

Hale had been ordered to hold his position for thirty seconds, not to sit, as soon he would be required to walk.

A man walked up to Hale, not kitted-out like the others. Grey, short, fifties, stocky, green jacket, a small firearm on his belt. He stood before Hale, looking up with sharp blue eyes boring into Hale's, probing, searching for answers, like those of María Díez.

"Who are you?" asked Grey Man.

"Charles Hale," said Hale, looking over Grey Man's shoulder to the men in the background. "I don't know what they..."

"Shut it. Look at me, concentrate," said Grey Man, interrupting, holding two fingers up to his steely eyes. "Who were those people in that place? Why were you there?"

Hale shook his head, felt tears welling up. "I, I…"

"Pull yourself together."

"I…"

"They were dangerous, heavily armed. Who are they? Who are you working for?"

Hale pushed the dressing against his head, stemming a line of blood that flowed down his cheek. "I think they're mafia … Russian. They pursued me in Spain, now they want me dead…"

"Lower your voice, don't shout," said Grey Man.

"I'm not shouting."

"Shut it. You are. You're deaf because of the grenades. Continue … Why do they want you dead?"

Hale felt groggy, thoughts muddled. He blurted out an answer, anything, "I ... I became embroiled with them. I didn't want to work for them, so I set them up. Some of their people died as a result."

Grey Man frowned, remained silent for some seconds, holding the stare. Finally, he said, "You're playing a dangerous game, sunshine, you know that?" He clicked a button on a radio held in his right hand, and then continued, "Have you been arrested before?"

"No," said Hale.

"Had your fingerprints taken for anything in the past?"

"No."

"DNA? Swab test, anything?"

"No. Where are they?" asked Hale. "The big Russian, and…"

"They're not feeling too good," said Grey Man. "Shut it and listen…"

Sirens wailed in the distance, some blocks away.

"This is what we're going to do," continued Grey Man. "Behind, there's a small window to the right of the garage door. Look now."

Hale craned his neck around to his left, felt sick doing so. There was the window to the right of the double garage doors, two foot square, yellowed with grime and partially blocked with gnarled stickers probably as old as the wrecks in the garage. Further to the right, a normal-sized metal exit door.

"Got it?" said Grey Man.

Hale turned back, nodded.

"Let's go to it now," said Grey Man. Another man, masked, this time with a balaclava, appeared to Hale's left, gripped his armpit. The three moved to the window, Hale dragging one foot, pain searing through his thigh.

He faced Grey Man, who stood before the window, which gave a restricted view out to the street. Grey Man's face was deadpan, serious, one side lit by muted orange streetlights streaming in through the window.

"Listen up," said Grey Man. "When you leave here, it's very unlikely that you'll see me again. But, if you do, in the street, anywhere, London, Scotland or Timbuk – bloody – tu, you ignore me, look ahead and move on. Understood?"

"Yes, but I…"

"Lower your voice, shut it. Nod or shake your head."

Hale nodded.

Grey Man paused, looked around, and then continued, "This night didn't happen. You erase it from your head. Anyone asks any questions, you deny everything, can't remember, no comment. Understood?"

Hale nodded.

"Good. If your mum, girlfriend, or president of the bloody United States of America asks you what happened, you deny all knowledge, you say nothing."

Hale nodded.

Radio chatter sounded from back inside the garage, *"Twenty and go."*

Grey Man clicked the handset. "This is what we do now," he said. "Lean forward, look outside, out the window. You'll see a lamppost, and further on, a bin. Next to the bin, there's a blue car, a Mondeo. Look now. See it?"

Hale leaned forward, saw the car, nodded.

"Good. Look at me."

Hale did.

Grey Man's eyes narrowed as he continued, "In ten seconds, you're going to walk out of here with this…" He grabbed a jacket from the man with the balaclava, shoved it into Hale's chest. Hale put it on. Balaclava moved behind, pulled Hale's hand away from the dressing, and wrapped tape around his head in one movement. "And this hat," continued Grey Man, handing him a beanie. "Put it on now." Hale did, struggling to edge it over the bandage.

Grey Man looked left out of the window towards the Mondeo, and then back at Hale. "When I say 'go', you walk out of this door, down the street towards the bin without looking back. Not fast, not slow, just normal and straight. When you get to the bin, you move to the back door of the car, you look at the door, open it and get in. Understood?"

Hale nodded.

"You don't look up. You don't look around, just at the bin, and then at the car door. Then you get in. Understood?"

Hale nodded.

Grey Man stepped aside. Balaclava pushed Hale towards the metal door buckled and scratched.

A voice on the radio crackled, *"Three and go."*

"Ready," said Grey Man. "And ... Go."

Balaclava opened the door. Hale stepped out into the chilly night, heard the door thump shut behind him.

The road was quiet, little traffic, apart from a truck and a taxi. A police siren wailed from a few streets away. A figure wandered in the distance beyond the bin, looked like a drunk staggering, shouting. The bandage slipped down, obscuring Hale's vision in his right eye. He ignored it, walked, steady, just as Grey Man said, towards the bin. Ten yards out, the Mondeo loomed larger. A figure sat in the driver's seat on the curb side, the car parked to face oncoming traffic, engine running, surrounding it with a small cloud of steam and smoke billowing into the cold air.

Three yards out, the sirens grew louder. Hale looked at the door, focussed on it. A second later, he opened it, lunged in, and slammed it shut.

FIFTY-FIVE

"Evening, sir," said the driver, who watched the road ahead, leaned over his shoulder to check behind, and then quietly eased the car into the street.

This man was dark, heavy mop of hair, spoke with a hoarse accent, a hint of cockney. "Be having you out of here in no time, sir," he said.

Hale clipped on his seat belt, drew breath, calmed himself. The car reached the end of the street, waited at a junction with traffic lights.

Hale shook, nerves on edge. A glow lit the sky in the distance ahead. Above townhouses and offices, it cast an odd signature in the murky night sky. Fire engines sounded. A blaze.

The man slotted the Mondeo into gear, moved ahead slowly, turned left onto a main road away from the street.

"What is that ahead?" asked Hale. "Is that the building I was…"

"Oh, don't worry yourself about that, sir. Bit of fireworks I'd say. Kids throwing bangers about."

Hale realised he wasn't going to get far along these lines of enquiry, so changed tack, "Where are we going?"

More sirens, and blue lights from both directions on the carriageway prompted the driver to look in the rear-view and side mirrors while speaking. "We're going up here a few miles, to the other side of town," he said. "Get you a bed and some rest seeing as you're looking a bit worse for wear there, sir."

A pain sat behind Hale's eyes, blinding, confusing his thoughts, muddling his words, but not enough to stem his curiosity. "Back there … those men. A man asked me questions, told me to get in this car, who was he?"

"That was *T*, sir."

"*T?*"

"Tango."

Hale paused. Looked at the man's face in the rear-view mirror. His eyes were relaxed, concentrating on the road. He wore a thick dark jersey, dark trousers. On the passenger seat there was some equipment, a compact rectangular unit.

"*Okay*," said Hale. "And who are *you* then?"

"I'll be *F*, sir."

"Don't tell me ... *Foxtrot*."

"That's the one, sir."

"Fine," said Hale. "So, who is *T* and who are his men?"

F said nothing for a few seconds, hauled the steering wheel around, leaning into the turn. A faint smile on his face. "Bit of advice, sir..."

"Yes?" said Hale.

"The man you mention, *T*," said *F*, straightening the car up, gunning the engine. "He should now be a figment of your imagination, and my advice to a good bloke such as yourself, is to let the little shindig back there slip from your mind, pronto. Then we're all good."

"I see," said Hale, looking out of the window, studying the streets. An unfamiliar area somewhere east of the city.

F was taking more turns, heading down side streets. Despite his banter, Hale noticed that his driving was accurate, at a considered, controlled pace, and he was ultimately vigilant.

The equipment on the passenger seat rasped, *"Nine Five. Hold."*

F looked about, pulled the car up to a curb in a residential street, killed the headlights, kept the engine running. He said nothing for ten seconds.

Blue lights flashed across the main road beyond an intersection behind.

Five more seconds, and then, *"Nine Five. Clear."*

F hit the headlights, pulled out into the street.

"We'll be having you sorted in your five star accommodation in ten minutes, sir."

Ten minutes later they pulled into a backstreet of no particular prominence, lined with ordinary Victorian terraced houses on three storeys, mostly red brick, some painted white. One or two streetlights illuminated the gloom, highlighting a vague drizzle in the air. It was quiet, but would soon be busy in the rush hour a few hours away. Hale guessed this was Shoreditch.

F pulled up to a white house guarded with black railings at street level. A gate led down some steps to a basement from where a light glowed. *F* cut the engine, looked straight ahead while he spoke.

"So here we are, sir. To your left is a house with black railings, see that?"

"I do," said Hale.

"Good. Listen carefully, chief, 'cos we don't want any mistakes, otherwise I get my nuts fried. Understood?"

"Yes."

"You open the car door when I say. Then you close it and go through the gate. I drive off and you never see me again. Heartbreaking I know, but you'll get over it. If in the unlikely course of events you do happen to see me at some place, you look the other way. We ignore each other and go our separate ways. Got that?"

"Yes."

"You'll go down them steps there, sir, and through the door at the bottom. It'll be open for you, just turn the knob and in you go. Inside, there'll be a short corridor. The light will be on. On the immediate right, 'guv, you'll see a white door. Move past that to the end, and on your left will be another white door with a 'No Smoking' sticker on it. Knock on the door, go in, and a nice man will see you."

"He will?"

"He will. Nothing to be afraid of, sir. And when you've seen the nice man, you come out, go back down the corridor and through the aforementioned white door. The one untarnished by said sticker. Understood?"

"Yes."

"Marvellous. In there you'll find a room with a bed, a shower, latrine for said use of, clothes, some money, and best of all, sir, some grub."

"Thank you."

"My pleasure. One thing, sir."

"Yes?"

"Tomorrow morning. The alarm clock is on the bedside table and set for 7:30 a.m. You leave exactly at 8:00 a.m. Try to cover your face with that hat or something as you ain't at your prettiest best at this present time, if you don't mind me saying. Then you join the commuters to wherever you might be going. You got somewhere to go, sir?"

"Yes, I can go to Essex where I..."

"Lovely. No need to tell me anymore, chief. Now have a good stay at this pucker hotel, and remember, when you've seen the nice man, you go to the room, you stay there, shower, eat, sleep and whatnot, and you don't come out until ... what time?"

"Eight."

"That's the one. Then you walk straight out and go to the Tube or buses, or whatever takes your fancy, and you don't look back and you never come back to this road again. Is that all plain as day, sir?"

"It is, thank you."

"Dandy. Well, I'll be bidding you farewell, sir. Please go now."

Hale opened the door, felt cool drizzle on his face, stepped out into the street, passed the back of the car and stepped onto the pavement.

The car drew away and was soon out of sight.

Hale entered the gate, walked down the steps to the door at the basement.

FIFTY-SIX

Hale twisted the doorknob and stepped into the corridor. Just as *F* has described, the white door was immediately to his right. The corridor was just ten metres long, painted with cream emulsion. A smell of cleaning fluid, disinfectant, and polish pervaded. The place was stark. Strip lights above and polished linoleum underfoot.

He walked slowly towards the end. He'd developed a limp on one side, tightness in his thigh and pain in the knee where Meathead's boot had pummelled it.

Apart from the buzzing fluorescents above, the place was quiet, unnervingly so. The end of the corridor was dim, and the door with the red *No Smoking* sticker loomed bland and anonymous, with no indication of what might lie beyond.

Hale knocked lightly twice.

His ears still ringing from the blast, he heard a muffled sound, the voice of a man from within. Hale turned the knob and edged the door two inches open. It then swung open wide, pulling away from Hale's hand. A man stood in the doorway dressed in a white coat.

"Ah, hello there. Expecting you," said the man, sixties, spectacled, grey hair sprouting from the side of his head at odd angles.

"Hello," said Hale, "I'm Char…"

"Yes, yes, very well, do come in."

The man, clearly a doctor, waved his hand towards a seat in front of a desk. Hale stepped into the small room, five metres square, well equipped with various stainless steel cabinets on wheels. Medical paraphernalia, an examination table, and other props reminiscent of a GP's surgery.

Hale took a seat.

"So," said the doctor, "let's have a look." He adjusted his spectacles, removed the bandage on Hale's head using scissors, examined him carefully, steady hands and an air of wisdom. "Hmm, marvellous. Yes." He stood back, looked Hale up and down. His commands were kindly, but direct.

"Stand please."

Hale got to his feet with a groan.

"Strip down to your underwear, please. Take your time."

Hale did so as the doctor returned to his desk scribbling something on a pad while whistling the theme to *Dad's Army*.

"Count down from ten to one would you?" said the doctor.

Hale did so, and then stood up straight in his boxer shorts.

"Marvellous. Turn around."

Hale did so, feeling giddy and little sick.

"And back again."

Hale did so.

"Hmm. Jolly good. Bend down, touch the toes, or thereabouts."

Hale did so.

"Okie dokie. So, did we lose consciousness at all ... during the recent escapade?" said the doctor, peering over his spectacles.

"Yes, the early hours," said Hale.

"And how long for?"

"Difficult to say. Seconds, or maybe some minutes?"

"Hmm." The doctor looked down, scribbled something, placed the pen on the desk, looked up and said, "Well, I'm stating the obvious, I know, but you've been banged around a bit old fellow, but nothing that alarms me too much. Nothing I haven't seen as a result of an everyday pub brawl. So, both of your eyes are swollen. The left is almost closed, looks nasty, but looks deceive. The swelling will go down, but the cuts above and below that eye, I'll have to suture in a minute. The cheekbone on that side seems to have potentially suffered a fracture, though I can't see any major deformity at present. You'll need an X-ray, possible CT scan. Where's your hospital?"

"Southend."

"Ah. I have a colleague there, good bunch. They'll sort you out and you need to go tomorrow. Can you do that?"

"Yes, I'm heading that way."

"Marvellous. They'll check out your legs and other bits and pieces, but you seem to be able to stand and walk, so I'll let those lucky people deal with all that. You should let them have my pub brawl story. You can do that for me, can't you old fellow?"

"Of course," said Hale.

"And that burn on your forearm. It's nothing, but they may ask. You did that before the brawl, working on the car. Those manifolds get hot in the engine compartment, don't they?"

Hale nodded.

The doctor rose, walked over to a cabinet and began banging draws and rustling syringes, bottles, and odd-looking implements. "So, let's clean you up and then you can be on your way," he said.

An hour later, 3:30 a.m., Hale closed the doctor's door, limped slowly back to the first door, plain no sticker. He turned the knob, peered inside. The light was on. Hale entered.

The room was small, blank walls, with a connecting shower room. A scene of precision. Single bed, pristine white sheets, towels, toiletries, and a change of clothes all carefully positioned. A jacket, shoes, socks, trousers, laid out in order. Hale noted the sizes of the clothes on the labels: 42 shirt, 34 trousers. His sizes. A bedside cabinet held a reading light and alarm with a small display indicating that it was set for 7:30 a.m.

Against the opposite wall, a dresser displayed various items positioned and spaced precisely, as if measured by a ruler. Food Package 1: sandwiches, fruit, tea for the evening meal. Food Package 2: breakfast cereal, bread, marmalade, coffee. Also, a brown envelope containing five hundred pounds, an empty wallet, a box of paracetamol, and *The Times* newspaper placed upon a small leather briefcase. Below the dresser, a mini fridge contained water, milk, and a bar of chocolate.

Hale removed his clothes and showered, being careful to avoid any water on his head or dressings. Every movement ached or sent pain across his back. The shower was hot and soothing. For the first time since his seizure by the Russians, he felt the hope of survival return, his mind no longer resigned to inevitable beatings, torture, and death. He spent little time looking at his face in the mirror. Too harrowing. He would be noticed in public, but a choice of hats and scarves were provided amongst the clothes to allow him to remain reasonably discreet.

Back in the room, he placed his old clothes into a black plastic bag positioned beside the bathroom door. An A4 sheet was sellotaped to it and printed with the words: *Old clothes and shoes*.

He ate the sandwiches ravenously, drank water, tea, and felt better still. He could sleep for two hours if he lay down immediately, but his mind kicked back into gear, racing through events. He flicked on a small FM radio provided on the dresser. The *BBC World Service* broke the silence with its considered, eloquent recital of the news from London. The male newsreader, voice deep, sombre, spoke of an explosion and fire in the north of London. Police and fire brigade were attending the scene. No clues were available as to the cause. Some bodies had been found. The standard line was issued: arson and terrorism not ruled out, an investigation would be under way once the site had been made safe.

Although Hale was the best witness to events that the investigators could hope to interview, he would be unable to answer questions he himself posed.

The call had been made to Baz at Victoria, but was he responsible in some direct or indirect way for the events that followed? Did Baz call the police, or some other party relating to his army connections? Or, was Hale followed by the police or Special Forces, and then freed by them at the club? This latter scenario could perhaps be connected to Hodgkinson, who might have had Hale tracked and tailed for some weeks with the help of María Díez. That would explain her unwillingness to detain him at Málaga.

The Baz theory seemed flimsy at best. Meathead trashed Hale's Spanish cell phone at the club by giving it some heavy treatment with his boot. Baz had the numbers of both cell phones (including the one dropped into the coffee carton at Victoria, courtesy of the Short Guy), but in the confusion, would this allow enough time to trace the remaining phone's geolocation? Cell phone tracking was an area of rapidly developing expertise within America's NSA and the UK's GCHQ – prowess that was drawing more than a little attention from conspiracy theorists and the press looking to break *Big Brother is Watching* stories. Hale's question in relation to the Baz scenario was clear: Hale's question in relation to the Baz scenario was clear: before the cell phone went dead under Meathead's boot, would an agency have the time and capability to assimilate the information and precisely track its last known position?

Weary, Hale slipped under the crisp white sheets, just managing to switch off the bedside light before entering a deep sleep.

FIFTY-SEVEN

7:55 a.m.

Hale stood outside his room in the corridor, dressed with the clothes provided and briefcase in hand. To his left, the door to the outside, leading up to the street. To his right, the corridor, quiet and empty, fluorescents still buzzing above. The instruction from *F* was simple: walk out of the door at 8:00 a.m., do not look back, and never return to the road.

Hale looked to his right. The doctor's door with the sticker remained closed, no noise from within. Hale took a few steps along the corridor, stood in front of the door.

Leave it, Charles. Go out into the street as instructed.

Curiosity tore at him. Perhaps just a quick 'thank you' to the doctor, before leaving. The reasonable thing to do.

He knocked lightly once.

No answer.

Knocked again.

No answer.

He tried the doorknob. It turned. He eased the door open a few inches. Inside, the lights were off, no sound. He opened the door and stepped in. Hale frowned, an expression that pulled at the stitches surrounding his eye as he glanced around.

The room was empty.

Hale stood in the centre and spun around three sixty. No desk, no examination table, no boxes, no doctor, no medical supplies.

Nothing.

At Fenchurch Street, Hale boarded the train and took a seat in the Quiet Zone, waited for it to depart, head throbbing, body numb. He assembled a cell phone of the pay-as-you-go variety, which he'd bought at a kiosk near Tower Hill. He slotted in the SIM card and sent a text to Baz:

'Baz, Charlie here. How's things? I'm on the train, heading home'.

Hale looked up as the train departed, thought of what might await him at Leigh-on-Sea. He watched the ashen walls of The

Tower of London flash by between modern office blocks, pubs, and industrial buildings.

Some cold thoughts occurred to him.

Firstly, he had no record of Marta's number, her whereabouts in Madrid, or indeed her surname. Her numbers had been recorded on the cell phones, both now gone. Maybe this is how it should end. Lover's lost to each other. A perilous relationship, which had no future anyway.

Secondly, he could perhaps afford a brief visit to the house in Leigh-on-Sea, but he must be vigilant, and then leave forever without being followed. The extent of the Morillo-Karzhov network within the UK was unknown to him, but to return to any familiar routine would be madness. The five hundred pounds cash on his person, minus fifty for the phone and rail ticket, would not last long. He cursed under his breath. Good old Charles Hale had returned to Blighty replete with money woes as usual.

As expected, his appearance was drawing attention. A woman, a smart commuter, began to take a seat, placed her briefcase down on the seat opposite. She glanced at Hale, and then moved further down the carriage. A cleaner, a huge black man hauling a plastic bag, made a quip, "Blimey, mate, good night out was it?"

"Unforgettable," said Hale, forcing a painful smile through his taut face.

Hale's cell phone sounded with an annoying default tone. A text reply from Baz:

'good 2 hear from you mate ... got work in Scotland for 2 wks building wall in castle. ur house is ok, dunno where lucy and debs are. will C U in a few wks for beer session. ill call u'.

Two roads from the house, Hale paid the taxi driver, stepped onto the pavement, looked around. Quiet, one dog walker. A postman rushed around lugging a red bag and listening to an iPod, distinctive with its white earplugs. The air was chilly, the morning sharp and fresh, typical of autumn on the estuary.

At the house, he walked up the path to the front door.

Baz was right about Lucy and Deborah. They were gone. The lawn was overgrown and the mail backed up as Hale pushed the door open. Inside, the air was dank, chilled, but still had a faint and distinctive smell of home. Memories flashed as he bent down awkwardly to retrieve the mail. He gave the batch a cursory glance. Bills, threats, statements, warnings, writs. The usual. No reason to trawl through them now. He placed them on the sideboard.

The ringing in his ears had abated, but still imposed within the silence of the home. Just birds tweeting in the garden, a distant hum of traffic, and the occasional blast from the *C2C* horn some miles away.

Hale's life had changed forever. He knew he must leave the house soon, before trouble returned in whatever form. The truth of Lucy's dealings with Ralph and the insufferable bores from Nerja was perhaps best avoided. If Hale broached the matter, asked questions, Lucy would become defensive, it would break down, and Deborah would pay the price of such a confrontation. No point in digging in the dirt.

Upstairs, he gathered a few possessions: a holdall, a watch, some paperwork, a few clothes. He gingerly descended the stairs, checked the front window in the living room for one last time. All quiet outside. He clutched the holdall and moved back towards the hall. Time to leave. As he did so, the birds from the back garden tweeted loudly, echoing around the kitchen. Hale thought of the kitchen, the good times with Lucy when they'd moved in, discussing their plans each morning over mugs of tea. Hale stopped in his tracks, walked slowly across the living room and into the kitchen for a final look.

Cold and dim, it had no signs of recent activity. No unwashed cups in the sink, no photos on the fridge, or any personal reference to Hale's bygone family existence. He lowered his eyes, pursed his lips, thinking of the future. He vowed not to make enquiries as to the whereabouts of Lucy and Deborah. That process would be handled in due course by solicitors. When – *if* – he came out of hiding.

As he made to leave, one item stood out of place near the toaster. An envelope, white, sealed, of fine quality paper. Text, black print was embossed on the front:

Mr Charles Hale.

Hale opened it, drew out a crisp folded letter. A simple paragraph, carefully typed:

Dear Mr Hale

You may remember we spoke in London some weeks ago. I have no idea when you might receive this letter, if at all. If, however, this does reach you, and you require assistance, you may wish to make contact.

*Yours sincerely,
Tony Hodgkinson, ICO*

Hale pondered the term 'assistance' and how the letter came to be resting on the kitchen work surface rather than with the rest of the mail at the front door. In the letter, Hodgkinson's intentions were predictably vague, and besides, was it the Branch Commander's place to assist criminals on the run? Hale thought not, so replaced the letter in the envelope, and filed it in his briefcase.

That afternoon, he located a guesthouse, *The Sunshine*, two stops east on the railway line at Westcliff-on-Sea. Here, he planned to stay for a week. Time to recover, let the swelling on his face calm down, visit Southend hospital.

A musty place of mock-Tudor design, the first floor room of the guesthouse overlooked an Indian restaurant on the corner of an unremarkable street running down to the seafront. For now at least, this was to be Hale's new home.

In daylight hours, Hale was able to lean out of the window, look south to see ships and tugs heading up and down the Thames. On murky nights, he could hear their foghorns sounding. The guesthouse was a discreet and convenient retreat. The owner had a few regular guests: commuters, city types passing through or using the train line for access to London, and a workman who repaired vehicles.

Hale used a false name, paid the owner cash, and no questions were asked. He nodded to the guests at breakfast, talked about the weather, told them about his 'car crash' and how lucky he had been to escape the pileup with his life. But nothing more.

Soon, the money began to run out. With a trawl around the Westcliff and Southend job agencies, Hale realised there was no local work attainable any time soon. Moreover, signing up to the agencies required form filling, residential addresses, proof of ID, details of last employers, and other information that Hale was loath to divulge.

He rang Pam.

"My God, Charles, where are you ... are you coming back?" she said, putting her entire switchboard of students and business whingers on hold.

"Looks like I'll have to," said Hale. "I had a few problems, and I'm afraid I look a bit of a state."

"Why, what happened to you?"

"It's difficult to explain on the phone, Pam. Things were okay in Spain. Then I came back and met up with some undesirables. Muggers, I guess you'd call them. My face is black and blue, but I'm okay otherwise."

"Oh God, no." Pam's sincerity touched Hale. Someone who genuinely knew him, able to express compassion. "You called the police didn't you? Did they get them?"

"It's being taken care of, Pam. An investigation and all that, but I'm fine. Look, anyway ... how's Stack?"

"Well..." The pause indicated the inevitable. "How can I say ... Grumpy."

"Nothing new there."

"Yes, but when your name's mentioned, he goes red. Actually, it's quite funny."

"Ah, good," Hale laughed. "I needed cheering up. Listen ... tell him I'm back on the scene and can do some work from a distance, you know, via the laptop. I'll need to acquire one from the college though, as mine died a death. I can do a day here or there, half days too, but at fairly random intervals and short notice. Bit odd, I know, but can you put that to him, Pam?" Hale sensed Pam jotting down the details the other end.

"Well, that is quite a demand on him, Charles," she said, an air of uncertainty in her voice. "I mean he's difficult enough at the moment."

"He'll be fine, Pam. Let him know that I'll give him a call prior to coming back in and that he should remember my last email to him. He'll know what I mean."

Hale left Pam to return to her switchboard. He ran through a short-term plan to stay alive, get money to eat, and pay the rent at various guesthouses that he'd change at regular intervals. Going back to work may be risky, but it was a measured approach. Varying the times at which he visited the office would make Hale difficult to track by any remnants of Karzhov's outfit.

Not having met Karzhov, it was difficult for Hale to comprehend how the mobster may react to the blitz at the club. Would he send more thugs from Spain to exact revenge, draw on existing 'talent' from within Britain, or back off and put it down to *The One That Got Away*? The evasive foe, Charles Hale. The boat handler who slipped through the grasp of southern Spain's most revered Russian gangster.

Hale somehow doubted that Karzhov would settle for this.

Two days later, a working Wednesday, Hale headed into London. His face now almost presentable, the amenable nurses at Southend Hospital had fussed over him, despite unconquerable queues of more worthy sufferers waiting in the corridors. A charity shop had provided a cheap second-hand suit for five pounds, and he now felt near normal.

Despite this pseudo-return to society and normality, the thought of Marta's predicament, her whereabouts, nagged at him.

Hale melded back into the commuter mentality, the routine, as if little remarkable had happened during the preceding weeks. No life or death sprint across the windswept beaches of Tarifa, no pursuit by mafiosos, no interrogation by top law enforcement professionals. Just the train, paperwork, the sports news, the daily grind. He watched the familiar mudflats of Benfleet Creek flash by. Everything appeared as it always had, and yet this was a false existence, unsustainable.

How long can you live like this, Charles?

FIFTY-EIGHT

The next station is Limehouse.

Hale dialled Stack, who picked up immediately.

"Martin Stack."

"Martin, it's Charles."

No reply.

"I'm coming in now," said Hale.

"Mm. Really?"

"Yes, really, and I'd like you to have a laptop waiting for me. I'll load the latest files when I get there and I'd like an office for two hours. That okay?"

"This is not going to last."

"That's correct, it's not going to last. But you're going to employ me on an informal basis for a month while we wind down. I need a cash advance now, and at the end of a month I'll leave. I'll accept a bonus, but I'll make no demand for a pension or payoff. A very reasonable deal. I get out of your skin, you out of mine."

"Where are you?" said Stack, his voice dower.

"Coming into Limehouse now. Remember my email, Martin. Do we have an agreement?"

"You're going to regret messing with me, Charles, you know that?"

"Martin, I'm shaking in my shoes. Now, I repeat, do we have an agreement?"

"Okay."

Five minutes out of Fenchurch Street, Hale closed the call to Stack. Then extracted the letter from his briefcase, unfolded it and made two calls: one to directory enquiries for the ICO number, and the second to Tony Hodgkinson.

He got the ICO switchboard.

"I'd like to speak with Tony Hodgkinson, please."

A pause at the other end, and then a woman's voice, "Sir, we don't have a name of that ... sorry, can you hold for a minute?"

"No problem."

A minute passed, and then, "Can you repeat the name please, sir."

Hale sensed confusion at the other end, repeated the name, "Tony Hodgkinson. Branch commander, I believe."

Another pause, a crackle. Then, "I'm afraid he's not available at this time. Can I ask who's calling?"

"I'd rather not reveal my name at this point. A sensitive issue."

"I'm sorry, but…"

"Charles Hale," Hale said, abruptly, impatient.

"Please hold."

Hale sensed urgency at the other end.

Five seconds passed, and then, "Tony Hodgkinson speaking. Mr Hale?"

"I received your note."

"Yes, we've been interested to know of your whereabouts."

"I'm flattered, but it seems you're only one member of my growing fan base."

"I can understand, and I assume some of this attention is unwanted. Am I correct?"

"I think that would be an accurate assessment."

"How can I help you, Mr Hale?"

"I'd like to meet to discuss the way forward."

"Fine. When?"

"Next week, it could be any time. I'll send a note to your office giving twenty-four hours' notice. I won't call again. Will that work for you?"

"It will. Make sure it's next week, Mr Hale, since time is of the essence. I'm sure you understand."

Hale closed the call.

Minutes later, he walked down the steps of Fenchurch Street's Crosswell exit, out into the cobbled road, taking a right, away from The Tower of London towards the *Connecting4Business* offices.

Just another commuter day, thought Hale, although now there is a difference.

I'm a marked man.

He climbed the stairs of the offices, entered reception. Pam was busy on the phone, letters in hand. She looked up at Hale. Her response rocked him, made him sad. She dropped the letters as he approached the counter, put her hands to her mouth in horror.

"Charles, oh God, Charles. What have they done to you?"

Tears ran down her cheeks. There was little to be said. He walked around the desk, embraced her for a moment, she sobbed at his chest. He shouldn't have come back ... she didn't deserve this.

The swelling and bruising had calmed over the few weeks since the blitz, and the outlook was good. After some months, the scarring would hardly be visible and the only reminder of that night. But he'd been deluded into believing that his appearance was in any way normal to those familiar with him, those who had worked with him on a daily basis for years.

Hale stepped back, held Pam's hand, made light of it, laughing, "Damn, I thought I looked great. Put my best suit on, just five quid from the charity shop."

Pam wiped the tears, giggled and shook her head.

"It really does look worse than it is, Pam," said Hale. "I'm fine, really."

Stack walked by with a bundle of papers, made a double take at Hale. Hale acknowledged.

"Martin."

"Charles."

Stack disappeared into his office leaving Pam and Hale to catch up for a few seconds. Her switchboard flashed, she needed to get back to it.

"Martin says you're leaving in a few weeks. Is that right?" Pam asked.

"It is. I have to move on from here. I'll come in briefly now and then leading up to the end. I'll call when I need to come in. Hope that's okay."

Pam, looked up, lightly shook her head, whispered, "What kind of trouble are you in, Charles? What are you running from? Maybe I can help."

Hale looked down at his feet, sighed, "There's so much to explain, Pam. You're a good person, you don't need to know the details, believe me. It's over with Lucy, and I met someone…"

"A Spanish girl?"

Hale frowned, looked around, feeling uneasy. Work had always been separate from his life in Spain. Always.

"You guessed?" he said. "I suppose with all of my trips, you worked it out."

"She called the office asking for you?"

Hale gasped, "She did? No, you must be mistaken ... when?"

"I'm not mistaken. Two weeks ago," said Pam. "I didn't understand her very well. She said very little. Asked where you were, when you were returning. Then she said goodbye and hung up."

"Did she say her name, leave a number?"

"No."

"Can you trace the phone records, get a caller ID?"

"No, Charles, it was a land line from abroad. No ID, and it's impossible to get more information on this system from a foreign call. I've been working on it long enough to know that for certain."

Hale puffed his cheeks out, gathered his thoughts. "Did Martin sort out the laptop for me?"

"Yes, in your office. The work's ready on a memory stick with the latest documents loaded. Also, paperwork from Martin, lots of it. Within five minutes after you phoned, he'd gathered it from me and dumped it on your desk."

"Good. Thanks, Pam."

FIFTY-NINE

Fax is dead. That was the view of most businesses. For the likes of *Connecting4Business* and the ICO, however, the machines lived on. Pam had delivered a note on Hale's behalf to the ICO by fax a week after his visit to Stack's empire, a Wednesday morning. And not with the twenty-four hours' notice originally stated, but just six.

From Westminster, Hale walked towards the ICO building at 15:55 p.m., five minutes before the meeting. In the reception area, he checked in and waited, standing, observing traffic in the street. He remembered his first nervous visit to the place months before. This time, he was not so much nervous, but weary, curious. Looking for answers.

Hodgkinson arrived, same suit, same polite smile. Just the vaguest hint of a raised eyebrow at Hale's injuries. Then more small talk about the weather until Hale sat opposite him in the same bland room. Hodgkinson laid a folder and notepad on the table, leaned back and fiddled with his pen.

"Have a nice vacation in Spain, did we?" said Hodgkinson.

Hale lined up an equally witty reply, but mentally retracted it, preferring to take an early lead in the dialogue, "Why am I here?" he said.

Hodgkinson smiled, "Please ... *you* tell me."

"The note. You broke into my house."

"The house is with the receivers. We contacted the lawyers involved, they have a key."

Hale said nothing.

"We are trying to protect you, sir," continued Hodgkinson.

"You are?"

"Yes, though I must confess that we do have somewhat of a vested interest in your activities, and in your survival, at least in the short term."

"I'm not psychic. Please elaborate."

Hodgkinson placed the pen neatly on the folder, leaned forward clasping his hands on the table, twiddled his thumbs. "I'd like you to meet a colleague of mine in a minute, sir, but before I do, I need to ask a question with regard to recent events in London."

"Events?" Hale shrugged, "Do continue. I'm, intrigued."

"Who are you working for, sir?"

Hale frowned, his eyes narrowed. The question jarred. Did Hodgkinson genuinely believe he was somehow conspiring with Morillo and Karzhov? "I really have no idea what you're talking about. Is it necessary to play games like this?"

"You may or may not be aware that we have an interest in an international crime figure by the name of Sergei Karzhov, a case we have been working on for some time. This man is connected with a Spanish associate – a partner, we believe – by the name of Berto Morillo."

Hale said nothing, waited.

Hodgkinson looked up, continued, "Well, it seems that by some remarkable coincidence, on the very day of your return to this country, one of Sergei Karzhov's London headquarters was razed to the ground. Furthermore, these headquarters were unknown to us prior to the fire – or shall I say, explosions – since Karzhov's men move bases regularly within the city and are notoriously adept at covering their tracks."

"How did you know they were Karzhov's headquarters?" said Hale.

"The bodies were identified – what was left of them – through DNA, and also, the weaponry inside the building was in line with our records. As was a van parked nearby."

"I did see something about this in the news, a club in north London. So, you believe I'm involved?"

Hodgkinson, picked up his pen, began scribbling something on the notepad. He said, "You know you can use a code word … if you wish."

Hale frowned, "A what?"

"We cannot offer protection or any other guarantee unless we have some indication, of your group. No matter how vague."

"Group?"

"Yes, for want of a better word."

"You *do* need a better word," said Hale, shaking his head, confused. "Are we in a movie here?"

Hodgkinson seemed frustrated, his demeanour turning icy. "Look, sir, we have good reason to believe that you were at the club in north London prior to those explosions. It's clear from what happened, that you – or your *group* as I shall call them – had intelligence of which we were not privy, and somehow worked to eliminate this faction. May I say that working *together* on these things helps the common goal."

"And may I say that I share no common goal, as you describe it, and belong to no such group. I'd like to know what evidence you have that I was at this club you mention." Hale had no idea where this was going, but yearned to know more. "Furthermore," Hale continued, "wasn't it you or *your* group, Mr Hodgkinson, who sent these people to storm the place…"

"People?"

Hale realised he'd made a blunder, remained silent.

"I made no mention of people. Care to elaborate?"

Hale remained silent, not sure how to respond.

Showing impatience, Hodgkinson sighed, and then said, "Look, we're clearly getting nowhere. Let me get my colleague and we'll speak, hopefully more positively, about the way forward." Hodgkinson rose to his feet, turned to the door. "Tea, coffee?"

"Tea, white no sugar, thanks."

"I'll be five minutes."

Hodgkinson left. The door closed.

Hale sat in the room alone with nothing to hear other than his own breathing and distant echoing footsteps of people in the corridor outside. He studied the face of his watch, mulling what Hodgkinson knew, his intentions.

One thing was clear: the branch commander was a precise man and his timing was uncanny. Hale watched the hands of his watch. Time elapsed: four minutes, fifty-five seconds, and counting…

The door swung open.

A familiar face appeared.

Rosa María Díez.

Instinctively, Hale rose, offered his hand. María Díez shook it, gave a faint smile that was quickly extinguished as she walked to the wall and dragged a chair across to the table. Strange, thought Hale, to see her dark complexion and striking features within these nondescript surroundings. Hodgkinson walked in, holding two Styrofoam cups while clutching his file under his armpit. In a rather elaborate performance, he placed the cups on the table, pushed one cup before Hale, carefully positioned his own, shut the door, and quietly took his seat next to María Díez.

During Hodgkinson's tea service charade, Hale had noticed that María Díez was staring. Uncomfortably intense. Her unblinking assessment at work, as if studying the position of the sutures that had been made around Hale's eye.

"So, we meet again," said Hale, taking a sip of plastic-flavoured tea. "You're looking fine as ever, Inspectora Jefa. Unfortunately, as you can see, the same cannot be said for me."

Hodgkinson smiled mildly at the remark. María Díez did not.

Hodgkinson, seemingly in an attempt to break the ice, coughed, retrieved a piece of paper from his folder, and began, "Let me explain," he said. "The Inspectora Jefa's people followed you from Málaga..."

María Díez wasted no time in leading, "Yes, we tracked you into the Airport," she said. "At London Gatwick, and then on the train to Victoria. Here, you went to a café with some men, no?"

Hale nodded.

"At this point you were followed by a woman. Did you know this?"

Hale shook his head.

"This woman waited for you to come out of the café. You did so with two men – they forced you out. Correct?"

"Correct."

"Then, we had the problem ... or my friend here had the problem."

Hodgkinson leaned forward, rather awkward in his delivery, "Ahem, yes ... we knew these people were tipped off from Spain by Berto Morillo's people, possibly Karzhov's, difficult to say. But it was our intention that we protected you, whilst leading us to Karzhov's operation. We know only Karzhov has operations in the UK, not Morillo."

"So, I was the bait," said Hale.

"We took precautions," said Hodgkinson, "but these operations are never without risk. The Inspectora Jefa's tail – the woman she mentioned – was one of the best, practically invisible to most. But there was a problem outside the station. We tracked you on CCTV, the Inspectora Jefa was in the control room, but in the confusion…"

"How?" interrupted Hale. "We spoke at the airport … she was in Málaga."

"She took a flight ahead of you."

"There was no flight ahead of mine ... as far as I was aware."

"A military flight."

"I see," said Hale, raising his eyebrows. This was clearly a large-scale operation, expensive. He paused, recalling the scene at Victoria, and then continued, "Outside the station, people were everywhere, pushing, getting in the way."

Hodgkinson nodded, slurped some tea, continued, "Yes, indeed. Too many travellers crowding the entrance, heading for the Underground station in all directions. But Sergei Karzhov is a cunning and careful planner. He'd placed two spotters in the area. They barged the Inspectora Jefa's agent – the one tailing you – to the floor, held her back and then fled."

"But you were tracking me on CCTV?" said Hale.

"Yes, we watch you," said María Díez, "but then lose coverage off the main street. You go behind some buildings, and then you are gone."

"We lost contact with you at that point," said Hodgkinson, "and then we picked you up the next day."

"You did?" said Hale, "Where?"

"Fenchurch Street, CCTV."

"How could you possibly do that? Rush hour, the place was packed with commuters."

"Correct, but only two moved against the flow at around eight thirty, heading up the escalators. One, a woman. Another, a man who fitted your description in height and build – a man who bought a ticket for Leigh-on-Sea, as flagged by the ticketing system. We knew you'd head home out of curiosity, to see your wife."

"Ex-fiancée," Hale corrected.

Hodgkinson glanced down at his notes, "Yes, I do apologise. At your home, we kept watch. We were concerned that you'd be taken by Karzhov's crew, or some other party connected with him directly or indirectly."

"The postman was with you?" said Hale.

Hodgkinson nodded. "Amongst others around and about."

Hale pictured the postman, of whom he had thought nothing at the time, but remembered that he carried a bag that day. Normally, they pushed a red trolley in his road.

"And how would this postman have helped me if two thugs from the great Karzhov had put in an appearance?" asked Hale, still confused of the motives behind Hodgkinson's activities.

"Well," said Hodgkinson, "I cannot divulge too much, but let's just say he would be delivering more than letters from the satchel he hauled with him."

Hale paused, looked at María Díez, "Very well, so what do you want from me?" he said. "To help you arrest a Russian drugs baron? I can assure you that I am not some kind of special agent, armed and dangerous. You're dealing with an office worker who likes to sail at the weekends. Forgive me if I'm wrong, but I don't believe this is quite the skill-set you're looking for."

"Remember what you have done, and what information we have about you," snapped María Díez, a vein of anger in her voice. "And my investigations, as I explained in Málaga – regarding Puerto de Santa María, about the boat, which was attacked – are ongoing and now heightened, with the help of my friend here and..."

"Now, we must work together, please," interrupted Hodgkinson, "because the three of us have an investment one way or another in this case and the safety of the girl is to be considered. I think we need..."

Hale jolted upright, frowned. María Díez delivered a look to Hodgkinson so severe it made him lean back, throw his hands up and sigh. The first time Hale had seen the branch commander ruffled in any sense.

"The safety of the girl," said Hale to Hodgkinson. Then repeated it, loud, to María Díez, "What do you mean by *the safety of the girl*?"

Hodgkinson moved to explain, but the Inspectora Jefa cut him off forcibly, holding her hand up. "We had been tracking her too," she said. "Berto Morillo is in Málaga prison, but we can only detain him for a certain time, and he has rights to make phone calls and meet people as we look for evidence to charge him. But his lawyers are putting pressure on us for his release, understand?"

"What are you saying?"

She paused, and then replied, "Try to realise that Morillo has extensive forces throughout Spain and he can *control* these forces from wherever he is. We know the girl fled to Madrid, but we believe Morillo's men found her, abducted her."

Hale felt his world closing in, the responsibility bearing down on him. They were mad to have run. Marta had been right: Morillo was tenacious, dangerous, connected. Their endeavours were flawed from the outset, and Hale had perhaps placed his own interests, rather than Marta's, at the forefront. He leaned forward on the table, held his head in his hands. He felt María Díez's hand on his shoulder as he fought to hold back tears.

Hodgkinson continued, "Mr Hale, I'm afraid you have to face the truth. The fact is that after the showdown on the Marbella beach and the fireworks display at the London club, you have become something of a celebrity in criminal circles."

Hale leaned back, took a breath to compose himself. "How so?"

"Well," continued Hodgkinson, "we have intelligence leading us to believe that Karzhov is on a mission to find the Englishman with these *talents*."

María Díez nodded in agreement, looked up at Hale, "And you have seen that Morillo is persistent as well," she said. "He has an emotional attachment with this girl and he used everything to find her. And now, yes, he has her. Karzhov is different, a more dangerous international criminal."

"Yes, I understand," said Hale, "but where is this taking us? I don't want to run forever, but as you can imagine, I don't particularly wish to spend my days in a Spanish or British prison."

"Where you will not necessarily be out of Morillo's or Karzhov's reach," added Hodgkinson.

"Exactly," said Hale, shrugging. "So, I'm screwed."

Hodgkinson aligned his papers, positioned his pen and cup neatly alongside, straightened his back, and then said, "You know, for political reasons, we cannot work *directly* with you. You understand that don't you, sir?"

"Go on."

"Well, you see, regarding Karzhov … the Inspectora Jefa and I have been working on this case for many years and we know that he has a level of respect for competitors in the business. *Partners in crime* I guess you might call them."

"I don't follow you."

"We believe he sees you as an enigmatic figure, sir. Untouchable. Possibly with some power by way of perceived connections you may have. I must admit, you do seem to have the knack of evading your pursers, and leaving dead bodies in the wake as you do so. Karzhov is the type of chap who admires such traits."

"And?"

"The way Karzhov operates is that he tends to headhunt such *talented* individuals and draw them into his network. Indeed, this is how he became such a force in the first place."

Hale shook his head, assimilating the information. He glanced at María Díez, posed a question: "Inspectora Jefa. Mr Hodgkinson. Do I read this correctly? Are you seriously expecting me to collude with a Russian mobster?"

SIXTY

Perplexed, Hale left María Díez and Hodgkinson with no further instruction or indication that any plan, supposedly to infiltrate Karzhov's operation, would materialise. He boarded the train back to Westcliff, knowing one thing at least: this was now political. The players in the game were powerful, holding cards close to their chests. Even the identity of all the players involved was vague, indistinct.

Hale had offered his cell phone number for further discussion. Hodgkinson had waved it off, said nothing. Perhaps such information was readily available within the confines of the ICO. The branch commander had also implied, with some foreboding in his voice, that he 'suspected' Karzhov would try to ascertain Hale's whereabouts and make contact. Also, that as far as the ICO was aware, Karzhov had no knowledge of Hale's temporary abode in Westcliff. Another blunder by Hodgkinson delivered on a plate, since Hale did not recall divulging the whereabouts of his (current) guesthouse to anyone.

A fact emerged from the meeting that drew on Hale's curiosity. Hodgkinson's outfit seemed at a loss to reconcile events at Karzhov's north London club.

Hale called Baz, who picked up after two rings.
"Mate, how's things and what's up?" said Baz.
"Oh, I'm fine. As I said, I'm back in the UK," said Hale.
"Yeah, got the text."
"Wanna meet up?" said Hale, pondering whether it wise to return to Old Leigh and *Ye Olde Smack*.
"I'd love to, mate, but this Scottish job is dragging on … I'm up here now for a while."

Hale heard voices in the background, men shouting, and wind buffeting. A rooftop or building site.

"Okay," said Hale. "So, just give me a call when you're back down."

"No problems, buddy. Are you okay down there in the civilised part of Britain?"

Hale heard a jeer in the background – a riposte for Baz's quip.

"Yes, all is good. A few complications ... but listen, Baz. I wonder whether you knew anything ... or had anything to do with that thing I was involved with. Did you hear about a fire in London?"

"What? Can't hear you too well, mate ... you say a fire?"

"Yeah, well, I was caught up in it and I thought – sounds ridiculous I know – you might have something to do with my ... rescue?"

Hale heard laughs at the other end, and then Baz calling over to his workmates, "Hey guys! Get this ... my buddy, Charlie, thinks I'm some sort of bleedin' *Backdraft* movie hero, pulling him out of a burning house or something."

Baz laughed, and then spoke to Hale, "Look, Charlie, you sure you're okay? It's not another woman making you go nuts again, like before with the French…"

"No, Baz, nothing like that," interrupted Hale. "I'm just working something out, but you get on now and we'll catch up for a beer when you're back."

"Smashing, mate, let's do that. Ciao for now, Charlie boy."

Hale closed the call, felt a fool.

Repeatedly running through events of that night at the club made things no clearer. Besides, he had been unconscious for part of the night, and the entire episode was becoming a blur. Newspaper reports were ambiguous, and now there were more pressing issues looming, not least regarding Marta, her whereabouts and safety. Hale's life, his future, seemed to be forming in a new and sinister way, potentially as an anonymous drifter with a new identity, someone who moved from job-to-job, town-to-town, paying cash, and making few friends.

According to Hodgkinson, Hale's strategy to work at *Connecting4Business*, albeit erratically and without regular pattern, was inherently 'unsafe'. A month, he had predicted, may be acceptable with great caution, but with no guarantees. Beyond that, simply reckless. Such was the power and influence that Karzhov and his cohort, Morillo, commanded even from afar.

The meeting had concluded with an odd delivery of cagey rhetoric of which executives at *Connecting4Business* would have been proud. It seemed that from the perspective of María Díez and

Hodgkinson, Hale's newfound status as a criminal, implicated in drugs trafficking and linked to a series of violent incidents and deaths, held certain pros and cons.

Hale had considered Hodgkinson's qualified gibberish on the return train trip, and concluded that the rationale was straightforward: Hale's 'status' as a connected criminal was potentially valuable to the ICO and to María Díez's people. Consequently, the downside was that, neither formal recognition, nor protection could be afforded to him.

It seemed that Karzhov was a master of commanding his troops from a safe distance. Unlike Morillo and Happy, Karzhov was wise enough to steer clear of anything smacking of a setup or personal spat, and would certainly have maintained a good distance from the 'beach party' at Marbella.

As a result, the ICO commander and Inspectora Jefa would have no conclusive evidence that Karzhov and Morillo were implicated in anything more than petty crime and bullying, the latter activities perhaps qualifying as extortion at a stretch. Nothing that would put them behind bars for years. Nothing that they wouldn't wriggle out of with the best international attorneys money could buy. Clearly, Karzhov was the brains and experience behind this position. María Díez had alluded to this fact. Get Karzhov, and Morillo would fall soon after.

Hodgkinson would not seek to protect Hale. Hodgkinson's position was clear: the ICO did not collude with criminals and Hodgkinson was not enlightened as to the full extent of Hale's activities, either recently or in his conceivably murky past. The north London blaze perplexed Hodgkinson as much as it did Hale. Hodgkinson seemed to suspect Hale's involvement in some other agency, maybe even another criminal organisation, and Hale was at a loss to convince him otherwise. In fact, the more Hale revealed to Hodgkinson, the more perilous his position might be, affecting any future potential entry into a witness protection program. The bureaucracy and formalities inherent in such a scheme would preclude Hale's involvement, and any evidence obtained, inadmissible in court.

Thus, María Díez's vocabulary, within the context of this meandering discussion, and certainly Hodgkinson's, did not include the words 'deal' or 'agreement'. It seemed that the best advice to Hale, which he may or may not heed, was to keep the lowest profile possible. Avoid any regular routines, use cash, different names, move on.

Become a drifter.

Hale had enquired: *And what of Karzhov and Morillo?* After all, it was Hodgkinson who'd implied that Hale potentially might afford some level of respect, even admiration, from the mafioso collaborators.

The *C2C* approached Westcliff, the bizarre meeting, and the return to London weighing on Hale's mind. His life had now changed beyond all recognition. Gradually, he must descend under the radar, perhaps never to surface under the name, or even appearance, of Charles Hale. As for Hodgkinson and María Díez, he doubted he would see them again. They'd washed their hands of the matter, the meeting perhaps by way of a gracious warning. Gratitude in some way for Hale's actions, inadvertent as they may have been in leading them to Karzhov's club, a club now blackened, charred, and the site of an ongoing forensic investigation. María Díez, had assured Hale that she and her team were committed to Morillo's case and the pursuit of Marta's captors. There would be 'ways' to exert pressure on the Spanish mafioso and she would be leaving no stone unturned to free Marta. Hale did not doubt her intent, but how long would this take? In a year from now, would he receive a call to inform him that Díez's team were extending their search to Latin America to find the woman of Morillo's obsession?

The thought motivated feelings of anger and frustration in him.

Hale had left the meeting with pleasantries, a convivial farewell from María Díez, but little indication that any further action on his part was necessary or advisable. Just a characteristically obscure phrase from Hodgkinson as he opened the glass doors for Hale:

"Goodbye, sir. One can never say how events will transpire, or who one might meet."

SIXTY-ONE

Late October. Some weeks had passed since the ICO meeting. Hale maintained a clandestine existence, yet flouted Hodgkinson's warning by staying on at *Connecting4Business* for a few extra weeks. He needed the money, but something within him also fed off the danger. An uncharacteristic bitterness seeped into his veins. Marta was in peril and he was helpless to intervene. Despite Hodgkinson's rhetoric, Hale was left out on a limb with no inside intelligence, no freedom, rights, or life of his own. And Regarding Karzhov and Morillo, Hale's attitude was shifting, taking on a new and dangerous stance.

So, come get me.

Westcliff was the better option as far as Hale was concerned. Although he was courting danger by returning to the locality, in his view he mitigated the risk of being found by way of local knowledge, and by rotating his stay at seaside guesthouses and more dingy accommodation in the backstreets of Southend.

The Sunshine guesthouse wasn't living up to its name, especially after the late October daylight saving clock change: dark soon after 4:00 p.m. When Hale wasn't commuting to and from Fenchurch Street, he read, and surfed British and Spanish websites for news of Morillo or the investigation at the north London club. He spent time looking out of the bay window of his first floor room, seated in a hard chair leaning back with a foot on the windowsill. Lights off, and for company, a bottle of *Arehucas* rum imported from the Canaries. He couldn't face British television or British liquor. Beer he could tolerate, usually from a pub, but no longer the *Cheshire Cheese*, his regular London haunt. Too dangerous.

At *The Sunshine*, the world outside became familiar. On the street corner, a few chefs emerged on a twice-hourly basis from the Indian restaurant, stood around, smoked cigarettes, shivering in the gloom. They'd skulk back inside before clientele arrived or the owner spotted them. Dog walkers fussed with undersized mutts bearing woollen coats. Commuters came and went from the station across the road. Hale now recognised most of them. Men in suits with briefcases and grey faces, couples holding hands who perhaps worked and commuted together, and secretaries, young and fresh-faced. All with jobs in the city. Lives safe and secure, unlike his own. The local traffic followed a regular pattern. Mostly working vans and modest cars, some firing up in the 5:00 a.m. frost or fog to beat the jam into London.

Regulars at the guesthouse also worked a familiar routine. Weekend commuters, salesmen, consultants, mostly on contract. They arrived late Sunday night and were gone the following Friday morning. They drove across the country to various hometowns, the details of which Hale did not enquire. According to the landlord, a born-and-bred Southender of sixty-five and keen gossipmonger, Hale had acquired a reputation as being a loner, rather unfriendly.

Hale was fine with that reputation.

Early November, Wednesday, 7:15 p.m. Hale sat at the window chair, two shots of *Arehucas* down, warming his insides. Same scene, same commuters, same dogs. Except one thing. A man, black, maybe Jamaican, medium build, beanie and thick jacket hanging around the restaurant area. He seemed to look about him, and then move on down the street, south, in the direction of the seafront.

Hale took a slug of rum, watched him go halfway down. The man stopped, lit a cigarette, turned and looked back. From that side of the street, there wasn't much to see. At that angle, he wasn't looking at the restaurant, and beyond that, the view comprised fences, undergrowth. The unsightly structure of the railway line would hardly warrant a first glance, thought Hale, let alone a second.

The man waited for some minutes, stamped out his cigarette and then walked swiftly back up towards the restaurant. At the restaurant, he turned away, heading east on Station Road towards Southend. Hale grabbed his jacket, ran downstairs, and pursued the man from a healthy distance out on the street.

Hale's mind was muddled with alcohol, but frosty air was drawn into his lungs, snapping him awake. The black man was moving fast, not running, but a brisk pace, his breath streaming behind like that of a car's exhaust. The man crossed Station Road, disappeared out of sight over the bridge leading to Hamlet Court Road. Hale made it across the bridge to the foot of the road, which was surrounded by shops and rose up a steep hill. He then stepped out of sight into the shadows of a shop doorway to recover his breathing. Hale spotted the black man powering up the hill in the distance, and then turning into a side street until lost from view.

Hale, zipped his jacket up to the neck, whispered to himself, "You're paranoid, Charles. Paranoid."

He walked back to the guesthouse, reflecting on events of a day one week before. He'd been travelling into Stack's empire, usual route, nothing much different, but was followed from the Crosswell entrance at Fenchurch Street station.

At the time, Hale had no doubt about it. But having pinned his 'pursuer' to the wall and caused a commotion, the guy turned out to be an Iranian mature student studying English. On his way to a job interview near *Connecting4Business*. The Iranian wasn't tailing Hale. He was simply lost. Some of the student's friends turned up to join the fracas. Hale apologised profusely, said he was under pressure (true), things were not so good in his life at the moment (true), and that he could do without police interest (very true). Fortunately, the Iranian students had better things to do than to argue with a rambling office worker, and left the scene.

Following his pursuit of the mysterious black man, Hale returned to *The Sunshine*, headed upstairs where the bottle of spirits awaited. "*Exposure*, Charles," he said, angry, throwing his jacket onto the bed, pouring a shot of the dark liquid. "Avoid it and lie low."

He'd repeated this mantra to himself over the weeks since the ICO meeting. And after all, just another week with Stack, and he'd hit the road, head somewhere else. Wales, Yorkshire. Get lost in some other community for a few weeks, and then move on again.

London two days later.

Hale entered a café on Leadenhall Street beneath the iconic glass 'Gherkin' towering above. He ordered a coffee and croissant, took a stool seat by the window, flipped open his laptop.

"Shit!" Hale said, too loudly, thumping his fist on the table. Embarrassed, he looked around at the barista, who appeared unperturbed by the outburst. The twenty-year-old shrugged as if to say, *Chill out, dude, no big deal.*

Hale returned his attention to the screen. A screen-blocking virus prevented the *Windows* machine from booting up. Hale was familiar with this type of virus from his experience at work. Out of office hours, students would often browse dubious websites, thus encouraging infiltration by malicious software. Termed 'ransomware', the screen-blocking variety usually made bogus assertions that the user was viewing illegal pornography or downloading copyrighted music. It then demanded payment of a fine for the alleged crime. A simple anti-virus scan would eliminate the devious software. The virus on Hale's system, however, was different and displayed an odd message on a plain blue screen:

[Blue Beach Café. Southend. Eastern Esplanade. Sunday. 08:00 hrs]

Hale shook his head. Strange virus. The message disappeared, the screen changed to white, and then displayed:

[Codeword: Azul]

After ten seconds, the screen changed to black and the machine booted into *Windows* as normal.

Hale knew the Blue Beach Café, a smart bistro on the seafront with a view across the Thames Estuary. The place attracted trippers and locals, a pleasant type of place. On a Sunday, however, it would not be open at 08:00 hrs.

Strange request.

Could be Hodgkinson, thought Hale, but more likely a trap by Karzhov to lure him into something. He should send a message to Hodgkinson. Verify the source. But surely Hodgkinson would never send such a message to Hale's laptop, and even if he had done so, would never admit to it.

Hale thought of the only sensible response: ignore the message, lie low, and avoid Southend at all costs. Especially on Sunday.

SIXTY-TWO

Southend Esplanade, Thorpe Bay, Sunday 07:55.

Hale watched the Blue Beach Café from one hundred yards out. The morning was cold, the sun just managing to lift the colour of the sky from slate grey to a pleasant yellow-tinged hue. He stood motionless behind a bus stop on the beach side of the main drag, a road heading into Southend Seafront and the amusements further west. Hale preferred this end of town. Quaint bed and breakfast accommodation lined the road overlooking what was either a vast beach leading to mudflats, or an attractive shore with moored boats bobbing up and down on the water. The choice of view depended on the state of the treacherous tides, which could leave the foolhardy or ignorant trapped by water, or high and dry on the flats.

Ahead in the distance, a few runners and dog walkers passed the café. Some cars cruised by, as did the occasional cyclist labouring into a light, chilly breeze. South, to Hale's right, the tide was well out, the River Thames just visible as a thin line of blue-grey. Hale spotted distant figures in the mud. A man three hundred yards out, standing stationary. Another, a cocklepicker, moved slowly through the gloop, others dug spades into the oozing mud, which stretched on to the horizon. Nothing out of the ordinary, no mafiosos with bulky jackets, no limos with darkened windows cruising by.

But this was no movie, and Hale had no idea what to expect.

He ambled towards the café, pulled his beanie down to keep his head warm, pushed his frozen hands into the pockets of his woollen jacket. The café was closed. No surprise there. The depressing side of an English seaside resort.

I should be in Paris, thought Hale, his mood plummeting. Cafés in the city open at 7 a.m., or earlier.

He circled the Blue Beach Café, now impatient.

Coffee and croissant in Paris. That's definitely where I should be. Not following up a bogus message planted on my laptop, a message leading me to a closed Essex café on a dreary November morning.

He walked in front of the building for a final time, nodded to a sprightly old man walking a small white dog on a five-metre lead.

The thing looked more like a ferret, but happy nonetheless. Hale turned, and then began walking back in the direction of the pier, cursing. He estimated the walk back to Westcliff would be around four miles. He'd rather be spending his time running, reading, or planning the week's choice of guesthouses to frequent.

But those humdrum Sunday tasks were simply a means to delay a return to the bottle of rum. Denial prevented him from any admission of dependence on this new friend that awaited him back at the guesthouse. He looked west ahead to the pier stretching a mile out into the estuary. He mused that he would run its length one day. Then Hale stopped in his tracks, turned around. Something occurred to him, seemed out of place. He looked across the beach, out to the mud flats. The cocklepickers remained. Silhouetted Lowry figures, hunched, digging. The figure perpendicular to the Blue Beach Café, however, stood astride, hands in pockets, stationary. Still three hundred yards out. He or she appeared to stare directly at the café. No spade, no bucket, just standing, looking.

Hale descended some steps onto the beach, shells crunching underfoot. The beach sloped down twenty degrees. He slipped occasionally on clumps of seaweed as a familiar stench filled his senses, that of mud and brine.

The figure remained. Hale assumed it was a man. Broad shoulders, no curves. The mud ahead appeared sticky and uninviting before him. Hale looked down at his footwear. Hudson lace-up leather boots from Jones Bootmaker. Fine for tarmac streets, even cobbled, but inadequate for the job of viscous mudflats. Regardless, he set out, stepping into the oozing mud, which immediately sucked at his leg, allowing icy water to seep into his socks. He drew one foot out, stepped forward, sinking into another squelching hole of dark mousse. Reminded Hale of Cadbury Mousse, a dessert he'd gorged on as a child. But this variety didn't smell or taste as good. He knew it didn't taste as good, since he'd sampled a few mouthfuls of the stuff playing in it as a boy, or later in life when falling face first trying to dislodge a grounded boat. And even during his misguided youth, he rarely ventured out in the treacherous bog beyond a few metres.

A hundred yards from the man and Hale was working, breathing hard, concentrating to prevent his boots from being ripped off and sucked under. The last fifty were the hardest through the relentless mire. Finally he reached the man, spent.

Hale bent over, hands on knees, recovering for some seconds. Then rose up and straightened his back.

"Nice morning for a walk," said the man, taking a drag from a cigarette. He wore a black beanie, shades, black woollen coat, black gloves. Indeed, even this man's skin was black. The only things not black about this guy were the whites of his eyes, his fine teeth, and thin white stripes on his Wellington boots.

"Possibly," said Hale, "if you have a couple of those," pointing to the guy's Wellingtons.

The man smiled, "Well, you see, I like the fresh air, nature."

"How nice. Who are you?" said Hale, still recovering his breathing.

"I'm Black."

Hale decided against a clever reply, "Nice to meet you, Black. I'm Char…"

"Let's just call you White, shall we?" interrupted Black. "I like to keep things simple."

Speaks well, thought Hale, maybe a university education. Neutral accent, low and confident voice, probably born in Britain. He had perfect skin, a dark velvet tone, but behind the shades, difficult to guess his age. Like many of those black guys, they always seemed to look young. Twenty, forty, no real difference. Somewhat annoying.

"So, we keep things Black and White," said Hale. "Fine with me."

Black looked around, across to the mouth of the estuary, took another drag, flicked the stub into the mud. It fizzled out with a dying puff of smoke. "Do you have a word for me, White?"

"*Azul*, I believe. Do you always choose such imaginative venues for your meetings?" asked Hale.

"Well, put it this way, White, if anybody wants to come running after me out here, they're quite welcome. And when they get here, and by chance they need to get away from me in a hurry, well they might have a problem." He laughed with a deep, attractive timbre.

Hale looked him up and down. Probably armed. A knife, small arms maybe, ammunition, all concealable under the coat.

"What about snipers?" said Hale.

Black shook his head, "They'd have to follow me here to sunny Southend and set up quick. And if they *did* set up real quick, say concealed in one of those guesthouses over there," he pointed over Hale's shoulder, "then they'd have to be a great shot at this distance, White. Especially as we have a little breeze today."

"So, we're safe," said Hale.

"We are. You know a few hundred years ago, smugglers used to come up here, ground their ships on the mud and throw parcels of tea to rowing boats. They'd wait for the tide, head off and…"

"Sorry to interrupt, old fellow," said Hale, "but can you enlighten me as to why am I standing three hundred yards out in the mud at eight o' clock on Sunday morning? I'm assuming it's not for a history lesson, and I'm assuming you're not out here to pick cockles."

Black eyed Hale, paused for a moment, smiled, "Well, my friend, you are indeed correct, however, there is a connection with my history lesson."

"I'm intrigued. Hopefully you can shed some light on the issue before my feet freeze."

"Ah, of course, White, let me get to the point." Black adjusted his collar, eased it up around his neck, pulled out a pack of cigarettes from his jacket pocket. He lit another, shielding the lighter from the easterly wind. Hale looked around, impatient. "You see," continued Black, "my friends and I know of another smuggler, a modern day smuggler, who also works nearby. Heads into Ipswich and Felixstowe and inlets around there, bringing stuff in from places like France, Holland, sometimes up from Dover. The leader of this operation – let's call him *Red* – stays in the background you see. He never does things the same twice. He gets his people to use different vessels at different times."

Hale shrugged. Black took a drag, blew smoke and breath into the breeze. "Let me explain," he continued. "Red moves a lot of product, hash, coke, and nasty stuff like heroine and other shit. He gets his people to swap it between vessels, say from a tug to a fishing boat. Also uses ferries or even those waste disposal boats. In the case of ferries, he often gets the mules to drive the load aboard in a car. Then they shift it about to a lorry or bus down below – every trick in the book to avoid the Border Force boys. And here is the key thing … he contracts different people, boats, and vehicles each time. So even if we do make a seizure..."

"You can't trace it back to him," said Hale.

"That's it, White. You know those eels that might be winding around your feet real soon?"

Hale looked down, uncomfortable at the thought.

Black smiled, looked straight at Hale, serious, "This guy is slippery just like them ... the most slippery and dangerous eel of them all. We have been tracking Red for years, and now people upstairs are starting to make noises about his influence in the smoke and beyond into the provinces. Red kills people who get in his path, we know that too."

"Sound like a guy I'd be delighted to meet," said Hale. "Why am I here, Black?"

"Ha! I like your humour, White, but let me explain." Black flicked butt number two into the mud. "The word is that Red is sensing the heat on him in and around Ipswich, so he's looking to diversify, break out of the area. Do more work south, around here. Furthermore, there is one vessel that Red owns and that we can trace back to him. *If* he uses it on a run. He always takes this vessel out with the same crew for fun, travelling around and shit. Sometimes, he gets his crew to take it down to Spain, France, to film festivals, high-profile crap like that for the rich set. But he doesn't use this boat for shipping product, not with his present crew anyway."

"I don't see where you're going with this, Black," said Hale, shaking his head, shivering in the cold.

"Well, White, it's quite simple. This vessel I'm talking about is moored up the Thames here, near Tower Bridge."

"And?"

"And, it's a sailing yacht."

SIXTY-THREE

The two men parted, walking at a ninety-degree angle to each other through the mud. That's the way Black wanted it. "You're heading in the direction of those amusements," he had said, "and I'm heading northeast to that pub there. Don't stop or look across, just keep going."

That's what Hale did – using the time spent squelching through the mud to reflect on Black's words. Black had advised that Hale do nothing different during the following days, or even weeks. One of Red's minions would somehow get hold of Hale's number. How this would happen wasn't clear. The number would then filter through the hierarchy to Red. And Hale knew that Red was in fact Sergei Karzhov, the Russian mafioso eel who drew criminals into his lair, predominantly enjoying the company of dangerous, influential ones, especially those who'd acquired unique skills. Hale's boat-handling cred, trail of death and destruction in Spain, and north London fireworks display more than qualified for entry on Karzhov's *Most Wanted* list. Hodgkinson had alluded to this theory, and now it seemed that Black was setting something in motion as a result.

That *something* would perhaps leave Hale with room for some improvisation, but involved the use of Karzhov's yacht for a drug or 'product' run. Hale should speak with Karzhov, and Black had said that he believed Hale would receive a call to arrange such a meeting. As Black had put it: "Karzhov prefers to see the whites of his subordinates' eyes before getting into bed with them."

During such a meeting, Hale should explain that he was looking for work. Boat handling, away from Spain. Suggest also that Spain was hassle, too many people on his trail. Explain that he was now working low-level runs near Southend, along the Thames, but that he worked in certain ways only. *Certain ways* meant that he used sailing yachts, recreational craft, as his cover. No powerboats or other vessels. Just sailboats *when* he could acquire them. And that was not always easy.

Just as Black had surmised, Hale received a call the following Monday morning. It was not from Karzhov, but a Russian who sounded like he'd undergone a laryngectomy and whose only English must have been based on a one-hour crash course.

"You meet this man, you have this to do," began the Russian. "Because not to do this would mean problem. And problem only one you have. Know it?"

"I beg your pardon?"

A heavy sigh at the other end, and then, "This boss of mine, you meet. Understand?"

"I see."

"Yes, you see him."

"Okay, where, when?" said Hale, suspecting that primitive words, without conjunctives, might be preferable in this instance.

"You know this hotel, *The Ritz*?"

"I dare say I do."

"What?"

"Yes, I know the hotel. Time?"

"Eleven at the night-time tonight."

"How nice. Well, it's been wonderful speaking. And will I have the pleasure of making your acquaintance tonight as well?"

"Uh?"

"Goodbye."

Hale cut the call.

10:48 p.m.

Hale strode along Piccadilly towards Green Park. *The Ritz* loomed ahead on the left. A distinctive landmark, chateau-style architecture artfully illuminated in the cold November air. At another juncture, Hale might have appreciated the grandeur, but not now. In no good mood, he walked briskly up the steps to the entrance, allowed a smart couple – sixties, dressed for dinner – to enter ahead of him.

Karzhov had ruined Hale's date that evening with the bottle of *Arehucas*. His patience now ran thin, especially in the knowledge that Marta remained captive.

Time to get this sorted.

Hale nodded to the doorman who eyed Hale suspiciously, and then opened the door. A blast of heat eased the biting cold on his face. He stepped into the reception area, waved away offers of assistance from the concierge. The foyer bustled with guests fussing with luggage or speaking to staff of differing nationalities. Nice place, thought Hale, glancing at the decor. Chandeliers, soft furnishings, tasteful decoration. Light and airy, not gaudy or stuffy. He'd maybe come here one day for tea and to 'people-watch', but not to stay, even if he could afford it. Not his style.

His heartbeat ramped up a notch.

Fact: he was here to meet a killer. A revered Russian mafioso, slippery, powerful, notorious. He thought of asking at reception for Karzhov. Then thought better of it.

Moving further into the foyer, he saw the Russian.

Karzhov was seated in an alcove off to the left, chairs and a sofa backing onto ornate statues, flower arrangements, and artwork. He sat on the sofa, legs crossed, flicking through a magazine. He couldn't have been more prominent. White suit, white tie, white shoes. Hale clocked two goons as he drew closer. Both wore grey suits, one built like a chest of drawers, standing, arms folded beside the sofa, the other on a nearby chair. The standing ape noticed Hale's approach, dropped his arms to his side and muttered something to Karzhov.

Hale stood before them, eyeing Karzhov directly.

"I'm Hale, you called me. Where did you get my number? No one has my number."

Karzhov took some seconds to place his magazine on the table, and then looked up. His hair was jet black, face pockmarked, the worst damage concealed by a neatly trimmed goatee and moustache. Fifties, maybe younger, inherently ugly. He wore glasses with tinted lens. A porn star wearing Foster Grants, thought Hale.

"Indeed we did call you," said Karzhov finally. "Do take a seat, my friend." He looked Hale up and down. "I see you're dressed for the occasion." He smirked to his sidekick, who'd adjusted his chair to face Hale. The goon's chest heaved as he laughed, wheezing.

Hale took a seat, looked down at his five-pound suit from the charity shop, creased and dirty.

"I feel comfortable wearing this," said Hale, holding eye contact with Karzhov. "And, besides, no one told me it was fancy dress, otherwise I would have come dressed as a milk bottle like you."

The ape moved in, his meaty fists ready to inflict some pain. Karzhov held his hand up, stopping him dead in his tracks. "I can't say I like your humour ... if that's what you call it," said Karzhov, his expression now hard, serious.

"At least I have a notion of the concept," said Hale. "I repeat ... you called me."

Karzhov paused, holding the stare, scratched his goatee and smiled, "Oh dear, we appear to have started off on the wrong foot. What a shame ... but shall we now commence discussions?"

Hale guessed that Karzhov was well educated, no doubt spoke a number of languages. Money was no object, so it was clear that his motives were not as clear-cut as those of Morillo and Happy Gary.

Hale glanced at the concierge to his right. The Frenchman seemed to be aware of the tension and sent a waiter over, another Frenchman who stood nervously nearby.

"A drink for your guest, Mr Karzhov?" asked the waiter.

Karzhov raised his eyebrows, opened his hand, "Mr Hale, I will treat you."

"How kind," said Hale. He looked at the waiter who was leaning over trying to fathom the English. "I'd like a rum, but I'm fussy. Do you have *Legacy by Angostura*?"

The waiter mumbled, but Hale didn't wait for him to continue, "We'll, I'd like that or something similar. Two inches splashed in the bottom of a cold tumbler. Cold, not frosted."

The waiter frowned, nodded, and then walked off briskly.

"A man with specific tastes," said Karzhov. "So, let's get down to business. I am interested in you, Mr Hale, since your reputation proceeds you."

"Precedes."

"Hm?"

"The word is *precedes*. Apologies. If only I spoke Russian, you could correct me similarly."

Rankled, Karzhov shifted in his seat, and then said, "I might warn you that I am not a man you should annoy. I assume you are aware of my position?"

Hale leaned forward, elbows on the arms of the chair, "Let's be clear. I don't give a shit who you are, but I'm aware that your colleague, Morillo, is holding a woman by the name of Marta. Where is she and when will she be released?"

Hale thought he may have revealed his interests too early, leaned back, twiddling his thumbs. Karzhov sniggered, glanced at the goon beside him, and then back at Hale.

"My dear friend, we will come back to this issue, I promise, but let me first make a request." Karzhov paused, took a sip from a small glass, something clear and misty. Pernod perhaps. "Who do you work for, Mr Hale?"

Hale sighed, looked above to the ornate ceiling, and then said, "People seem to be asking me this question on a regular basis, and to be honest, it's becoming a little tiresome."

"Well, this is not surprising is it not? You seem to have acquired a reputation. And I am interested in certain events. Events that involved considerable force, where people died, where…"

Hale cut him off, "I don't work for anyone. I am a boat handler, I work boats. That's it ... simple."

"Yes, I'm aware of this," said Karzhov, swilling the remainder of his drink around. "But I can only assume you have some very interesting connections. And you wish to continue in this business, am I right?"

Hale nodded.

The waiter returned with the drink. Hale picked it up from the table, downed it in one before the waiter had time to say a word. "This is *Legacy*?" said Hale, eyeing the waiter.

"Yes, sir," said the waiter, nervous, hand trembling on his tray. "This is what you did order, no?"

"Where did you get this, in-house or did you send out for it?"

"Sir, we had to send out…"

"It's good, thank you. Get me another."

Hale eyed Karzhov who seemed puzzled by the distraction. The waiter walked off.

"Yes, I do work the boats," continued Hale. "But is there any swift way you can get to the point here, because if you haven't done so by the time that guy comes back and I've downed the second one, I'm gone."

"I understand, a busy man. I like that," said Karzhov. "Can I ask you, Mr Hale ... can I call you Charles?"

Hale shrugged.

"Charles, might I ask what line of work are you currently undertaking?"

"What interest is this of yours?"

"Simply that we may be able to combine our interests."

The waiter returned, placed the glass on the table. Hale thanked him, didn't touch it. The first shot had worked its way into his bloodstream, a calming effect, allowing him to concentrate on Karzhov.

"I work boats – sailboats – on the Thames," said Hale. "The area I work ranges from the mouth of the estuary up to Tilbury Docks, sometimes further in, towards the city, that sort of area."

"And what is the nature of this work?"

Hale paused, shook his head lightly, continued, "Pleasure cruises, rich old Americans. They like to come out in the dead of night in the British winter on a sailboat. They enjoy viewing the lights of oil refineries and other industrial works from the river in shit weather."

The ape whispered something in Karzhov's ear. Karzhov waved him away as if his comment was that of an imbecile.

"I see," said Karzhov, leaning forward, elbows on knees, clasping his hands. The first time, he had deigned to make any physical move on behalf of his guest. "You must have clientele with curious tastes. But, this is of no interest to me. My interest, however, is in your skills, and your territory."

"Go on."

"Before I do, you must tell me something of the incident at the beach. It seems to have caused my colleague some embarrassment and this is not something I am happy about."

Hale felt his mouth dry, reached forward, took a slug of rum. Then another. Fire descended his chest and into his stomach. "That was unfortunate," Hale said. "I was doing boat work for a man."

"The idiot called Happy Gary?"

Hale shrugged. "As I said, a man. This man was supposed to pay your partner, Morillo, for an *inconvenience*. Then people could move on with their business. It seems that the negotiations broke down somewhat."

Karzhov puffed his cheeks out, smiled, "And it seems that you are a master of understatement, Charles."

Hale knocked back the remaining rum, replaced the tumbler, eyed Karzhov. "So, are we finished here?"

Karzhov shook his head. "No, we are not. It just so happens that you will be working for me now."

"I will?"

Karzhov nodded. "You see, Charles, I have some boat work available. And because I run a profitable concern, I require skilled people, not fools."

"I work the Thames and Channel area, nowhere else," said Hale.

Karzhov seemed to ponder the idea for a moment, nodded, "No problem."

"For each run, I receive fifty grand sterling, no counterfeit. I don't know what crap you're shipping, I don't care, and you never tell me. One run spans two days of my time, no more. You source the boat and crew."

Karzhov nodded.

"One more thing."

"Yes?"

"I work with sailing boats only."

A glimmer of a frown crossed Karzhov's brow. He leaned over and whispered to the seated ape, who mumbled something back in Russian.

"Why?" asked Karzhov.

"I don't like power. Where possible, and depending on the weather, I sail. Yes, even at night. Quieter, less suspicious. Ask yourself: who would ship stuff in this way? I only use the motor if it's flat calm."

Karzhov raised his eyebrows, leaned back on the sofa, uttered more words to the ape. Some debate seemed to form between them, until Karzhov addressed Hale, "I can do this. I have a vessel and I have people who do this type of sailboat work."

"Okay, but be clear on this," said Hale. "I don't trust you. So one question for you…"

"Yes?"

"Why would you trust me?"

"Oh, but that is simple," said Karzhov. "If you cross me, you die. Accidents happen at sea as you are aware. But remember also, the girl will feel some considerable pain before she dies too."

Hale gripped his fists, felt his face flush red. "You shitbrain," he said, loudly enough to quell the hubbub in the foyer.

The ape moved again. Again, Karzhov waved him back.

The concierge came across, leaned over, humbly whispered in Hale's ear, "Sir, the guests. Please if you would calm…"

"It won't happen again," said Hale.

The concierge moved away, seemed to hold his hand up to placate an elderly couple seated across the foyer.

"Let's make a deal," said Hale, drawing breath.

"I don't do deals, Charles. People follow my instructions."

Hale ignored the comment. "The deal is as follows. Your poodle, Morillo, frees Marta after my first boat run. I'll halve my fee if the girl is released."

"But of course, and no, I will honour the *full* fee. I am a man of my word," said Karzhov, appearing satisfied with proceedings, more so than at the outset. This angered Hale. He tried to focus, but anything that pleased the Russian, riled him.

"Tell me," continued Karzhov, "what is this word, *poodle*, you speak of?"

"Morillo," said Hale. "He's your pet dog. Put a lead on him and you can take him for a walk."

Karzhov's face contorted, and after some seconds, lightened. He imparted the comment in Russian to the ape, who frowned, and then laughed, his massive frame shaking.

"Charles, you are an interesting man," said Karzhov. "Berto he is a great friend, but he has a thing for certain women. I call it a weakness and I have told him about this, but he is learning ... and so will you. When you have finished some jobs for me, you will understand that you are better off working with professionals."

"How reassuring. I'm sure I'll have a glittering résumé as a result."

"Yes, of course, and now we are done here."

Karzhov fastened a button on his Jacket, rose to his feet. Short, thought Hale. Five foot, five. "We will be in touch of course," said the Russian, offering his hand. Hale took it, squeezed. Let him feel sinews and muscles formed of a lifetime hauling ropes and anchor chains.

Unperturbed, Karzhov nodded to the ape. They moved off along the exquisitely carpeted hall towards the dining area.

Hale walked towards reception, called the concierge over.

"Sir, can I help you?" said the Frenchman.

"Yes," said Hale. "That nice old couple over there." He nodded in their direction.

"Yes, sir?"

"You know Mr Karzhov?"

"But of course, sir. One of our best..."

"Wonderful. Well, I've spoken to Mr Karzhov. He is a very good friend of mine, you understand. He insists that you deliver your best bottle of champagne to them, a bottle of that rum I ordered, and some flowers of your choice. This all by way of apology for the unfortunate scene earlier. We are businessmen, under pressure. I'm sure you understand."

The Frenchman's face warmed. He drew a note pad from his pocket, began scribbling. "Yes, sir, of course I understand. I will get on to it…"

"And Mr Karzhov would also like to pay for their stay here tonight, plus breakfast tomorrow morning. Can you deal with that as a matter of urgency?"

"Yes sir, right away."

"Thank you, goodbye."

Hale zipped his jacket up to the neck, stepped out into the freezing air and headed along Piccadilly. The meeting had gone to plan in terms of Black's ideas, but something ate at Hale. It ate at him even more than the dire risk to his own life he was proposing to take within Karzhov's world.

The plan to set up Karzhov might kill Marta.

María Díez had assured Hale that all measures would be taken to extricate Marta from the grip of Morillo's people. But the Inspectora Jefa would need to free her before any boat run, before Karzhov's arrest, before his people could bear influence on Morillo. And before Marta was tortured and killed. Hale assumed Black's people were also aware of Marta's perilous situation.

Hale would put his own life on the line with one boat run for the Russian. But a question remained.

Just how good was María Díez?

SIXTY-FOUR

Hale rejected the first two dates sent by Karzhov's yacht crew. Both were poor choices for weather, and especially tides. The timing was awry. On the Thames, they'd either get it right, or go against up to nine-knots of tide and anything the wind threw at them.

The day was set by Hale for Tuesday, the first week of December. He sent a text message to the crewmembers:

'8:00 a.m. Tuesday. Prepare the boat. Do not be late.'

Plenty of time to catch an outgoing tide from the yacht's mooring in the city, and then sail on to Sheerness not far from the mouth of the estuary. Here, they would rendezvous with a fishing vessel, load the cargo. Then head ten miles back across the Thames northwest to Holetown Creek, a quiet inlet to the west of Canvey Island. At Holetown, they would moor up against a jetty in the dead of night and unload to a waiting van. Once Karzhov's assignment was on the road, they'd cast off and run the tide back to Limehouse.

The plan was solid in theory and the forecast good: light airs, visibility typically dull and grey, but no fog. They'd need calm seas for the fishing boat rendezvous and no delays were possible, since the tide was the enemy if it turned against them ... a ticking clock.

Tuesday, early morning.

Hale descended the steps at Fenchurch Street station, walked to the Tower of London, and then a few hundred yards east to St Katharine Docks, a marina development nestled amongst red-bricked apartments, shops, and restaurants.

The yacht, *K2*, swayed gently against the wharf, watched from afar by Hale seated at a window stool in a café. He had arrived fifteen minutes early to wait, observe. Two crew wandered about on deck, smoking, laughing. They tended the ropes, hauled sails out of the hatches and unfurled them. They were competent, knew the boat and the gear. One had a potbelly and thick black beard, the other a chain smoker with a weasel face. They were vigilant, continually looking around the dock. Waiting for the skipper to arrive.

Alert with the caffeine boost, Hale hauled his bag over his shoulder. Inside the bag, just clothes and food, nothing that could be traced back to him. In his front pocket, a pay-as-you-go cell. In his rear pocket, a wallet within a plastic bag, twenty pounds in change, and an unmarked key to *The Sunshine* guest house, nothing more.

Hale approached *K2*, the impressive fifty-foot ketch, steel hull painted white, wooden decks, kitted out with digital radar and other electronic paraphernalia attached to the rigging. He threw his bag onboard, catching the attention of the weasel, who flicked his cigarette butt into the sea.

"Ah, you must be…"

Hale cut Weasel off, "Don't do that."

"What?"

"You threw your shit into the water. Don't do it again."

Potbelly arrived upwind of Hale, who detected his odour. "You smell bad," said Hale eyeballing him. "Go get a shower now. We leave in ten."

Potbelly's English was limited explained Weasel, trying calm Potbelly, whose face was now purple in the few patches not concealed by his beard.

Potbelly walked off.

Weasel continued, "I am Kurtz, and my friend…"

"I don't care. You are A and he is B, okay?" said Hale, pushing past him to manoeuvre into the cockpit ahead of the mizzen mast. "I'm here to do a job, not to make friends with you. We're casting off in eight minutes with or without B, so go tell him his new name and to hurry."

Weasel shook his head, walked off, climbed off the pulpit at the bow and onto the wharf. A detail had not gone unnoticed by Hale: a sheathed knife under his coat at the waist as he extended his arms.

Hale reconnoitred the boat in the crew's absence. A tidy vessel, expensive fittings, but too many gadgets for his liking. Too much to go wrong, and at sea things go wrong.

Fifteen minutes later, they motored east along the Thames. Hale stood on the foredeck, pulled out a hip flask, took a slug. It eased the morning fuzz in his head, an otherworldly daze. Something he'd acquired through weeks of irregular sleep patterns, paranoia, stress, and alcohol. He looked ahead at the glass towers of Canary Wharf looming out of a light mist, steam rising from their summits in the chill air. Thought about the ants below, crawling along pavements, ascending the edifices to take their seats for the day's work. Home to conglomerates and the kind of corporate monsters to which Stack would kowtow.

Hale's thoughts turned to Lucy and Deborah, but these were soon banished, replaced by those of Marta and his rage at her predicament. Anger at Karzhov, and at himself, dominated his soul.

Hale's mood was darker these days, undeniably so. Prepared to admit it to himself.

You're damaged goods, Charles.

Hale sensed chatter behind, caught the whiff of cigarette smoke, called out to the crew, "Put the sails up." He remained looking ahead at the looming metropolis.

Silence from behind. Then, "You want sails up? There is no wind," said Weasel. Hale heard Potbelly laugh.

"Yes there is. Put them up, now."

"But, in city? The wind is all over…"

"Now!" Hale turned to face them, his voice raised to counter the pumping diesel engine. "This a sailing yacht, and we're going sailing. Put the rig up, cut the engine, and sail."

Weasel stood silent for a moment, frowning, conferring with Potbelly at the helm.

"I asked your boss, Sergei, for a sailing crew, not a couple of bus drivers. Sail goddamn it or I call him." Hale held his cell phone in the air. Unbeknown to the crew, he had no number for Karzhov.

Hale moved further aft, amidships, while Weasel darted across the deck, adjusting lines, working winches, hauling halyards. The two Russians shouted, argued while trimming the sails in an attempt to make the boat stable. They killed the engine, leaving an odd stillness. A pocket of silence surrounded by the noise of the city. Tugs and barges motored by, purposeful. Skippers looked across from the bridges of their vessels. Some shook their heads, cynical. Others, more amenable, smiled, waved at the odd sight: a yacht, full sails hoisted, in just five knots of variable wind, in the city, in the rush hour.

"Tack," said Hale.

"I try to do the tack, boss, but…"

"Shut up and tack."

Hale watched the wind on the vane above. It veered ninety degrees, and then backed thirty. All over the place as it funnelled through the skyscrapers, gusted hard, and then dropped to nothing in seconds.

"We cannot control this."

"Sail!"

K2 was in irons one moment, heeled over at thirty degrees the next.

"This madness, boss."

"Sail!"

Hale watched the crew. They were efficient, knew how to sail, already working hard and getting tired. Hale worked them for another hour with *K2* making little headway.

At the Millennium Dome, Weasel took the helm while Potbelly made his way forward. Hale knew what to expect. Potbelly would moan, say this was not part of the plan, that they were behind schedule and Karzhov would ask for blood if they failed to make the pickup. Hale had calculated the time, the tides, the weather. As much as one can. Hale spoke before Potbelly launched his rant, "Drop the sails, start the engine. Do it now. Move."

Potbelly cursed something in Russian, something that would probably insult Hale's mother using the crudest language imaginable. Hale didn't care, pulled out a sailing jacket as the day drew in cool with damp murk edging in from the east.

That afternoon, *K2* wallowed in the brown waters a mile off Sheerness near the mouth of the estuary. The sails flapped impotently in light airs as Hale perused the chart down below. They were playing for time, waiting for dark. The crew demanded a rest, but Hale declined, leaving them to talk at the helm, smoking, eating cold pasties and stale crisps.

Soon it was black, freezing, and the night settled into a misty millpond. No stars in the sky, but visibility moderate, between two and five nautical miles.

10:00 p.m.

Hale had made it clear to Karzhov: Hale was the skipper, and it was his call to abort at this point if conditions were not good.

Conditions were good.

Hale's first run for the Russian mafia was on.

SIXTY-FIVE

Midnight.

K2 wallowed in eerie darkness under motor, the shoreline to the south lit by an orange blur through the mist. Ahead, to the east, Hale spotted navigation lights. Then heard the thud of a diesel engine. He'd been tracking it on radar. The fishing vessel was on time.

Potbelly and Weasel took positions on the foredeck, bracing themselves against the steel shrouds as Hale positioned the yacht, edging the vessel broadside to make a clear target for the fishing boat.

Within minutes, figures were seen on deck of the approaching vessel, huddled against the rusting metal of the bridge. They wore dark oilskins and woollen hats, distinctive figures who worked the ropes as they came alongside. This was an old, hard-worked vessel. Its red and white metal hull bore the scars – dents and repairs – of many storms and collisions.

Hale held *K2* steady and glanced across to the bridge of the fishing boat. Not much to see other than the glow of a cigarette butt and a dark figure at the wheel. The swell was light and the fenders compensated for any movement between the vessels.

Hale leaned out of the cabin, called, "Okay." to Weasel. Loud enough to be heard above the diesels, but not enough to carry far across the still waters. The two skippers held the boats together with deft helmsmanship, rather than risk tying up with ropes. This technique was simpler if they needed to make a run for it. Moreover, if a sudden swell or wash from a tanker arrived, they'd avoid becoming caught up, entangled.

The men on the fishing boat hauled heavy burlap sacks over the gunnels onto *K2*'s deck. Potbelly received them, pushing the sacks behind, while Weasel dragged them to the forward hatch, letting them drop with a thud into the cabin below. No subtlety here, just haste. Items crashed around below decks, dislodged by the falling contraband. Hale was unconcerned with the damage, but pondered the scale of the haul. This was a huge stash by any standards, commensurate with Karzhov's status and wealth. Clearly, this man undertook nothing in small measure.

Hale scanned around in the blackness, felt a chill of fear run through him to add to the biting night air. If they were seized by a Border Force boat in this position, the skippers and crews of both vessels would go to jail, released only when they were old men.

The last of the sacks hit the floorboards. Potbelly gave Hale a thumbs up. Weasel threw a small package across to the crew on the fishing boat, waved them off. Hale eased *K2* away. The fenders squeezed against each other momentarily as the boats parted.

Soon, the fishing boat was a hundred yards astern, chugging back east. Hale swung the helm around, setting a course for Holehaven Creek ten miles northwest of their position. The swell built, and a light breeze with it, hardly enough to generate a ripple on the black water.

Potbelly and Weasel fastened the forward hatch and gingerly made their way aft to the cockpit. Hale gunned the engine, creating a wake behind, looking to get across the channel swiftly. A container ship crossed them ahead, the lights from its bridge towering above and illuminating *K2*. The ship steamed on as *K2* negotiated its wake.

Too close.

Hale cursed as waves crashed over the bows. Potbelly fell hard on the floor, rolling around like a seal.

"Get up, for chrissakes," said Hale.

Then silence.

The lights of Canvey Island on its easternmost point loomed on the starboard bow. Some distance remained, but the wind and tide was favourable. Hale let Weasel take the helm, bent down into the darkness on the floor and rummaged around in his bag. He hauled out a bottle of *Stolichnaya* vodka, turned to Potbelly, shoved it lightly into his stomach and patted him on the arm.

"You guys did good," said Hale. "Take this and drink it sometime ashore … my way of thanks."

Potbelly studied the bottle, murmured something, seemed perplexed.

Hale grabbed the helm back from Weasel, checked the radar. No vessels in the immediate vicinity. A few large ships anchored out near the mouth of the estuary, but nothing moving, nothing coming their way.

Thirty minutes later, Potbelly and Weasel were halfway through the bottle of *Stolichnaya*. As Hale had predicted, they'd moved to the foredeck and gone to work on it.

Hale leaned out of the cockpit door and called out, "Sails up, now!"

Two faces peered from behind the mast. Potbelly spoke first in a slur, "Boosss you..."

"Now," said Hale. "Sails – all of them – up now."

Weasel stumbled about, holding on to the rigging, working the ropes, unfurling the foresails. Potbelly manned the mainsail, but was unsteady, slamming against the mast in the swell.

"Boss," said Weasel. "Whyyy we ssshail. No wind, what?"

"We sail in," said Hale. "I'm the skipper and we go in under sail, quiet, no engines. Got it?"

Weasel shrugged, looked across at Potbelly who shook his head, picked up the bottle from the coachroof. The bearded oaf took a deep gulp, handed it to Weasel who did the same.

The lights of Canvey Island seafront cast a glow above the seawall defences. Ahead, the inlet to Holehaven Creek, and beyond, a massive network of lights towered into the sky from the Coryton oil refinery. *K2*'s sails were set, flapping as they motor-sailed. Hale killed the engine. The yacht wallowed in silence, a faint breeze edging them along on a broad reach.

Despite a sense of foreboding, Hale felt calm for a moment. The dark and peaceful silence eased his mind. He absorbed the sound of the wake playing against the hull, the clang of the bell on the Chapman buoy a mile astern, the occasional flap of the sails.

I may have my freedom now, he thought, but for how long?

How long until his actions caught up with him?

As they pressed on, the seawall dipped away and the inlet to Holehaven Creek emerged to starboard, its mouth black and ill-defined. They drifted on. Ahead, the hum of the refinery works invaded the stillness. Their destination was almost upon them.

Hale swung the wheel, brought *K2* around to starboard, searched the gloom for the jetty. A hundred yards in and the dark line of its wooden structure appeared, reaching out from the seawall fifty yards across the grey-black creek. The lights of the nearby *Lobster Smack* pub rose up into the mist, lighting the gloom from behind the seawall defences.

"Sailssh downnn?" said Weasel, now off his face, drunk.

"No. Remain under sail. Keep them up," said Hale. "Here, you take the helm, take her in. Then we drop the sails ten metres out. Ten metres, understand?"

Weasel grunted, swayed as he grabbed the wheel from Hale.

"You," said Hale, keeping his voice low, pointing to Potbelly. "Go aft, take the mizzen sail down. Then get the stern line and tie her up when we're in."

Hale moved forward.

K2 was thirty metres out, drifting on a run, virtually no wind. The sails bumped and flapped, causing the booms to swing across and snatch violently. Hale heard Weasel's curses from the cockpit, battling to align the boat.

Twenty out, Hale gave Potbelly the thumbs up to drop the sail on the mizzen. Hale released the halyard on the mainsail, which fell around the deck. Then gave the signal for Weasel to bring her around to port alongside the jetty.

Hale released the Genoa halyard. It too fell untidily to the deck. The bow made contact with the jetty. *K2*'s forward quarter nudged the wooden upright of the structure, which creaked and moaned in complaint.

Hale jumped onto the jetty, bowline in hand. He glanced along the length of the wooden structure. At first, nothing to see, but then some movement ashore beyond. A dog, a man, something. Potbelly was amidships, staggering forward, gesticulating wildly to Hale. The yacht was at an angle to the jetty, needed hauling in by the stern line. Hale ignored him, wrapped the bowline around an upright post, tied it off with an ugly knot, hauled his full weight onto it.

Now only one thing left to do.

Sprint.

SIXTY-SIX

Hale fled. Jumped from the jetty onto the sloping concrete and hardened tar, which comprised the sea defences. His heart pounded, and though he pumped his arms, his legs wouldn't respond, felt like jelly.

Voices behind, shouts. He sucked in cold air, felt his heavy-weather jacket chafe his armpits, slowing him. A nightmare. You want to run from terror, but you can't run, can't even shout out.

He looked ahead, battling to focus his breathing. *Think, Hale.* He pushed harder, up the slope onto flat concrete, the base of the old seawall. To his right, the new incarnation of that wall blocked a view to the Thames, the stretch they'd just sailed. He thought about form, about swinging his arms higher, controlling his stride, his breathing.

But this was no Sunday run in the park.

This was his only chance. In his head, he heard Rupert taunting: *Screw up now and you're in prison, Charles.*

Behind, more shouting, louder. Then blue lights flashing, illuminating the gloom around him and lighting the black groynes, which poked out into the Thames like witches fingers. Dogs Barked.

Something big was going down back at the jetty.

Oil refineries to his left. Strange noises emanated from the industrial mass and played with his mind. The path ahead was now dangerous, the section lit only by the refinery lights. He gasped, cried out. His lungs were shot. Thought of the pain. It would go away. It would. *Keep the pace.* The gravel underfoot, pebbles, small rocks, jabbed the underside of his sailing shoes. Soft soles, inadequate for this work.

One look behind, he allowed that. The scene was awash with flashing lights. Dogs barked, fierce, intense. Shafts of lights forged up into the sky from the jetty area. A helicopter droned, its blades thumping a beat in his chest.

He pushed on, stumbled, smashed into the gravel scraping his hands up to his wrists. Any running form or technique was now lost. His head swung wildly, mouth open, grabbing breaths in the panic.

He moved down the seawall, a short cut across Thorney Bay beach. He recognised the place. He was making ground. But the terrain, shingle, slowed him. Running through treacle. He fell again, face first, yelled into the shells and sand. Then hauled himself up.

Back up onto the seawall, through a gate, over to flat concrete, the river lapping to his right.

Think, Hale, breathe. You keep going, you never give in. You keep moving.

His right ankle throbbed, must have turned it.

He regained some form, settled into a steady breathing pattern. Cold sweat ran down his back, he felt his calf muscles tighten. He kept the pace until he saw the landmark, a building, round, white. The Labworth Café.

He reached the building, ascended the steps beyond, which headed inland. Then settled into a walk, sucked in air. Frenzied gulps, his breathing crazy. Now cramp pulled at his stomach.

He tried to walk normally, inconspicuously, and then descended a tarmac ramp leading down to the seafront amusements and arcades below. Gaudy lights flashed around, though most places were closed for business apart from a late-night snooker bar.

His breathing settled.

At the foot of the slope to the right, a small white van was positioned, sidelights on, music playing from within. Hale approached the passenger side, opened the door and hauled himself into the warmth, slumping into the seat, exhausted.

The van pulled away from the curb, quietly drove on.

"So, Chuck, can you tell me why I'm picking you up from Canvey bloody seafront at four in the morning?" said Baz, working the wheel to turn onto the main road towards the town centre.

Hale said nothing for a few seconds, and then, "Well I'm afraid not, Baz. Thanks for the lift and everything, but we all have our little secrets, don't we?"

SIXTY-SEVEN

The next day, Hale checked out of *The Sunshine*, headed into London for a brief visit to Stack's empire. The last visit until further notice. Maybe this time it was finally 'goodbye' to Pam and *Connecting4Business*. He'd demanded cash, walked into Stack's office, grabbed the envelope, and walked out without a word.

Pam shed a tear, wished him luck and Hale didn't make it any more painful and promptly left.

He roamed around Tower Hill, aimless, light-headed from caffeine and lack of sleep. The plan was that there was no plan.

Not yet.

He headed for the Underground station where he'd usually pick up a free paper at the entrance. But this time, he stalled outside the *Isis Bar*, a swish annex to the five star *Grange City Hotel*. Through the large window, he spotted a television on the wall. *Sky News* was reporting something about a drugs seizure in Essex. The news ticker wasn't clear on the screen. Hale entered the bar with its dark wood and comfortable surroundings, took an easy chair and ordered a coffee while watching the television. More details were coming in about yesterday's report, a raid on Holehaven Creek on the Thames near the estuary. A massive cocaine haul connected with a known organised crime ring was seized from a sailing yacht. The yacht was believed to be owned by Russian millionaire businessman, Sergei Karzhov. The crew was arrested on the vessel, as were three men believed to be receiving the haul, waiting in a van nearby. Karzhov was arrested at one of his London apartments in Kensington.

Hale leaned back in the leather armchair, closed his eyes. A vague smile on his face. He sensed the barman walk across and stand beside him. The bar was empty – he was probably bored. "Is the coffee okay?" said the barman. "Can I get you anything else, sir?"

Hale kept his eyes closed, "Coffee's lovely, but wondered if you could spice it up with something?"

"Certainly, sir. Brandy, something like that?"

"Make it vodka. Your finest."

Two weeks later. Hale remained in hiding. Just as Hodgkinson had advised, just as Black had warned, just as Hale had promised himself.

Let it run its course. Let the dust settle.

He stayed in lodgings, inland from Westcliff, sometimes over at Leigh-on-Sea, wore different clothes, changed the patterns. Private lodgings were discreet, and only occasionally would he use guesthouses. But he stayed in the area, needed some roots, needed something to hang on to mentally. Like a murderer returning to the scene of a crime, somehow he couldn't detach himself completely.

Money was tight, informal work scarce, and it seemed Baz sensed Hale's predicament. The cockney builder knew an old-timer fisherman down at Old Leigh who needed a helping hand to move wood, haul boats, tidy the yard. Cash-in-hand, no questions, no paperwork.

Hale took the job, despite the danger that he was too close to his old home high up on Marine Parade. He wore a hat and overalls, cut his hair, and never returned home up those long steps. December's cold wind, a brand only the British coastline can deliver, bit into his flesh each morning. Yet, Hale relished the opportunity of this new life, a new beginning.

But there was a problem. No call from Hodgkinson, nothing from María Díez. And the questions rankled, especially regarding Marta.

Where was she? Alive?

The rain lashed Old Leigh one morning. A westerly gale, wild and squally, the cobbled streets awash and only hardy souls venturing out with dogs along the front. Hale hid in a greasy spoon café, waiting for the torrent to abate. Later, he'd clear anchor chains, driftwood and logs from the yard, and breathe dank sea air down into his lungs. The old timer would sit in a hut with his collie dog, both barking orders from a distance.

Hale's cell phone rang. He took the call to hear Baz on the line, "Mate, you wanna beer tonight?" Hale thought he should not, since *The Smack* was a habit. And habits were bad news.

Defiant, he flouted his own rules, "Okay, see you there at nine."

And at nine that night, Hale stood with Baz at the bar in *Ye Olde Smack*, the same as ever. Karzhov and Morillo's people might be seeking Hale, but perhaps Baz was a decent bodyguard to have around, for one night at least.

"I've been thinking," said Baz, holding his pint of ale up to the light, inspecting the hue of the liquid for no apparent reason. "Just how much debt did you get into? I mean it seems it's all gone down the pan for you. Lucy, the house ... the whole ball game."

Hale surveyed the empty pub, mulling the question. A fire roared in the grate, the storm outside rattled the wooden door on its latches. After the trauma of the preceding months, it was good to feel the ale work into his blood, to speak with someone he knew and trusted. Just like Rupert, Baz would understand.

"It started with Céline," said Hale.

Baz smiled, nodded. "*You don't say*," he said, emptying his glass and waving the barman for another.

"We had a thing about going off doing stuff, spending cash like water flowing out of a tap," continued Hale.

"Hm, I've 'bin there too," said Baz.

"But then it went downhill. She got into bad stuff. Smoking cheap weed, and then got caught up with heroin, some shit like that. She started hanging out with this junkie boyfriend and I vowed never to see her again. I was hurt, you know how it is?"

Baz shrugged, "Course I bleedin' know how it is. Go on."

"Céline was in with the wrong crowd. But despite my appalling finances, I sought her out, got back in touch. I got her away from the jerks who were plying her with drugs, uppers, downers, you name it." Hale paused, looking down at his beer as he brought the memories back to life. "Her pillock father practically disowned her when he realised what she was into, but I managed to get her on a rehab thing in the Caribbean. Antigua. Lucy didn't know about it. The first instalment of the course cost me ten grand."

Baz raised his eyebrows, "Ouch."

"Yes, ouch," said Hale. "But guess what?"

"It didn't work?"

"Correct. So I sent her on another out there."

Baz said, "Twenty grand."

"Yep. Then guess what?"

"You didn't send her on another?"

"Yep, two more. Forty grand, and it worked."

"I bloody hope it did. She must've got a great suntan as well."

Hale smiled, laughed it off. "I couldn't let it go, Baz. Just had to get back in there and sort her out. You know what I'm like..."

"I do, you nutter. So, where is the French woman of your dreams now?"

"Paris. Married to a decent guy, a teacher. They have a kid. Sometimes I call her … it's all cool."

Baz shook his head, pursed his lips. "So all that about never seeing her or calling her again … that was bullshit?"

Hale remained silent, shrugged.

Baz changed the subject, "I'm concerned, Charlie, because you're jumpy as hell. What are you running from, mate? Who? All these guesthouses, chasing around like a lunatic and stuff. What shit are you into?"

Hale picked up the second pint from the bar, downed a quarter of it, and then eyed Baz. "I trust you more than anyone, Baz, but this is something I've got to work through by myself." Hale smiled, prodding Baz in the chest. "One day – probably when we're old men propping up the bar like this every night – I'll let you know, and then you can let me know more about these fishing trips of yours."

Baz's friendship eased the pain of isolation, but Hale was sinking. He knew it, but was succumbing, helpless. The drinks were coming earlier, and harder. Mean stuff, cheap spirits, scotch, vodka. Sojourns with the local fishermen at Old Leigh would often happen at mid-morning: tots of rum with milky tea served in a metal mug, chipped and dented. Hale was building a reputation with them, something he'd need to address before word got around and trouble arrived.

On some days, he'd take leave of the yard unannounced, head into London, hang around odd places. Backstreets in Soho or Shoreditch. Catch a jazz band. Spend money in bars and pubs. The loner, avoiding conversation, watching over his shoulder. Preferred rain to sun, and he came out in darkness. The night owl who enjoyed the splash of rain on wintry pavements. In terms of his mental state, Hale was in a dark place, a place in which he was increasingly at ease.

Detached, anonymous.

Alcohol numbed the inner turmoil, until its effects waned. This, however, was remedied easily by a simple action: take more. Hale became adept at concealing his state of inebriation, able to purvey an outward persona neither social nor unsociable. Just another guy on the train, in the bar, passing through.

On the twentieth day of December, the anger erupted inside. Why had he not received news from Hodgkinson? Black would know how to contact him, no doubt about it. They were not keeping their side of the bargain. Denial, though, prevented Hale from addressing the fact: there never was any real bargain.

At 10:03 a.m., after a few shots of rum, he rang the ICO from the boatyard. A woman on the switchboard answered immediately in an East London accent. Hale said, "Can I speak to Tony Hodgkinson, please. My name is Charles Hale."

A pause at the other end, and then, "Can you repeat the name of the person you wish to speak to, please."

Hale sighed, enough to be heard by the woman, "*Tooonnnyy* Hodgkinson."

A tap on a keyboard. "I'm sorry, sir. There is no one here by that name."

"What? He's the branch commander. Please try again."

"Sir, I'm sorry…"

"I said *try again*. I met him a few weeks ago, so please check your records, *again*."

A pause, longer this time, and then, "Please hold."

Hale glanced around the yard, holding the phone to his ear, forced a smile to the old man who was sitting, throwing sticks for the dog.

She came back on the line, "Sir, we have no record of that name having ever been registered here. You said you met? You must have met someone el…"

Hale cursed, smacked the phone against the side of his head. Somehow, the call remained connected.

"I'm coming into your office," said Hale, and then closed the call.

Two hours later, he sat on the *C2C*, which was quiet apart from a few Christmas shoppers bound for the Oxford Street scrum. He watched the glass towers of the city approach, keeping his mind clear of Hodgkinson until he was at the ICO. There, he would be able to explain rationally who the man was, where they'd met, and how the switchboard operator was mistaken.

Hale arrived at the building, walked in, calmer now, thinking it through.

"I simply have no record of a Mr Hodgkinson," said the receptionist on Hale's arrival at the desk. This was a different woman, stern, with a Scottish lilt.

"Please check again," said Hale, drumming his fingers on the counter.

"I'm sorry, sir…"

"Show me the log book, please. I signed in. Inspectora Jefa María Díez and branch commander Hodgkinson would have done so too. October fifth this year. It was in the morning and that was the last meeting we had."

The woman, now ruffled, moved across to a filing cabinet, drew out a book and placed it on the counter. She flicked through the pages to the first week in October.

"You can see here, sir, there is no entry and…"

"Great, okay then … can I see the interview room?"

"Sir?"

"I was interviewed by these people on that day ... I can even show you the room."

The receptionist directed Hale to a waiting area while she made a call. Five minutes later, a suit with a security guard appeared.

"Mr Hale?" said the suit, looking addled.

Hale shook his hand, nodded to the guard.

"We'd be happy to show you to the room you mention, but then we must ask you to leave," said the suit.

"No problem," said Hale. "I see the room, and then I leave."

They strode down the corridor, polished and clinical, just like before. Spoke about the cold snap, the weather, just like before with Hodgkinson. The suit knocked on the interview door. There seemed to be noise from within. The door opened. Hale stepped inside followed by the other two.

A plump man stood by the opened door, "Good morning, folks. Don't get many visitors 'ere do we ladies?" he said. Two women, forties, were seated at desks, one hammering away on a computer keyboard, the other filing through an impossibly high stack of folders. They nodded, smiled, uninterested.

Hale turned to Plump Man, "May I ask how long you have worked in this office?"

Plump Man's eyes rose to the ceiling. Taking some seconds, he sat down, leaned back on his chair, which creaked under the load as he swung from side to side. "Well let me think," he began. "Rose 'as been here longer, in this room. But me, well, going on four years. You know, we could do with a break. I mean look, no windows, and as you can see, it's a bit cramped and..."

Hale stared at him blankly until the big man's ramble petered out, leaving an awkward silence in the room.

Hale shook his head, frustrated, turned to the suit, "Thank you, I'm finished here."

Covent Garden, Christmas Eve.

Early evening brought a penetrating cold, an impending frost, as couples and families huddled in the darkness, gazing up to Christmas lights. Around the market, people gathered in the melee to hear carol singers and buskers. Shoppers charged about with branded bags they'd gathered from earlier shopping sprees. Lovers huddled in the night air, laughing, moving out of the cold into cafés and bars, their breath streaming behind.

Alone, Hale ambled in darker cobbled areas near the Bow Street theatre area and Opera House. The scent of vin chaud mixed with roasted chestnuts hung in the air. He stood stationary for some minutes, listened to the music and shouts of excited children. Then hauled his trenchcoat tighter around him, pushing the scarf up to his neck in an attempt to trap the icy air out. He thought of Céline, and how they used to meet here, wondered what she would be doing now. Probably out in the streets of Paris with the family, taking in the atmosphere, savouring the night. Then of Marta. Colder thoughts, bitterness at how he'd been betrayed by Hodgkinson and Black. And María Díez, who seemed unobtainable, untraceable. No way to get through to her department, despite his continued efforts. Apparently, she was back in Madrid, but Hale's repeated calls had returned only vague replies and long distance shoulder shrugging.

He should have known.

These people had used him, and then turned their backs. Cruel world.

He banished the subject, thought of the coming year. This loneliness and isolation would pass. It was time to move away, go further north as he had originally planned. He should have done so weeks ago.

He moved through the crowds towards Covent Garden station, joined a group of Italian students who stood watching a busker. He looked on as they giggled at the statue that was not a statue, but a figure seemingly sitting on thin air. He laughed with the students and they exchanged some words. Enjoyed the few seconds of company, made him feel human again, part of society.

He came here to be with people. Christmas Eve alone back at the guesthouse would be have been troublesome. Later, of course, he would return to the bottle of spirits, but for now at least, he was near sober, near normal.

Some minutes later, he entered *The Cross Keys*, the traditional drinking well a few blocks from the market and away from the bustle. Inside, dim, warm and inviting, a fire roared and people gathered by the bar in long coats, shopping bags at their feet. The place served food, but this was a drinkers' pub at heart, serving any kind of ale you'd care to sample. Hale took a stool at the bar, thought to himself that the scene here wouldn't have been much different a hundred years ago.

A pint of ale appeared before him. It soothed his mind as well as his throat as it slipped down, slow and easy. A few old men at the other end were doing the same, as was a man who had edged in beside him, still wearing a thick working jacket and woollen hat.

Despite the risks and advice received, Hale would return to Spain one day. To Andalucía. But the new year was ahead and his life in the north was foremost in his plans. In the coming year, things would form themselves. He would continue to lie low, remain alone for a while. Slowly, things would work out.

Hold it together, Charles.

The figure beside left the pub without a word, leaving a half pint of beer. Hale exchanged a shrug with the barman, who removed the glass.

"This yours?" said the barman, holding up an envelope.

Hale looked up, shook his head. "Where was it?"

The barman pointed to the bar where the man had been seated. "It must be his," said Hale. "Give it to me ... I'll go after him."

Hale grabbed the envelope, ran out into the street. He looked about, spotted the man. Jacket, woollen hat, walking swiftly along the street to his right. Hale pushed through the shoppers, out into the street, broke into a jog.

"Hey!" It was somehow pointless shouting, but he did anyway, "Hey, you left this..."

The man turned off into a side street. Hale ran up to the junction, looked down the street into a throng of shoppers. The crowd pushed past Hale at a crossing on the junction, a bottleneck. He stood up on tiptoes, trying to see over the mass of people.

The man had disappeared, no sign of him.

Hale returned to the bar, sat down at the same place, waved at the barman. "He's gone," said Hale, handing him the envelope. "Maybe put it behind the bar ... I guess he'll come back for it sometime."

"Don't think he's been in here before," said the barman, flipping the envelope between his fingers, and then muttering, "Charles Hale."

"What?"

"It says Charles Hale on the front."

"I'm Charles Hale."

"Okay, job sorted," said the barman, returning the envelope to Hale, and then walking off to serve a customer who was waving money in the air from across the bar.

Hale perused the envelope. Good quality, dense, the letters of Hale's name embossed on the front in black ink. He ripped it open, pulled out the crisp letter within. It was folded precisely. On opening, it was blank, apart from one line typed in the centre:

[24 December. Gatwick North. Arrivals. 18:54]

SIXTY-EIGHT

Money was tight, as was the time available to travel from Leicester Square Underground station to Gatwick Airport. There were questions to be asked, to be considered, before taking any actions in Hale's new world. But he didn't ask them, didn't consider them.

He had barely enough time to make the trip, and barely enough cash for a return journey back to Westcliff.

I shouldn't go, it isn't safe.

Hale boarded the Circle Line Underground train. The office party crowd was out in force. Men wearing creased suits, some drunk, in ebullient mood. Women in expensive coats and thick makeup, laughing, some holding plastic cups of cheap white wine. Hale liked the atmosphere, stood in the aisle, observed from a distance.

At Victoria, he moved swiftly out of the Underground, up to the mainline station, passing the café where he'd been abducted. Bad memories. He moved on, not looking back, dodging crowds of travellers hauling cases, queuing for tickets. Couples kissing, hugging, waving goodbye.

The Gatwick Express was departing soon for the thirty-minute journey. He cursed as people fussed at the turnstiles, studying tickets, wrestling cases and rucksacks and colourfully-wrapped boxes of Christmas presents. He edged past, bought a ticket at the machine, ran down the platform and boarded. The train was crammed, no sitting room available, but Hale didn't mind.

The lights of central London flashed by, soon merging into the dark of the countryside. People shuffled by, pushing, apologising. Hale apologised in return, holding English reserve, politeness within the scrum.

It's Christmas. Be nice, Charles.

The effects of the ale subsided. Hale's mind cleared and thoughts of what might await at Gatwick tormented him.

The meaning of the note.

The train arrived at Gatwick South. Standing by the door, Hale was one of the first onto the platform, and soon climbing higher on the escalators. He boarded the shuttle metro, viewing the aircraft on the stands and the landing lights of others blinking on their approach.

The Gatwick North Terminal hall was quieter than Hale had expected, echoing with the noise of trolleys being pushed, chatter, and announcements. A throng gathered around the Arrivals area. He looked up at the incoming flights. Nothing of relevance. Some flights from Paris, Munich, Brussels, Egypt, Edinburgh.

18:50 p.m.

Hale stood at the end of the stainless steel rail, watching the automatic doors of the Customs Area swing open, and then close, letting couples and groups emerge into the hall. Taxi drivers and chauffeurs held up cards expectantly, moving into position amongst the awaiting crowd. Passengers were greeted by grandparents, holding hugs, smiling, shedding tears. Businessmen, some preened and smart, others unshaven and drawn sauntered by. Airline staff moved swiftly on, away from the airport, home for Christmas. Holidaymakers, hopefuls, still with sunny climates in their psyche, wore shorts, hauled on warmer jackets, fell into the arms of loved ones. Children ran out, holding presents and balloons, their excited laughs repeating against the walls of the terminal building.

Hale waited, looked about, checked his watch: 18:57 p.m.

The stream of passengers thinned. The doors swung open less frequently, until finally they remained closed.

Silence.

Hale stood, looked down at his shoes, cheap and worn, pondering the long trip back to Essex. He shook his head, turned and moved to leave.

Time to go.

He adjusted his jacket, tried to compose his thoughts. This was no time for anger or bitterness. Rupert's voice in his head: *Mean thoughts will take you down and dirty, old boy. They'll dominate you, if you let them.*

Not now, not on Christmas Eve.

Hale walked away, slowly at first. Loathe to accept the lonely night ahead.

To his right, the doors swung open.

He paused.

A tall security guard emerged, carrying a case. He was accompanying a woman. Hale moved back to the rail for a moment, looked on.

This woman was dark, did not look British. She wore a long coat hugging her slim figure and a coloured scarf gathered around her neck.

This woman's hair was black, shining.

This woman caught Hale's eyes.

This woman dropped her hand luggage. The security guard picked it up, followed after her.

This woman moved faster, almost running. Running towards Hale.

This woman smiled at Hale, a warm smile.

This woman was Marta Fierro Almazán.

###

About the Author

Born in Surrey, England, James Smith was brought up in the USA and South Africa before his globetrotting family returned to Essex in the late 1970s. Following college stints at Chelmsford and Leicester, he embarked on a career in the computer business. This, however, was short-lived as he spent much of his time and energy surfing, writing, recording music, and filmmaking. He now directs independent feature films and develops writing ideas, many of which are based on experiences from frequent visits to Andalucía.

Visit the author website
http://jamessmithwriter.wordpress.com

Printed in Great Britain
by Amazon